"Ain't That Bout'a B*tch"

"Ain't That Bout'a B*tch"

Ms. Betty

Rev. date: 11/13/2014

Contents

Preface 7

Acknowledgements 9

Chapter 1   Once A Good Girl's Goin Bad, She's Gone Forever.........11

Chapter 2   Hands In The Air 23

Chapter 3   Knock Knock, Guess Who 45

Chapter 4   Mistaken Identity 70

Chapter 5   Rats, Basketballs And Baby Mommas 80

Chapter 6   Floating On A Memory 92

Chapter 7   Surprise 94

Chapter 8   Brick Ho House To Freedom 106

Chapter 9   Hoes To Housewives 130

Chapter 10   Tuck Duck And Roll..146

Chapter 11   Crystal Balls On The Wall 156

Chapter 12   It's Electric 163

Chapter 13   Dreamed Deferred 172

Chapter 14   Love Or Love Of Convenience.....................................179

Chapter 15   Back To The Basics 212

Chapter 16   Ole Faithful..229

PREFACE

Ain't That Bout'a Bitch, is a book about life, dating and relationships that have actually happened to me, but could have happened to any woman. The experiences I have gone through, some good, some bad, some that still has me waiting on Ashton Kutcher to come from around the corner and scream that I have just been punked. None the less, all have been a true learning and spiritual growth experience that has helped me to heal and help others. I place a humorous spin on each and every story to make it relatable and easy for those who may have or still be experiencing some of what I have gone through and to know that there is a silver lining around every dark cloud and not to give up on finding true love and happiness within.

When I started writing this book, I didn't even know that I was writing a book or had any real intentions of writing a book about my personal life. I'm a very private person and never thought what I had experienced would or could make a difference in anyone's life. The more I fought not to peel back the layers pain, shame, the guilt and fear to write and tell my life experiences the more I wrote and poured out my tears, blood and soul on these pages and healed in the process. I remember there was a time I use to pray daily and ask God to show me my purpose in life and to give me the wisdom to recognize it and walk in the path chosen for me.

Upon writing this book, I started reflecting on my beginning, which almost didn't happen, but God! My mother was 30 when she went to her doctor and found out she was pregnant. Without missing one beat. The doctor told my mother she was pregnant then turned around to his appointment book and said just as calm, "I'm scheduling you for a 9am appointment next Tuesday at my other clinic for an abortion!" After my mother kicked him in his back and walked out his office mad as hell, she was fine until about her 7 month in pregnancy. She started hemorrhaging very bad and had to be hospitalized for 2 weeks. The doctors were never able to find out what was wrong or what made my mom start to hemorrhage, but they were able to save my life. I'm a few months old when my family went to the beach for family day and was just hanging out. My mom who can't swim was on shore relaxing, my sister who is 13 years older than me was in the water doing her thing and my dad was in the water up to his knees holding me. A crab grabs his toe and won't let go. At that very instant, my dad thinks he is Joe Namath. He falls back, calls an audible and throws my ass into the deep end of the beach like a football. TOUCHDOWN! My mom goes into a frantic mode and starts beating on my dad while that crab gets a better grip and on my dad's toe and does not let go. My sister starts diving in and out different parts of the water looking for me. When she comes out the water the last time, she has me in her arms. I'm laughing and giggling like my dad was just playing when he spiked my ass into the deep end. We won't even get into the abuse my sister use to lay on me! With my sister being the oldest, she has tried to take me out of here a few times her damn self. But I stood strong and here I am, to tell you my story of hurt, pain, struggle and growth!

In all aspects of my life good, bad or indifferent, I have never had any regrets of anything I have done. As Winston Churchill so aptly stated, "All men make mistakes, but only wise men learn from their mistakes."

ACKNOWLEDGEMENTS

First and foremost, I would like to give all honor, praise, glory and thank you to my Lord and Savior Jesus Christ. Without him I am nothing! Trust me, God is still working on me and working hard. So bear with me as I continue to grow and share more stories with you.

To my mother, thank you for giving me life and laughing at me when I tell you things but for also pushing me just as hard as you laugh! Thank you for your love, support and undying dedication to me and all my dreams and for not beating my rump after I turned 8. To my father, thank you for your undeniable love, support and dedication to me is priceless!

Xlibris Publishing, Thank you for allowing me the creative freedom to pursue my dreams and purpose in life and actually see it come to pass.

To all my family and friends that supported me from the beginning when I was just starting out and not sure if I should embark on this journey, thank you for being that ear, backbone, shoulder and the best support system ever.

Special thank you's to; Ms. Ashley Sweets of *5 Star Salon and Spa* in Delray Beach, Fl (Crystal Carter) for always keeping me classy and sassy. Still revoking you and your momma's match making license and setting it on fire! Nicole (Markeisha) of *Dolly's New Image* for always being there no matter what. Mr. Julian Noel of *J-Love Designs* for my custom made jewelry and for being the best camera man in the dead of heat in South Florida. Jlove0483@gmail.com. Ms. Erica O'Neal of *Graphics by Erica* for such a beautiful work of art with my book cover. We have more work to do my sister! graphicdesignsbyerica.com

Gino Richardson, I have your triple D midgets and a case of Ripple on ready! Dr. Carmelia Speed you mean more to me than you will ever know or understand. Cuzzo Pamela Mills your words were like fire shut up in my bones. Mr. Maurice Gardner of *Gardner Photos and FX*, your special re-touch to my pictures made the difference and kept me from jumping off the curb. Charles Arness, words cannot express the gratitude I have for you and all your help. Deidre Gent, you already know how much you mean to me!

Last but not least, a huge, sincere heartfelt thank you to the men who made this book possible. If it weren't for you and all that you brought to my life, Ain't That Bout'a Bitch would have been a fleeting thought and I would have never found my purpose. You are the real MVP. Thank you!

CHAPTER 1

ONCE A GOOD GIRL'S GOIN BAD, SHE'S GONE FOREVER

My mom was a deputy sheriff in Gainesville and always worked shifts, which worked out perfect for me, especially when I started high school at GHS. Getting out of school at 2:30 and home by 3:30 was complete and total freedom when she would work evenings and especially midnights! When she worked evenings, I would get home just shy of her leaving for work, which gave me plenty of time to straighten up the house, get all pretty and hit them streets or have company over. There was always a gathering at my house on NE 11th Terrace, either playing cards, grilling, hanging out or making out. There was never a dull moment when Mom Dukes worked evenings or midnights. Being a teen, my mother never knew a lot of the things that would happen once she left for work, but now that I'm older and live hundreds of miles away, I figure I'm safe from an old dirty south ass whoopin with that one special "Brown Bomber Belt" that never ever seemed to break, it just got stronger.

At this time, I'm 15. Just got my learner license, a brand new beeper, short cut and I just knew I was the shit. I was dating this slightly older cat named Don Juan. I think he was about 19 or 20. He use to do alright by me financially and spent a lot of time with one another doing all kinds of fun crazy shit. It was the 1st semester of my of 9th grade year in 91'. I was home recovering from having my gallbladder taken out due to gallstones. We saw one another a few times when my mom wasn't home. He wasn't exactly what she wanted me to date, but girl you know how it is when you're young. You think you're in love. You know everything and think he is the finest thang since sliced white Wonder bread. He was a little nickel and dime d-boy. Still living in the hood, living the local d-boy life with dreams of being the next Tony Montana but wasn't really raising no real hell in them streets.

This particular night that he calls, my mom had left a few hours earlier for work. Before she left she told me she was going to pick up my birth control and would drop them off on her lunch because she wanted me to get back on my pills ASAP. He calls and asked, "Boo, are you ok? Do you need anything? Are you hungry?" It has been over 4 weeks since we last had sex and my young hot ass was geeking like a true crack head because not only am I missing him, I think this is the best head and sex by far (boy did I learn the difference!) So I tell him I am hungry and asked him to bring me something and come lay in bed with me and watch TV. I'm not feeling well, I just wanted that "special touch." He slides thru, has his boy drop him off and take off with his car. One thing leads to another and it is on! That night seemed like we made love like in the movies, sucking, fucking, slurping, kissing, caressing, eating, beating and a car door slam! We had already finished and was just lying on the floor in the afterglow when I heard the car door slam. I jump up, whisper scream to him, "Get cho black ass the fuck up, get cho shit and get in my closet, my momma is here and you know she don't like yo ass!" You would have thought I had Carl Lewis in my room with how quick he picked up his shit and ducked off in the closet, sucked in behind my heavy winter clothes.

I would have had him go out the back sliding glass door or even the side door of the den, but my ole Super Negro Swift like SWAT momma was already in my room by the time I put on my robe. I hobbled out the bed acting like I had just woke up to go to the bathroom. The first thing out her mouth is, "What the fuck is going on in here, I've been calling you all damn night to make sure you're ok and you ain't answered the phone?" I had turned the ringer on my phone off because I was talking to several people at the same time and didn't need any awkward phone conversations. I think I see my closet door move slightly so I jump up real quick and respond, "Ma, I took a pill and went to sleep coz my stomach was having severe pain, so I fell asleep and that's why I ain't answer the phone. Did you pick up my pills?" My momma quick as hell on her feet. I'm trying to slide past her pistol toting ass to go to the bathroom. My mom asks, "Where did this KFC box come from and who fucking stankin ass drause is these?" I turn around. My eyes zoom in like a camera lens and I see his white Fruit of the Loom men drause in the middle of my floor, the only thing my re re ass can think to say is, "Ohhh those are mine, sometimes wearing men drause is real relaxing." I was young at the time and that's all my young dumb ass could think of.

Everything is moving so fast, yet in slow motion, as I try to move past my momma and act as if everything is ok. Except my Super Negro Swift like SWAT momma does a quick shake spin move past me and snatched my closet door open and step back like she finna swing. She turns to me as I see my friend standing butt bookey ass naked in the closet. His hands filled with his clothes and trying to cover his ding a ling. That didn't last long. He dropped the clothes and put his hands up like his ignant ass was under arrest. My mom turned her head to face me, I'm standing there with my face on stuck. It is at this very moment I truly realize this is my last moment on earth. My mom bust out and said to me with a very serious face and calm voice, "Bitch, I know this little ugly ass dick ain't what got you acting like you ain't got good got damn mutha fucking sense? I shoot bullets bigger than this lil mutha fucker." I don't respond because I don't know if she is going to shoot me or if the Brown Bomber Belt is just going to mysteriously appear in her hand and she starts issuing out ass beatings like candy on Halloween night. She turns back to him and tells him in a very calm voice, which I know is the voice of death, "If you don't get yo black, raggedy ass the fuck out my house in 5 seconds, I will blow your mutha fucking brains out!" He didn't say one word! He didn't get dressed. He didn't say bye. He didn't kiss me, shoot me a bird or nothing. He flew past me so quick, fast and in a hurry, my hair and robe moved in the breeze.

I'm still on stuck. I can't say anything. I'm not sure what the hell is about to happen and I don't want to get hit because I'm still recovering from surgery and I probably wouldn't know how to act being that I got my last ass whoppin when I was 8yrs old. My mom turns to me with a total look of disgust on her face and says, "Since you wanna be grown you lil bitch, you need to get the fuck out my house, leave my house and car keys and go with him and do what the fuck you wanna do since you wanna be grown!" Now remember I told you, this nigga ran past me and out the house so got damn quick, hurricane Katrina had to pull over and slow down and say DDAAMMNN.

I put on some clothes, dropped my head, looked at my mom really pitiful and walked out the house. Where the hell am I going? I ain't got no money, no car; his ass has become one with the wind and gone. I sit down beside the big oak tree in our front yard and just shake my head and say, "Ain't this bout a bitch." My mom is coming out the door speed walking to her car, when she yells to me, "Get cho black ass back in that got damn house and I will deal with you in the morning when I get off!" I ran my fat ass back in the house so damn quick. You would have thought I had never lived in the house before, everything felt fresh and brand new. It seem like morning came so damn quick or I didn't sleep one, because I was too worried about what morning would bring when my mother returned home from work. By the time my Super Negro swift like SWAT momma had made it home, the house was spotless, laundry done, breakfast was still cooking and I was trying my hardest to look soo hurt, sick and in need of care that she wouldn't beat me with the Brown Bomber Belt. My mom didn't fuss, cuss or even whoop my ass with the Brown Bomber Belt, she simply came in asked me if I was ok, ate breakfast took a shower and went shopping with a coworker of hers and actually brought me some items back from the store.

We never spoke of the incident again. Guess she felt sorry for me as I was young dumb and full of, well you know what the old folks like to say . . .

The young man and I continued to date for another month or so, but he never came back to my house. If he thought he felt the presence of my mom somewhere, he would stop doing whatever he was doing, leave whatever he was about purchase and exit stage left like Snaggle Puss. We eventually broke up. He went to prison and I went to college. I often wonder whatever happened to him, but then again life goes on . . .

After me and the ole speed racing closet hider broke up, I was single for a while just really chilling and hanging out doing normal teenage shit. It's now my 2nd semester of 9th grade and I'm taking drivers ed with the coolest drivers ed teacher ever at GHS. He was country as hell, drove an old Cadillac and use to always say some of the countriest shit. One day after drivers ed, which was not too far from my house I start walking home. I see a red Geo Metro creep past me, go to the corner and make a u turn. I keep saying, I know this car but I'm also replaying Boyz in the Hood in my head when the dudes in the red Hyundai circle the block and kill little Ricky in a drive by. The red Geo Metro circles back around. Slows down and pulls up beside me. The passenger window rolls down. I'm scared and trying not to take off running coz I don't want to get shot when I look and notice a familiar face. I stop. He smiles. I smile and he asks, "Do you need a ride home? I am going your way." He know where I live at, he has dropped me off before. I play coy as usual and say "Yes" as I'm batting my eyelashes. He drives me home, walks me up to my door and holds small talk before asking me for my number. We exchange numbers and the journey starts and what a journey it was.

Things are going rather well between Sincere and I, he would come pick me up from school, bring me lunch and meet me at my house after school, just really be there all the time. There was one time I came home mad and damn near in tears because this one boy always picked on me and use to always want to fight me and I couldn't figure out why. One day me and ole boy squared off, when the teacher came round the corner broke it up but threatened to write us up if this kept on. I went home and told Sincere all about it. He was to cool bout the situation, all he did was nod his head, said "uhmmm mm". At first I was mad as hell because he wasn't saying or doing anything, he was just cool and nonchalant. I didn't think anything else of it until I went to school the next day. The boy who always wanted to fight me was sitting on the wood fence in the back hall of GHS. When he saw me he jumped down and said in the shakiest voice ever, "You go with Sincere?" Before I could answer, because I was completely thrown off, he asked another question, "Why you ain't tell me you was his girl? We cool, whatever you need, I got you!" I didn't know what to say or think. This was a shock. Just yesterday he wanted to fight me and now he wanna feed a sista. That was just one of the many ways Sincere use to take care of me.

Sincere, who is 4 years older than me, was an up and coming dope boy from 8th Ave or as we like to call it, Out East. He use to trap out of some of the nastiest, dingiest, crack head filled shanty shacks on 1st Ave. Whenever I was looking for him and he wasn't at home with his mom, sister and 3 little brothers I could always find him on 1st. Sincere was a very handsome, 6'4, chunky, 275lb light skinned teddy bear. He always kept a low haircut, unless he was in the trap and that money was getting good and he didn't want to leave. We fell in love instantly and was always together doing something. My mom knew what he was doing and wasn't really feeling that, but he begin to grow on her with his sweet charm and ole school manners. Our first two years together were the best, even with him trapping a lot he never let the streets or anything going on keep him and I apart. Things begin to take a turn for the worse when I start going to Santa Fe Community College for high school dual enrollment my junior year of high school. I didn't change. I was still the loyal and faithful girlfriend I had always been. Going to school and straight home. In the beginning, I never wanted to be in the streets acting reckless. I'm a lady. I represent my mother and I never wanted Sincere to look bad or crazy in those streets. Apparently he didn't get that same memo.

One day goofing off on campus, I was in the student activity center where everybody hung out, black, white whatever we all would just duck off in there and cut up listening to music, playing cards and chilling, when a girl comes up to me and asks, "Ain't you the girl that go with Sincere that be on 1st?" Where ever I went and someone asked me if I was Sincere's lady, I would cheese like an idiot because I loved being recognized as Sincere's lady, guess it was that naïve love. I smiled at the girl an respond, "Yes, that's my baby. Why?" Once she put her hand on her hip, smacked and turned her lips up, I knew it was about to be some bullshit, "I thought it was you, well my homegirl wanted me to tell you she is having his baby!" In my mind what lame ass chick sends her friend to deliver your baby announcement to the main lady? I don't break the smile on my face to dare give this bitch the satisfaction that I'm hotter than hell right now. I ask her with a smile and pleasant voice, "Who is your homegirl and why would she send you of all people to tell me something so personal?" Trying to be slick the heffa says, "You'll see!" and then ran her ass out the student center. I don't break my stride. I kept kicking it in the student center because my next class started in 30 minutes which would not give me enough time to make it cross town and find out what the fuck is going on. One thing when it come to a man, don't ever miss your money or your education, because a nigga gonna be a nigga til God pull the trigger!

I get home, change clothes and hit his house on 8th Ave like gang busters. His mom is home, whom I adore because she was always real and bout that life. I storm in, see her and instantly show my respect and give her some love and head to the bathroom where he is taking a shower. Soon as I lay my eyes on him, I wanted to hit his ass in the head the shower rod and just beat him to sleep in that tub. He instantly detects my attitude and says, "I just gave you an allowance I know you ain't back for more?" Perfect segue to this bomb I'm finna drop on his ass, "Ohh so is this how you take care of the step mother of your future kids? Who the fuck is she that is about to drop your lil bundle of joy?" He stops mid stroke of washing his body. Looks crazy as hell while trying to think of how the hell he can dress this up. I continue to stand there, trying to give him the opportunity to say something, I can't take the silence anymore, "MUTHA FUCKER WHO IS SHE?" He washed the soap off his body real quick, steps out and finally says, "Can we talk about this outside?" I'm on his every freaking move. I'm so close to him that I could have easily gotten dressed in his clothes with him. We went across the street to Duval Elementary which was directly in front of his house. As we walk, he keeps his head low while rubbing his rough as concrete hands together. Finally speaks up and says, "I don't even know if it's my baby or not. She let me use her house to cook and package my dope. Sometimes she lets me sell it from there, but it ain't nothing going on I swear. I did fuck her once. You and I had just had a fight and I got drunk and went over there. I ain't mean to sleep with her, it just happened because I was mad at you. It ain't my baby!" Did this simple ass bastard just tell me, he was mad at me and drunk so he slept with her? I hauled off and hit the shit out of Sincere. I know it didn't hurt but his wanna be actor ass jumped like I hit him with a brick. I'm going off like a firecracker. We are walking and all Sincere can do is keep saying that this baby ain't his then switch it up to it might not be his, but he has yet to tell me who she is. In his feeble ass mind, since I'm not in the streets, he thinks I want know who she is or find out who the hell she is. Oh how wrong he was!

Since finding out about the baby and new chick, I start taking time to go out all while still maintaining my studies. Oh it felt so good going out with the girls, especially my right hand, Boo'Fawnda! We use to tear that road up, because Gainesville is a very small town where everyone is either related, or they know everyone and word travels quickly. We always had a blast hanging out in Gainesville but I never wanted Sincere to know my business. Things get better between Sincere and I for only a short time before he gets back into his old habits again. Missing for a day or 2. Not where he say he is and I keep hearing about this baby. Threats of having my ass kicked by the alleged baby momma and I have still yet been able to correctly pinpoint her ass, but don't worry its soon to come. I was always cool with all of Sincere's friends. So it was rather odd that when I pulled up one day and asked "Where is Sincere?" everybody head dropped like a dead leaf from a tree. I stood there with my hand on my hip and asked again, "Where is Sincere?" The snitch of the crew with the pretty eyes kept his head down and said in a low voice, "He ain't here. He is out cooking!" Well well well, I knew what cooking meant and there were only a few places I knew where he cooked, but I had already been by there so that only left one place, the potential baby mammy! I slow roll past Amoeba house and I don't see his car. I keep rolling down the back roads to E. University Ave and BOOM! There sits his car, backed into some bushes trying to hide. I make a mental note and keep on rolling. I need my allowance at the end of the week, seen some hot shit I wanted in Orlando.

Things remain the same but get worse. Amoeba hasn't had the baby yet, which is what I'm waiting for. She is still sending empty promises and funny ass threats. Sincere is growing in the game. I'm still in school getting ready for my senior year. I had left school early one day, went and got my hair done and went home. I was on the computer doing some homework when I look out the window and see Sincere pull up, but he doesn't knock on the door. He walks to the side of the house and grabs the water hose. I don't think anything of it, because I know the tan colored Saab would run hot often. I walk to the front porch and wait for him to walk from the side of the house to his car with the hose. This high yella fat fucker bypasses his car and walks right up to me and sprays me from head to toe with the water hose. I'm shocked, stuck and soaked! When I do come out of shock and realize that my new hair doo is gone, my dress is drenched. I come out of my shoes and get ready to charge him. He pulls up his shirt to show me his pistol then says, "Ohh so you wanna talk to somebody else? I'll show you about trying to leave me and see somebody else!" All I can do is nod, point my finger at him and say, "Touché mutha fucker, Tou mutha fucking Che`!" I walk back in the house, change clothes and make a bee line to the hair salon. I already felt a part of me dying, even though I was trying my hardest to hold on. Her pulse was fading fast with very slow deliberate breathing. My mother use to always tell me, "All men lie and cheat baby, just find one you can tolerate and live your life." Never!

Amoeba has the baby, a little girl. Remember Sincere is high yella and if you close your eyes and look at the inside of your eyelids, that is the color of Amoeba. I waited a few months, pulled right up to her front door and knocked. When she opened the door, you could see the surprise on her face. Even though I wasn't in the streets heavy, I knew plenty of people who were. They hipped me to who she was, where she lived, where she worked and who else she was sleeping with. Amoeba was an older, very dark skinned drag queen looking chick. She understood the dope game and was always cool with the younger dope boys. Those old heads had already ran through that ass and knew what she was all about. She stood there for a few minutes looking real stupid in the face. She is now face to face with the same little girl that she had been going around town saying she was going to whoop. When she saw me I brought all of my ass to her front door step! After standing in that hot ass sun long enough, I said, "Hi Amoeba, how are you? I hear you have been wanting to kick my ass since you was pregnant, well here I am!" She starts to giggle in a real nervous giggle and said, "I ain't never said nothing like that, I don't even that much about to you want to fight you. Who been saying that?" She had sold all these wolf tickets while she was pregnant. I bought $100 worth of them and I was coming to redeem them to see if I won a damn thing. "Amoeba, I ain't here for no bullshit, word on the street is you are fucking Sincere, you want to fight me and you just had his baby, so what is the truth? I'm here so break the shit down to me so I can understand." We are still standing in this damn doorway when she replies, "Me and Sincere do go together and he told me y'all had broken up. I had the baby 3 months ago." No fight was about to go down, so I back down just a tad just in case she try to do a punk ass sneak attack, "Amoeba we haven't broken up we are still very much a couple, but since I'm here let me see this baby you claim is his." When I walked into her section 8 house right off 8th Ave, she had the cheap black faux leather furniture in the living room on the right with all the black and gold accessories from Aarons Furniture. The nastiest kitchen to the left. At the end of the long hall was her bedroom with an addition on the back of her room which is where she kept the baby. I know you're wondering how I know all of this to a tee? Instead of this fool bringing the baby to the door, I walked in her house and asked where the baby was.

She pointed and I walked through ole girl house like I lived there. I go into her bedroom and its clothes, drause and everything all over the floor. I just shake my head and continue a few more feet and walk into the little additional room attached to hers and see the baby laying on her side in a crib. I don't want to wake the baby up. I totally understand how it is to get them little boogahs to sleep, but I need to see and hold this baby for myself. Amoeba has finally come down the hallway, with nothing in her hand and ain't saying a damn thing. I bend over the crib, pick up the sleeping baby, cradled her in my arms and knew right then, she was not Sincere's baby. She was black ass Amoeba and no facial features what so ever of Sincere or his family. I put the baby back in the crib, rubbed her back so she could drift back into a deep sleep. I motion for Amoeba to walk out the room. When we make it to the living room I'm shaking my head and I tell her, "That's as much Sincere baby as it is mine! She is dark as hell for one and you know Sincere family got some strong genes and she don't have none of his momma or sister in her. His momma been told me that ain't his baby." I start to walk off when she nervously say, "That is his baby, you just gotta give her some time to come into herself." All I can say is a quick, "Bitch please!" When I walked out that door that day, I never heard another word about Amoeba talking about whooping my ass, wanting to fight or anything negative. When we would see each other in public, she would speak. I would wave and that was it.

I find Sincere and have him follow me to the back of the park across the street from St Patrick school on NW 16th street, I give him a hug to make sure he don't have his gun on him. I grab his hand. Very romantically walk him away from his car just in case he has his gun stashed in there somewhere and I punch his ass dead slap in the face. I found a big ass rock close to a tree. I grab it and stand there on ready. I'm going off on his ass about lying to me about this chick Amoeba and her new bundle of joy. Sincere never hits me, never makes a move for his car, he just stands there and takes everything I dish out. I wanted to hit his ass again, but I ain't wanna push it and have my ass handed to me. I broke up with Sincere right then and there. I was tired and had far too much going for me. I had already started meeting like-minded men who offered me more and afforded greater opportunities for growth and learning. Sincere would pass by the house daily like a merry go round. Call the phone private and hang-up, and send messages through my friends who didn't mind because he was paying them. That was the first time Sincere and I had broken up the entire 3 years we had been together.

I'm in my senior year and still doing the high school dual enrollment program at Santa Fe Community College. I'm gearing up for graduation and going on to college and living my life like its golden. I'm home one Friday night with my best friend from elementary school. She was staying the week with me because her mom went on a cruise and didn't want her home alone the entire time she was gone. My mom had gone to work on the evening shift and called later to let us know she would be pulling a double and to see if we need her to bring us anything. Hell nah lady, we are cool in the gang! Erin and I start making plans on what we were getting into that night, when there is a knock on the door. We don't see a car. I go to the door and look real intense at the figure standing at the door. It's Sincere. We haven't talked in over a month and I started ignoring all the private calls and declining the gifts and messages sent through my friends. I ask Sincere through the door, "What do you want?" He just stands there looking crazy and I stand behind the door looking crazy right back at him. We do this for about 10 minutes, before he finally says, "Can I come in and talk with you? I just want to sit down and talk to you." I open the door, ask Erin to give us some privacy. She goes into my room and starts watching TV. Sincere and I go into the den. I sit in the big blue recliner in the right corner by the window and he sat on the couch. We watched TV for about half an hour. Sincere is sitting there looking uncomfortable as if there is something highly perplexing on his mind, but he isn't quite able to put his thoughts into words. He keeps tapping his right foot, so I ask him with serious attitude, "Do you need to use the bathroom, because you know where it is." He looks at me crazy and finally speaks, "My intentions were to come here and kill you. Wipe down this entire house of all my finger prints. Walk out the front door just as I came in, lock it and then show up to your funeral next week crying harder than your mom. Your only saving grace, besides your big mouth ass friend in the back, is when I look at you I realize how much I'm in love with you and how much you mean to me. I know you only talking to that nigga Oliver with the blue box Chevy to get back at me about what you're hearing in the streets, but that shit better be over tomorrow or I will kill you." He has just pissed me off royally and I want to cuss his ass out and run past him to my pistol. Something tells me I won't make it, so I sit there and nod my head and ponder what he has just said. I was talking to Oliver. Not because he drove a box Chevy, but because he was nice, a gentleman, knew how to treat me and worked at UPS. I asked very politely, "Sincere, baby are you finished?" He nods his head. I stand up and start slowly walking towards to den door and light into his ass, "Don't you ever come to my house again threatening me about some bullshit you are caught up in. You love them streets and the hoes in em, so you can have that. I'm happy living my life without you and I hope you feel the same damn way. Yeah bitch, you showed me your little pistol last time you was here and wet up my damn hair and clothes and you just threatened me again, let this be your last time ever talking to me like that. You're pushing me to a place I don't want to be, so I suggest you get ya shit and get the fuck on! I tried being with you and being good to you but these streets have you and I ain't one for competing with nobody, whether on my level or not." Sincere sat there for the longest not saying one word, I can't lie and say I wasn't scared because I was. I didn't break my stride to let him know I was scared as hell. I got tired of looking at him and hearing him breath. I started walking towards the front door now because I'm feeling like I'm safe and say, "It was nice seeing you, please take care of yourself. I'll see you around sometime." He got up, walked towards the front door which I had gapping wide open, stopped and turned to me and said, "Just as long as you know I own you!" All I could muster up to say was, "Bitch please!" and slammed my door.

Erin was still staying with me and having a ball, when I invite Oliver over for a little play time. He comes over, parks his car in the front yard on the grass and just as we are about to get down to business I hear loud pounding beating on the door. My heart falls into my pinky toe. All I can think is, it's my momma again and she is coming back with a vengeance. Erin peeps around the corner to the living room window and see that a car has pulled all the way up to my front door with the high beams on. We can't really make out who it is. Erin and I go into the 1st bedroom where the light isn't as bright and we both gasp for air at the same time. It's Sincere out there acting a pure damn fool with a car full of his old homeboys from 1st Ave. I send Erin to the front door and tell her never open the door, just tell him that I'm not here, that I hopped in the car with somebody and took off. I really don't know what the hell I was thinking because my car was in the driveway and Oliver's car was parked in the front on the grass. Sincere ain't trying to hear none of that. He rants and raves all while beating on the door for about 20 minutes before the fellas pull him back into the car and speed off. When I see them speed off down the road, I pull Oliver punk ass up from under my bed holding his clothes close to his chest like a girl shaking like a leaf in a tree and tell him to get the hell out of my house. I never spoke to Oliver sorry ass again. How he let two women go investigate what the hell is going on and never try to investigate or protect us? Glad I never give his simple ass some. Sincere strikes again, now it's on! Men can dish that bullshit but when a woman plays their game but with her rules, men can't take it. Ohh well, Once a Good Girl is Goin Bad, She's Gone Forever. Things were never the same between Sincere and I mean, ever again.

My entire senior year Sincere and I were broken up. No contact, no phone calls, no nothing. I graduated, but didn't walk. Since I attended all my classes on a college campus, I felt grown and didn't want to walk with people I didn't really know. Do I regret not walking with my high school graduating class? No, not all. I take summer A off to get a break from school and just kick it. I start school in Summer B and that is when my life takes a turn down a dead end street. I met this really fine, suave, handsome man one night at the local hole in the wall club and I fall head over heels in lust with him. He blew my mind among other things and had me completely gone with his sexy, sweet charming self. ~~Ain't That Bout'a Bitch~~

CHAPTER 2

HANDS IN THE AIR

Sincere and I had broken up for the 1st time due to his constant desire and love of the streets and all that the streets and the hoochies had to offer him. I said I wasn't going back. This break up was permanent because there was another baby on the way from one of the girls who he claims was only going to get the dope and cook it up for him, nothing more, and nothing less. Well apparently a baby got cooked up in one of those crack pots. Yes, another baby followed after Amoeba's baby, but it wasn't with Amoeba!

Since I never wanted kids, I kept it moving and I graduated from Gainesville High School June 1995 after completing my last 2 years in the high school dual enrollment program at Santa Fe Community College. It was a great experience that I so thoroughly enjoyed and took full advantage of. Attending my junior and senior year on a college campus. Driving to school. Going to class later than those in regular high school. I fit in perfect on campus. I have always looked and acted more mature than my age, which is why I always dated older men. I had been out of a high school for a year and was currently working towards my degree in Mental Health Counseling, living at home with my mom and enjoying life to the fullest. The local hot spot in Gainesville was, is and will always be Fletchers. It's a little hole in the wall club, with one way in and one way out. Picture windows in the front so you can see who is at the bar and another picture window by the DJ so you can see who is about to pass out from the heat, funk and liquor. No ventilation, except for that oversized gym fan in one corner of the club that you never feel unless you are standing directly in front of it with all of your clothes off. Somebody auntee ole 1969 floor model TV in the adjacent corner. The worse female bathroom in the world. Yet the best, strongest and cheapest drinks, with DJ DL were always bumping some hot beats. Don't come in there with your new hairdo because you bound to sweat it out and you don't have to dance to make that happen. Just walk into Fletchers and you were instantly drenched as if you had just came out the pool. This is the local hot spot no matter the season, whether any other event is going on in town. You are going to have a great time while trying to fight your way to the dance floor, meet some interesting people and most definitely be entertained beyond your wildest imagination.

I had just finished and submitted a grueling research paper and needed a night out with some serious fun, drinks and local crack head entertainment. I call my homegirl Boo'fawnda and told her it was time to hit the streets. Normally I would have said lets hit the turnpike and tear Orlando down, but I wasn't in the mood for driving. Now hold on, let me tell you about my ace. My slider. My true ride or die. Always right there no matter what day or time it is. Boo'Fawnda is about 5'5. Very beautiful, light brown sister. She has the prettiest doll face, with some long, thick black hair, which is always laid. Her nails was always on point, well as her clothes. Sista never stepped out the house with anything out of place. She always dressed to the 9's no matter where we were going. From first glance, she has a bright, white, chessire cat smile. Get her timing wrong or do something stupid and you would have thought you have just went to battle with one of the Hell's Angels.

I called Boo and explained everything to her and she agreed that we both needed a night, as she had a grueling week as well. We get dressed. Our make-up is beat for the gawds honey. Our clothes look as if we had just stepped out of a fashion magazine. Boo'Fawnda comes to my house, scoops me and we head to Fletchers. We get a perfect parking space right up front, so we can look through the big picture window and see who is already in there, as well as see who is walking up. We finally decide to get out and make our way to the door, when he steps out of nowhere.

I get out of the car. Fix my clothes to ensure I'm on point and looking my absolute best, when I look up into his face. There he stands. 6'4. 275 lbs of pure solid light bright and damn near white sexiness. We lock eyes. Smile. Stare for a few minutes before he walks into the club. I'm standing there with this deer in the head lights look on my face. Boo'Fawnda keeps calling my name and finally slaps me across my back to get my attention. I shake it off. Walk into Fletchers and instantly start having a good time. The music is contagious with the hard bass beating through the speakers. When you finally make it in, you couldn't help but to start dropping it like it's hot or backing that ass up. The drinks seem to be magically floating through the air, as they are all over the place. When you walk into Fletchers, the bar is directly in front of you on your right. You have a 2 tables and 2 chairs lining the wall directly in front of the window and 2 additional tables and 2 chairs lining the wall on the left as you head into the dance hall area. I stop to the bar and order my usual. A $3.50 Funky Monkey. Don't knock the drink until you have had one or 2. It's a fruity drink with about 5 or 6 different liquors in it that is sure to get you right after the first sip.

With drink in hand, I dance my way through the thick crowd of people blocking the door to the dance area. I slide my way in. Start dancing a little harder to the music and sipping my Funky Monkey even more. I scan the room. Wave and blow kisses to many friends that I see in there that night. I look in the corner by the fan and see him. Again. He nods and smiles. I nod. Bat my eyes very coyly and smile, quickly turning away as to make a dramatic statement. The night continues on with more of the same. Once you get to the dance floor area, there is no room to walk around and mingle. For one its small as hell and secondly it's too got damn hot to do anything else but breathe.

I have watched him all night. Not once did he entertain any women. He stood in the corner by the fan enjoying his drinks. He set his table with a full bottle, bucket of ice and chaser as to not have to go back and forth to the bar. A few fellas that we mutually knew approached him and showed love. As I watched him, he watched me. Fletcher's closes at 2 am, as all the clubs in Gainesville do. As the time started getting closer to 1:30 am, the crowd started thinning out.

I'm talking and laughing as usual, when I feel a lite tap on my right shoulder. I turn slowly, thinking he has finally approached me to ask me out, only to see a short, black ass Darth Vader looking round dude asking me if he could take me to breakfast. I politely tell him no thank you and turn back around to my homegirl and keep talking. As I'm about to hook back up with Boo'Fawnda and leave, I get another tap on my right shoulder. I think to myself, if this is the same little dirty foot Michelin man, it's about to get ugly. With a smirk on my lips, attitude on the tip of my tongue ready to spit 50 rounds of this AK mouth quickly, I turn around. Just as I'm about to let the attitude loose, I realize it's him. My lips turn into an instant smile. The attitude instantly melts like butter in a hot skillet. He bends down. He comes close as if he is about to kiss me. I lick my lips. Slightly pucker as to not seem overly eager. He bypasses my lips and leans into my ear and says, "Hi beautiful, my name is Benny! What is your name? I have been watching you all night since our brief encounter in the parking lot!" Now trust me. Not only am I taken aback that he speaks proper English, but just to know that he was man enough to step up and properly introduce himself. I reply very coy, "Hello Benny. My name is Betty and the pleasure is all mine!" We chit chat a few moments longer before we are ushered out the door by mean drunk ass, teeth missing Bruno. As everyone tries for the last time for an early morning booty call, Benny and I are deeply engaged in a very deep and intellectual conversation about the current news, education and various other interesting subjects when he asks, "Would you like to continue this conversation over coffee and breakfast?" Not only am I sexually stimulated, but he has also peaked my mental interests. There is nothing sexier than an educated man who can teach you new things and open your mind to broader horizons. Now, hear me and hear me good when I say educated. Education does not always mean college educated. Some of the most intellectual and most influential men I have ever met, were only armed with common sense and they went further in life than those with a doctorates!

We meet at Denny's on University Ave and the corner of NW 13th Street. He got there before me and grabbed a booth in the back. I know you are wondering where in the hell is Boo'Fawnda right? Hell Boo was with me the entire night, but upon formally meeting him and engaging in some mind stimulating conversation, I didn't even know Boo was alive let alone born, but we was together the entire night. Before we walked into Denny's, Boo had already expressed her dislike of him. She said it was something about his pissy red ass that just didn't set right with her. Boo and I are close in complexion, yet she like those straight from Africa colored brothers I'm really more partial to my light bright damn near white brothers. We walk in. See him. I wave. He motions for us to come join him in the back. I slide in first, to be able to sit next to him. Boo slides in behind me as to be able to sit on the end for easy exit. We all engage in small talk. Benny is trying to be the consummate gentlemen and not have my best friend feel left out. Benny taps me on my right thigh to get my attention, then leans down close to my ear. I love it when he does that. He smells so damn good and the sound of his voice with a slight southern drawl accent, yet it has the tones of a well-polished man. He asks, "What is your friends name again, as I don't want to appear rude?" I gently rub his left thigh and very seductively reply, "Boo'Fawnda!" Benny then says, "Boo, I hate that you are sitting here with us. Is it ok if I call a few of my friends over to the table so we can all have a great time?" I don't wait for her response when I just blurt out, "YES, that would be awesome!" It just so happen that all his homeboys were already in the restaurant and just a simple hand wave away. The booth went from being occupied by 3 people to 7 people quickly.

Now don't get me wrong, we were having a great time laughing, eating and just chopping it up but Benny had some facially and vertically challenged friends. In between laughs Boo kept looking at me like, "I hope don't nobody see me with y'all and think I'm with any of these fools!" The really only cute one was Ernie and he wasn't really all that cute, but his sense of humor made up for the bell pepper nose. Open gate spaced teeth. With bad acne at his age. Ernie is trying his hardest to get at Boo. Making up funny shit to say. Complimenting her on everything and just generally making small talk and being friendly, but she is not having it. Boo is talking mad shit to him and made him pay for her breakfast versus Benny who had already said he had all of our meals that morning.

It's time to leave as it's getting late. All of us are yawning like the doors at Wal-Mart. I lean in and tell Benny I have had a great time and I look forward to hearing from and seeing him again, when he says, "I was hoping to wake up with you in my arms and start my day off with your beauty, magnetic smile and energy. Now as I said earlier, there was already a strong sexual attraction as his body, color and intellect is pure kryptonite to me. I explain to him that I live with my mother and that I was riding with Boo and that is was far too late for us to get together for an evening of passion. This is what my lips were saying while my coochie had already climbed out of my panties and into this pants and was having the time of her life. He agreed and left the subject alone. I wrote my home number and beeper number down on a napkin. Slipped into his hands quietly and tapped Boo and told her I was ready to go and to slide out. Benny and Ernie pay the bill. We all walk outside, continuing our lively conversations and just enjoy each other for the last few minutes before we say our good byes. Boo and I hop into her car and get to giggling, laughing and replaying the night like a scene from one of our favorite movies. We pull into my yard so I can get out, when we see a car pull up behind us. Neither one of us get out, just in case we need to ram the car and get away. We wait for a few minutes when the interior light in the other car suddenly comes on. We both squint our eyes and look really hard to make sure we are seeing what we see. I look at Boo and Boo looks at me, when we bust out laughing and say, "Benny and Ernie!" Benny gets out the car first and slowly, but ever so sexily walks up my driveway. I'm playing this thing cool, but the lord knows I want to jump his bones like he is a trampoline. I meet him halfway up the driveway and he grabs me around my waist and pulls me close and whispers in my ear, "I want you and I'm not taking NO for an answer!" Girl, when I tell you I almost climbed his tall ass right there like a squirrel on a tree trying to catch a nut. I looked at my watch. It is now 4:30 am. My mother is due to get off at 7 am and she will be pulling up in the yard no later than 7:30 am.

Be my luck, this is the time she comes home with a yard full of coworkers to have an early drinking session to talk about all those arrested. Who is sleeping with who? Who had to use force? Cracking jokes the entire time over breakfast and drinks.

My hot ass is thinking quickly. I'm like; I can knock his little old ass out real quick. Send him home sucking his thumb, as well as get a lot of this pressure off my ass from school and not being broke off in a minute. I grab Benny just as hard as he has grabbed me. I look him dead square in the eyes and say, "You might as well have Ernie sit in the living room to wait for you. I will be finished with your sexy red ass in a matter of minutes!" He laughed, kissed me on my forehead, patted me on my ass and walked over to Ernie who was still sitting in the car. He said something. I couldn't understand or really care what he was saying. I was talking to Boo'Fawnda and telling her to call me at 6 am to make sure I get this nigga out my momma house before she get home. Boo agrees, gives me dap and backs out the driveway. Ernie blows the horn and pulls off. I'm standing in the middle of the driveway, totally confused as to why in the fuck did Ernie just toot his horn and pull off. I look at Benny in total bewilderment and ask him, "Uhmmmm why in the hell did Ernie just pull off? I told you to have him sit in my mom's living room and wait for you, because what I want to do damn shol won't take long!"

Benny had this aura about him, like he always bets on black and wins big! He flashes that million watt smile, grabs my hand ever so gently, leads me to the front door, takes the keys from my hand and used the appropriate keys to unlock the door as if he had been there before. Benny opens the door, stands to the side to allow me in first, then he follows. When Benny gets in that door, girl I thought a wild lion tiger mixed with Magilla Gorilla had attacked my ass. Benny was all over me like a cheap suit but with style. We make out in the living room. Touching. Fondling. Deep passionate kissing. Dry humping and more kissing. We finally leave the living room and make it to the hallway. We are bumping along the long hallway, kissing passionately and trying to get clothes off of each other. We finally make it to my bedroom, which is semi clean. I had tried on so many clothes, shoes and different clutches that night until it was unreal. It finally dons on me that I have clothes, shoes and clutches all over the place. I stop dead in my tracks and yell, "Stop! My room is a complete mess. We can't do anything in here!" Benny looked at me like I was crazy. He threw all that shit on the floor directly in front of my closet. Picked me up, threw me on the bed and did every and anything he wanted to do to me. I was in heaven. We both fell out from a night of pure ecstasy.

When I finally awoke the next morning, I was totally immersed in Benny's arms, feeling like I'm on top of the world. I look into his face, there is a calm happy look upon his face, even in his sleep. I rub his beautiful curly hair, stroke his yellow skin over his high cheek bones, and rub his very built masculine chest while gently raising the covers to take a quick look at what has my cooda throbbing so early in the morning. I'm in total ecstasy when my black ass look at the window and realize the sun is up. Shining bright. Birds chirping. I hear people happily walking down the street. I violently shake him, calling his name in a high pitched whisper, "BENNY. BENNY. BENNY!" He starts to move, he opens his eyes. Looks at me and says, "Good morning beau." I stop him mid-sentence placing my hand over his mouth and explain to him that my mother is home. I hear the shower running, I jump up. Grab his clothes frantically and very quickly. I remember what happened the last time she caught a boy in the house! I pack his shit so quick, look both ways out of my bedroom door to make sure the coast is clear, run him out the side door of the house and tell him to go south towards NW 23rd Ave and call Ernie. By having him head south, that kept my mom from seeing him as he left the house. It was all a way to keep my secret a secret that is if she ain't sitting in one of the other rooms looking out the window to see what is going on. I give him a quick kiss, rub that dick real quick, I ease the door shut. Run back to my room and make sure everything is straight in my room.

I walk into my mom's room while she is still in the shower and say, "Good morning mommy. Why didn't you wake me up when you got home?" I was trying to play this shit off and pick her brain at the same time, as she just seemed too damn calm in this shower. She replied, "Hey baby. Mommy know you been under a lot of pressure with school and I know you went out last night, so I just let you sleep." Man when I tell you, I almost did a damn triple double cartwheel.

I was in the most awesome mood. I told mommy I would cook us breakfast. Now my momma know I'm not the best cook, but she obliged. I know to cook a little bit, but not the big stuff. My mom was big on education and having your own, just in case a nigga get to tripping. You can pack your shit, tell him to kiss your ass and keep it moving. Never ever missing a got damn beat! I applaud my mother for installing that value in me. I don't have any regrets of being independent and able to walk away from anything that does not add value to me.

I went into the kitchen. Cleaned the few dishes in the sink that remained from the night before. I started a pot of grits first, took out the eggs and bacon. Pulled the cast iron skillet from the oven. Turned on the eye of the stove to start getting hot and cook the bacon. All the while I'm preparing me and my mother's breakfast, all I can think about is Benny and the wonderful few hours I had with him and do my own rendition of James Brown dancing. I never did get Benny's number, I only gave him my beeper and home phone number. I pondered that for a few minutes and was like fuck it, I'm good. After breakfast, mommy and I both went to bed and crashed. I finally woke up about 3 or 4 that afternoon. Shortly after I wake up, my phone starts to ring. My phone only rung in my room. My mother and I always had separate phone lines, with separate phone numbers. My line was mine and private and the same for my mom. I rolled over and answered in a very exasperated voice, "Helllo?" I was hoping it was Benny but it wasn't. It was Boo, who was supposed to call me at 6 am. When I realize its Boo, I click but in a quiet voice as to not alert my mom to what I had already gotten away with. I click and say, "Bitch, where the fuck was you at 6 am? Why you ain't call me? You know my momma came home and Benny was still in here slobbing, snoring and pooting like he pay the mortgage!" Boo thought that shit was funny as hell and in between laughs managed to get out a quick, "I'm sorry girl, I came home, took my clothes off and laid cross the bed thinking I could get back up to call you. You see how that worked out for the both of us!" We laughed about all the activities of the night before and how Ernie was all over her. Then here came the million dollar question. Boo asked, "How was your early morning desert with Mr. Benny?" I was too damn excited to tell her all the juice, but I had to make sure my mom was in a deep grizzly bear, hibernation sleep before I start telling this story. I told Boo to hold on real quick. I put the phone down gently. Eased out the bed to make sure it didn't make any noise. Slowly opened my bedroom door and damn near floated on air down the hall to my mom's bedroom. Before I could get in real good ear shot of her room, I heard her in there shifting gears like she was driving a semi-truck. I stuck my head in the room long enough to see that she was comatose.

I glide back to my room and damn near did a triple axel getting back in the bed to fill Boo in on all the happenings. I told her how the romance started in the front yard, with him taking my keys and opening the door like a perfect gentleman. Once that door shut, all hell broke loose. The deep kissing. The touching, caressing. Deep breathing. Heavy sweating and all this before we even have all of our clothes off. Benny was a perfect gentleman in his approach, his delivery and even his ending. Just telling her about my time with him was getting me all worked up. The phone beeps. I go crazy, hoping its Benny. I tell Boo that I will call her back soon as I get off the phone with him. I click over. In my sexiest voice I say, "Hel-lo!" The voice on the other end says, "Damn baby . . ." As soon as I recognized the voice, I just hung up. If only call block was available back in the day, a lot of headaches would have been avoided. I called Boo right back and we made plans to hook up later that day and hang out after we got a few more hours of sleep.

By the time I got up, it was late in the evening, but the sun was still up and shining bright. I called Boo and as she was just about to call me. We had both just gotten up and was about to hop in the shower. I told her to be ready in about an hour and I would slide through and scoop her up. I get funky fly fresh. You never know we were going to end up. I pick my girl up and she is funky fly fresh as well. We bend a few corners before we end up at one of our mutual homegirls house. Soon as we walk in the door the party starts. Drinks. Good food and my beeper constantly going off with a number I don't know. I ignore it at first because whoever it is can wait especially since they waited this late to contact me, plus I know it ain't Sincere because his ignant ass would just show up where ever I was. With a few more drinks in me and an hour or so passed, I call the number back and asked that infamous question, "Somebody paged me?" The voice on the other end that responded didn't sound like a voice I recognized, especially after he said what he said, "Yea, I got your number off the men's bathroom wall in Fletchers!" I'm totally taken aback. I know good and got damn well my number ain't on no damn men's bathroom wall in the hole in the wall jook joint, well at least I hope not! My eyes get big. My mouth drops open. I put my hand on my hip and I curse this bastard for the old and the new, then I hang up. I tell the girls what just happened and they raggedy asses fall out laughing. We get back to chillin when my beeper starts going off again back to back. It's the same number. I ignore it. My beeper keeps going. I finally call the number back and as soon as I hear them answer, I part my lips. take a deep breath to light into his ass again, when the voice on the other end sounds slightly familiar and screams, "Whoa, whoa, whoa Betty, this is Benny. Benny Blanco. I was just joking. I was just joking baby, please forgive me."

The biggest smile comes over my face. I toss my hair back and sit down on the couch like a little school girl. I ask Benny, "Why in the hell do you play so much? I know you can't think I'm some quick, cheap thrill with all the nasty things you did to me last night?" He just chuckles and does a quick moan in approval. We chit chat for a few then he asks, "What are you and your girls doing right now? The fellas and I are about to BBQ and I would love for you to come chill with me." I ask the girls real quick do they want to ride over to meet my friends and his friends. Everybody declines because it's Sunday and it's late. Everybody either has school or work tomorrow. Boo was the only one ready to ride. He gave me directions and I told him we would be there shortly.

Boo and I head cross town from Smokey Bear park to SW 34th Street to the Bee Hive. We pull up and there is a yard full of cars and people. I don't see Benny. I don't see Ernie. We sit in the car with it running for a few minutes, just in case we are in the wrong place. Just as I'm about to place the car in reverse, Benny and Ernie come walking out the door with pans of food to go on the grill, Benny sees me and yells, "Hey baby, get out the car and come on." Boo and I look at each and without saying one word, we were thinking, "What in the hell have we gotten ourselves into now?"

Boo and I are known to getting ourselves in some of the craziest situations, with no regard to the danger or outcome, so this outing was no different. We get out the car. Straighten our clothes up and make sure we are on point. You already know how women are when a new woman comes around that they don't know. So you know me, Imma give a fucking show and pose for a picture or two. We walk up. Pleasantly greet everyone. All seems fine and normal until Benny runs his light bright ass over to me and gives me the biggest hug and longest kiss. The dagger eyes started. The whispering started. My hand started to the small of my back. I always carried my pistol there, just in case some dumb shit popped off. Living in Gainesville, you never know! Benny introduced me and Boo to everybody and tried his hardest to make lite of the situation. He could see and feel the tension that was brewing. Which only got worse as the evening went on.

Benny was doing his absolute best to be the utmost perfect gentleman in this situation. He played hostess with the mostess, cook, bartender and man to me. Eventually the tension subsided when someone broke out the cards and said SPADES! Benny fixed my plate and had me sit behind him while he beat asses all around the spades table. We laughed. Cracked jokes. Ate like some cute pigs and enjoyed the rest of the evening. It was something about seeing and spending time with Benny in this capacity that made me care for him. Care for him a real sincere way. I think he was feeling the same way, with all the attention he was giving me and how genuine he came across. People started leaving. Taking overly filled plates of BBQ and side dishes. Filling up their cups of straight liquor. Waving good bye in a hurriedly fashion, as if no one sees what they are doing. Boo and I help Benny and Ernie clean up and put the food away, just as we are sneaking little bites to eat and packing our own plates to go. The night ends on a wonderful note, filled with fun, laughter, deep gazing eye stares. Quick booty rubs. Sneaky dick grabs. Passionate kissing, all while cleaning up. Ernie and Boo go outside and sit by the fire pit talking and actually becoming better acquainted. Benny and I stay in the house and recreate our own 5 alarm fire.

Monday comes and there is more of the same from Benny. Highly attentive and very affectionate. Each day we talk, we begin to communicate on a deeper level. Learning more and more about each other. Family. Past relationships. Future plans and desires. Likes and dislikes. Needs and wants. The more and more we talked and spent time, the more and more we became closer to one another. The week has passed and Boo wants to go shopping. She know good and got damn well I ain't had no real shopping money since Sincere and I broke up and I really didn't want to ask my mom, because the first thing out her mouth is, "What the fuck you need clothes and shoes for when you have 2 closets full of clothes?" I had heard that speech so many times, I could recite it myself in my sleep. Benny called and asked me to swing by and spend some time with him. You already know I was at his front door before I hung up the phone. We chilling when I tell him what me and Boo want to do. Before I could blink my eye, Benny put $500 in my hand and told me to have fun. I looked at him with a strange cock eyed look on myself. Just as I parted my lips to ask him a question. He kissed me and said, "You never have to want for anything, long as you are my lady!" I ain't need to hear another mutha fucking word. I kicked back and got real comfortable under the right side of his body. I laid my head in chest. Inhaled real deep and drifted off to sleep with his right arm wrapped around me.

Boo and I hit Orlando first. When we couldn't find exactly what we wanted. We rode through Daytona to see what they had and hit 95 north going to Jacksonville. When we hit Duval County it was on. We hit every store and had a freaking blast. We had clothes. We had shoes. We had matching purses with plenty of money left over to ball out when we got back to Gainesville. We go home. Get clean. I slide through and scoop Boo up. As usual my dog was clean as a mosquito dick. We hit Fletchers. It's thick as hell with all the usual's in there. No Benny. No Ernie. No beep. No message from any of the clique I see in the spot. No worries! We had a blast that night and did our usual of getting drunk on someone else tab and breakfast on they ass too. We went home and got ready for the park at T.B. McPherson on Sunday.

Sunday comes and goes with no word from Bennie. I still don't stress it. In dating Sincere, I know what is like to date a hustler who makes major moves. I know when that call come, they have to move and move like the wind with no trace. Sunday comes and goes. Monday and Tuesday come with no word. Now I'm looking a little crazy, because I at least figure he would have sent word by one of his homies. I still don't stress it too much. I keep it moving like a G and continue to do me. Friday late night, I'm home chilling in the bed watching movies. My beeper goes off. I don't rush to it. I think it's one of the flunkies that I gave my number to. Then my beeper starts going off back to back. I roll over to get it off the night stand to shut it off, when I accidentally hit the button to see all the pages and its Benny's special code. At first, I jump to call his fuck ass. Then I say, "Nah, let his ass sweat and get a tan waiting on me to call him back!"

I place my beeper on vibrate and stick it under my pillow thinking that will slow down the aggravation it is causing. The entire time I have it on vibrate, Benny is blowing my shit up. I get frustrated as hell and take it in the living room and place it under the cushions on the couch. When my movie is finally over. I get up. Fix me something to eat. Grab a cold one. Go back in the room and watch another movie. When it's over, I go get my beeper from under the cushion. The battery light is flashing like a caution sign. I check all the mixed texts. Each and every one is from Benny. By the time I call him back. You can hear the sleep in his voice, with the serious eye boogers. The phone rings one time before Benny answers. He wrestles with the phone and groggly says, "Hello?" I'm thinking to myself, *this bitch got the game all fucked up and twisted.* I respond with a quick, hasty, nasty, "Yeah, you paged me? What you want?" Benny tries to come with a soft, somber, childlike voice and say, "Baby please forgive me. I had to go out of town unexpectedly and didn't have time to call you before I left or once I reached my destination. It was rock and roll once I got there." I'm listening to all this shit and instantly think to myself, *"This nigga must think I'm some kind of fool and don't know any damn better." You're gone the entire week and weekend, probably with some other chick. Doing gawd only knows what.* I reply with a simple, "Uhhhhhuhh, yeah whatever. When did you get back? What did you bring back for me?" I just wanted to see what the hell he would say and produce. You can't shoot me no bullshit, empty ass lie and not have something to back it up with. There is silence on the phone for a few minutes. I aggressively say, "HELLO." In the phone to try and get his attention after my last question. Benny plays the game just as good as I do. He slowly and grasply responds, "Yes baby, I'm sorry I dozed off. What did you say?" I quickly responded, "When did you get back? What did you bring back for me?" He did that ole player caught up in some shit cough and came back quick, "Baby you know I got something extra special for you!" That's all I needed to hear. I told him, "Ok, yeah. I guess I'll see you later. I'm going to bed." I just hung up the phone and didn't say another word.

Saturday rolls around. Boo calls me because you know we're trying to tear up the streets. I tell Boo my pockets looking kinda lite. Sincere was a true hemorrhoid in my virgin ass, but he always took damn good care of me. With his absence, I was getting a reality check. My mom took care of all my needs and a lot of my wants. But all that unnecessary bullshit I wanted, moms wasn't going for it. Especially since I was older and thought I was grown. So you already know I wasn't trying to fix my bowl mowf ass to go down that hall and ask her pistol toting ass for shit. Just as Boo said she had me, I get dressed my phone beeped that there was another call on the other end. I tell Boo to hold on real quick. I click over and say, "Hello." In my sexiest voice. I'm hoping its Sincere. Low and behold it ain't. DAMN! It's Benny. He quickly says, "Baby, I know it's the weekend and you and Boo want to go out. Come by my brother PePe house and get some money. I don't want nobody doing shit for you!" On the inside, I'm doing cartwheels, but I play the shit cool and respond, "I don't know about that. I ain't trying to show up over PePe house and one of your bitches show up coz I don't have time for the bullshit and games Benny!" This bitch actually had the audacity to try and catch a fucking attitude and say, "Well fuck it, I don't care if you drink or eat since you don't know how to act!!" You already know I snatched an attitude big and wide as my ass. He had me hot as fish grease on a Friday night in front of a church trying to raise money for their building fund. I quipped back in a quick stern voice, "Bitch, don't get it twisted. I don't need yo fuck, pussy ass. I got my own mutha fucking money and will never ever bow down to you or an mutha fucker with or without money! Miss me with that shit and I'll holla at you when I'm down and out!" I hung up that phone so mutha fucking quick and hard, I heard something rattle in the phone. I was never broke. I always had money. Just not the amount of money I felt I should have. I was never in need of a bitch to take care of me, because I always knew how to save my money thanks to my mommy and Tee Tee. One of the most valuable life lessons my Tee Tee ever taught me was, *"You never ever let a man, woman or child. Black, yellow or white handle you and think they have you bent over a barrel. Always have you some money stashed away somewhere and play ya cards close to your chest."*

Boo and I went out that night. Of course we went to Fletchers. There wasn't and still aren't many places for the black people to hangout in Gainesville. Don't get me wrong. There is always a local club promoter doing some grown and sexy event or throwing a concert for the latest hot entertainer, but it isn't an every weekend thing. We go to Fletchers, grab our favorite drink, a Funky Monkey and make our way to the crowded dance floor area. We are having a dam good time, vibing to the ferocious bass beat. Being extra cute sipping our Funky Monkey drinks. I'm good and toasted. I feel a hand on my right shoulder. I don't think anything about it. Someone is always bound to touch you to try and get by you so they can get to the dance floor. When the hand remains on my shoulder.

I get worried that it's someone who is about vomit or fall out. I grab the hand on my right shoulder with my left hand. I grip it hard to ensure I have control of whatever they are about to do. I turn my head to the right and all I see is a stomach. I look up. It's Benny. He is smiling and cheesing like he wasn't just missing for an entire week or that he had just talked to me like he had lost his ever loving rabbit ass mind. I snatch my hand from his and turn back around and keep dancing.

Benny stands there all night like my personal bodyguard. I don't move and neither does he. Its last call for alcohol at 1:45 am. Boo and I second round of drinks have now dwindled down to the last few little pieces of ice. We have to make a pivotal decision right now. Do we get another one and ride out or just call it night. When we make the decision to make a run for it and grab something at the country, bootleg after hours spot. Benny and Ernie walk up with 2 fresh drinks. We gladly take the drinks. Thank the fellas and walk outside to stand in the parking lot and watch all the happenings before we leave for the afterhours spot. The usual baby mommas fighting each other while the dude ain't nowhere to be found. The crack head popping up like a jack in box trying to get that last, late night hustle on. Benny is on me like crazy, asking to just talk to me. He was making a scene and embarrassing me. I'm not one to make a scene in public. I never know who is in the crowd looking. I finally step behind the oak tree in the dark. Place my hands on my hips and ask very sternly, with my teeth clinched so tight, air couldn't slip through, "What the fuck do you want Benny? You was gone for an entire week, no word from you or the fellas. Then when you do pop up you talking shit to me like you thought I was just supposed to take that. Who the fuck do you think I am? I'm not her or them, so get your shit together!!" Benny is just standing there, looking down on me like he just want to karate chop my ass in the throat. Girl, his eyes was slaying me left and right. You already know them red ones is my weakness and he was making me so weak. Standing there, in all his sexiness glory. Smelling good. His slacks and dress shirt hanging from his body like they were tailor made to fit each and every muscle just right. I was praying he didn't touch me, because that would have made my wanna be mad ass, soft as wet tissue. Benny was smooth with his approach. He moved in closer, as if he was ready to strike to kill. I backed up slightly folding my arms, smirking my lips to make it appear as if I'm boiling. When in reality I'm already weak girl, wanting and needing his ass to touch me. He leans in a little closer and says in the sexiest voice, "Baby, I know you're highly pissed with me and you have every right to be. I just want to hold you in my arms and make it up to you, but I know if I touch you right now you are going to let my ass have it. So how about this? Find out what your schedule is for school and let's plan a little mini getaway with just me and you. Everything on me!" *Duhh mutha fucker. Who else was going to pay for it?* is what I wanted to say, but I played hard and cool and calmly replied, "Uhmmm I will see what I can do." As I turn to walk away and go find Boo, Benny grabs me, pulls me into his body and holds me tight and kisses me like I have never ever been kissed before. Once again, my little cooda is out of my panties and in his drause having a grand time. When we finally let go of each other and I come to, Benny is in the car with Ernie his best friend and PePe his brother peeling out the little dirt parking lot. Once I get my damn sense back. I find Boo and we ride out to the country bootleg joint and I'm quiet the whole way there, damn!

Monday comes. I check my school schedule and managed to do the assigned work before hand, turn it in and get the entire week off. I was only taking 3 classes at the time anyway, so it wasn't that big of a deal to get work knocked out. I call Benny and tell him the news and he sounds highly excited like a kid on Christmas Eve ready to open up all his gifts. Benny tells me he is going to rent a car and take care of some last minute stuff and then he will come scoop me up so we can leave town no later than noon on Wednesday. I oblige and handle things on my end as well. Wednesday comes. Benny calls me early that morning and tells me to be ready by noon and that he will call me as soon as he is on his way. I oblige and go back to sleep. I get up about 10, shower, double check my bags and make sure my hair and makeup is laid. Noon comes and go. 1pm comes and goes as well. No phone call. Now, I'm getting pissed and just want to lay into his ass something decent. About 3:45 my phone rings and it's Benny. Before I can part my lips good to start going off, Benny says, "Baby, I know you're mad as fuck and so am I. I was hoping to be on the road by now but something came up and I need your help." I'm looking rather perplexed because I'm wondering what could have come up that you need my help all of a sudden. I ask the million dollar question in a very exhausted voice, "Benny what has supposedly happened now?" He takes in a deep breath and that's when I should have just hung up the phone, but my nosey ass wants to hear this shit. He says, "I let PePe hold the truck to go run some errands and he got caught up in something at Alachua General Hospital and I need you to come pick up the extra set of keys and go pick up the rental truck. It's in the parking lot right by the emergency room entrance." My first question was, "Why would I drive my car to AGH? Leave my car? Pick up the rental? Come back to pick you up? Then drive back out to AGH and pick up my car when I can just take you to pick it up and we head out from there?" He had an answer for everything. Benny says, "No baby, I need you to go pick it up because I have some business to take care of and I don't want it to hinder us from getting on the road." I'm like whatever at this point, so I ask him where he is and he tells me PePe house, which happens to be right around the corner from me. I hop in the car, speed round the corner to Tree Trail apartments and get the extra set of rental keys from Benny. There is a look on his face and in his eyes that I have never seen before and my gut instinct tells me to run!

While driving to AGH, my mind, body and gut keep telling not to go. The closer and closer I get my mind is still saying not to go. I pull into the ER parking lot. I see the burgundy Nissan Pathfinder but there isn't any parking over there, so I drive a block away and park. Once at the hospital everything is beautiful. The wind is blowing nice. The birds are chirping. The temperature is perfect for my little mini getaway with the man I have been seeing for a couple of months now. With those thoughts in my head, I get a little extra pep in my step and make a bee line to the truck. I have the key in hand. I hit the alarm button. Open the door. I place my right leg and hip in the driver seat. Stick the key in the ignition just as I'm about to lift my left leg up to place in the truck all I hear is "PUT YOUR MUTHA FUCKING HANDS IN THE AIR . . . GET OUT OF THE TRUCK . . . TURN THE TRUCK OFF . . . GET ON THE GROUND . . . GET ON THE FUCKING GROUND!" I'm stuck. I can't move. For a few seconds. I don't see anything or anybody. All I can do is hear all these voices yelling all these different commands at me. I keep my left hand in the air. Slowly lower my right hand to shut off the ignition. With keys in my right hand, I slowly exit the truck with my hands in the air. I walk sideways but backwards towarda the car next to me in a slow pace as to not alarm them and they shoot me prematurely. Police from Gainesville police department came from all over the hospital. It seemed as if they descended from the shallow, short roof like they were mountaineers. They popped up out the ground like a Jack in the box and out the bushes like flies. I had never seen that many cops in one place in my life. I have both of my hands raised, as they have their weapons cocked and aimed at me still yelling all these different commands. My dumb as a box of rocks ass yell back to the police, "It's ok, I'm not stealing the car, I have the keys! I have the keys. The car is rented to my boyfriend Benny Blanco!"

One officer is coming in close for the kill and screams at me "GET ON THE FUCKING GROUND!!" You could see the fire in his eyes to destroy me. As I'm dropping to my knees to get on the ground and lay down on my stomach, the officer comes in and takes me down with force. Placing his knee in my back. Forcing my hands behind my back to arrest me. He aggressively places the cuffs on my wrists. Snatched me up like a dirty sheet and places me against a police car that apparently sped into the parking lot when I was in a daze, as I do not remember ever seeing a police car. I'm leaning up against this hot ass police car, a female officer comes over and pats me down. While she is frisking me, I ask, "Ma'am can one of you please call my mother? She works for the Alachua County Sheriff's office?" The female officer never responds. She just placed me in the back of the squad car and shut the door. I'm sitting there in the back of this police car with a million thoughts running through my head about to drown in my tears. I'm watching the officers high five one another and mull around like they had just captured the #1 most wanted criminal for the FBI. I'm thinking to myself, "What the fuck did I just get myself into?" My mind is going fast as hell but at the same time in slow motion. I'm trying to replay everything over and over again in my mind, well as figure out what the fuck is going on and how am I getting out of this. I can't go to jail. I'm far too cute, plus I'm supposed to be heading out of town on vacation with my man. Ohhhh shit, my momma!! I had never ever been to jail in my life. I had never been arrested. I have never been in trouble, well besides minor speeding tickets and that one car accident. Nothing like this before, especially with my mother being a sheriff deputy. None of the police are talking to me. They just have me sitting in the back of this damn squad car. No one has read me my rights. No one is doing anything but inspecting the vehicle, taking finger prints and pictures of the outside and inside of the car.

About an hour passes and I'm still sitting there when I see two plain clothes detectives walk up. The first one looks at me and shoots me the nasty look. The 2nd one walks up. We lock eyes. He is staring at me and I'm staring right back at him just as hard. He squints. I squint. When I finally recognize who it is, I start bumping the window with my right shoulder and nodding my head for him to come in my direction. The 2nd detective was a close friend of the family and knew me and my mother very well. He walks over to the car, opens the door, leans in real close and says, "What the fuck are you doing here and in the back of this police car for Christ's sake? I know you don't have anything to do with this do you?" Now I'm getting somewhere because I still have the slightest idea as to what the hell has happened. I'm in tears now because I see someone I know and I feel as though I have a pretty good chance of going home. The tears start flowing down my face like again. I look up at him dead square in the eyes with my voice cracking I say, "Eric, I don't have the slightest fucking idea as to what is going on here. All I know is I came to pick up the car for my boyfriend so we could go out of town on vacation. I get here; get in the car and ohhhh my God Armageddon starts. They arrest me and throw me in the car and no one has said anything to me. I swear, I swear to God,

I don't know what is going on and I for damn sure didn't have anything to do with this!" Eric looks at me, shakes his head and says, "I know you didn't have anything to do with this and you're not under arrest, they just have you detained to get a better idea of what's going on. Let me talk to the officers and I will be right back with you." Before he can shut the door I yell, "ERIC, can somebody please and I do mean please take these cuffs off me and may I have something to drink. I have money on me, I just need these cuffs off and a drink to cool down?" The look in Eric's eyes was one of light in at the end of the tunnel. He nodded and called for the female officer to come uncuff me. Eric walked off and soon returned with a cold Pepsi from the vending machine and then he disappeared into the hospital.

I'm still sitting in the back of the police car, but at least I don't have any cuffs on me. It seems like a freaking eternity has passed. It has been 2.5 hours. Eric finally emerges from the hospital with tapes and a stack of papers in his hands. He walks over to his car and places the items in and then walks over to the squad car where I am, opens the door and asks me, "Do you know or are you associated with Pepe King?" I respond, "Yea, I know Pepe" with a confused, puzzled look on my face. Eric then asks, "How do you know PePe?" I'm getting worried but I answer, "I'm dating Pepe's brother Benny. I don't know him like that, but I have seen him a few times when Benny and I are spending time." The look on Eric's face when I said who I was dating made me feel like I had really just fucked up really bad. Eric is screaming at me, "WHAT THE FUCK ARE YOU DOING DATING THE LIKES OF ONE MR. BENNY BLANCO? DID YOU KNOW THAT THIS TRUCK WAS USED IN THE COMMISSION OF AN ATTEMPTED ARMED BANK ROBBERY ON AGH CREDIT UNION BY PEPE?" He walks off for a few minutes, paces the parking lot and comes back and asks me, "Do you know how many times Benny has been to prison? Do you know how many times I have arrested him my damn self and sent him to prison for credit card fraud, theft, robbery and other fucking crimes that can send your pretty little ass to prison for a very long time and you and I both know you ain't built for prison and your momma would die if not kick your ass to sleep!" Ok, now work with me and get the oxygen tank and a fucking pamper because I had just pissed and shitted on myself. When Eric said all that, I was done. My heart stopped because all I can see is me going to prison with my momma foot stuck in my ass. She is doing long, hard time with me because they could not remove her foot from my ass. I'm looking around all crazy, trying to gather my mind and I ask Eric, "Say what? Are you serious? I thought he was just street hustled like a dime bag or 2 of weed. I didn't know he was stealing people's credit cards and robbing like that. I know nothing about any bank robbery or any other crime, come on Eric you know me and you know I'm a straight laced kid." Now as I'm telling Eric this, I sitting with my feet on the ground facing him and I turn my head to the right and see a Dodge Omni that looks oddly familiar ride by real slow.

Eric asks me several more questions and verifies that to his partner that I was nowhere near this place or had anything to do with this failed botched attempt of a bank robbery of a damn hospital bank. For some reason his partner had a serious hard on for me in having something to do with this damn attempted bank robbery. I'm still sitting on the side of the police car waiting, hoping and praying to be released by Barnaby Jones wanna be, when that raggedy Dodge Omni passes by again. This time, it rides by slow enough for me to see who is in the got damn car. PePe is driving with a beard on his face looking like Osama Bin Laden youngest son. There is some fat light skinned dude in the passenger seat that I have never seen in my life and here goes Benny in the backseat of this small ass clown car with his knees in his chest, a hat and sunglasses trying to look inconspicuous. Just as I jumped with excitement and had just took a deep breath and parted my lips to call Eric and Barnaby Jones to the car and tell them to go bend the block to apprehend their culprits, Eric walked over to the car and said, "Betty let me tell you something and you better fucking listen to me like I'm your fucking momma and daddy. I saw the tapes from inside and outside and I don't see you anywhere in them. I know you and how you were raised, so I already know you ain't involved in this shit, but if I ever and I do mean ever find out that you are still dating Benny Blanco I will make up charges to throw you in prison for life just because I can! Do you fucking understand me?" With tears running down my face mixing in with snot and boogahs going into my mouth, I dry heave and say, "Yes sir, I understand. If I'm free to go, can someone give me a ride home?" Eric said, "Hell nah, call Benny and tell him to come pick you up and that somebody wants to talk to him!"

I know, I know, I know. You are trying to figure out why I didn't tell Eric and the Police Academy squad that PePe and Benny was circling the block like vultures ready to swoop in for the leftovers. I was so fucking heated and pissed with everything that had happened. How he got me caught up in some bullshit that could have potentially sent me to prison. Harmed my family or even put my mom's job in jeopardy, I wanted revenge! There was nothing the police could do that would remotely add up to what I had in mind for his high yella smooth talking ass. I walk up the drive of the emergency room parking lot. Make a left as if I'm going to the bus depot to catch the bus, but I duck off between some buildings and bushes and walk the long way back to my parked car on the other side of the hospital. Trust me, I waited almost a damn hour before walking to my damn car just in case they jump off the roof again on my ass. I get in the car, sit there and just loose it. I'm mad. I'm scared. I'm angry. I'm hurt. All I can do is think of where to find his ass and put a hollow point in his temple.

I finally make it home. I'm blowing Boo'Fawnda beeper up back to back to back to back. I don't even think to stop and call the house phone and see if she is home, I just start paging her. She never calls me back. About 15 minutes later, Boo sky blue 2 door Regal slides up in the middle of my momma yard. She just walks in and says, "What the fuck is going on? Where have you been? I've been beeping you all damn day and you ain't answered? Now you're blowing me up and shit." I just bust out crying, slobbing and snotting all at the same damn time and tell Boo everything that has happened. She starts crying, then she beat me getting mad and was ready to fuck Benny ass up. We talk for a few and then reality really hits. I need to call my mom and tell her everything that has happened.

It ain't never ever took me that long to call my mommy. I picked up the phone at least 10 times and put it back down on the kitchen table. Boo finally picked up the phone and dialed the number. She held the phone until my momma picked up. Soon as I heard my mommy voice, I bust out in tears. I can't talk. All she hear is crying slobbering gibberish. She asked me if I was home. I was able to get out a, "Yes ma'am." All I hear is something about she is on her way. I'm more scared of what the hell she is going to do to me than anything. Her car skids up in the yard right behind Boo. My mom walks in, Boo is on the couch and I'm sitting at the table. I tell my mom everything that happens. I'm crying and still snotting. I even tell her how the bastard had the nerve to ride by the damn crime scene several times and never ever once stopped to turn him or his brother in. My mom, grabs me and gives me the biggest hug and kiss ever and reassured me she was not mad. She said, "We all get caught up with a raggedy ass nigga in our life from time to time. I just hate this raggedy mutha fucker tried you like this but don't worry about it baby, mommy got this one!" She went in her room shut the door. I heard her talking but I didn't stress her phone call. I was just thankful that she believed and trusted me to know that I didn't do anything wrong and I didn't have her size 12 in my ass!

For weeks, Boo and I looked for Benny. We never ever saw him again or heard from any of his friends. It was as if they all had made tracks in the wind. A few months have passed now and I get a call from my mom saying she and a few of her friends at the jail are under investigation. I'm confused and I asked more questions, but she just said to stay up and we would talk when she got off at 11. She was currently working the evening shift. I was pacing the hallway, worrying like crazy until my mom came home. When I saw the lights pull up in the yard, I ran to the door. I opened the door and was like, "MOMMY, what is going on? What happened? Mommy took off her utility belt, took off her uniform shirt and grabbed an ice cold beer from the freezer that I always placed up there for her. We sit down at the kitchen table when she says, "Benny called Eric and explained everything to him and how you didn't have anything to do with the attempted armed bank robbery and that you never knew he was a thief. He turned himself in a few weeks ago with Eric as he had some outstanding warrants here and a few other counties in Florida, Alabama and a couple for Georgia." My face is on the floor in 1000 pieces. I don't even know what to say. A few other counties, Alabama and Georgia?

Ok, remember the week he was missing and told me he was out of town on business? Well he was out of town on business. He was sitting in a Tallahassee jail on an outstanding warrant for the same crime of forgery, uttering forged instrument, bad checks amongst a plethora of charges. He sat there on that warrant until a bond was set. Well let's go back to his entire criminal and prison history. This is Benny Blanco complete prison history. It reads like someone's college transcript. 5/88 -6/88 is his first time in prison. I'm guessing he violated probation as it was only for a month. His 2nd time in prison was from 10/90 – 11/92. 3rd time 12/93 – 6/95. When he got out 6/95 is when I met him and dated for a hot couple of months. His 4th time in prison was from 1/96 – 4/99. 5th time 2/02 – 6/06!

My mom continues to tell me that Benny has filed a complaint against our friends that work at the jail, claiming that they were abusing him and treating him less than. Benny is claiming that officers are beating him and that they are allowing the other inmates to beat on him as well, they aren't allowing him to eat, among a list of other trumped up charges. The complaint went to the major and was dismissed. Apparently that wasn't enough for him, so he sends it up to the Secretary of Corrections. Now he is trying to really get people fired and for what? The case sat up there for a few weeks. An investigation was conducted and it too was thrown out! Shortly after all of that, Benny has his day in court for his outstanding warrants and is sentenced to prison, yet once again. I never hear from or see Benny again, but I did see his mammy in Winn Dixie on North Main Street. This snagga toof heffa had the nerves to grab my left arm as I throw her a quick wave and slide past her and she says, "Betty why did you do my son like that?" I'm always respectful of my elders and I was trying to remain respectful as much as possible, but Snaggle Puss kept going and I lost it. Before I knew it, I said, "Bitch are you serious? Your cock loving son got me twisted up in some shit that could have damaged my family well as my future. You gave birth to his raggedy ass when you should have swallowed his sorry ass. Since you all up in my business, please find yourself all up in a dentist office and leave me the fuck alone!" She had me so got damn hot, I was crying because I was ready to fight. It wasn't until she walked off that I noticed the crowd of people who had gathered. I gathered myself and quickly left. I never saw her again either and thank goodness I didn't, as I would not be responsible for what happened the next time.

I did a recent check of the Florida department of corrections and see where Benny Blanco is back in prison for the 6th time since 10/2010 and is not due for release until 2017! You don't even have to ask what the charges are, as they are the same that they have always been.

My homegirl Boo'Fawnda is doing wonderful. Boo graduated college, had an excellent career in Social Work before getting married to a wonderful Christian man who moved her away to another country and has Boo living like the true queen she is.

Now, I know you're wondering what ever happened to Mr. PePe King? He was eventually caught and from what I last heard, he did go to prison for his attempted armed robbery of a got damn hospital bank. ~~Ain't That Bout'a Bitch~~

CHAPTER 3

KNOCK KNOCK, GUESS WHO

After the entire Benny situation I didn't want to date, go with, hold hands, hug, look at or even remotely think about another man. Even though Benny and I were together for a few months, it felt like I had been drug through the Vietnam War and over glass for damn near 10 years. I never went to jail for any of the foolishness Benny had me caught up in. My name was cleared and Benny went back to prison in 1996. He was sentenced to 5 years, but only did 3. I focused solely on my studies in order to complete my degree in Mental Health Counseling. I dated here and there but nothing serious, just pretty much chilling and building my stable up of dudes who I liked but no real desire to be with any of them.

Sincere started coming back around in a strong way and I was avoiding his attempts to come back in my life like The Matrix. One day he caught me off guard and came to my job with my favorite food, some of the prettiest lilies, wine inside of water bottles and sat in the front lobby until I couldn't take it anymore. I brought him back to my office. We moved all the furniture out the way and made a very cute and cozy picnic on the floor and talked. We ate and just reconnected like we did when I was young and in love all those years ago. In all the time I had been with him from 1992 until that time, that little girl he first met and drove home from the driving range on NE 12th Street had died and been reborn into the woman who sat before him. Sincere was not ready for Ms. Betty. By the time Sincere and I rekindle our relationship, he was major in the streets and making some serious big boy moves. Meanwhile, I'm starting out my professional career as a Sr. Health Coordinator with a grassroots HIV/AIDS agency. Sincere still kept all of his professional life away from mine and kept that same respect for me and my family whenever he came around or we went out on our dates and out of town for mini vacations. Things are going great between us. My allowance picks up again which was great for me. I went back to school for another degree in Psychology with a minors in Substance Abuse. Suddenly while I'm going back to school and working like a damn slave for this grassroots agency, I became ill. I go to the Doctor and I'm diagnosed with diabetes and placed on 5 different medications to get everything under control and also told that I can't have any children. I didn't get upset about not having kids, shit I was concerned about getting this diabetes under control. One week into taking the meds I can't keep any food down. I'm losing weight, my hair is falling out and I'm pale white, always tired and just out of it. Sincere sees me like that and freaks out, my mom freaks too and they rush me to the hospital with all my meds. The hospital runs all kinds of test and come to find out I don't have diabetes. I just have an elevated level of testosterone and overly elevated amount of lactic acidosis. The doctor had originally prescribed 2500mg metformin daily, along with aldactone and some other meds. The ER doctor told us that had I waited any longer I would have died. The amount of lactic acidosis built up in my body was off the charts. They put me on an IV for a few hours, kept checking me and eventually sent me home. Sincere was so damn scared I was about to die, he did everything I asked of him for and I was loving it. We could be watching TV, I would cough and he would jump and ask, "Baby what's wrong? What do you need?" I use to laugh until one day he asked me that and I told him I wanted a new truck. A Tahoe!

Sincere gave me the money the following week. I went to Jacksonville and got my burgundy Tahoe trimmed in tan! I was still sick as hell when we went to pick it up but I pushed that baby all the way back to Gainesville and rode out like a champ. Things are going well between us which of course is throwing me off because I'm just waiting for something to pop off. Sincere put some music in my truck so I just knew I was the shit then, I'm bumping with the big dogs. At the time he had the green machine Pontiac and I had the Tahoe so we was complete. The grassroots agency closed its doors due to bankruptcy in late 1999, so Sincere increased my allowance until I found another job. I started working for the state Department of Health in 2000 working in HIV/AIDS/STD department and loved it. One day while out in the field, I went looking for Sincere because he was late with my allowance. When I did find him, he was on his 4 wheeler in front of Amoeba house with the fellas. I see her car but don't pay that shit any attention. I pull right in her yard directly in front of Sincere and wave for him to come here so we can talk in private. You know I ain't one to show out in public. This Negro had the nerve to wave me off and say,

"Man, get out of here I'll deal with you later!" Who in the fuck do this nigga think he talking to is what's rolling through my mind. I wave for him to come to me once again and this time he starts slick rapping since he got an audience. The fellas laugh and I get hotter than an overheated radiator with no water. I throw my hands up, nod my head, and place my truck in reverse backing up slowly trying not to hit the trees behind me. I slam on the brakes throw my truck in drive, punch the gas and hit that damn 4 wheeler head on. Sincere is scrambling trying to turn it on while the fellas are screaming and trying to get me to stop. I'm pressing forward full speed ahead, pushing the 4 wheeler with Sincere still on it towards the ditch behind him. Just as I have him cornered, Sincere turns the wheels to the 4 wheeler and the back tires hit a tree. I'm steady pushing on the gas and he steady praying the wheel don't slip off that tree. I see the fear in his eyes. I stop, crank my music up and slowly back out of the yard just as if nothing has ever happened. I bend a few corners and head home hours later, only to find my allowance in an envelope in between the storm door and the front door. One day that little boy will learn to stop playing with me.

Sincere never changed and I never believed he did. We grew up together in a comfort zone. Always knowing we would be there for one another no matter what each other did. I was always his safe haven from the streets and gold diggers. He was always my loving cuddly teddy bear who took care of me and any situation I needed help with no matter who ever or whatever was going on. We are still kicking it after the whole allowance fiasco and once again, I had to reiterate how crazy I am when I start hearing in the streets there is another baby. One story said the baby was already born, another story says ole girl was still pregnant. Since I can't make heads or tails of it, I let it ride and figure when the time is right, it will be revealed to me. After a grueling day of STD clinic and seeing roughly 30 people, I'm bone tired, but I have class that night in Jacksonville. I head out from work and stop to get some gas from the cheap gas station on NW 23rd Ave right next to Smokey Bear Park. I leave the truck running, with the music bumping. I'm filling up my gas tank when an old 84' Regal pulls up smoking and back firing. I turn my truck off with the quickness to make sure we both don't blow up. As I'm standing at the pump, I see the girl get out the regal and have to lift the door up to open and close it. You know how those old heavy car doors are once they are out of place, you have to lift them up to open and close or your ass is subject to fall out on the wrong turn. I see this but don't pay her no attention. A few moments later she comes on my side and asks, "Ain't yo name Betty who go with Sincere?" I'm tired and have been through this drill before, ain't no more smiling from me when you mention his name. I respond, "Yea, I'm Betty.

Why?" She feel cocky now since her homegirl has put $10 on pump two and says, "I don't know if you heard or if he told you but I'm pregnant with his baby!" Now I'm smiling and ask her, "Really? What's your name baby?" She so retarded this bitch starts rubbing her flat ass belly, smiling with that one gold tooth in the front and says, "My name is Rah'feekiey and I'm with Sincere now!" You already know, I don't say one word because I can't afford to lose my career over an assault charge on a pregnant hoe. I finish filling up my tank, get the printed receipt from the pump and in the calmest voice I can muster up I say, "Congratulations Feeky boo! You live in Phoenix Apartment's right? I hope y'all have a healthy baby and live out the rest of your days in paradise, but I need you to understand one thing. I didn't have to fuck Sincere and get a baby to get this truck. I don't have to have a baby to get my weekly allowance nor do I have to run up in another female face and tell you or her anything about me, because y'all already know who the hell I am. So please, next time save the drama for him and not me!" She was standing there looking at me as I jumped back in my truck smiling the whole damn time. Since she was standing there I figured I would give her something to look at, I turned my music up and beat the roof off the Tahoe as I pulled out from the gas station. You know just as soon as I got further down the road I called Sincere and went in. Girl I was so deep in Sincere ass, I felt like a tampon. When I got out of class that night at 10 pm, Sincere was parked next to my truck and trying to talk. I'm not one to make a scene in public, so I told him let's just go home and talk about it then.

When we got to my mom's house, I was standing in front of Sincere while he was sitting on the driver's side with his feet on the ground. He was trying to explain to me that he has never slept with her, she just help him to do his dirt, yada yada yada. The more he talk, the madder and hotter I got. Just as I was about to say "Fuck it" and walk off, Sincere comes out his mouth and said, "Bitch, if you just shut the fuck up and listen you will understand!" I broke 3 fingernails pass the meat that night jumping on Sincere's ass, there was blood everywhere. I never let him get out the car, I kept him inside the car and hit him with everything I had in me. I see the blinds in the living room move, but I think it's the AC kicking on because at that time of night my mom is normally sleep. I keep fighting and wailing on Sincere and not once did he ever hit me back, he was just blocking me from hitting him in the face. A few seconds later I hear "CLICK CLICK!" I stop fighting, stand up never moving from where I'm standing. Sincere damn near knocks me to the ground screaming, "Ma, oh thank God! Ma please come get her she is crazy and jumping on me for nothing!" My mom has come to the end of the drive way with the shotgun in her hand, just standing there. I'm froze because I'm not sure what the hell she is about to do. My mom finally asks, "Betty what the fuck is going on out here? Is he hitting you?" I shake my head no and answer in a quiet little girl voice, "No ma'am. I'm jumping on him because he got another girl pregnant and she had the nerve to approach me at the gas station before I went to school tonight. I couldn't take it ma so I hit him a few times." My mom let out a quick "uhmmpph", turned around with loaded and cocked shotgun in hand and walked back into the house like it wasn't nothing. Before I could blink my eyes good Sincere had jumped back into his car and peeled out of there so damn quick the dust was still floating. I don't even think he stopped at the stop sign. I was the only one left standing outside trying to figure out what the hell just happened.

You know that mishap was short lived, Sincere came back like clockwork the next day spending time and doing the normal stuff he did to make up. The weekend comes and we hit The Royal Blue night club which was the hottest spot in Gainesville at one time. We're nestled in a corner close to the dance floor chilling, having drinks. A few people came up to handle business and I'm looking at him like "I know you ain't crazy and done lost your mutha fucking mind?" He gives me some money, I walk over to the picture booth and let Parker the snitching powder head take a few pics of me. Soon as I walk in the area where you take pictures, I see Ms. Rah'Feekiey with one of her homegirls who she tries to tap on the sly. I speak and say, "Heyyyyy girl what is you doing in here with that special bundle of joy in your belly?" She is smiling from ear to ear with that one gold tooth in the front of her head rubbing on her flat belly once again. She says, "Girl I had to let Sincere know what time it was, until he propose to me I'm grown and can do what I want to do, he got me fucked up!" I laugh my ass off and agree with her, because apparently she didn't get the memo that Sincere was in the club with me and I didn't dare say one word. I let her and the homegirl take their pics first, hell I even complimented her on the pics. I sashay my ass up there and do my own rendition of a big hip Naomi Campbell and tore it up! Once I finished taking my pics, I walk back to my cozy corner with Sincere where he had a fresh drink waiting for me. I gave him my pics to look at and tell him his baby mamma was in here. He blew me off. Just as those words left my mouth Feeky boo walked by. With cat like reflex I jumped out the corner and grabbed her, when she turned around and saw Sincere her mouth dropped. Sincere stepped in front of me and went the fuck off. She tried to step up and say something but when I saw Sincere ball up his fist I stepped in between them to keep him from bashing her head in. Sincere's cousin and brother came and pulled him away, Feeky boo sped off and Sincere was trying his hardest to not catch a fresh one in the club and started explaining. I didn't care anymore. I had my truck, music, weekly allowance, still doing me and didn't have to have sex with Sincere unless I wanted to. So what did I care?

A few weeks pass and its Tuesday, STD clinic day. For some reason I stayed up front with the doctors and medical assistance that day and goofed off. When the clerks brought the charts to the back of the clients who had checked in, I went through them just to see what kind of day we would have when I came across a familiar name. Normally the medical assistance do the work up on the client before the doctor and I see them. I didn't have to go in the exam room with the doctor, I just use to like to go and be nosey especially when he would stick the extra, long wood stick cotton swab in the urethra of a man and turn it 10-15 times to the right and then turn it 10-15 times to the left to ensure he got a good sample for stat lab. The men would act all brave and strong while I was in the room but as soon as I walked out you could hear them let out a scream that would curdle your blood. There are too many funny stories about STD clinic day that deserves a book all on its own. Anyhow, I see the name of the person I know and tell the medical assistant, "I got this patient don't worry about it. When I finish with her you can check it and make sure I got everything you need." She laughed and said, "Ok Betty I got cha!" I grabbed the chart and started calling her name from the back where we sit, While walking towards the waiting area I say, "Rah'Feekiey. Ms. Rah'Feekiey please come to room 2!" As I was rounding the corner she was as well and we met face to face at the corner. Feeky boo eyes got big as silver dollar pieces and her mouth dropped but never said a word. I led her exam room #2. Introduced myself, told her what I did and what I was about to do before the doctor came to see her and that if she tested positive for any STD's, she would see me again and we would need to delve deeper into her sexual history and partners. She damn near pissed on herself. When it comes to my career, I'm the consummate professional. Not once did I mention anything about Sincere or anything that had happened between us for the past month or so. Just as I'm about to conclude our work up before the doctor comes in to perform his part, Feeky boo grabs my left hand and says in the most pitiful voice, "Betty, I just want to apologize for everything. My baby ain't from Sincere, even though we did fuck twice. The first time we fucked it was when I let him cook up at my apartment and the second time was when we went out of town for a pick up. I never meant to cause all this drama and problems. I'm sorry!" I patted her on her hand and told her, "No worries, we good!" I got up and walked out just like I had never seen her a day in my life. I was so used to hearing all that shit when someone I knew or had an issue with came into the STD clinic and saw me. I took and still take my career very serious and no amount of dislike for anyone will ever make me jeopardize my job. Welp, low and behold I have to go back and see Feeky boo who has gonorrhea and we now need to start dishing out those sex partners! This heffa in there crying, snot running into her mouth, boogahs on her arm from wiping her face and all I can do is ask, "How many sexual partners do you have? Do you sleep with women? Do you use IV drugs? Have you ever had sex for money? Have you ever had anal sex?" The questions go on for about 20 minutes and trust me, I wasn't trying to be mean. I was actually doing my job. A job that I was damn good at. Sincere name never came up but a host of other dudes I know name did and thank you sweet baby geesus in a manger, I was not into hood dudes. After that day at the STD clinic, I never saw or heard another word from or about Ms. Rah'Feekiey again.

Sincere and I get on and stay on good terms for a while after the whole Feeky boo fiasco for a few months. I knew the other shoe was to drop soon, so all I was doing was enjoying my benefits and waiting. I'm still doing me and dating, going on trips out of town, taking mini vacays and enjoying my double life when I hear about another baby from another random hood chick.

A year had almost passed since Sincere and I had broken up for the 1,000 time again due to his constant infidelity and infinite baby making skills. I was always dating and seeing other people because I always knew his fuck ass was doing his thing. I was never ever worried about being without a man, because there was always one in the stable that just needed to be groomed and brought out for show.

This one particular guy I was kicking it, wasn't in the stables but he was cool enough to kick it with for the time being. He was fairly decent built, dark skinned and cute in his own way, older gentleman with the prettiest salt and pepper hair. We dated for a few months and all was cool until one day the unexpected happened and I really didn't know how to bounce back from that.

I started dating this really sweet man who was 66 at the time. To look at him, you couldn't tell he was that advanced in his years. Very well rounded man with a big generous heart, well-educated with enough common sense to lend to the less fortunate and the stamina of an 18 year old. There wasn't a morning that went by that he didn't come see me before we both went to work, have breakfast and sometimes fool around. My sister Lucy would drop my nephew off in the morning so I could take him to day care since she had to be to work very early. One morning my older friend was coming up the driveway and my nephew who couldn't have been no more than 4 at the time said, "Here comes grandpa!" We fell out laughing and that was his name from then on, Grandpa. This particular morning Grandpa says "Baby, let me just suck on your tidday a little bit so I can get my mind right for work." He is sucking my tidday but it didn't feel or sound like a regular tidday suck. I rocked on for a few more minutes before my mind got the best of me. I eased to the right and turned on the light so I could get a better understanding of what the hell was going on. He was down there sucking my tidday with his mouth moving like a cow chewing curd, slurping and huffing like he had just ran a marathon. He was trying to keep his false teeth from falling out while sucking my tidday all while trying to keep me from noticing what was going on. You know what a regular tidday suck feel like and when some is trying to hold on for dear life. I started beating his ass in the head like it was on fire so he would stop. I gave him a kiss on his cheek and sent his ignant ass to work. I was too out done and didn't know what to say or do. I didn't see him for a few days after that and to be completely honest I wasn't mad. I had dated older men before but never ever experienced anything like that. Sometimes I wonder is he dead and if he left me anything in the will. Hell my tidday never did recover from that day and need to be compensated for the injury. Shortly after that incident, grandpa and I stopped seeing each other. I met another young man and the fireworks went from there. Sincere wasn't far. He just knew he couldn't control me, but he always let his presence be known and sometimes felt!

My nephew is the only boy in this family of all women, so I would spend a great deal of time with him doing different things such as the movies, dinner, going to the pool and anything else fun I could think of to spend time with him and let him know that his auntee loved him dearly. One particular day I was taking him to see the new Ice Cube movie, "Barber Shop", when I see a black Lexus GS400 on 6th street right next to 5th Ave driving towards me at a slow speed as if he was ghost riding the whip. I start to honk the horn because I think it's a friend of mine that I have been trying to get in contact with for a couple of days so I can let him know what is the latest on a little situation we had going on. I stick my hand out the window and gesture for him to meet me on the side access street by the GPD police station. His Lexus slows, with my Tahoe facing south and him north. We roll down the windows and are both taken aback when we realize that we are not who we thought each other were. Yet, we are instantly attracted to one another. I apologize first and explain how I thought he was a friend of mine who drives the same type of car and when he explains the same thing. As I get ready to say my goodbyes, he states, "You are absolutely gorgeous and I would love to see you again. Is it possible we can exchange numbers?" We never get out of our cars, we are just able to see each other's faces, we exchange numbers and head to our destinations.

A few hours later, my phone rings and its Charles. He asked how was the movie and lunch date with my nephew and other little idle chatter in getting to know one another better. Charles asked that fateful question, "Would you like to meet for dinner and drinks? You know we really didn't see one another and I would really like to get to know you better." I agreed as you know I would. We agreed to meet at Outback at 9. I hurried and got my nephew clean and packed up. Drove like a bat out of hell getting down the road to my sister house in Orange Lake. I slowed down to about 5 miles an hour and made my nephew do a stop, drop and roll out of my truck, so I can make it back home to get ready for my date.

I get all dolled up in a nice cool relaxing multi colored summer dress, with some matching flat gladiator sandals and a coordinating clutch. I let my hair down, as it is particularly breezy in Gainesville that night. I wanted to have that gone with the wind look and effect. I get to Outback a few minutes early. I want to see my date as he walks up so I can make a quick assessment and decide if I want to spend the time, energy and effort in grooming him for the stable, because this dating thing is getting harder and harder. I finally see his black Lexus drive in and circle briefly searching for a parking place, when he finally parks. My stomach starts fluttering like I had an entire soccer team in my stomach running the entire field trying to score a goal, when I see this tall, light bright, well built, slightly bow legged, low clean cut fade man from God. His face was nicely chiseled, with a perfectly edge goatee and fresh from the barber shop tape. His cologne was a subtle hint of "Fuck me to sleep and how do you want your eggs in the morning?" As he got closer to me, his smile kept getting wider and brighter. Upon reaching one another we embraced as if we had not seen one another in months and was happy to back in each other's arms. When we finally let one another go from what seemed like forever, Charles just stands there looking down on me like he is a prisoner on death row about to devour his special ordered last meal. I'm looking up taking in all this beauty before me, when my neck catches a crook. I'm 5'3 and he is actually an astonishing 6'11.

We make our way into the restaurant and ask for seating on the patio, to enjoy the beautiful weather and become better acquainted with one another. The evening went rather well, full of laughs, great conversation with no holds barred on any subject. Charles explains that he plays basketball overseas and he is currently home on vacation due to his season has just ended in Spain and he is home trying to relax and get back to American life for the next few months he is home. I explain to him that I work for the Alachua county health department as an infectious disease specialist, which entails me investigating people who are infected with

STD's and HIV. As most people always did, Charles asked, "What exactly do you do?" I tried to explain in the best layman terms available. "Well Charles, when people come into the health department and test positive for any STD or HIV or at their private doctor's office, it is my job to investigate how they caught the disease. I ask the tough question of who are you having sex with? Do you sleep with men and women? If you sleep with men, are you a top or bottom? Do you perform oral sex? If so, do you use condoms? Are you a prostitute? Are you into anal sex? And all types of questions as such." When I finished explaining that, Charles sat there with his mouth open looking at me as if I had just told him he had an STD. I reassure Charles and show him my most recent HIV negative results that I always carry with me in my wallet. At times due to where I worked and having access, how my love life was going, I would test myself twice a year. It felt good to break out my HIV negative results like the big joker in a spades game.

Charles and I thoroughly enjoyed one another and agreed to continue seeing each another in hopes of something greater. We spent a great deal of time doing all the cute couple activities and having fun beyond measure. We had yet to have sex, but the sexual tension was there for sure. His dick would get hard and knock windows out of cars as we passed by, which was nothing in comparison to the oceans I was leaving behind wherever we went. Charles could touch my arm in the most innocent way and I swear my coochie would chew through the seat of my drause in hopes of getting to him. Charles and I had been seeing one another for several weeks now. The feelings, emotions and desires grew beyond measure. The first time we had sex, it was totally explosive. We sucked, licked, bit, chewed, felt, fingered, caressed and pleasured every inch of each other's body without regard for anything.

The day we made love for the first time, Charles had called me earlier in the day while I was at work during one of my clinical rotations. Clinic rotations were, when I would see all clients who came into the STD clinic and tested positive and needed immediate investigation on determining who their sex partners were and so forth. When Charles called I was knee deep in gonorrhea with a generous side of stank bacterial vaginosis. He asked what did I want for dinner and if it was ok if he came to my house. I was so flattered and of course obliged. Charles then asked if it was ok for him to come by my job and pick up my key. He wanted to have dinner and drinks ready for me when I came home. When he gave those details, I was almost in tears but I couldn't let him know that. I told him to call me when he was outside by my truck. Charles came and looked so good as he was standing by my truck in a pair of jeans and fitted shirt showing all of his muscles and pure unadulterated sexiness. I gave him the biggest hug and kiss as I slide the key into his left hand with my right hand. I couldn't wait to get off work. As clients kept coming through I was asking the bare minimum questions, and giving out free rubbers with meds like I was giving away free government cheese.

When I made it home, I was surprised to see his black Lincoln navigator in my driveway. This is a car I have never seen or knew he had. All the windows in the house are open and an aphrodisiac aroma emitting from my home. I sit in my truck taking all of this in mentally when I gather my personal effects from the car and head to the door. I hear the locks turning and the door opens with Charles standing with a glass in his hands looking ever so sexy, dressed in absolutely nothing but a smile. I stop dead in my tracks. I see this monster hanging from his body calling my name like a poltergeist. I come back to my senses very quickly. I don't want the neighborhood women clawing at my door trying to get what I want. I run to him, give him a passionate kiss as I shut the door with my right foot and throw all my stuff to floor with no regards to breakage. After kissing for what seems like an eternity, I finally pull away, grab my straight Hennessy on the rocks from his hand, take a big sip and look at my dining room table, which has been set with takeout food and candles. I wasn't even mad that there were food cartons sticking out from the garbage can. Just the mere fact that he thought enough to get some Winn Dixie grocery store flowers and take out and have it all set up for me meant more to me than any jewel in the world.

As I'm standing there marveling over what he has done, Charles says to me, "Baby, the bath tub is waiting for us and I don't want the water to get cold, so come on and let me undress you and take care of you!" Girl my mouth is on the floor and my coochie has once again eaten through the seat of my drause like a mean ass junk yard dog trying to get to him. I asked him about the food getting cold and stale and Charles responded to me in the sexiest sincerest voice ever, "After I'm through with you, if you still want to eat, then I have not done my job as a man, now sit down on the couch so I can take your shoes and socks off" I sit down on the couch, sipping on my drink and Charles rolls my slacks up, takes of my black loafers and gently slides off my trouser socks, kisses each foot and then leads me down the hall to the bathroom and when he opens the door. My word, the sweet gentle aromatherapy smells hit my nose. The tub is filled with bubbles and rose petals on top of the bubbles in the tub. I put my glass down and start to undress myself, when Charles grabs my hand and says, "You have had a hard enough day of taking care of everyone else, now it's my time to take care of you and all your needs and wants!" I don't have on any panties or slacks. My overly aggressive coochie has eaten all of that up and spread herself open so he could enter with ease.

Charles starts to unbutton my blouse and he takes it off with such delicate care and ease. My goose bumps show with excitement as my mouth is unable to move to utter a word. Once he has my blouse off, he kisses me on my forehead. He starts to unbuckle my belt, slides it off. Unbuttons my slacks and he does only what a real man knows to do, he slides his hands into my slacks, runs his hand to the top of my ass and as he runs his hands from the back towards the front by way of my hips and slowly but surely slides my slacks down, kissing my thighs as he bends down. I'm standing there in my bra and the waist band of my eaten drause due to my overly aggressive coochie. Charles is looking at me with the most devilish look on his face. His monster has risen and had started tapping me on my forehead saying, "I hope you know, it's about to go down and we will rise as the victor, good luck!" I stand there waiting for his monster to stop tapping me on my forehead. Charles unsnaps my bra with one hand like a pro. Slides my straps down, pulls my bra off and just like clockwork a few folded dollars and change falls from my tiddays. I shake my head and bend down to pick up the money in embarrassment, when Charles stops me in mid bend. Gets on his knees and gently bites my coochie through my panties and starts to pull them down with his teeth. I'm about to faint from the anticipation and anxiety of what is about to happen next. Once my panties are on the floor, I step out of them and follow his lead to the bathtub. Charles enters the rose petal, bubble filled tub first, and then takes my hand to assist me in. We embrace, kiss passionately and caress one another's body before Charles turns me around to have my back against his stomach. He holds me close as if he is protecting me from danger. Continuing to follow his lead, he sits us both down in the tub at the same time and caresses my body in the hot water as he asks me about my day.

I'm melting in this tub like a snowball in hell. Never in my life have I experienced such romance and intimacy without the sex. We continue to talk and talk, when he stands up and requests me to stand up as well. Charles grabs my wash rag, soaps it up very well with my Caress body wash and commences to start washing my body. He washed my face, neck, back, chest and even knew to have my prop my leg up so he could wash Ms. Precious. He rinsed my entire body just as well as he washed it. In return I washed him and was trying to get in a few sucks and licks, each time I tried, he would always stop me and say, "There is a time and place for that lil lady!" We are washed, rinsed and dried off when Charles starts to lotion my entire body with my cocoa butter oil infused lotion. This is where everything takes a deep left turn for the better, well as a phone call was made to them people with the pretty white hug me jacket as I was gone!!

Charles made love to me like no man had ever done to me. He took his time, kissed, caressed, licked, sucked, touched, rubbed up against, teased and pleased my entire mind, body soul and spirit. He took his time with me and took pleasure in learning me and my body. Not once did he ever make the experience feel cheap or rushed. We laid in bed, which was full of wet spots, talked for a few before, ate the food he had brought, had a few drinks and then we fell into a deep comatose sleep. When I awoke the next morning, Charles had a dress picked out and ironed for me with my breakfast and lunch ready. I showered, ate a hot home cooked breakfast with my sexy ass man. I got dressed with his attentive hands all over me and we left that morning feeling like we had just conquered the world.

I was on cloud 9 all damn day. Normally when I'm in the field hunting down HIV patients I'm always feeling some type of way, which is not a good thing. Onc, it's hard to tell someone that they have been exposed to such a deadly disease and not be able to tell them who may have possibly infected them. Secondly there are a lot of times in trying to locate certain clients, it's like chasing the wind. I'm in the field having a blast of a day due the lasting impression Charles has left on my heart, mind body and soul when I get a phone call from the little fella Telly, whom I was kicking it with before I met Charles. It has been some time since I last spoke with, called or even spent time with him.

Telly was just a few years younger than me, didn't have the money I liked. He looked ok and was cool enough for the time being to get me through my dating drought, especially since Sincere and I had broken up again. Telly worked at the Wal Mart warehouse and drove a little loud Honda Accord. You know the one, with the special muffler to make that annoying ass sound as they switch gears. It was highly aggravating to ride in, but going to the late movies or going to little eateries from time to time was cool. We kicked it, had some good times, but as I said earlier, he wasn't what I liked or really wanted.

One night Telly and I was supposed to go out, when he calls me around 6 something on that Friday evening and tells me that the axel on his car has just fell from the front of his car as he is on his way home. Now don't get me wrong, I do have my blonde moments from time to time, but that damn shol wasn't one of them. I give a quick eye roll while calling him a lying son of a bitch under my breath and ask, "Babe are you ok? Do you need me to come get you?" Of course he gives me delayed paused stuttering response of, "Uhmmmm no baby, I'm good a friend of mine with a tow truck is coming to get me." Now trust me, this nigga ain't had no damn friends with a truck yet alone a damn tow truck. So I let him roll with that lie like water off a ducks back. It's now Saturday afternoon and I haven't heard from Telly since Friday, so when Charles calls and wants to spend some much needed quality time with me, I jump on it like a lion on fresh prey.

It's a beautiful, breezy, cool sunny Saturday in Gainesville with everything pointing to a wonderful day with Charles. I get up, clean my house, shit, shower and shave in preparation for whatever Charles has planned for us. You just never know with him. Charles shows up a couple of hours later looking sexy as ever in some basketball shorts showing off his ever so sexy slight bow legs or hell it could have been just the way he stands with that fucking monster in his pants. I would always ask him what was the name of the cologne he would wear and he would never ever tell me, but it was always a mixture of "Fuck me to sleep and how many kids do you want?" He always smelled so got damn good. He had some grocery bags in his hands, which is the norm because he never showed up to my house empty handed. I take the bags and place everything in their proper places. Charles makes his way to the kitchen after taking off his shoes and placing them in the room. He comes to the kitchen and makes us some drinks and we take them to the bedroom to watch TV and chill. As usual we are talking about every and anything under the sun, just enjoying one another's company when he tells me that he has to make a trip overseas to check out a great opportunity for him and his upcoming basketball season which could prove to be even more lucrative for him. Instantly, I become upset because I'm so use to him being with me and making my life and days just that much easier.

Even though he brought groceries to the house, knowing good and got damn well I don't know how to cook, we head out for dinner and drinks at Longhorns to try and cheer me up. We have a great time at dinner discussing our past, present and most definite future and head home. On our drive home, Charles decides he wants to switch positions in the car. He pulls over not even a block from Longhorns on Archer Rd and tells me to switch positions with him and to drive us home. In my mind I'm thinking he can't be drunk because he isn't a drinker like my alcoholic ass is. I'm slightly confused but in my mind I'm finna bump the music and flex. No matter if we are in his Lexus, Navigator truck or my Tahoe he would always drive.

I get in the driver seat, adjust the seat and get ready for takeoff when the fool pulls out my right tittie and starts sucking my nipple like the runt of the litter fighting for his life. I'm taken aback, but I keep my composure because we are behind dark tint and stopped at the red light on 34th Street and Archer Rd, when he decides to pull my right leg up and finger me all while sucking my tittie. I'm gone and ain't paying attention to shit until some inpatient ass fucker behind me honk his horn like they are in the 100 yard dash. My right nipple is still in Charles mouth with his hand still in my pussy as I hit the gas with my left foot and try to maintain a certain driving decorum. I'm tearing up the road trying to get home quickly as possible. I speed into the driveway, I don't think I came to a full complete stop before I threw the truck into park, snatched the keys out the ignition and ran into the house. We ripped each other's clothes off right there in the living room and got straight to business. Charles dick never tasted or felt as good to me as it did right that evening. It was like he was on auto porn star with a double dose of the energizer bunny and no sight of him losing any stamina.

We were all over the house with no regards to the windows, blinds and curtains being open. We continue to make love all over the house, but I can't help but hear a muffler ride and up and down the road multiple times. At first I blow it off as it's somebody who is lost because at this very moment Charles is eating my pussy so got damn good, while one hand is pinching my nipple and the other hand is fingering me like he is digging for gold. I'm all in the moment moaning and groaning and busting nuts all on his fingers and in his mouth, but this got damn car keeps riding up and down the street and it sounds as if the person driving is hitting the gas pedal harder and harder to make it known that they are there. Charles has no clue what is going on or that I'm trying to figure out what the hell is going on when all of a sudden the loud muffler is gone. I get on all fours and start sucking Charles dick and rotating his balls in and out the rotation when I hear the grass and small hedges crumpling outside the bedroom window. My mind tells me not to worry about it and keep doing what I need to do as my man is going to be leaving the country soon for business and will be gone for a few weeks. The more I suck and massage Charles dick and rotate his balls in and out my mouth, the harder and harder he gets. Charles is gone and I'm right there with him. I finish getting Charles sloppy wet and hard I climb onto his dick like spider man climbs a wall.

I'm hearing grass steady crumpling and hard breathing like dry heaving from crying, when all of a sudden there is a hard knock on my front door. Charles grips my hips, continuing to thrust his hard dick deep inside of me when he says, "Baby don't you dare get cho ass up and take my pussy anywhere, fuck whoever out there!" When he said that I busted at least 3 nuts and kept riding. There was another knock at the door, but I kept riding my Clydesdale like a champ. I hear the grass crumpling again, but this time as the grass is crumpling there is a pounding knock on every window around my house with a few knocks on the door as they circle my house 3-4 times. The whole time I know who it is, I'm just hoping that the idiot gets the drift that I'm busy thoroughly enjoying myself and not about to stop. This fool is steadily running around my house knocking on all the got damn windows and doors. I'm just hoping Charles don't get mad, but I was just about to show my ass in a few minutes.

Now I'm pissed. They have fucked up my got damn riding groove. I hop off and give Charles dick a few quick good sucks and tell him, "Keep it hard baby, I'll be right back!" I storm to the front door like Sophia did in The Color Purple marching through the corn fields. I'm butt bookey ass naked when I snatch the front door open. There stands Telly crying with snot and tears running into his mouth. I look at his ignant ass and very sternly ask him through my clinched teeth, "What the fuck are you doing to my house when I know good and got damn well you see I have company?" He just stands there and looks at me all crazy like I did something wrong. Telly still hasn't said one word. I ask him again, "What the fuck are you doing to my house? I know you have seen, heard and witnessed that I have company and that we are thoroughly enjoying ourselves?"

What Telly didn't know is, a friend of mine had called me and told me they saw him at the movies with some girl the same night we was supposed to go out. That happens to be the same exact day the axel fell off his Honda. Yet, he was at the movies, driving his car and had some chick with him. I know you have to take what people say with a grain of salt, especially when they are telling you about your mate, but I had no reason to doubt my friend. They had never lied to me or on me about anything. Funny thing is, the same outfit they told me he had on the night before, was the same exact outfit he showed his monkey ass up to my house in. Now remember, I hadn't heard from him since Friday, when the supposed axel mysteriously falls off this Honda. So he finally mutters, "Is this how you do me? I really cared for you and had big dreams for us!" That shit didn't faze me, I have heard that shit all my damn life. My anger is turning me on at this point. I lift my left tidday and start sucking my nipple and tell Telly, "Look, we did what we did, had what we had and now it's time to move on. I know you were at the movies last night with some other chick and how ironic is it that you have on the same outfit from last night. I'm happy and in love with someone else." Right as I say those words, Charles walks right up behind me butt bookey ass naked too. It surprised me because I didn't even hear him walking up. When Charles walked up behind me naked, he put his left arm around me and stood to my right and asked me, "Is everything ok?" I'm really turned on now and ready to jump off the roof on that dick as soon as we finish handling this business. I look up to

Charles, rub his dick and look at Telly and then back to Charles and say, "Yes baby, everything is just fine, somebody who is lost and needed some directions." Telly is just standing there looking at Charles package like "DAMN!" When I break his concentration with a few finger snaps and ask him, "Is there anything else I can help you with? Telly is just standing there, never saying another word as I shut the door. I don't have a grain of remorse in me for him as I turn my attention and affection back to Charles.

When we return to the room, Charles and I talk about what had just happened and I told him everything. To my surprise, he wasn't angry he was actually laughing and said, "I can understand why ole boy was standing in the door crying and running around the house like Carl Lewis, you got some good ass pussy and head! I hope to never be on the receiving end of your words, because you are one evil ass little woman. If I was him I would have choked your ass!" He couldn't do nothing but laugh. I'm sitting there wondering who in the hell he thought was gonna choke me? I keep my Correct a Nigga Pistol close by for such occasions. Charles and I continued to enjoy the rest of our evening and each other as his time to leave for overseas was nearing and I was dreading the day. We made plans to communicate daily and even video chat as time permitted due to the time zone difference.

Charles and I continued to date when he went overseas. We talked, email and video chatted as promised, but I knew the inevitable was coming. At that time in my life I knew I couldn't handle nor maintain a long distance relationship such as this one. Mentally and physically I want and need that person there daily and I had already prepared myself for a breakup upon his return. Charles returned from Spain 3 weeks later and we had a blast making up for the lost time. We did some of everything and went everywhere, but I knew there was something he had to tell me he just wasn't sure how to break it down. Charles finally told me he was heading back to Spain for their basketball season which last 8 to 9 months! The money he would make for those months was great money especially living overseas where the money isn't taxed the hell and back like it would be in states, plus he was not only a seasoned NBA baller, but a veteran of playing overseas. We remained together the first season, upon his return things were different. Not because of anything on Charles part, but all because of me. I was not moving to Spain, nor did I get my passport to go visit him in Spain. We had a deep, sincere heart to heart and mutually agreed we would break up but always remain the best of friends.

Charles was always there for me whether it be lending an ear, his gentle arms or whatever it was I needed at the time and trust me, there have been plenty of times Charles was there for me and I will always love him.

Charles and I break up and move on with our lives, slowly but surely I put my life back together. I had never loved someone as intense and hard as I had loved Charles. It took me a minute to comprehend what I had just walked away from and why. I didn't date for a minute because I never found a man who could fill Charles shoes. Since I couldn't find someone to fulfill me as Charles did, I fell back on my ole Sincere. He had been sniffing around the whole time I was with Charles and I wasn't paying him any attention. Whenever things got real rough in them streets or he had to beat a chick up, I was always the mommy who always made it better. I remember when 9/11 happened. I was rushing out the back door to go teach an HIV104 certification class for some nurses when I stepped off the sidewalk wrong, broke my ankle and rolled up under my truck with my skirt over my head. My program administrator was the coolest man ever, he helped pull me from under my truck like a piece of loose paper. He helped me get in my truck and prop my left ankle up in my rolled down window as we waited on the information to come back from workman comp. I was so embarrassed and told him, "Bill, I can't put my leg up in front of you I have on a skirt and my ankle is fine." He was so cool and country at the same time and said, "It ain't like I ain't ever seen drause before!" I miss my family at the health department.

At the same time I was laid up with my ankle, Sincere was laid up with no dope! He was sicker than I was. After the 9/11 terrorists attack everything went on straight lock down. No dope was moving over the water, the air, bus, train or hump back crooked leg donkey. I was the first person he came running too trying to figure out what the hell he was going to do. He had dope but not enough to last him past a month or so. His money was on point but he wanted to make sure he still had dope to go out and money to flow in like water. Sorry Charlie, I can't help you that is not my area of expertise. That was a rough month or 2 for him because I didn't care what was going on, I still needed my allowance and I was going to get it. Things eventually clear up and his connect calls him and they work it out. On the other hand Sincere and are cool but I'm hearing rumblings in the street again, about a baby and a different chick. I sit back because I know eventually it will come to me and I will bring it to his ass. When I did my dirt, Sincere could never pin point me or who I was dating unless I wanted him to know. I didn't have my business out there in the street and I loved to date out of town. There were times I would hit the highway or the open skies, shut off my phone and just enjoy paradise. One day while Sincere and I was chilling, I casually ask him, "Baby are you seeing someone? He quickly and adamantly answers, "NO" I take that and wait a few more minutes after affectionately rubbing on his belly, kissing him all over and just trying to show him all the love in the world, I ask, "Sincere is there somebody who is pregnant that I need to know about?" He turns to me and looks so cute and innocent, for a split second there I saw the young boy I had fell in love with all those years ago when he says, "For the first time since the first time, there is nobody else just you and there ain't a baby unless your're finally pregnant and going to give me one." Shit, he knew better than me that I was not spitting out a baby for him or anybody. I knew he was lying but I let it play out.

One day while in the field I called Sincere boo hoo crying. A girl who I had went to school with and was near and dear too tested positive for HIV. It wasn't my case but when the name came across the board of immediate contact as all previous contacts have been unsatisfactory, I jumped on it. I went to her house to talk to as a friend first then as a professional because not only was she pregnant she had an unsuspecting boyfriend who she was sleeping with unprotected. When I asked her about her use of protection, this heffa had the nerve to tell me she douche each time before they have sex to clean out the canal. I was in tears when I left there. The baby was born a few months later HIV negative because she got on medication quickly, but I never knew what became of the boyfriend, because we lost contact shortly after this episode. Sincere and I are at lunch when I tell him what is going on and why I'm so upset. He could never deal with me being upset, crying or sick but he listened to me this day and reassured me that all would be fine and I should not worry. I did what I could as a friend and a concerned professional. I went home had a drink and Sincere shows up later, looking crazy like he had done something. He pulled a box out of his pocket opened it and never asked "Would you marry me?" all he said was, "You pick a date and we'll get married!" Huhh? What? Where in the hell do they do this at? Is that how you ask me to marry you after all these years? All the fights? All the women? The gun battles and lets not mention all the little bastards you have created since we have been together? I stand there with my lips twisted to side and wait for him to put it on my finger. When he did, it was the prettiest 5 row diamond pyramid ring I had ever seen. Unpucker your lips girl, hell it was a pretty ring and being the fact of who it's coming from it was the prettiest diamond ring, just wait till you see it, you gonna want one.

It's now late November early December2002 and it seem like STD's are the new Christmas gifts cause my ass has yet to have any damn down time to goof off in the field like I normally would because I'm steady running the road asking all the personal questions about who you sleep with, are you bi, do you do anal yada yada yada. I found myself waking up in the middle of the night asking those same questions and getting mad as fuck.

Sincere and I have been engaged now for a few months and all is fine even though I'm still hearing the mumblings in the street about this baby and chick. Nobody is really bringing me a real bone to chew on, so I do my usual and sit back and wait for it to come to me because it's coming. Since I had been so busy with work and school it was kind of hard to see Sincere, especially with him doing his thing in the streets. We get some time in here and there and make some of the sweetest plans to bring in the New Year together and then take a weeklong vacation away from everything and just focus on us and our upcoming nuptials. I wasn't thinking about or planning no damn wedding because I already knew something was about to jump off, I just couldn't quite put my finger on it, but I played the roll! It's New Year's Eve and I want to bring the year in right. I find an all-white pant suit with a vibrant bright red corset, matching stiletto red shoes and coordinating clutch. I get my hair laid earlier that Tuesday afternoon in preparation for the night. I'm laying down that evening trying to get some shut eye before that night because I know we are about to shut down the Royal Blue. Sincere calls and tells me there is a change in plans, he will meet me at the club because he needs to handle some business. I'm cool with that because he has never handle business around me, no need to change the game plan now since we are engaged. I start getting ready and since my sister Lucy is at my house, I leave my truck home and have her drop me off at the club since I have been drinking and GPD are known to be some assholes. I get to the club and it's packed and bumping as usual. I find Sincere sitting to the right in the pool table area having a drink. We greet one another as two lovebirds should with hugs, kisses and so much affection as I flash this pyramid diamond ring baby. Something is off, but I don't say one word.

We stay in the pool hall area for a while enjoying the music, talking and just doing us when I see some unsavory dudes walk in and motion for Sincere. He gives me a kiss, tells me he loves me and he will be back. Some time passes and a few drinks later I need to show off this outfit and shake what my momma gave me. I hit the dance floor, jamming my ass off, when I look up and see Sincere leaning in and talking to a chick I know. I can't focus my eyes just right to tell you who she is. I walk closer to the area never being seen by Sincere or the chick. I now recognize it to be, stop and it hits me. This is the chick who I have been hearing about that Sincere is supposed to be going with. I see him do a quick fake move to the bathroom so I make a move back to the pool area and low and behold here he comes, talking about things took a little longer than expected. I play the role and act like I haven't seen anything, all the time in the back of my mind I keep thinking, *"Sincere know I will pop off in this bitch at the drop of a dime because I'm looser than a magnum rubber on a small soft dick!" Why is he playing with me?* We sit and chill over there for about 30 – 45 minutes when the DJ announces for everyone to get their drinks and grab someone special because we are just a few minutes away from 2003! Sincere sends the cute little waitress to bring another bottle of Hennessy and ice so we can properly bring in 2003 together but soon tells me he needs to use the restroom. I oblige but mentally I'm on ready!

Sincere gives me the biggest kiss, tightest hug and tells me he loves me and can't wait for our wedding day. I smile, and tell him the same thing all the while plotting on how I'm about to pop off on they asses. He heads out to the bathroom and tells me he will be right back. I fix me a nice glass of Henn with no ice and no chaser because it's about to get nasty. I finish my drink, peep around the corner and see Sincere back over there by the bar with Tabora laughing it up like they are so in love. The countdown is about to start 10, 9, 8, 7, 6, Sincere is still over there with Tabora holding hands 5, 4, 3, 2, 1 HAPPY NEW YEAR! Everybody is celebrating, hugging, kissing, drinking and enjoying the birth of 2003. I smoothly walk up on Sincere who has his back to me and Tabora horse shaped, egg head ass has her eyes closed. When I hit Sincere with a right hook everybody is caught off guard. He jumps back ready to fight until he sees me. He is stunned just standing there for a few seconds I guess trying to think what the fuck he needs to do now. I'm going off and trying to get to his ass. Tabora is over there standing still mumbling something when I scream, "Ohh don't worry bitch yo ass next. Ho you know me and you know this is ain't nearly what you want!" Sincere is trying to rush out the side door with his cousin and Tabora is fast on his heels. I wasn't worried about them leaving. If you had ever been to the Royal Blue you already know you have a better chance of catching the lottery than getting out of that parking lot when it's packed to capacity. I head back to the pool area grab my clutch and phone. I call my sister to come to the club quick. I go to the back where I see the green machine trying to get out the parking lot but he can't because of how the cars are parked and ain't nobody trying to leave the club, hell the party is just getting started and it's about to be in the parking lot.

As I'm walking up to the car I hear Tabora hollering and cussing and clowning. She is who I want first because I don't know if I will ever see her again but you can best believe Sincere will be back. Why Sincere has his driver window down as he sees me approaching him, I will never ever understand or know what the hell he was thinking. I have my clutch and shoes in my hand, I throw the clutch on the ground and one shoe and just as quick I throw that shit on the ground I jump through the driver window and punch Tabora in the face a few times. She is screaming and trying to block me. Sincere is trying to grab me but can't get a good grip on me. His cousin is sitting in the back looking like he watching a movie until Sincere holler, "FRANK COME GET THIS CRAZY BITCH." What the fuck did he say that for? When Frank grabs me and tries to pull me out the window I start kicking at his slim ass. He grabs my legs and pulls me off Tabora but when I slide by Mr. Sincere I made the nigga eat my high heel like it's something good to eat. I tag Sincere in his left eye a few times. I hear him screaming with blood running down his face. Tabora still over there screaming like a white woman in a horror movies and Frank calling for someone to help him get me out the damn car. When I'm finally pulled out the driver window Sincere is somehow able to pull out the parking lot. I see my sister Lucy who has my niece Brooke in the car. I run and jump in her car beat the dashboard and tell her to punch it and catch the mutha fucker because I ain't finished whooping on his ass. Sincere is speeding down 13th street heading north towards 39th Ave. By the time we catch up with him, Sincere is stuck at a red light. Before my sister car can come to a complete stop I'm out the car and running up to Sincere's car like the jump out boys. I'm running as fast as I can and get to the trunk of the car before the light turns green and Sincere peels out of there like a NASCAR driver. I lose my footing and slide across the entire 39th Ave like a baseball player sliding into home plate. SAFE!

When I get up from sliding all across the got damn road, my beautiful red corset is now hanging down by my belly. My tiddays are flapping in the wind. The knees of my white suit are scraped to hell and back and full of blood. I'm hot as hell, drunk and ready to fight. My niece is in the back seat crying which made me feel so bad. Whenever I was going to do dirt I never let her be with me. I would drop her off to the house and promise I would come back and get her so she wouldn't see anything bad. I get in the car, my sister is laughing, Brooke is crying and I'm ready to fight. We get to my house and I'm trying to get the keys to my truck to go and find his ass because I'm finna put a bullet in his brain for sure tonight. My momma is cussing me out telling me I ain't finna go nowhere, my sister is doing the same and Brooke is steady crying. I don't know what happened next but I know I woke up the next morning in my bed still in my ruined white suite and dusted red corset. My body was sore as fuck like I was a punching bag for Mike Tyson. I stayed in the house that entire day nursing my body because I gotta get my ass up the next day and go deal with ozzing coodas in STD clinic and I wasn't in the mood for that. The week comes and goes with no word or sight of Sincere, which is perfect because I'm trying to roll through my mind what fucking movie did he watch that gave him that simple idea to bring in New Years with two women at the same bar, when your fiancé has no idea about the other chick, because apparently he missed a few scenes and blanked out during the planning process. The weekend comes and I'm getting ready to go out of town and free my mind when I see an unknown car pull up to my house. I sit back and wait to see who gets out just in case I need to get ready for whatever. Low and behold it's Sincere and I'm thinking what could he possibly be over here for. He rings the doorbell, I take my time in answering. When I do open the door I don't say one word, I just stand there with a look of "Bitch what" on my face. He stands there for a few minutes and had the unmitigated gall to say, "We can't seem to get our shit together. I want my engagement ring back!" Here I am ready to fight, I have my pistol in the small of my back just in case I need to go into instant correct a nigga mode ASAP. When I hear him say those words and look dead ass serious, a calm I had never ever experienced came over me. I straightened my head and posture, unfolded my arms and calmly as I could I said, "You can get this ring back as soon as you can give me back all the pussy I have given you!" This raggedy bastard stood there with a look like he was carrying the 2, minus the 1 adding 12 to see if it was possible. I backed up slowly, opened the door and went back in my house, to never hear from Sincere again.

Welp that was short lived. The FEDS started kicking in doors a few months later looking for Sincere and a few other big boys around town. I didn't know anything about the raids until Sincere called me all up in arms and panicking and worried. The day he calls me we had been apart for about 3 – 4 months and I was at work trying to calm my nerves because this big tall amazon ass woman who had just give birth to an HIV infected drug baby had threatened to beat my ass if I didn't leave her property. I had to work like hell to calm her down, keep her calm and get all the information I needed. As I was holding her baby gathering all of her information, you could see the thrush in the little innocent baby's mouth, the involuntary shaking of its tiny frame from her drug abuse, panicky cries. You know you can't beat no crack head when they geeking for that drug, so I played it cool and did my job. When I get in the truck, the last thing I want to hear about is the FEDS are looking for you. So what, maybe they'll be able to tell me where the stash is and who all these extra women are and where are all these damn babies. He asked me to speak with his lawyer and find out what he was up against and be his buffer as usual. NOT! That shit was no going down this time. I told him to find someone else to do it. I had a lot of shit going on at the time and didn't need any additional drama. He found some chicken head to do it and as soon as she talked to the lawyer she put his business in the street. I agree to see him one last time before he turns himself in and it was one of the saddest days ever. We cried, laughed, reminisced and promised to remain in each other's life. At a time like this I wanted to ask him but I figure this might be a bad time to ask him about the rumblings in the street about a baby being born. I keep quiet because I know it will soon come to me, just as everything else did. We spend our last few hours together never going to sleep just holding one another. I offered to stay the night. At first Sincere was all excited then he instantly got worried that the feds may come kick in the door while I was there and he didn't want that to happen to me or for me to see him getting arrested. Sincere turns himself in the next morning. A part of me is sad because the man I have been with for over 10+ years is in jail and headed to federal prison for God only knows how long. The other side of me is elated and feeling like he got what he deserved for all the shit he took me through for those 10 years. Was I wrong to feel like that? I don't know and to be honest I don't care. I got off work and went out on a fabulous date.

A few weeks pass before I can visit him. The feds want to try and keep him and all the other people they rounded up as separate as possible. They have Sincere housed in Union county jail. I trek all the way out to the boonies to see Sincere with butterflies in my stomach, tears in my eyes and questions in my heart. I go through all the necessary security measures and wait for the officer to escort us into the visitation room. My stomach is jumping all over the place. I had never been in a jail, even though I almost was fooling with Benny. The officer takes us in the room, tells us which number to sit at and wait for our loved ones to come in. I sit at #3 and I'm wearing the paint off the door staring at it waiting for him to run through the door. He finally comes through the doors and the tears flow for the both of us. We do the prison movie thing and hold our hands to the glass and say we love one another in the phone. He is telling me everything that the feds are telling him, who he thinks snitched on him which is a story all in itself and how the feds watched everything. We have been in visitation for about 40 minutes and the conversation is great. The entire time he has been locked up all we have had was constant phone conversation, so it was nice to see him and know that he has not been abused. Sincere had just finishing giving me a compliment, telling me how much he missed me and apologizing for everything he has done to me and took me through when the visitation door swung open with force and there stands a chick holding a brand new baby! We are the only black people in the visitation room. That pretty much rules out the black ghetto chick standing in the door looking crazy, holding a newborn baby is coming in there to see Big Bubba with the confederate flag tatted on his neck! I drop my head, close my eyes and shake my damn head and laugh. Here is the baby that I had heard the rumblings about. Sincere eyes have gotten wide and he is shaking his head saying "NOOOOO please don't leave me, I just want to see my son. I was in here when she had him. I'm not with her Betty, she was just one of the girls who I got caught up with when I was in the streets, I swear I'm not trying to hurt you I just want to see my son. Can you understand what I'm saying?" Actually I couldn't understand a damn thing he was saying because this ghetto heffa was standing right behind me and steady asking, "Are you Betty, huh? Are you Betty? I seen't yo truck outside." I can't hit this girl. She has a newborn in her arms and I'm sitting right here in the got damn jail. I stand up, give Sincere that look of, "You lucky there is glass between us because you already know we would be tearing this shit up" and I storm out of there madder than a wet hen.

I didn't see Sincere anymore after that visit. We talked every day all the time. Shortly after Sincere's arrest, his brother was arrested on some serious state and federal charges and that broke Sincere's spirit. A few weeks later I moved back home to St. Pete and started over with my new job. Sincere and I remain in contact via mail and phone. The day Sincere was sentenced he called me and sounded so depressed and unsure of anything because not only was he sentenced to 15 years, his brother was looking at some serious state and fed time. He ran from the police, hit a police officer, had a gun and so much dope in the car. Sincere just felt like his life was over but mine was just beginning. This ain't the last we hear from Sincere. ~~Ain't That Bout'a Bitch~~

CHAPTER 4

MISTAKEN IDENTITY

My dad has always been a character and spotty otty ever since I can remember. He always had the gift to gab, meet and make new friends easily with no hesitation; and maintain those friendships for many years and let's not talk about the women! My father has very smooth caramel colored skin, cheek bones of an Indian and the charm to tame the baddest king cobra. My dad and I have a very close relationship and the more and more I'm around him I start to see where a lot of my character and genetic makeup derive from. Some great, some good, some so bad til it can't help but be good.

My mother and father got divorced when I was very young. He remained in St. Pete while my mother, my older sister and I relocated to Gainesville. I was able to always maintain a relationship with my father and would split summers, spring break and Christmas between him and my mom's baby sister house in St. Pete. All depending on what was going on, what outings were planned and what food was being cooked, is what helped to determine where I wanted to be that day or week. As time passed my father remarried a very loving, supportive, understanding and patient woman; whom I do regard as my mom and treat her as such. Coming up as a child, I always saw my step mother take care of everything and ensure everything was properly done and if it wasn't right, she made it appear as if it was. She came from the old school where women truly took care of their husband, house and children without any regard for self. She truly takes care of everything. My step mom can work a full 8 – 12 hour day, come home cook a full meal, wash clothes, clean and make sure all in the household are clean, fed and got some where to lay their head that night.

She has been that way since I was a little girl and I have always admired that in her, but at the same time wondered why she works so hard with all these able body Negros in the house, especially my dad?

Over the years, she and I have most definitely become very close and spend a lot of time together. When I tell you we do everything together, I mean it. When I come into town, my step mom is my ride or die shopping and club hopping partner in crime.

Before I moved back home in 2003, I use to go home at least twice a month and spend the weekend with my dad and just have a blast with my folks. One weekend, I come into town late Friday night around 1:30 – 2am and my step mom slept on the couch in the den waiting for me. When I walked in she sat up and said, "Bet Bet, is that you?" I quietly responded, "Yes ma'am." I didn't want to wake my dad, not that he could really hear anything over that 69' back firing Pinto snoring he does. I put my luggage in the spare room, go into the kitchen where my step mom is fixing the both of us something to eat. If you were raised in the South and have a parent raised in the old days, then you can understand and relate to how southern people treat you. Whether family or guest, no matter what time it is, you are gonna get something to eat and drink. I had already been out all night partying and drinking by the time I get to my dad's house, but I can tell my mom wants to talk. We sit down in the den, eat and pour us some Parrot Bay. That was our drink at the time. It's about 4am and we're both doing the ole people nod, when I say, "Mommy, I'm going to bed, I need to get this drunk off of me." She says, "Ok, I guess we can talk later." I'm feeling bad now, so I said, "Mommy come sleep with me tonight and let's talk, we haven't had girl talk in a while." She perked up and went in her room changed clothes and I changed clothes as well. We get into the bed and she starts telling me that today is the 5th anniversary to the day when she caught my dad cheating on her. I sit straight up in the bed, look at her with a look on my face like "who just farted and walked off." We both get comfortable as she gets ready to tell me the story. I'm shocked because I know my father is a charmer and attracts the ladies, I just never thought he would cheat on my step mom. She is truly the doting wife. She has my father completely spoiled. She works a full day's work, comes home cooks complete meals or warms the hell out of some leftovers. Cleans, washes and dry the clothes and puts them away. Ensures all of his meds are in place when he needs to take them. When they go out of town she packs all the bags and makes sure everything you need and don't need is in a bag. She makes sure everything in that house is complete and she even aides with the care of his mother who is up in age.

To put this into better perspective, one year, we did Thanksgiving at my tiny 1 bedroom, 2nd floor apartment in Pompano Beach. It was a lovely apartment with wood floors, granite countertops, stainless steel appliances and a mixture of neighbors from the gulleiest of projects and some from the most suburban areas.

Now, don't get me wrong, I'm hell with some chicken breast or fish on a George Foreman grill and some canned veggies but when it comes to cooking like my parents, you will come out better chewing on a dog's rubber toy, because that's exactly how my food will turn out. I knew they were coming, so I went to Publix and ordered the precooked Thanksgiving dinner with all the trimmings. The precooked dinner included a 12-15lb cooked turkey, mashed potatoes, dressing, cranberry sauce and gravy. It didn't sound too bad. I called my dad and step mom and told them what I had did and my step mom was like, "Uhmmmm ok Bet Bet, Imma bring some stuff with me to just doctor it up." I was like cool, but I should have known better. When my parents finally showed up for Thanksgiving, they had a 60 gallon marine cooler full of greens, hog maws, mac and cheese, spiral ham, homemade glaze for the ham, dressing, ribs, all the southern breakfast foods, sodas, tea and of course the most important beverage of them all, Vodka and Tequila! When I tell you, I had to take racks out of the fridge to make room for all that food. They were at my house for 4 days and we never had to go out for anything. My step mom brought everything we needed and didn't need. I was able to eat Thanksgiving leftovers well into the end of the following year. So when I say my step mom takes care of my dad and ensures he has everything he needs and don't need, it's no joke!

Mommy tells me one night my dad had gone out, and stayed out real late, later than usual and she was tired of waiting up for him so she went to bed. When she finally heard him coming through the door about 3am, she turned over on her back so she could get a better look at him. When he came into the room, the moon was shining very bright that night for some reason through their bedroom window. My dad slides into the room. Trying to be extra quiet and stopped directly in the path of the bright moon light, so my mom is able to see him turning his cell phone off and gently taking off his clothes. My mom noticed that when my dad got down to his boxers, there was something very red on the front of his boxers but she couldn't quite make out what it was. She couldn't take it anymore. She shot straight up in the bed and screamed, "What the fuck is that on the front of your boxers? What is wrong with you?" My dad, being the snake charmer he is and quick thinker on his feet quickly looked down in disbelief and shock. Sprung his head back up to look at my mom and replied, "Ohhhhhh shit, I'm bleeding!" I have my face buried in 2 pillows crying, snorting and trying to muffle my screams of laughter. My mom grabs my shoulder and asks, "Bet Bet, why are you crying, are you ok?" I quickly replied between sobs, "Mommy, I'm so sorry for what daddy did and I'm not crying from sadness, I'm crying because it's funny as hell and I'm trying not to scream and wake him up. She was like, "Ok, but there's more." I'm in dire need of a depends pamper because that liquor is trying to come out but I don't want to wreck her flow of this story by getting up to go the bathroom.

She says after he shot her that quick lie, she jumped up out of bed and said, "Nah nigga you ain't bleeding but you finna be because I'm finna beat yo ass mutha fucker!" Now my step mother isn't a fighter like my mother, so she wind milled his ass until she got tired and he got tired of ducking and flinching. I'm on the floor, slobbing like a Jerry Kids reject, yet trying to be considerate of her feelings. As a woman we all have felt the pain of your man cheating on you unnecessarily especially when you are doing everything in the world to keep his stankin rusty ass happy. Till this very day, the only color lipstick she wears is blood red.

About two months before I moved back home to St. Pete, I came back to St. Pete for 3 back to back interviews and to spend time with my folks. I knew right after the interview was over, I had the one job that I truly wanted and had already been praying for. Shortly after I finished with the last interview, I started looking at apartments and waiting for my parents to get off. My step mom called me and told me she was on her way home and to start heading that way. Before I can ask her if I need to pick up anything, she hangs up, so I hop on I-275 and flush home. I get home and mommy is already there with some chicken wings, fried rice, egg rolls and some other stuff. We eating, chilling and I'm telling her all about the interviews and about which job I really wanted. The look on her face is one that I have seen many times before. She wants to talk and we can easily and freely talk since my dad isn't home yet. I ask my mommy, "Should I fix our favorite drink so we can really talk before daddy gets home?" Girl, she kicked them sneakers off, unbuckled her pants, slid that bra off thru her shirt and said, "Hell yeah Bet Bet, I gotta tell you this one before your daddy gets here because he hates this story!" I washed my hands, fixed 2 strong drinks and plopped down in the oversized chair next to the couch where my mom was laid out on sipping her drink.

Whenever my parents get ready to go out of town, she packs his clothes, meds, whatever snacks he wants and her stuff as well. She will lay his clothes out on the bed to match them up, and then add the shoes to ensure the entire outfit looks good, all the while he is in the den watching TV, picking his damn teeth and nodding while the TV is watching him. I get it, I just ain't there yet. I'm trying to wrap my mind around this, but it just ain't there or I have yet to meet the man who inspires these actions out of me.

Every year they go to Alabama for an annual Black Tie affair. My step mom is busy packing gowns, suits and all necessary items for this 4 day event. They make it to Alabama and she realizes that she forget a pair of his reading glasses, but pays it no mind as they are known to share each other's glasses from time to time. They get settled in the hotel room and my step mom has laid everything out for the Friday evening event and starts to freshen up first. My step mom wears a partial crown and uses poligrip when she wants to ensure that she is gripped tight and will not be experiencing any sudden accidents of teeth flying out her mouth. My step mom hops in the shower, while my dad was outside talking to some friends. My dad returns to the hotel room and starts to brush his teeth while watching TV. He waits for my step mom to get out of the shower so he can hop in, but his mouth becomes stuck. He tries to remove the tooth brush, but to no avail it will not come out. He starts to panic and runs into the bathroom where my step mom is now drying off and aggressively mumble some Geechee talk to her and she is like, "What man?" So he mumbles some more Geechee talk to her and they walk out the bathroom into the main room where the sink is, when he holds up the tube left on the sink. My step mom asks my dad, "What the hell is wrong with you? All this fucking mumbling and shit!" My dad who still can't talk is just mumbling "UURRRRRRHHHHHHH UUGGGGGGGG AAHHHHHHHH (while holding up the tube)." At this point my step mom is laughing her ass off and has to sit up before she chokes on her drink, she says, "Bet Bet I promise you when I figured out what the fuck was going on, it took all I had not to run out the room in tears laughing! I went over to the coffee maker, picked up the coffee pot and put some water in it and placed it back on the maker to heat the water up and asked your crazy ass daddy, "Man, why in the hell did you brush your teeth with my Poligrip? "He was still mumbling and carrying on like a crazy man. I'm trying to put the hot water in his mouth to loosen the Polygrip, telling him to swish it around in his mouth. Instead of him doing what the hell I tell him, he steady trying to argue with that mumbling shit."

It took about 20 minutes to get the glue to loosen up because she didn't want to get the water boiling, but just hot enough to get it loose. The whole time she is telling this story, we are both dying laughing and making the most of girl time before my dad gets home. My step mom is sitting up sipping on her drink and laughing just as hard as me. She says in between laughs your daddy asked me, "Why in the fuck did you leave that shit on the counter?" My step mom is quick on her feet like Ali and she quipped back, "Why in the fuck didn't you read the got damn tube?"

I'm literally crying because this is normal conversation in our house with these two. Once again I need to pee, but I refuse to wreck the flow of this conversation because my dad should be walking through the door any time now. She said my dad says, "You know I can't read without my damn glasses." My step mom said by now she is pissed that he is blaming her for his non reading ass for brushing his teeth with her Poligrip, because he is interfering with her getting dressed, so she angrily responds, "You better start reading or doing something before you fuck round and gargle with a douche!" Just as she finished telling me the story, I'm literally in tears, almost on the floor dying laughing just as we hear the locks on the front door turning. I quickly get up; wipe my face with the bottom of my shirt. I try to stop laughing but I can't. I finish my drink and try to make it to my room before my dad gets in. We meet right in the middle of the living room and he looks puzzled as he asks, "What's wrong with you Bett?" I make it seem like I'm upset about something and that we will talk later. I can't bear to stand there and keep looking in my dad's face, because I can see the Poligrip in his mouth. I just slide down the hall to my room and take a quick nap before dinner.

I finally moved back home to St. Pete in 2003 and moved onto Coquina Key Island where my dad lives so I could be closer to him. I was getting settled into my condo, with the Gulf of Mexico serving as my back yard. I was getting re-acclimated to my hometown and all my family that lived there. I had been in the condo for a few months getting everything just how I like, wanted and needed. I got the job I wanted and knew I had after my interview, and was very happy with my new job as an AIDS Drug Assistant Program Social Worker at the Pinellas county health department. At times it was mentally draining and emotionally challenging, as you get attached to your clients because you want to do more. You get attached to your clients even though I know that is a great big no no. There are times that their life and struggle will get to you so bad because there is only so much you can do. So a lot of my time was spent getting my place all nice, cozy and of course relaxing with some libations.

The time that I didn't spend with my dad or other family members, I would go out. Shop. Hit a local hot spot, just to break the monotony of work, home, parent's house and church. It seem like every time I went shopping, to the movies or just out cruising the town taking in some air and clearing my mind there was always this one guy. He had a really nice body, fixed up older car, sexy build, magnetic Denzel Washington walk and a smile that look like butter wouldn't melt in his mouth. We would always see each other at various places around town and always in traffic.

Neither one of us would make the first step to kick start this thing off, so it was always simple flirting. I dated off and on, but no one of particular interest that I wanted to keep around. I guess because I always had this guy in the back of mind constantly wondering about him, Mr. Wonderful.

A year had passed and I had been to all the supposed upscale clubs in St. Pete, Tampa and all the little local surrounding towns. I finally decided to stop by the local hole in the wall club in St. Pete, which was run by the Nite Riders van club. I was dressed rather classy yet seductive but still classy. I go in, grab a seat at the bar and order a Hennessey straight, light on the rocks and survey the scene before moving in closer for a possible kill. From afar I see this tall sexy, well-built body holding up the wall and slightly moving his body to the ferocious bass beat. I keep my eye on him because something is telling me this is the man I have been flirting with for an entire year and neither one of us have made a move. After 3 drinks, I slowly get off the bar seat. I pull my dress down over my hips, wiggle them slightly and slowly stroll to the dance floor to see and be seen as I make my way to the other side of the bar to an empty table. As I dance and casually move to addictive beat on the dance floor, trying to make it to the other side of the club. I feel the eyes of that tall sexy, well-built man who is holding up the wall in the corner wearing me out with his eyes. I coyly look up, smile and bat my eyes as I throw these hips around people on the dance floor and make it to the chair. I'm sitting there enjoying the crowd and music, when a waitress approaches and says, "A drink has been ordered for you. I just need to know what you want to have?" I look at her with serious confusion and ask her, "Who ordered the drink for me?" She was cool as hell and was like, "Girl just take the damn drank, niggas now a days don't want to buy a bitch a loaf of bread, let alone a damn drank!" I couldn't do nothing but laugh and order my Hennessey. The waitress came back with my drink. She casually nodded in the direction of the dude who had been checking me out all night. I smiled and said, "Thank you."

Now this is my 4th straight Henny Hen. No food since earlier. I'm feeling pretty damn good, like I could out dance Michael Jackson and actually catch a leprechaun. I decide to make my move. I get up. Drink in hand. I casually stroll over to him and gently stroke his arm and say, "Thank you love for the drink. What is your name?" He is a lot taller than I thought or remember. He leans down. I'm enjoying the aphrodisiac cologne he is wearing and hearing his deep voice vibrate in my ear. He holds me around the small of my waist and pulls me close to him. My body shivers slightly as he gently tells me in my right ear, "It is my pleasure to provide you with whatever you desire. My name is Jerald. What is your name?" My eyes roll with fever as I'm enjoying feeling his body against mine. I wrap my right hand around his freshly shaven, tastefully faded head to bring him in closer. I seductively tell him, "My name is Betty. Please tell me why it has taken so long for us to finally meet?" He looks at me a little puzzled but rolled with it. We kept talking and drinking throughout the night. The DJ spins one of my favorite songs. Soldier Slim "Slow Motion." Lawd that Henny told me I was part Jamaican and have some dutty wine up in my ass. I was grinding and dancing on this poor man like I was a jackhammer to concrete.

Ohhhh we danced, touched and grinded. We had a little mini soft porn going on in that corner and it was something serious. The song stops. We're out of breath. Jerald is knocking people's drinks off the table from across the room because he is so damn hard. I'm 3 sheets in the wind and trying to make sure I still look good as the lights to club are now starting to come on, because it's time to close up for the night. We stayed in our little cozy spot for a few more minutes, which was still slightly dim. We exchanged numbers and promised we would get together for a date. I leave out the club first happy as hell that I have finally met and have a date with the man I have wanted for some time. I slide by the little jook joint after hour's food spot. Grab a hot greasy bite to eat and head back to the island. I have the windows down, bumping Solider Slim's "Slow Motion" thinking about Mr. Wonderful and wondering why everybody in the club was looking at me with the damn side eye as I was leaving the corner with ole dude?!?! Like they ain't never been in a dark corner with somebody having a moment.

I wake up late Sunday afternoon. I missed church, nursing a pounding headache and slight hangover, still trying to put all of the events from the night before back together. I check my phone and notice I have several missed calls and a few missed texts. I'm looking for one in particular missed call or text. Being that my blind as a bat ass didn't have on my glasses, I overlook the missed call and text from Jerald. I instantly call him back. We talk for a few and reminisce about the night before. We make plans for the day and I tell him where I live and what to have for the guard at the gate. I'm so excited! I straighten up my house. Shave all major body parts and get ready for my own personal Denzel Washington.

It is now about 4pm. I'm dressed very sexy. Hair laid. Make up on point. Damn near open casket sharp. We are going out for dinner, drinks, movie and just spending time together getting to know one another better. All I kept thinking is, this is the man who has flirted with me for a whole freaking year and now I have him. The guard from the front gate calls! I have a few minutes left to get the girls in place. Make sure my make-up was on point. Ensure my outfit was perfect. I open the sliding glass door to the balcony so the wind from the Gulf of Mexico can blow in like a perfect scene from a movie. Practice a few quick poses. BBOOMM! There is a knock at my door. My stomach drops. I instantly get gas. I prim and prop quickly and glide to the door as if I'm on a conveyor belt to the gateway to happiness.

I open the door and there he stands, about 6'5. Tall, dark, thick, well built, well dressed. Smelling like a woman's sexual dream of ecstasy, carrying a bouquet of red roses. I was so very flattered. I smile. Reach out for the bouquet and to give him a warm and inviting hug with a kiss on the cheek. He smiles. This mutha fucker is missing all 8 of his top teeth.

Now you know I stopped dead in my tracks. My face is twisted like a Rubik's cube! I backed up from dude like he had shitted on himself like the little baby from Bae Bae kids. I didn't know whether to invite him in or push his toothless wonder ass down the stairs, shut my door and act like I ain't know or see shit. He pulled the Billy Dee move from "Lady Sings the Blues" and said, "Do you want my arm to fall off?" With the way I'm feeling and thinking, "Hell yeah it would match yo ole empty parking lot looking ass mouth." I invite this fool in, take the roses and forcefully throw them on the kitchen counter. I keep saying to myself is, "How the fuck did I get tricked with the toothless boy wonder? Is this a joke or some mistaken identity?" I walk back into the living room. Plop down on the couch across from him sitting on my two seater. We strike up small talk when he asks, "Are you ready to go? Do you know where you would like to go eat?" I almost got up and Jackie Chan kicked that nigga in the back of his fucking head for asking me such a dumb ass question. As I try to come up with the appropriate way to answer him, I keep staring at him to ensure this is the same dude I met the night before. I keep staring and staring, steadily replaying the night before in my mind. The only thing that really sticks out is, every time I would pull away to try and look in his eyes, he would just grab me tighter around the small of my back and pull me closer to his body and whisper in my ear. Then it hits me like a ton of bricks. Now I know why the people were looking at me crazy when I walked out the club last night after being in a gorilla lock with him.

I didn't know how in the hell I was gonna get out of this. I was already dressed. The girls sitting up and out and my face beat to sleep. Just as I was thinking of what to say, my home and cell phone started ringing at the same time. I excuse myself and check each phone in my bedroom. I answer the phone. It's somebody I had recently met and wanted to go out with and get to know better. While I'm on the phone with him I'm changing clothes. I'm finna tell this fool that somebody in my family has something bleeding and hanging off and need immediate medical attention. I run back into the living room trying to look as dramatic as possible and fighting the urge to super glue some Chicklets in his damn mouth. I explain to him that my dad is rushing my step mom to the hospital because she just fell out and he can't wake her up. At first he looks a little puzzled and then he asks, "Do you want me to go with you because I know this is tough to deal with?" Hell mutha fucking nah bitch, I don't ever want to see your empty parking lot looking mouth ass ever again." That's what I really wanted to say but I was polite as I was turning off the TV, closing my sliding glass door, grabbed my keys and purse and said, "Right now is not the best time for me or my family, I will give you a call in a little while and let you know how everything is." I walk downstairs with him. Give him a half parting hug. Get in my car and speed out the parking lot as if I'm really going somewhere. To be honest I don't even think my car was in drive when I kicked dust up. There are only two bridges that can bring you on the island and let you off. Where my condo was located, I was right at the north bridge which is considered the 1st bridge. All I had to do once I came out from the condo, was make a right. Go over the bridge and hit it. What I did was, make a left like I was going to my dad's house, to be with my dad and step mom and go with them to the hospital. Being that I got in my car first and peeled out of there like a NASCAR driver, I was able to make the left and park in the cut at the 7-11 and wait to see his car pull out and head in a different direction. When I saw him leave, I waited a few minutes. Hit the back streets to go off the island on the south bridge. Circle the block a few times. I went back home, changed clothes and went out with the other dude.

The next day, I got a call from the human resource manager for Broward County Health Department. I was offered the position for Jail Linkage Program Coordinator. The lady couldn't get all the information out before I accepted the position and told her my start date. You know I got a bad habit of telling them my start date when I'm trying to get the hell up out some shit. I turned in my resignation letter. Got a letter from my job so I could break my lease, brought all the boxes, tape and supplies I needed, had my shit packed in a week, hired movers and was gone! This situation is what made me move down to Ft Lauderdale and never look back. I have gone home plenty of times and never saw him or the original really fine handsome dude I mistook Mr. Toothless Wonder for. Do I wonder how he is doing and if he has gotten some teeth? Hell nah . . . ~~Ain't That Bout'a Bitch~~

CHAPTER 5

RATS, BASKETBALLS AND BABY MOMMAS

I move down to Ft. Lauderdale and graciously accept my new position the Broward County Health Department. In learning my new job and coworkers, I'm learning my new city and loving every minute of it. There is always so much to do in the tri county area. A plethora of cultural diversity and food to match. No matter which city you go to, there is a beautiful beach and shopping to match the wondrous beauty of south Florida. Please don't let me forget the non-driving snow birds and immigrants. I have never in my life been so afraid to drive on any highway in this great country, but when you come down here baby of that's a whole different world and you bet not be in a hurry anywhere and have the slightest attitude because you may get ran off the road.

Every weekend for the first 3 months I was in somebody club having a blast and meeting new and more interesting people. I had gone to Miami a few times but never really knew exactly where to go besides South Beach or Coconut Grove because I wanted to make sure I didn't end up in the wrong place at the wrong time and end up on the First 48. One day one of my coworkers overheard me talking on the phone telling someone I wanted to go down to Miami for this concert at one of the local clubs but wasn't sure if I would go because I didn't want to be down there alone, when normally I hit the streets straight solo. She came over to my cubicle and said, "I live in Miami and have an extra ticket to that concert. You are more than welcome to it." I don't really know ole girl like that. She seemed cool from the few brief interactions we had in the office, so I'm thinking she don't want to lose her career so she just might be cool. I accept her offer, exchange numbers and get ready for the concert.

It's the day of the concert and I go to my coworker's cozy little apartment in Over Town. Uhmmm sweet baby Geesus in a manger. I had heard of it and had been warned to never go over there once it's night time. I ask LaBreeka if it was ok for me to follow her home right after work and get dressed there. Once off I-95, I roll the windows up and just take in the sights. One of the neighborhood stores that we passed had been in Trick Daddy and Dj Khalid videos. One of the project apartments had been featured in Ace Hood video. I felt like I was on a Hollyhood tour of Miami. We pull into LaBreeka's complex and it was one of the newer apartments built to try and bring up the neighboring property value and attract people and business back to the neighborhood. I felt a little at ease until we got out our cars and hit the breezeway to walk upstairs to her 2nd floor apartment. It was the same scene from every hood in America. A table with an over excited game of spades going on. The neighborhood hot girls practicing the latest drop it like it's hot dances. The resident crazy check dude who scares the shit out of me every time no matter where I am. Some older lady hollering out her window to LaBreeka that the UPS man had dropped off her clothes that she had ordered and a few little friendly flying critters hanging out in the breezeway. We make it to the 2nd floor where LaBreeka apartment is. She opens the door and people start to scatter like roaches. Her two teenage sons had some friends over, her cousin and her young daughter was there, well as LaBreeka crack head sister begging LaBreeka to take her to the store so she can steal so she can make some money. My head is spinning like a merry go round trying to figure out what the hell I have just walked into and to make sense of everything going on around me. We get dressed and head to the concert and what a blast I had. Girl the club was packed to the got damn moon and back with nothing but fine, good looking, well dressed, chivalrous, well-spoken men. I was in my element and loving it. LaBreeka and I turned that place out and developed a tight bond. When the concert was over we was still crunk and wanted to keep partying when LaBreeka suggests we hit this other club close to the American Airlines Arena. I was sold when she said that because that's down town, more of the type of men I like and more fun. We freshened up our makeup and hit I-95 full speed ahead. I don't know the streets or my way around Miami but I notice that Breeka got off an exit before her house and turned down a few back streets and ohh my Geesus! She had me in the heart of Over Town down the main drag where it was just a bunch of stores, abandoned buildings, and two pool halls next to one another with enough Negros to shoot a trilogy for a Tarzan movie. I eased my seat belt off just in case I needed to make a quick getaway and run like the wind. We circle the block a few times to survey the scene to see who is out there. Not that you could see anybody because it was so many got damn people. We finally get a good parking spot in front of the abandoned buildings facing the two pool halls. Oh my Lawd, the show that was being put on that night. Somebody had the music bumping crystal clear with the bass thumping. Some good looking thug boys standing around watching the movement of everybody in close proximity. The crack heads putting on Broadway musicals and dance competitions and Breeka breaking her neck to get into this twilight zone, mind numbing atmosphere. Once again I ask myself, "Betty what the hell have you gotten yourself into?"

I finally get out and follow Breeka everywhere she goes. I'm walking so close to Breeka that I could actually have walked in her shoes with her at the same damn time. She found that shit so funny when I'm on the verge of tears because everything that I have heard about Over Town after dark is running through mind like movie credits. We walk around outside meeting all of Breeka's friends and family members and local neighborhood celebrities when Breeka's takes me into the 1st pool hall and it's just as live in there as it is outside. Breeka is introducing me to all her friends that are on the inside when he stands up. I break my neck following his rise to greatness! I saw him when we walked in. He was sitting in the corner dress prep boy casual yet very distinguished but when he stood up that was another story. From my measurement he looked to be about 6'8, 275lbs. Flawless pecan tan complexion and the straightest whitest teeth that produced a smile that would give the sun a run for its money in brightness. A body that was chiseled by Zeus himself. After watching him get up and glide across the room I turn my attention back to Breeka and another round of friends that had walked in when "He" approached.

He glides up to LaBreeka and says, "Bre who is your friend?" You know I got to batting these eyelashes and clutching my chest like a southern belle. Breeka turns around and nudges my elbow with hers and says, "Lavache this is my homegirl from work, Betty. Betty this is Lavache." I extend my hand to shake his when he grabs my hand and gently kisses the back of it and says, "What a pleasure it is to meet such a beautiful woman in a place like this. Would you like to go outside and talk some more?" I felt safer inside then out, so I kind of shook my head no with a raised eye brow look of concern on my face, Lavache and LaBreeka both laughed at me when I didn't find shit funny. Even though the party atmosphere was live and in full effect I just kept having that feeling I would end up with a bullet in a my ass cheek that the doctors couldn't remove. How would I explain that my momma as to why I was over there in the first damn place.

We step outside and go across the street to his car which is parked in the same parking lot as Breeka and mine but closer the abandoned building so we could actually see everything that was going on. Lavache and I talked for what seem like forever and it seemed as if we had known one another for just as long. Lavache actually is 6'11, 330lbs. Plays basketball overseas with a very small team. There was the possibility of one kid. Owned his own home, own car and was 27. We left the club, went and grabbed something to eat and went to the beach and talked all night. No sex, just pure mental orgasms all night. When I made it back to Breeka house the next morning, you know she wanted all the details but before I let her know anything, I needed to know what she knew since she did tap my elbow the night before. So I told Breeka, "Spill the beans heffa. What's the deal with Mr. Basketball overseas?" Breeka put in to tell me that he is a local neighborhood celebrity because he has gone overseas to play basketball. Originally from Over Town and was known to get into a lot of fights, even with women but has since calmed down. She wasn't sure if he had a chick or not or if he had any kids even though she has heard some foot dragger was supposed to be having a baby and that should would find out more for me. We talk and chit chat a little more before I leave the war zone of Over Town and head back to Lauderdale.

Lavache and I talk all that weekend and make plans to see one another again and soon. I was really starting to dig him with the way he spoke and actually put actions into his words. LaBreeka and I on the other hand had grown very close, which is very odd for me. All of my friends are male because of the natural things I like and prefer to do. I love muscle cars and will hit a car show in a heartbeat and get the biggest rush from the sound of the big block engine and the mere sight of a custom rebuilt engine. I love football, especially college football. Give me my favorite cigar and drink and I'm in heaven whether in a sports bar or at home with the grill crunk while watching FSU dominate the gridiron. Not a lot of women are into that because they are so busy being catty with one another or trying to keep tabs on a Negro that ain't paying their ass no got damn attention, trying to hate on the next female and I just don't have time for that. In hanging out with Breeka she was cool as hell. She use to keep me laughing and up on the latest. Where we differed at and I would always change the subject out of respect, because I never wanted to say anything rude to her or make her think I was judging her because that is not me at all. She married a man in prison who had life without the possibility of parole and would spend the majority of her paycheck sending it to him among doing other things to take care of him and I just never understood that nor do I want to, but we always remained cool. Yes, she married him while he was in there. They met through a mutual friend and things just took off from there. They got married while he was in prison. Had a little make shift reception in prison, but was unable to consummate the marriage because he is in prison. Lavache and I spend time the entire following week together and I'm in absolute heaven. He had a beautifully decorated 3/2 condo in a well-manicured part of Kendall which is worlds away from Over Town's over dilapidated property. You can tell there is a great deal of history over there that needs to be restored and loved forever more. Even though he is highly affectionate he never ever made a move to try and have sex with me nor he make me feel uncomfortable. The sexual tension is truly building and growing stronger and stronger. In the midst of spending time together and fighting the urge to make love, I need to get some clarification on this possible baby that he briefly mentioned because I'm not trying to be side blinded by no crazy deranged baby momma who thinks I'm trying to take her baby daddy. When the time seemed right. I rubbed his arm, gently scratched his back with my fingernails and nuzzled up to him real lovingly then flat out asked, "So, do you remember when we were on the beach you vaguely told me about a possible kid? Do you care to elaborate on that for me please?" He took this long exaggerated breath, looked around like he was hoping the words would just magically appear out of nowhere but they never did and I sat right there with my hand under my chin with my eyes on the sparrow waiting on my answer. Lavache finally responds, "Well see, what happened was" I should have ran then but his sexy, too tall, possible hammer in his pants is what made me stay and hear him out. "One night at the same club I met you at, I had just come home from overseas and was just in there chilling with my friends, drunk and wanting to kick it when a girl I knew from the neighborhood fell through and was saying all the shit a nigga wanted and needed to hear. One thing lead to another and I knocked her off. No feelings, no love, no nothing. Now she claim she pregnant from me and I don't think it's mine. If it is she just after my money." Ok, yada yada yada, I felt like I was back with Sincere when I heard him say all that. The girl ain't get pregnant by herself and if she was after his money, he was the dummy who left the bank open for her to get it by not using a rubber! I let that pass and get ready so we can go out to dinner.

That night we had dinner at one of my favorite steakhouses, Smith and Wollensky on North Miami Beach. We sat out back by the water, which is my favorite place to sit because you get to see the passing boats, the big beautiful mansions and the ambiance is to die for. It seems as though the more time we spend the closer and closer we are becoming and I'm so loving that. We finish up, make it back to the house and the mating call starts. I go into the living room, turn the TV on and put my feet up to make some room in my belly so I can eat the dessert we brought home along with the leftovers. I hear Lavache running water in the master bath but I don't pay him any attention because I'm good and full and ready to go to sleep and fart. Just as I get good and comfy here he come in the living room butt bookey ass naked with a killer shark hanging from his body. Lavache had washboard abs, slightly bowlegged which I never noticed before and sexy as hell. I'm sitting there just staring at his crouch after looking him up and down several times. Once I came too he didn't even have to ask me to follow him. I was in the room butt ass naked getting into the tub. Fuck all the romance, I wanted his ass! The tub was full of bubbles with some slow music playing and candles lit. I was naked standing there waiting for him when he came around the corner laughing his ass off and said, "Damn I can't be romantic to you?" I was so horny and ready to release this sexual tension that had been building since we first met. All the romance was out the window. Once we got in the tub I had to explain to him that there are times women just want a nutt as bad as men. Some are women are bold enough to tell you and others not so much. We have a great time in the tub but baby when we got out, I thought I was in the fight of my life.

Lavache dries me off and rubs my entire body down in lotion. The way he did it was so smooth and non-sexual. It was as if he was trying to engage me mentally for a battle I had no idea I was getting ready to enter. Once Lavache finishes lotioning my entire back side, he turns me over, stands me up from the bed and took total control from there. Lavache had me bent over the bed, on the floor, on the dresser, on the wall, on the ceiling. OMG this man was fucking me so good, so hard and in positions I had never ever thought of or experienced that he had me faking a coma just so he would stop and leave me the hell alone, but that shit didn't work. He stopped for a few minutes to put me in a different position when I tried to crawl away quickly and just jump out the window taking my chances with a broken arm, ankle and leg, this fool grabbed my ankles and drug me back to him like a fisherman reeling his prize catch, cause I was for damn sure fighting. Oh my goodness girl, I ain't never look for ice before like I did that night. I got a hand towel, wet it and stuffed it with ice cubes. My poor little cooda was tore up like a game of Jinga. As much as I liked him, I was truly hating him at that very moment. Every time he tried to cuddle and show me some affection I would pop his ass dead square in the head and threatened his ass. Even though I had the entire igloo ice box on my cooda, I was really digging Lavache and enjoyed that night.

A couple of months had passed and all was going fine between us. We are spending time and traveling doing our thing, becoming closer and closer but I notice there are more and more phone calls coming in from the baby momma. I know, I know, she was there before I was but I needed some clarification as to where the both of them stood with one another and where the boundary lines lie. I had already been through enough with Sincere and all his baby mommas and not to mention all his extra affairs, so this shit ain't sitting right with me. I tell Lavache, "Sweetie if we are to have anything moving forward, you will need to set up a sit down meeting between you, myself and your baby momma because something just ain't right and I'm not going for it. Been there and done that sweetie, it ain't going down again!" He agrees and within a few days, we all meet up at TGIF. I need to hear from her where she stands and what she is looking for from him and myself, because all the calls in the middle of the night and ain't nothing wrong with her was not going to cut it. Lavache starts the conversation with introducing everyone and reiterating the purpose of the visit. He tells me in front of her the same story he told me a couple of months or so ago about how he came home, they hooked up and that was it no relationship or anything. Broom Hilda, the baby momma agreed. Lavache then goes on to explain that he respects her decision to be with other people and she needs to respect his decision to be with another woman and that if the baby is his, he will gladly accept his responsibility but she needs to respect his house and our relationship! I think I had just nutted a few times when he stood up and took charge of the situation, because I just knew he was going to hoe up, but he didn't. Once again, Broom Hilda agrees and says she will respect our relationship and that she is not interested in being with him. I'm at peace and ease and never had to say a word. Broomy never has anything to eat and leaves once our conversation is over. We stay eat and Lavache says, "I know you were thinking I wasn't going to stand up for you or us, but I'm really feeling you and want this. After Thanksgiving, I have to go overseas to check out 3 different teams that my agent says want to see me. I may be gone for about a month or so and I just want to know that you are in my corner no matter where I am!" Well, been here before and I know this ain't finna work, but I go along for the ride since I'm already in it. Thanksgiving was coming up and I had no plans of going to St. Pete or Gainesville to see my family because we had already worked it out that I would split my time between the two for Christmas.

I had already met Lavache's mom and grandmother and treated them with a high level of respect as I do everyone's elders. No matter what they say or act towards me, I always show respect and hold my tongue. Lavache grandmother didn't really care for me and she always let it be known with some real slick shit always coming out her mouth whenever I was with him when we went over to hot match box ass apartment in Over Town that she shared with his mom. I never said anything, just smirk smile, nod my head and give him that look of, "We only finna be over here in Pakistan for a good 10 minutes and then we roll out like the tide!" He never gave me any problem about not staying long, he never apologized for her behavior towards me nor did he apologize to her because we didn't stay too damn long. Thanksgiving is here and we are house hopping showing love to all of his friends and my one and only little friend down in Over Town, LaBreeka. We nibbled at each and every house we went too and unsmirk your face, he already knew my ass don't know how to cook. Which is why he made phone calls all week to see who was cooking besides his mom and grandmother. I was dreading going to their house but I had to suck it up. Everywhere we went the party was in full effect. Music, enough food to feed Ethiopia and Somalia at the same time and never run out for a few days. We make it to the hot match box in Pakistan. Lavache opens the door and allows me to go in first. I smile hard and say, "Happy Thanksgiving mom and granny! Love you and thank you for allowing me to spend Thanksgiving with you." Lavache mom was very sweet when I said that. She walked right up to me and gave me the tightest hug and told me she love me too. His grand mammy walked on my absolute last nerve. She never gave me a hug nor greeted with some form of a pleasantries but said, "This ole bitch probably just hungry and want something to eat, you know she don't know how to cook!" She didn't try to hide that shit under her breath or nothing. I instantly look at this tall bastard who turns his head quick as you can blink and starts rubbing his ear, like he ain't heard shit she said and starts looking at a TV full of snow. How did she know I ain't know how to cook? I shot him a look to let him know I will deal with him when we get in the car. His mom came in with the quick sweet recovery and said that dinner would be done in a few. Lavache puts in a DVD for us to watch because they didn't have cable. As we were waiting for the DVD to start, there was a continuous CLICKITY CLACK CLICKITY CLACK CLICKITY CLACK. This was not normal pots and pans clanging in the kitchen. You automatically know the distinctive sounds of pots and pans clanging. I look in the kitchen where the noise is coming from thinking that I could get a better understanding of what that noise was. Nothing! There was the noise again, CLICKITY CLACK CLICKITY CLACK CLICKITY CLACK but this time it sounds like it's more than one making that noise. I look at in the kitchen again. Nothing! I look at Lavache who is now about to push the color off the remote to get the movie to start right dammit now. I gently tap his left leg and ask in a whisper, "Baby, what is that noise coming from the kitchen?" Lavache did not want to look at me for shit. I tap him more aggressively and ask him in a more stern voice to get my point across, "VACHE! What the fuck is that noise in the kitchen?" You know how when someone ask you something in front of the wrong person and they trying to shoot you that side eye to say, "We'll talk about this later" that's the side eye action he was trying to shoot me, but I refused to let it go. The movie finally starts and it's showing just as bad as the got damn TV with all the snow. Now I'm highly frustrated. I hit this fool one more time because the sound just came back and in full force. Lavache drops his head shaking it and slightly turns to me and mouths, "Babe don't say nothing. Its rats! The rats over here in OverTown are horrible and my grandmother has a few." A few? More like a few hundred. Bitch they move with military precision like they are the spokes persons for the Army, A Few Good Men! I already had my purse on the couch with me. Just as I was about to pick my feet up off the floor his mom stuck her head out the kitchen and said that dinner was ready. Before I knew it, I quickly said, "Oh no ma'am I'm not hungry, we been eating at every house we stopped too!" Once again, ole gangster granny strikes and says, "What dat bitch said? I know she ain't say she didn't want nothing to eat?" I was too damn busy looking for rats to come out the kitchen with Chek sodas, overflowing plates and a toothpick in their mouth to even remotely pay her ass any attention. In my mind all I could see was a rat finishing his dinner, climbing up on the couch next to me, sucking his teeth with a toothpick hanging out on the side, rolling over and rubbing his belly talking about, "You just don't know what you missed. She put her drause off in that food. You should have been here last week when she make dem neckbones!" Once I saw that in my mind, I was too ready to go and she had a nasty ass attitude. I told Lavache to get a to-go plate for him and HIM ONLY and get me the fuck up out of there. He can always come back to see them next week when I'm at work before he head out of the country. I was too tired of her slick ass mouth and her roommates on 4 legs. Girl if you could have heard how they was moving through kitchen, boot stomping, throwing their hands in the air and calling out cadences. After that last episode I never went back to her house and it wasn't no love lost, trust that.

A few weeks past and his trip overseas is pushed back which worked out fine because Broom has now gone in labor. I was at his house when she called from the hospital, so I told him to go handle his business and I'll see him later in the week. I went home and he went to the hospital. He called me a few hours later to let me know he was the proud new father to a healthy, bouncing baby boy! "CONGRATS" is all I could get out. It was the dead of night and I was in a coma. He said the baby looked just like him and Broom and the baby was doing fine. Once again I congratulated him and went back to sleep. I let a week or so pass so he could spend time with the baby and make sure Broom had everything she needed and would not be a pest. Was I wrong for thinking and acting that? Hell nah, because I know how petty these simple ass heffas can be.

The baby ain't even a month old and here come the crazy phone calls again. One night after a very long and stressful day of dealing with office and street politics, I went down to his house to chill and enjoy him with no stress, plus he was getting ready to fly out the next day to go out the country. The phone is blowing up off the hook and I lose it before I know it and went off quick fast and in a hurry, "Listen I have no ties to you or anybody else and I refuse to go through this shit. If you can't get her and this situation under control I'm out. I'll miss you but fuck it, I don't care I'll get over you!" He answered the phone and I could hear her on the other end of the phone cussing me for everything and claiming the baby was missing him. I started packing up the few items I had over his house and made my way to the door when I hear him say, "Broom I was just with the baby and you all week, you know there isn't anything between us. We have had this conversation before, get this shit together and stop calling!" Before he hangs up I hear "CHILD SUPPORT!!" The two very words that scare a man worse than getting hit in the nuts. They argue back and forth for a few more minutes when I'm half way out the door and Lavache grabs my arm and snatches me back in. They finish arguing and he is trying to explain. I ain't trying to hear that shit because I have heard it all before. He may not be actually fucking her or want to be with her, but life is short as hell and I want to always be happy. I explain to Lavache, "If she acting like this now, what the fuck you think she is going to do later as the baby gets older? I know you don't think this shit stops? Ohh no sir, it kicks into overdrive and I just don't have time for you, her or your WWHHAAPP!" Before I could finish my sentence this bitch slapped me so hard, I could have sworn there was an infinity swimming pool in my right eye with all the water that had welled up in it. When I shook that shit off, it was Junk Yard Dog and Nature Boy Ric Flair all up and through his mutha fucking house. I was able to get into the kitchen. I grabbed a butcher knife and told Lavache, "If you come any closer to me I promise you on the life of yo raggedy ass mammy, I'll cut you every which way but loose. Don't you ever put your hands me or any other fucking woman like you some got damn body!" I ease towards him, he eases back. I keep a tight firm grip on the knife and keep it in front of me as I ease towards the front door. Lavache backs away from me with our eyes in dead lock, never blinking or looking away. He makes it to the edge of the couch and sits down. I make it to the other side of the dinner table and head towards the door when he bursts into tears like 4th of July fireworks. I don't pay that shit no attention. I make it to the door where my bag is laying on its side. With the knife still in my hand, my eyes on him, I bend down slowly pick up my bag and walk backwards out his house, never to see him again.

I make it home and check my body for any cuts, scrapes or bruises. I'm perfectly fine except for a little skin peeled off my knuckles from the fight I was just in. I can deal with the skin scrape. What I wasn't going to deal with was an ass whoopin from a man when my own father has never ever laid a hand on me. What the fuck was he thinking? It came flooding back to me what LaBreeka had told me about when we first started talking, that he would fight a woman. I guess he wasn't expecting me to fight his tall ass back. Where the fuck he got that from? He got some good licks in and you can best believe I did too, but my fat ass wasn't in the same shape I was when I use to fight Sincere and needed a damn 2 minute corner break with the way Lavache and I was fighting. The next day Lavache left the country to be scouted by the 3 teams. He called and texted a few times after our fight but I would never answer calls from his phone and especially from numbers I didn't recognize. There was nothing more for us to talk about since you don't know how to talk with your mouth, but with your hands. The following weekend I slide down to LaBreeka house so we can talk and I fill her in on everything and she is on the floor. Shortly after the fight with Lavache, I resigned from my job and moved back to Gainesville to regain my footing and get back on my grind. LaBreeka and I remained in contact and the best of friends. I would roll down to Miami on the weekends and kick it with her.

The last time I saw LaBreeka she filled me in on the latest with her and what she had heard about Lavache. Lavache was no longer playing ball overseas. He was back in Over Town living with Broom Hilda, had another kid and was doing bad. LaBreeka wasn't looking her absolute best either. LaBreeka was the type of Miami chick who was always up on the latest hair, clothes and everything especially with her sister boosting. LaBreeka tells me she is HIV positive, no longer working with the health department and still married to her life without the possibility of parole husband. I cried and cried when she told me that. I have several friends who have this deadly disease and don't really understand the ramifications that come along with this disease and lost some very close people to me as well who are infected with this monster. Even though Breeka worked with me in the HIV department, she was just a clerk and did not have a real sense of the disease either. I asked her questions and she asked me questions. The main question I asked was, "Do you have an idea of who could have possible infected you?" without a shadow of a doubt Breeka responds, "Yes, my husband!" I know you're trying to figure out she got it from him if he is prison. If you happen to date or be married to a top dog in prison you can still be privy to some of the outside life. They had it set two weekends out the month they would be set in a certain area of the visitation room and she would be allowed to sit on his lap and ride him. As she is telling me this, my eyes well up and my stomach becomes nauseous as hell. I couldn't take it anymore. I told Breeka I had to get out, let's hit the beach grab some drinks and just enjoy the moment.

When I left Ms. LaBreeka that was the last time I ever saw or spoke with her again too. ~~Ain't That Bout'a Bitch~~

CHAPTER 6

FLOATING ON A MEMORY

When I moved back to St Pete in 2003, I met this really cool guy and we use to hang out and do all kinds of fun stuff before I met the Mr. Toothless Wonder. Time rocked on with a few bad dates and I moved down to Ft Lauderdale and we lost contact. One day after a few years, I get this email from lil buddy and it just so happens to be the weekend that I'm coming up to St Pete to hang out with the family. We exchange numbers, chit chat and agree to hook up and spend some time and catch up on all the latest that is happening in each other's life. The night I was supposed to hang out with him, I was deep in the streets with ole friends and new ones, drinking (as usual), spot hopping and partying like it was 1999. I completely forgot about lil buddy until he blew me up in texts. So I politely respond back and told him I will see him when I leave the club.

By the time I get to lil buddy house, the sun is trying to come up, the birds are chirping, I'm sleepy as hell and doing one mean version of James Brown, while ranging his doorbell like a crack head trying to get into a free crack giveaway. He finally answers the door and I shoot pass his ass like a lightning bolt and flood his toilet like I'm a Hurricane. We talk, fool around and I drift off into a wonderful dream, of me just as happy as I want to be running and jumping running through a field of wheat, with the sun shining on my face, the wind blowing thru my hair. I come across a toilet in this field that I'm running thru in my dream. Of course I take a seat on this wonderfully soft and plush toilet, in the middle of a wheat field and start to pee pee. And ohhhhhhhhhh what a wonderful piss it is. Its long, strong, steady and sending chills up my spine until I feel someone tapping and shaking me, almost violently. I awake to find myself not in the glorious wheat field, but in the middle of the bed of lil buddy who I went to see. He was tapping and shaking me, calling my name trying to wake me up and in the sweetest voice he says, "Baby, baby wake up, your peeing in the bed." I jump up and in my embarrassment and amazement I have turned this poor mans bed into a swimming pool. I hop in the shower to wash up and when I got out, he has a towel and one of his T shirts waiting for me. He was so sweet, kind and reassuring that everything was ok and things happen as he finished cleaning up the bed. I'm completely out done and don't know what to do. I tell ole buddy I'm going to my mom's house and I will call him later. He says, "Why don't you come back and we do dinner?" I'm looking at him like are you fucking serious, but I politely accept as I Chicago two step out his front door. The day rocks on as I try to get over my hangover and drunken embarrassment, when he sends me a text that read, "Hey sexy, wut r ya doing? Are we still on for dinner?" I'm still embarrassed. I don't know what to say or do. I told my mom what happened and she laughed so hard, I almost put her in a nursing home that day. I reply back a few minutes later and say, "Hi hun, of course we are still on for dinner tonight. I'm just getting up about to hit the shower."

You already know I really don't want to go have dinner with this man. Even though I took a shower, lotioned up, put on clean clothes and my most expensive perfume, in the back of my mind, I'm thinking, Am I going to smell like pee pee? Will I be able to order alcoholic beverages and not have him say, "Hey lil Pissy pants, know your limit!" So he hits back with, "I'm about to run to the store, do you need me to pick up anything?" In my mind, I'm thinking wow, how sweet and accommodating of lil buddy is, especially after I have turned his bed into an Olympic swimming pool and he still wants to date me and spend time. In trying to keep it light in hopes that he might sense my embarrassment and cancel the date I respond, "No sweetie, I don't need anything from the store. I'm just tired and want to sleep but thank you for asking!" With that response I'm thinking I'm in the clear, this Negro texts back and says, "R u sure? Coz I can always pick you up a pack of XL Huggies!!"

When I read that last text, I was done. My eyes had stretched to the size of semi-tractor trailer tires. I had to make sure no one else read that shit but me. I didn't respond, I never left the comfort of my mother's house and I never ever saw or called him again. At times I do wonder if he ever had another drunk chick sleep over his house. If he did, did he make her sleep in the living room on an air mattress? Did he eventually get a new mattress? I don't know, I just know I never spoke to him again and left his ass floating on a memory. ~~Aint That Bout'a Bitch~~

CHAPTER 7

SURPRISE

I moved back to Gainesville from Ft Lauderdale early 2005 after resigning from my job at the Broward County Health Department as a Jail Release Linkage Coordinator. You remember, the job I had took there after meeting the bowl mouth toothless wonder in my hometown St. Pete. When I moved back home to Gainesville, I quickly got a job with Planned Parenthood as a Safe Passages Program Coordinator, working with at risk young girls in the aspect of reducing the rate of unplanned teen pregnancy and STD's. I also trained and mentored the volunteers and college interns and continued to teach health education classes.

I stayed in the duplexes on NW 6th Street and was known for throwing a spades/fish fry party with the quickness. I would supply the fish, grits, fries and sometimes my mom would make them melt in ya mouf hush puppies. All you would have to do was BYOB. At each party my mom was always there. She was the one who did all the cooking for the parties, plus all my friends loved her free and open, humorous spirit. This one particular party, it's a house full of friends and coworkers from the Alachua county health department and friends from all over. We got the music bumping, the card table is on fire. Fish bones are piling up, lips looking like they just been coated with a fresh bottle of Armor All. Everybody is having a blast when all of a sudden I hear a scream from the living room and all I can think is, "Something has happened to my mom." I run to the living room from the kitchen to see everyone standing up and gathered in a circle. I'm getting pissed because I'm thinking, "Why in the fuck are y'all standing around looking at my mom on the ground?" When I'm able to get closer and see what's really going on, my mom isn't on the floor. She is actually in the middle of the floor teaching the women and the only two men who ain't on the spades table, how to ride dick to get your bills paid. I scream, "MAAAAAA, what are you doing?" One of my coworkers grabbed my arm and said, "Hush girl, yo momma breaking that shit down on how to work dem hips on a nigga!" I'm looking at her with my face scrunched up like notebook paper. All I can think is "WTF? Is my coworker about to fight me about my momma??"

Now for those of you who don't know my mommy. I'm built and look just like my mommy when she was young before she had me. She always likes to tell me, before she had me, she didn't have a stomach and she could still wear hot pants. She has the large chest, small waist. Big pretty round hips. Ass and thighs for days. Some would call us a shit brick house. She can dance, move and rotate that ass like a roller coaster, all while holding a conversation. I peek through my friends and hear my mom say, "When you really want to get a good grip and make him know this ain't no damn game, ball ya fists up. Put them right in the middle of his chest, pick your hips up and grind, roll and ride that dick like this!" The girls are looking in amazement, while one of my homeboys dick has gotten hard and he screams out, "That's what the fuck I'm talk'um bout!!" All the while I'm looking like a deer tied to the front of a hunter's truck. I don't know whether to take notes or dismiss this got damn class. I say, "Mommy, I need you in the kitchen, we outta fresh fried fish." My momma hollered back, "Y'all better eat what the fuck in there, I'm in the middle of something right now." I don't know why I said that, because everybody got they ass up from the spades table and was in the living room trying to see what she was doing. I sat back and watched my friends and coworkers imitate every move my mom made, laugh and ask her other questions. All I could do was shake my head and say, "Lawd Geesus take me now!"

This is when things go deeeeeeeeeeep left. One of my coworkers loved to bring her man to every and any gathering because she wanted to keep an eye on him. He was known to cheat on her something awful. Even when he went anywhere with her, he would flirt with the other women there, but you couldn't tell her nothing. She loved him dearly and couldn't bring herself to leave him no matter what he did. I had already told her this was not the environment for him. It was going be a good mixture of men and women, but not a good spot for couples coz people are going to be trying to get their grind on. Well, none the less she shows up with him and all is fine at first. He was vibing with everybody and even got in on the dick riding class. I finally get my mom back into the kitchen to cook some more fish. Everybody came back to the spades table. All is fine until my mom hears her song. Since the fish is in the pan cooking, my mom decides to go back in the living room to dance to her song. I'm bullshitting in the kitchen on the spades table when I hear a male voice say, "Hell yea, that's how you work that shit!" I just shake my head and say, "What is she doing now?" I slowly walk into the living room with my head hung low, like I'm about to get a whooppin and see my mommy giving my highly insecure coworker man a lap dance. She got her ass in his face, working it! He slapping her ass and putting money in my momma pants. The crowd goes wild and those heffas is back on the living room floor showing they own skills. Dropping it like it's hot, testing out the newly acquired dick riding skills and having a blast. I look over to my coworker and she is just sitting there with a half-smile and I'm thinking "Ohhhh Lawd, I don't wanna hafta knock this hoe out about my momma." I walk up to her and whisper in her ear, "Girl, I'm so sorry if it's a problem I can get her to stop". She said, "Hell nah, he excited as shit because I won't dance for him like that. Imma tear dat ass up when we get home, hell yo momma fun as shit!"

My momma finished his lap dance when her song went off and went back into the kitchen to finish cooking like she had just come home from Sunday service. She had his money in her pocket and ain't did shit but dance with all her clothes on. That's a bad mamma jamma!!! Needless to say, the party lasted on a little while longer, with everybody bellies full, drunk, horny and ensuring I had another party soon.

I get to work early Monday morning. I went looking for my coworker who was looking for me at the same time. We met up in the hallway and she greeted me with a big huge hug and said, "Thank you girl, I had so much fun and can't wait to get with you and your mom again and have a blast. All he could talk about was your mom on our way home and girl he tore my ass up, Thank you!" I told her she was welcome and I will be sure to invite them to the next party I was throwing, which was my mom's surprise birthday party. As we part ways, all I'm thinking with a big kool aid grin on my face, "He tore yo ass thinking about my sexy brick house ass momma." ~~Ain't that Bout'a Bitch~~

The date was set, Friday September 16th, Gainesville, FL 8pm. Be there or be square! All phone calls, emails and running around town making the last and final preparations for a phenomenal surprise birthday party for my mom, to rival all parties, had been completed! My mom's baby sister, Tee Tee came to town from St. Pete to partake in the festivities, well as be the designated driver for my mom, because we all knew what to expect. All of my mom's oldest closes and dearest friends and coworkers, whom I was able to get in contact with, made it and was even gracious enough to assist in the final preparations before the birthday girl got there. I made sure to invite my mom's friends from Gainesville Police Department and Alachua

County Sheriff office of all levels just in case one of the neighbors decided to be some punks about the music and traffic flow.

My sister, niece and nephew along with my aunt was at my mom's house trying to keep her occupied until I arrived. She was under the impression we were just going to take her out to dinner. I was running a little behind schedule, because I was trying to ensure the guests who had arrived early, were comfortable and knew where to find whatever they would need until I returned. I arrived at my mom's house, everybody started sniggling and giggling, because I walked in with red exotic fluffy handcuffs and face mask. My mom who has thrown back a few beers is looking at me with her face scrunched up, asked me in a very strong voice, "Where the fuck you going with that bullshit?" We all laugh and I responded, "Inmate, I'm here to take you to your birthday celebration, so cuff up or go to the hole." My mom who is a retired sheriff deputy was all too tickled when I told her that, but I should I have known I was going to pay, because she was laughing a little too hard. She obliged, cuffed up and I put the mask on and allowed me to guide her to my car. Once in the car, she asked, "Where are we going?" I told her it was a surprise and she would see once we got there and not to ask me again. I forgot I had allowed her to bring along the beer she was drinking when she was at home, she finished the rest of the beer and started bussing me upside the head with the beer bottle talking bout don't talk to her like that. All I could do is what most black children do when getting a whoopin, duck, dodge and block the hits. She finally stopped and I was able to make the phone call to let them know we were on the way and right up the road from my house. Ready, set, GO!

The duplex I lived in on NW 6th Street, a main highway in Gainesville with ample front, side and back yard to entertain a host of people. The grass was cut and well-manicured. Tiki torches in place. Tables and chairs delivered with their appropriate covers. Liquor table in place and full with chaser, as all my parties are BYOB. Gift table set and filling up quickly with plenty of presents. Balloons placed in the respective places. Speakers on deck blasting the tunes. All that was left to do was the delivery from the caterer and have him set it up. The guest had started to arrive and my front and side yard was filling up quickly. People started parking at the now closed Melody Club and walking over with their arms full of gifts, and smiles bright enough to light up the dark sidewalk. The music is pumping, people starting to drink, eating appetizers, dancing and just naturally enjoy themselves awaiting the birthday girl. The phone call was made, everyone got into place and anxiously awaiting for me to pull up. I pull into my yard, honk the horn and I can see people scattering like roaches when the lights are turned on. I get out of the car, walk to the passenger side, open the door and grab my mom by the middle of the handcuffs, lead her from the passenger side and say, "Ok inmate, I need for you to comply with all direct orders or suffer the consequences!" My momma went off, "I got yo got damn inmate and as soon as you take these got damn handcuffs off me, Imma show you an inmate and beat your ass!" I'm dying laughing, because she has no idea what is about to happen. To ensure my safety, I leave the handcuffs on, hold up one finger and start a silent count to 3. 1, 2, 3 and I snatch the eye mask off and everyone screams "HAPPY BIRTHDAY!"

Once my mom is able to catch her breath, take everything in, she turns to me and said, "Ohhh you got me!" I'm crazy, but not that crazy. I asked my mom, "Is it safe for me to take these cuffs off you?" All she could do was laugh and say, "Yea." I took the cuffs off my mom and it was like a family reunion. She was hugging all of her friends and coworkers like she had not seen them in years. The old friends and coworkers, I had tucked them off in the back of the crowd, so when she saw them it would be like Christmas. Once she made it to the back where I was standing, I said, "Mommy, look who just dropped out the sky", my mom looked up in total amazement and started to cry when she saw a table full of old friends and coworkers that she had not seen in 10 years or more. My mom, who had never had a surprise birthday party, was in total amazement and very happy, all she kept telling me was, "Thank you!"

The night is going along perfect. Everyone is eating, drinking, playing cards, dancing and enjoying this unusually cool and breezy September night. My mom is just a natural social butterfly and people naturally love her. She was walking around all night, talking, hugging, kissing each and every person, dancing and just enjoying the night. The time had come to open up her birthday gifts. Now, when I tell you about some of these gifts, each one has its own history and story to itself. Lieutenant Walker from GPD, who has been a long and dear friend of the family for years, came up to my mom as she was sitting at the gift table and personally gave my mom his present. He walked up in an ole sexy cowboy walk, with some jeans on and a nice shirt. Handed her the gift bag and stood back with his right hand on his right hip as if he had his hand on his service pistol and was expecting her to have an old Wild West shoot out with him when she opened his gift. When Lt. Walker came up to my mom, she looked and had this amazing smile on her face that was just priceless. She stood up to give him a hug, to show her gratitude and appreciation. Lt. Walker jumped back in shock and screamed, "Don't bite me!" My mom hadn't even opened the gift and he thought he was in trouble. My mom is a fighter, but if she felt you were getting the best of her by locking up, she would bite the pure'dee dog shit out of you. There have been a few times Lt. Walker and my mom locked up and she bit his ass and then busted that ass with them hands. One time she left teeth marks in his back for 2 weeks. We laughed. They hugged. My mom sat back down and finally opened the gift and just dropped her head and laughed till she cried, all while the gift bag in her hand. One of the other guest yelled out, "Show us the gift!" When my mom pulled out a big pack of silver duct tape, everyone hollered and then my mom proceeded to tell the story behind the duct tape. When she finished, everyone was in tears.

Years ago, when I was still in elementary school, my mom's car broke down on us and for a long time we had to walk everywhere, catch rides or catch the bus. My mom's oldest sister had recently gotten a new car and she gave my mom her old 79' Buick Regal. Welllllllll, the old Buick had been subjected to the harsh elements of the sea water of St. Petersburg the sides had started to rust. The rust was so bad on the side of the Buick; we had to cover it with duct tape. It seemed like it took two rolls of duct tape for each side of the car. Lawd, if it rained it would rain in the car and we would be swimming. As time went on the car ran like a charm. It was just the outside looked a mess. One morning I was getting in the car so my mom could take me to school, I stepped into the back of the car. Just as I placed my foot down on the floor board, my foot kept going. I stopped, look around to see who has seen this. I'm embarrassed as hell. I scream for my mom to hurry up and come see what the hell just happened, because I'm scared. She comes out the house, locks the door and slowly walks her ass to the car and when she gets closer to me, she yells, "What the hell is wrong with you, yelling all crazy and shit?" I don't say one word. I just continue to stand there with my leg caught in between some rusty ass metal and my Ked covered foot standing on the ground. When she finally realized what was going on, she made sure I was ok first. Then she burst out in this thunderous bear laughter like some shit was really funny. I ain't see shit funny. My leg is the one that is being held captive by some spiked, rusty ass metal. My mom goes back in the house and grabs some pliers. She bends the rusty metal up as to not scratch or puncture me and then pulls me from the back seat. She makes sure I'm ok before having me sit in the front with her. She takes me to school and she goes to work. When she gets home from work, a thick, strong piece of plywood had been placed over the hole and we kept right on riding like it wasn't nothing. And that is the story of the duct tape. Lt. Walker use to help buy duct tape for the car and kept telling my mom to get rid of it because it was a death trap. When your money funny and the jokes it's telling ain't paying the bills, you gotta do what you gotta do. And we did. We rode that car until we got one better. Thank you God!

The night progresses with more of the craziest gifts and some of the nicest most heartfelt gifts. Somebody gave my mom a glowing, dancing penis that moves and dances off of your hand claps. Another gift was an animated dog that once turned on with fresh batteries, will hump your arm, leg or wherever you place him until he gets off and he got a moan game that is on point! Somebody gave her a penis necklace that resembled a Hawaiian lei that she wore for the rest of the night. The gift table went on for over an hour with some great gifts and some gifts that made all of us step back and say WTF? None the less, it was all in good fun and love.

I didn't hire any dancers, but one of my friends P.G. who came and was just having a blast and loved my mom to pieces decided him and his close friend would do a dance and semi strip tease for my mom. He gave me the CD with the song he wanted to dance to and had me clear the car port of everyone except my mom. Everybody cleared the car port, got behind the fence and I started the CD. Missy Elliot "Loose Control" starts playing and everybody is bouncing. My mom who has had several Michelob's and Hennessy on the rocks is sitting in the chair like a little kid saying, "Bring on the fucking show!" Well dammit man, P.G. and his homeboy slide up to my mom like they are on freshly waxed tile floors, gyrating their hips at a fast speed. Pulling up their shirts. Making their abs roll like a deep ocean wave. Teasing the hell out of my overly aggressive cougar momma not knowing who they were dealing with. The rest of the ladies are behind the fence and they are screaming. Throwing soaked drause over the fence at the fellas, trying to get at them. They look damn good throwing that dick, as if Luther Campbell was there himself singing the song. P.G. and his homeboy was dancing, grinding and taking shirts off, unbuttoning pants showing boxer drause, when P.G. got to close to my momma and she snatched his little ass up like the last homemade biscuit at the family reunion and was trying to lick his stomach. OMG, the crowd went wild. Me and my niece ran over to P.G. and pulled him from my mommy's strong bear grip and screamed, "NOOO mommy, don't do it!" She knew P.G. but that liquor told her he wasn't gay and she could have him that night as her fresh fish boy toy. P.G. big massive 6'6, 285lbs sexy, charcoal colored boyfriend said different that night. He was standing close by watching the whole thing and shooting dagger eyes at my mommy. The dance finally ended. I allowed my mom to hug P.G. briefly. I didn't want to cut the big boyfriend like a fresh caught fish. The night went on with more fun, laughter, drinking and just plain ole good home grown, country fun.

At the time, I was dating a long shoreman from a small local country town close to Gainesville. I had invited him and told him to bring his friends and kick it with me and my family. So all the country boys came and we had a blast. There were about 5 spades tables going. Music bumping. Cake cutting. I'm participating in as much as I can. I'm always being the hostess with the mostess. I'm in the house getting ready to pull some warm food from the oven when the long shoreman I'm dating runs into the house and frantically tells me, "Betty, you need to come get your momma right now!" I instantly panic. I grab Ms. Yvette and ask her to finish getting the extra food ready to take out to the food table. I need to get check on my momma. Ms. Yvette oblige without even blinking an eye. I run out the door following my dude. He takes me to the darkest part of my front yard which is covered with some very tall trees and no street lights. As I run up to the situation, I see my mom leaned up against a tree with her right arm propped up on the tree and her left hand propped up on her left hip like she finna pull a belt out the sky and beat the shit out of a kid, all while she has on this got damn bright pink dick necklace. I run up. Out of breath. Heart beating like a drum in the FAMU famous drum line and ask in a very low but stern voice, as to not alert the other party goers that there is an issue, "What the fuck is going on over here? Mommy, are you ok? Tommy what the fuck are you doing to my mom?" I'm heated and have quietly slid out of my shoes. I'm ready to fight Tommy big too tall ass. One thing about me, I don't fight my family, but I will fuck you up about my family. My mom, rolls her drunk ass head towards me and says, "Baby, don't worry. Ain't nothing going on over here that I can't handle!" I see right now I'm about to put her grown ass in a nursing home full of women. I can't get a straight got damn answer out of her. I'm only 5'3, so now I turn my attention to Tommy big 6'6, thick, sexy, chocolate brown, well groomed, well dressed ass, that smells something good and say, "Tommy what the fuck is going on? Are you bothering my mom?" All the time this is going on, my dude is standing behind me, sort of on my right side and not saying one word but he has a smirk on his face. His smirk is angering me to the point, I'm about to pick up a brick and smash his ass. Before Tommy can answer, my mom says, "Baby ain't nothing going on, I just told this tall sexy ass man that I would lick his toes, elbows and asshole!!" OMG, I thought Jesus had just came and took me home to Glory when I heard my mom say that. My heart stops. My mouth falls open. Tommy jump in and say while rubbing his hands as if he just ran up on a bag filled with $1 million dollars, "Betty, don't worry, I plan on doing the same damn thing to your momma fine thick ass too!" Ohhhh Lawd Geesus, take the wheel because I'm about to lose it. I slide my shoes back on. Wipe my face with my hands, look around to make sure none of the other party goers are close by to witness what just happened. I place my right hand on my hip and point my left index finger towards the house and I say to my mom with clinched teeth, "If you don't get yo ole chunky monkey black ass back to that got damn house and in some light where I can see you, I know something and I ain't even playing with your grown cougar ass. GEEETTTT!!" When she starts moving back towards the party, I turn my sights back to Mr. Tommy and tell him, "If I even think you looking at my momma I will smash yo ass. Get back over there and play some fucking spades as if your life depends on it, because right now it does!" My teeth was clinched so tight, my jaws, teeth and temples went to throbbing. OMG. What if I had woke up and went to my mom house for breakfast and found Tommy there, butt bookey ass naked cooking breakfast like Ving Rhames in the movie Baby Boy and ask me how did I want my eggs? Ohhhh hell nah, it was about to be a problem. I turn to Mr. Merchant Seaman and just look at him. I can't get one word out of my mouth. He sees the anger boiling and immediately says in a childlike voice, "Baby, let me go fix you a drink. Come on, it's alright!"

I get back to tending to the needs of the guess and having a blast when I lose sight of my mother again. I scan the yard quickly and see Tommy too tall ass on a spades table tearing their ass up. So he is safe for now. I walk around the entire duplex. I don't see her. I walk into my apartment and look in both rooms, slowly as I don't want to walk in on a surprise! I check the bathroom and find her there. The mixture of beer and Henny had caught up with her. She looked up at me and said, "Hey baby, mommy is so sorry for getting sick at this wonderful party you have put together for me!" I walked into the hallway to grab a wash cloth. I wet it with cold water and placed it on the back of my mommy neck, to help cool her off and stop her vomiting. I rubbed her back and reassured her all was fine and I'm just glad she was having a good time. I asked her, "Mommy, how were you drinking Hennessy when I brought you Michelob's?" She stood up. Re wet the wash cloth to wash her face. She got some Listerine and gargled and said, "I don't know who was giving me Hennessy. It seem like no matter where I turned, when the cup or bottle went empty somebody was steady replacing it, and you know I was drinking at the house while I was waiting on you to come pick me up, so something was bound to happen." We both laughed as we walked out the bathroom.

I look at the clock and it is now 3:15am and this party is still going strong. I walk outside and see people that I don't know. I walk up each to one of them and politely ask, "Hi, excuse me. Do you know someone here? Do I know you?" Like clockwork, they each tell me, "Nah, I don't know anyone here and I don't know you, I just saw the party, parked and walked over. Is it cool for me to stay?" I laughed and told each one they could stay, eat, play cards and relax. I tell mommy to go say her goodbye's to her friends. I'm going to pack her and my Tee Tee some food and cake and send her drunk ass home. My Tee Tee is my mom's baby sister and my favorite auntie of all. She is always the one who hangs with us, cracks jokes, will fight in a heartbeat, shoot you and then take you to Church on Sunday like it ain't nothing. Tee Tee helps me walk my drunk ass mommy to the car. We give our hugs, kisses and say our I love you's. I put mommy in the car. Place the food on her lap and kiss her again and tell her how much I love her and I'll see her in the morning.

I get back to the remainder of the party which is still going strong and live. One of Tommy's friends comes in the house looking at me all frantic and I'm thinking, "Ohhhh Lawd what now?" Tommy's friend Cleve says, "Betty, you need to come quick and get your friend before he get hurt!" I'm looking crazy, because everybody there is good. With my head cocked to the side and my eyes squenched I ask Cleve, "What friend? What's wrong?" Cleve say, "Ya homeboy that I think work with yo momma asked if any of us had some weed. We know he the police, but because he here we think he aight, so we let that nigga smoke with us. Soon as this nigga get high, he start asking if anyone of us want some head?!?!" Just as Cleve gets the last word out his mouth, I hear loud voices like it's about to go down. I run outside. I see all the country boys standing up ready to get it in. I run up. I grab my mom's coworker. I apologize to the fellas and reassure them that everything is fine and to please continue playing cards. I fumble around in his pockets, grab his car keys and place his drunk high ass in his car. I don't say one word. He sits in his car for a few minutes looking at me like a scolded dog. I stand there the whole time with my arms folded. Never saying a word. He finally starts his car. Backs out and drives home. My mom's coworker is an openly closeted bi sexual man. I know your trying to figure out how is he openly closeted. Well he was open and honest to only a few of us and remained in the closet with everyone else. He had been married for 30 years. Retired military, two adult sons and worked for the sheriff office. I'm guessing he felt that he would not be welcomed with open arms. His sexuality always seem to come out when he was high, drunk or both. I was so embarrassed. I just grabbed a chair and sat in the corner of the yard with my head hung low like I did something fucked up.

The party is finally over. I greet each and every guest with a goodbye hug and kiss. I ensure everyone has taken to go plates and had a great time. Each person assures me they had a blast and can't wait for the football party the next night. The last guest leaves my house at 4:52am. I didn't wash my ass. I didn't wash my feet. I didn't change clothes. I locked my doors and crashed on the couch.

I get up early Saturday morning and head over to my mom's house to check on here and make sure her and my Tee Tee were ok. I walk in and find my Tee Tee sitting at the kitchen table eating some form of breakfast. I give her a hug and kiss, walk down the hall and see my mom sitting on the side of the bed putting lotion on and she looks all bright eyed and bushy tailed. So I ask my Tee, "Does she remember anything from last night?" Tee Tee just laughed and said, "Hell nah! She tried to make me hold the cake while driving her drunk ass home and when I told her NO, she tried to bribe me by saying she will let me where her penis necklace!" I fall out laughing. What kind of bartering is that? My mom comes into the kitchen with us and we are telling her everything from the night before and all she can do is laugh and say, "I did that? NOO?!? For real? What happened?" We start going through all the gifts and laughing all over again. I see stuff I want, so I scoop it and keep it moving. Tee leaves town and mommy gets some rest as we have a football party that night. I run some last minute errands in preparation of the UF against Tennessee game.

The house fills quickly with people. Some from the night before and a few new people. The table is set again with plenty of food. The cooler is re-stocked with ice, beer and chaser. The TV is blasting the game and tunes are playing in the background. Everybody is having a good time as usual. The Gators win. It's getting late and people are now starting to leave. I tell mommy to get ready so I can take her home and get some rest and that I'll see her tomorrow. Sunday comes. I get up and go to church. Emmanuel Missionary Baptist Church on 8th Ave. Service was awesome, what I could remember in between naps. On my way home, I call my mom and check on her. She is still in bed and I told her I would be over later, as this was her weekend birthday celebration. I was getting ready to move south and I wanted to ensure me and my ole girl had a blast before I moved.

It's about 6pm when I slide over to mom's house. I get out the car and instead of using my key, I rang the doorbell. I don't know what I was thinking, but I was trying to surprise my mom and take her to dinner. Mommy comes to the door with mix match house shoes on. Satin cap on her head cocked to the side like a .38 pistol. Eye crust and a unit on her face when she snatch the door open. I'm standing there looking at her crazy because she is looking at me crazy and not letting me in. I ask, "Mommy why aren't you dressed? You know I'm taking you out to dinner tonight!" The look on my mom's face got stronger and did her famous hand on hip move and said, "Bitch is you crazy? Where in the fuck you think we finna go? I ain't going out to no damn dinner, hell I'm still trying to get this drunk off my ass from Friday and Saturday night and I gotta go to work tomorrow. If you don't take yo crazy ass home and sit down some where I know mutha fucking well!" I'm laughing and ask my mom, "Can I come in mommy?" As my mom is shutting the door in my face, she hollers back,

"Hell nah, you go in ya own damn house. Nite nite mommy love you now take yo ass home!" is the last thing I hear as she shuts and locks her door and slides her fat ass back down that hallway to get back in her bed.

She calls me the next day from work and tells me how much her and her friends enjoyed her birthday party and full weekend birthday celebration. She apologized for kicking me out her house the previous day, but she said she ain't young no more and cant party like she use too. A few weeks later, I'm all packed up. Truck loaded. I moved to Ft. Lauderdale to start my new job. ~~Ain't That Bout'a Bitch~~

CHAPTER 8

BRICK HO HOUSE TO FREEDOM

It was a bright, beautiful, hot, humid Friday morning in October 2005 when I drove up to the now defunct Broward Correctional Institution in Ft. Lauderdale, Fl. AC blasting, stomach jumping like 25 kids amped up on high octane sugar on a trampoline. It was my very first day working in a prison. A maximum security prison as a law librarian. I walk into the admin building. There was a very timid, soccer mom beautiful woman holding a clip board in the lobby of the administrative office with an infectious smile and warm demeanor. There were some people already seated when I walked in. She walked up to me with her right hand extended and said, "Good morning, I'm Warden Becky! It's a pleasure to meet you." In my mind I'm thinking, "Who in the hell let June Cleaver run a maximum security prison?" I warmly grab her hand with a firm handshake and say, "Good morning Warden, my name is Betty. The pleasure is all mine. At the time I applied, interviewed and accepted the job as Librarian, I thought I could actually use my degree with another population of people who would benefit from my vast years of education well as experience.

Don't ask me what in the hell made me want to do something like that, but I did. At times it was rewarding. Even though on the compound, the other inmates made me want kill their ass one by one with my bare hands. I had a wonderful staff of murderers, kidnappers, muggers, drug dealers, car thieves and bad check writers. In all honesty I truly did enjoy my library crew as they taught me a lot about the prison world verse the real world we live in. I was new to the whole correctional institution and how it works. My staff taught me the entire 33-8. Which is the Bible of the penal codes, rules and valuable policies for the department of corrections and trust me it was a truly beneficial learning information that helped me a many a time. Every day was truly a learning lesson about something that we in the civilized world take for granted.

Coming home every day most definitely made me appreciate the little things I took for granted, like using the bathroom. On the days that I had to drop a stinky bomb, I would make the other inmates go back to their pod, lock the doors and keep my staff there. I would close the bathroom door and lock it for privacy. So one day one of my older inmates who was in there for insurance fraud asked me, "Ms. Betty why do you shut and lock the door when you go in there to take a shit? I was sort of taken aback. It's just common sense and courtesy to shut and lock the door. I respond in a puzzled manner, "Because it's rude and nasty to take a shit as you say, with the door wide open while you guys are in here!" All my inmates bust out laughing and was damn near tears with it. I asked, "What in the hell is so funny?" Another ole head calmly said, "Ms. Betty I can respect what you're saying but you have to remember how we live. Our bathroom don't have doors for privacy or anything else. It's just like a stall in a public bathroom, so we see, smell and experience everything that happens in the bathroom. You can keep shutting the door, we won't bother you but we smell shit, stank pussies, bad body odor and the whole 9!" I'm curious how they get rid of the smell when someone takes a shit and what the pods and bathrooms look like because I still had not been to a dorm to see what one looks like, so I asked, "When someone takes a shit, how do you get rid of the smell?" She responded, "Wipe, courtesy flush and repeat!" I felt so bad for them, so I asked, "What about when you take a shower?" Another inmate answered and said, "Well Ms. Betty when we do take showers, you don't even have a full shower curtain. We have a half a shower stall that just covers you from your shoulder to your knees." I thought they would at least have some form of privacy. Even taking a shower was not private or easy. Simple stuff like having privacy at home to take a shit, being able to sit out on porch or balcony when the evening is very nice with the wind blowing verse going inside a hot, stuffy, hormonal filled prison dorm.

As we became more and more comfortable with one another and developed a high level of trust, once a week we would have Crack Story Time and the girls would tell me some of the craziest, most entertaining stories that should have been made into TV series. One day, it was Crack Story Time and I ran out my office and slid up on one of the desks in the main library like I was playing baseball and sliding into home plate. Once on the desk, I start swinging my feet with great anticipation like a little kid waiting for Santa Clause because I know this story is going to be just as good as the rest. One of my favorite girls, who I called Halley, because she was light skinned with good hair and a very pretty girl, was telling us this crazy story about this one particular time she was prostituting on Biscayne Blvd in Miami trying to get some money for crack, liquor and a place to stay for the night. Halley is cracking up by now and doing her famous crack head clicking sound and leg kick movement as she gets ready to tell the story. Halley says, "This white guys pulls up in this big ole pretty truck and he asks me, "How much darlin?" I told him $50, so he says "hop in." I get in the truck and he says "I'm kinda small, you're gonna have to make it grow a lil bit darlin". I'm already looking crazy because I don't wanna be putting in no whole lotta work for no $50. So I told him to pull it out and let me see it. When he pulled that shit out, I said "Got damn, I ain't no mutha fucking magician I can't make that shit grow". I'm in tears and laughing so hard, one of my inmates comes up to me and starts patting me on my back to make sure I'm ok. I wave her off. I didn't want one of the officers to walk in and think the inmate was attacking me and they take her to the hole for no reason. I gather myself and ask, "Was it really that small?" Halley says, "Ms. Betty, I would have been sucking the hair around his dick instead of his dick, it was just that small!"

As I was becoming more and more acclimated with my new job and my work crew, don't think I wasn't also looking at the sexy, single, eligible officers on the compound either. Working in that environment, you want to be linked to the strongest alpha male on the compound verse the one who is scared of all the inmates just in case something went down, so that's what I set about looking for. The 1st one I looked as was medium height, light skinned, well-built and sexy as hell, well he was sexy long as he kept that hat and mirror shades on. In talking to him and watching his body movements, he was soft and not what I was looking for. The next one was kinda cute. He was short, brown skinned, nicely built with the wide shoulders and small waist as if he worked out all the time. Being that the library was directly in the center of the compound with a 300 degree angle I could see just about everything and it always seem like when a fight was about to go down and officer assistance was needed, he was always the 1st one on the scene but the last one to jump in because he had to pull out his workout gloves. Carefully put them on. Fit each finger in its proper setting and then stand there with his hands on his hips like he supervising the damn fight. So I passed on him immediately without ever talking to him. Now the next little fella seemed kinda clumsy, yet sweet in a naïve way. He was about 6'4, dark chocolate, bald head and well built. Turns out he was truly a gym rat. He walked slowly along the compound on his toes with an unconcerned aloof look on his face. Quit often you would see him sitting on a bench with an inmate in the shade holding a long conversation and appearing as if he was truly enjoying himself. I looked at him but didn't really pay him any attention until one of my staff came and said, "Ms. Betty, are you single, dating or married?" Not thinking much of it, I answered her with a quick "No" as to go ahead and hurry her out of my office. The next few days I see Sarge Aloof floating by the library smiling, waving and sometimes stopping in to see if all was fine. Still didn't pay him that much attention until I saw him sprint across the compound. Snatch two of the biggest manliest looking inmates apart from a HBO PPV fight. He broke the fight up and had both inmates under control until the other officers could arrive and get both inmates cuffed and sent to the hole. The day that happened, my staff and I ran to the east window and watched everything unfold as we always did when something went down. Once everything was all said and done. I was still on that window looking out waiting on the sequel. The only thing that happened was the big fella who seemed aloof walked by on his toes as usual. He waved. He winked. No sweat on his body. No dirt on his uniform. He didn't appear to even have an elevated heart beat or anything. I was instantly turned on and curious to know more.

My inmates went home at 2 and I use to have them lined up faithfully every day at 1:50 in 2 lines so that when the officer came to pick up my work crew along with inside grounds and the kitchen crew, they could keep right on trucking with no problem. The left line was for those inmates who lived on east side of the compound and the right line was for the inmates on lived on the west side of the compound. The officer would escort them to a certain point and have them march single file down the side walk to their respective pods. One particular day Sargent Aloof decides he is going to swing back by the library before he leaves for the day and talk to little ole Ms. Betty, the fresh fish at the brick whore house. I call all jails, prisons, police stations and hospitals the "Brick Whore House". Just about everybody is sleeping with someone or a few people on the job, regardless of being married or not. When entrusting your life with someone on a daily basis in life or death situations, you tend to build bonding relationships that at times can turn sexual due to the stress or other factors, hence the name "Brick Whore House."

When my inmates left at the end of the day, I would finish up any paper work that was needed, go over to the mail room and get the current day's mail delivery, make copies of legal work for the inmates and deliver to their individual dorms. When I finally make it back to my office, I would lock the library doors, duck off in my office sort and read the magazines and chill til 5pm, because at that time I had done my 8 and it was time to hit the gate! One Friday afternoon Sargent Aloof decides to come back by. I was just about to walk out the library and head over to the mail room with my rolling cart. He tries to open the door but notices that is locked. He is knocking with one hand and has the other hand and his face pressed against the door looking in to see if I was there. I see him looking in and start to wave my hand so he sees me and tell him to hold on as I walk to the door. I'm unlocking the door and open it to let him in he is all smiles and over joyed. I think nothing of it and as he is walking in, I smile and ask, "Hey Sarge! How are you? What brings you to my side of town?" He was just smiling and takes a seat in one of the chairs while I'm standing there with my cart ready to go pick up my mail and make some legal copies of an appeal for an inmate and drop off to them. Sarge Aloof responds, "I was just stopping by to check on you and make sure all was fine since you're new to corrections life." I don't talk to many people that work there, well not about any personal information so I'm curious as to how he knew this information. I play it cool and jump over the comment trying to keep the conversation short, even though I would like to know more about him, but on this particular day I was trying to get what I needed done so I could try to slip out the compound undetected. I had a date that night, so all his rah rah at that time was going in one ear and out the other. I made a move towards the door and said, "Well Sarge I'm heading over to mail room to make my daily pick up and make some copies for an inmate, so I can make a quick getaway." When I start to unlock the door, ole Sarge asks, "Well is it ok if I tag along and get to know you?" I oblige and we walk the compound making my rounds walking and talking. He was so helpful in pulling the cart, lifting all the heavy packages, he even made all 300 copies of legal appeal papers for the inmates and came back to the library and assisted me in getting everything set up for my staff the next day. Sarge Aloof shift ends at 3. By the time we hit the Sally Port to turn in our keys it was 4:30pm. He is steady by my side just talking away as he walks me to my car and finally asks me for me my phone number. We exchange numbers and respectfully part ways. I think no more about him as I'm now thinking about the inmate gossip hotline that travels faster than the speed of light. I was mentally bracing myself for the eye rolling, tooted up noses from the female staff on the compound and the million questions from my inmate staff.

I made it to work early Monday morning after having a fun filled weekend. I clear the metal detectors with ease. Bypass a full body pat down and walk through the 2nd door of the Sally port when I'm greeted by Sarge Aloof! He asked me simple questions about my weekend as we walked and took a seat on the bench in front of the library and continued talking as we waited for count to clear and the inmates to be escorted to their respective jobs. Count clears. The inmates start moving and we end our conversation. He put a very big smile on my face that remained for the rest of the day even with the barrage of questions from my inmate staff. "Uhmmmmm boss what's going on with you and Sarge? Why was he walking around the compound with you on Friday? Did y'all go out this weekend? Did he call you, coz you know we saw him walk you to your car and exchange numbers?" I'm cracking up laughing because not only are they asking me all these nosey ass questions, but they were dead ass serious and wanted answers. We were all sitting in the main library in the chairs like girlfriends having girl talk before we start our work day, when one of my older inmates says, "Ms. Betty remember a week or so ago I came and asked you if you were single, dating or married?" I think back and nod and agree, she then says, "Sarge had stopped me earlier in the day and has asked me to find out what was your status!"

Now I wanted to know more and who better to ask about ole Sarge Aloof. So I asked and they spilled the beans. He is head of the SRT, that's short for Special Response Team for riots and other dangerous situations at the prison. Sometimes he would get called to another prison to assist with issues. He was one of the most respected yet feared officers on the compound. He use to date a nurse at the prison but she started dating Sargent Puff right up under his nose. Well the only problem with that is, Sargent Puff was a woman! One day Sargent Puff, who stands a hot 5'0 even in her boots even got mad, pulled her blonde hair up in a ponytail and ran up on Aloof who is 6'4 and said she had to get some stuff off her chest about her ole lady and he better listen. He laughed, patted her on her head and walked right past her like she wasn't even there. I died laughing because Sgt. Puff is a sweet little timid white woman who you can't even imagine swatting a fly. You can tell she ain't got no fight game and would be the last person you want as backup.

The day moves along smoothly and my inmates leave for the end of the day. Sarge Aloof slides back by the library and walks with me again as I make my evening rounds. As we are making our rounds Sarge is acting rather strange like he wants to say something but he has yet to get his words together. Sarge just asks, "Since you don't have any plans tonight, would you like to go out for drinks and dinner?" I laugh and look at him and say, "You have some nerve to say, since I don't have any plans tonight." The look on his face was of total shock and embarrassment. He quickly tried to cover up his mistake and say, "Oh my God, I'm so sorry because that isn't what I was trying to say. I meant to say if you don't have any plans, but if you don't want to go it's cool and I totally understand." I didn't respond until we had made all my rounds and he lifted all the heavy stuff and even had him buy me a snack from the staff canteen before I answered him about going out with him for dinner. Once we finished with dropping everything off and getting the work ready for my inmates the next day, I respond very sarcastically but in a humorous way and say, "I guess I can go out with you since I don't have shit else to do and it is my time to do a good deed for a mentally challenged person this month, I guess I can meet you for dinner at Mangos downtown. I'll meet you there at 8:30, buh bye!" Once I said that I opened the door and showed Sarge out and locked the door behind him. He walked off all slow like he was happy, yet trying to figure out what the hell had he just said.

I get to Mangos a little after 8 and Sarge had already gotten us an outside table on the patio. He looked good in his work uniform but he looked especially yummy in his regular clothes and he smelled good. There is nothing like a well-dressed, good smelling man who actually can hold a conversation; that is a turn on to me in the biggest way. We had a great time at dinner and getting to know one another better, as well as him schooling me on the true fundamentals of corrections, being that I was civilian staff and not trained as an officer. We continued to date and see each other often and really begin to enjoy one another amid all the gossip, lies and foolishness. The female officers that had been trying to get with him long before I got there. Female officers that never ever came to the library or had one word to say to me was now all of a sudden so friendly and coming into the library carrying bones. My grandma always said, "Be leery of the dog that carries a bone because it will damn shol tote a bone!" I overlooked them a lot of times and kept running my business while they ran their mouth like a star running back.

Several months had passed and we were going strong in our relationship and part time living with one another when his lease was coming up for renewal and he suggested we live together, since I lived in Broward and was closer to our job. I had met all of his family including his two daughters and the mother of the youngest one whom he claimed to have been divorced from for several years. When his daughter would come and stay with us for the weekend, we would go pick her up from her mothers house. Sarge would be in the house helping his daughter get her stuff together, the mother and I would be outside engaged in great, laugh filled conversation. Being that I come from blended families it was always important for me to ensure that everyone got along for the sake of the children. His ex and I got along just fine and it was never an issue for us to come pick up his daughter. The issue I had was, she would call every morning at 6 am on the dot! I would listen to the conversation intently to ensure I picked up on everything. There were also mornings his phone would ring at 6 and he wouldn't answer that call which stood out as odd, especially with a call coming in that early. So one morning after her usual phone call, we were both getting ready for work and I asked him, "If y'all are divorced and you have a pre-teen that can call you and talk on her own and ask for whatever she wants or needs, why does her mother call you every morning? What is there to talk about?" He didn't have a response nor a lock on his phone at the time, so I let it go but when he hit the kitchen to make our lunch I hit that phone and got all the numbers I needed. We always took separate cars to work as our hours were different. With Sarge being an officer his shift was 7a-3p and with me being civilian staff, I had regular 8a-5p hours but would buck at 4 if I could. I made sure that the numbers went with the correct person and went along with my morning as if nothing ever happened. The phone calls kept coming with him doing the usual. One day while at work I put in my own investigation on both situations. Once I got my inmates all set with their work for the day. I locked up in my office and started digging. I got online and found the marriage license but there was no sign of a divorce decree. I searched the tri county area of Dade, Broward and Palm Beach. No divorce decree found!

I waited until my inmates left for lunch to call the other number that calls at 6am that he loves to ignore. My inmates left and I walked over to the staff canteen to grab my lunch and a cold Pepsi. I walked back into the library picked up the phone and dialed the number. The voice on the other end in a real ghetto voice said, "Hey baby, I tried calling you this morning but I guess I missed you again!" I'm completely thrown off. I never said anything, not even a hello to this person, so I respond, "Uhmm excuse me, who is this?" She responds, "This Earlene. Who are you and why are you calling me from Sarge job?" I smiled hard as hell because she just opened the door and I walked right on in. I respond, "My name is Betty and I'm Sarges live in girlfriend. I'm trying to figure out who you are and why you call him every morning at 6?" There is silence on the phone for a few seconds, so I say, "HELLO?" Earlene finally gets back on the phone and says, "I didn't know he had a girlfriend. I wondered why he would always call me from work and I could only see him for a small amount of time, hell I was just with him yesterday." I had to ask because I needed to know, "Are y'all having sex?" Earlene busted out laughing and said, "Yep, he just ate my pussy yesterday!" I got so fucking mad, I could have shitted a brick house. I wasn't mad at her but him, because he had kissed me in my mouth when I walked through the door when I got home and ate and fucked me the same night he had been with ole Earlene. I was quiet on the phone for almost a minute when Earlene said, "HELLO! Betty, are you there?" I was too out done because the only pussy I love to taste is my own. Threw clinched teeth I muster up a simple, "Yeah, I'm here." Earlene says, "Hold on real quick lemme show you something." She clicks over and when she clicks back over there is a phone ringing. When they pickup you can hear all this noise in the background. The voice on the other end says, "H dorm, Sarge Aloof speaking!" I don't say one word, I think I may have stopped breathing to make sure he didn't hear me on the phone. Earlene then starts to talk and says, "Hey boo I really enjoyed you yesterday. I just wish you could have stayed longer. You know how I am after you eat me!" This black ass back to Africa, punk, lamp shade built bitch had the nerve to respond to Earlene and say, "I love how you taste. You know I love eating your pussy and then when we fuck I be in another world!" I tilt my head to the side, squint my eyes as if that will help bring some clarity to what the fuck he just said. That is the same exact shit he says to me. I am standing up pacing the floor ready to tear some shit up when Earlene asks, "Well baby when will I see you again?" I'm so fucking mad I have tears in my eyes and I'm ready to fight his ass, but I can't because we are at work and I can't risk going to jail. I'm planning and plotting and figuring out my next move, especially since this bitch had just recently moved in with me. Sarge responds, "Maybe this weekend, but I'll call you later and we will set something up. I gotta go. The inmates are coming back from lunch now so I'll call you later muah muah!" Did this big rusty bitch just blow kisses through the phone like his name is Soldier Boy? He hangs up, Earlene whispers, "Hold on." Earlene clicked the line to make sure he was off the phone before we finished our conversation. When she clicked back over she said, "I didn't call him to make you more madder than you already is, but I just wanted you to know that I wasn't lying to you!" The phone was silent for a few minutes, but she knew I was still there. I lifted my head. Dried my eyes, stood still and said, "Earlene, I knew you weren't lying and I appreciate you being woman enough to talk to me and tell me everything. Sorry we had to meet under these circumstances, but its all good. Please take care and maybe we'll get the chance to meet. We both bid our goodbyes and hung up the phone.

5pm couldn't get there quick enough. I finished my work and even helped my staff do some shit to try and pass the time quicker. Nothing helped, just made it worse. When my staff left and shift changed at 3, I made a quick run for the mail and left at 4. Where I lived in Ft. Lauderdale, it always took me an hour and some odd minutes to make it home. I swear that day I was home in 30 minutes. When I walked into the apartment Sarge had his ole ugly ass sitting in the chair watching tv getting ready to put on his gym shoes so he could go work out. When he saw me walk in that early with a semi mean mug on my face, he knew something was wrong but little did he know just how wrong it was. I asked, "So Sarge, when was your divorce?" He went to stuttering like a car with a bad carburetor and said, "Uhmm I think Jun urrgghh Jul noo I think August!" I'm steaming now because this bitch has the nerves to stand in my face with a straight face and stutter another lie. I get in a fight stance and ball up my fists and scream, "WHEN THE FUCK DID YOU GET DIVORCED?" He said in a low voice like a child, "We haven't gotten divorced, we have just been separated for 10 years." I'm so mad and ready to fight but I can't move. I can barely breathe but I remain standing in my fight stance and scream, "NOT ONLY HAVE YOU LIED TO ME AND HAD ME FUCKING A MARRIED MAN, YO BIG DUMB MUTHA FUCKING ASS HAD ME IN THIS WOMANS FACE LAUGHING, KEE KEEING AND KICKING IT LIKE ALL IS GRAVVY BABY. NOW I KNOW WHY THE FUCK SHE WAS LAUGHING IN MY FACE!" He doesn't say anything. I'm pacing the floor because he ain't saying anything and I'm about to lose it. He gets up out the chair and starts walking towards me and says, "I'm sorry I didn't tell you I was still married but separated because I was afraid you wouldn't want to date me and I'm really crazy about you." I didn't say anything, because that was the perfect Segway into this next situation. I tell Sarge to go back and have a seat because there is something else I want to talk about. He sits down and looks scared out of his mind. I ask, "So Sarge you say you crazy about me huhh? Well tell me this, where were you yesterday when you got off?" Sarge starts looking all around as if he is hoping his lie will just float down from the sky. He doesn't say anything for a few minutes, so I ask him again, "Sarge, where the fuck were you yesterday?" I'm so fucking mad because this bitch ain't saying nothing but just sitting there looking stupid, so I asked, "Do I need to call Earlene so she can tell you where the fuck you were yesterday?" This bitch still just sitting there not saying nothing. I lose it. Remember Sarge is big, cock diesel ass man. I walk in the kitchen pick up a frying pan and swing batter batter swing and cold cocked his ass in the head. He didn't flinch. He didn't budge. All I heard was "TING" and saw a dent in my frying pan. I stood there waiting on him, I was ready for whatever was about to go down. He stood up and looked at me with a dazed look. I screamed, "COME ON MUTHA FUCKER, COME ON! You got me looking stupid as fuck again as you ate this bitch yesterday, fucked her and then brought yo raggedy ass home and kissed me in my mouth, ate and fucked me too. That ain't the fucked up part, what's fucked up is sitting on the phone listening to you tell her the same damn thang you tell me and then you blew kisses in the phone at this bitch. So if you want to get down, you better fucking come with the get down bitch coz I'm ready!"

———

He starts pacing the floor and looking at me, never saying anything. He walks into the kitchen and grabbed a bottle of water and walked back into the living room where I was still standing, ready and waiting for his ass to pop off. He sits back down and says, "I met her a few months ago at the American Legion. She works there and we just struck up conversation. I wasn't looking for anything or even trying to cheat it just happened. I know you don't want to hear that I'm sorry but I am sorry, I never meant to hurt you. I promise I'll never see her again."

I know he thought that ended everything and made it all better. I jumped up on his ass like a squirrel to a tree and went to swinging on his ass again. No matter how hard I thought I was hitting his ass, I wasn't hurting nobody but my damn self. My hands, wrists, arms and everything was hurting but that didn't stop me from fighting him. Not once did he hit me back or try to get me off of him. He stood there and took every single lick I laid on him. When I got tired, I slid down his tall ass like a fat kid on a slide and went back to cussing his ass out. I walked away from him and grabbed my purse and keys. BBBOOOMMM fell right on my got damn head. There was some water on the tile that I didn't see and busted my ass. That really wasn't the type of exit I was looking to make after I had just whooped his ass and cussed him out. He ran over to me to make sure I was ok. I can't lie, I was seeing double and my head went to throbbing like a drum. He was trying to touch me and get me up. Even though I was groggy from the fall I was fighting his ass off of me. It took me a few minutes to get myself together and when I did I hauled ass but not before I yelled at Sarge and said, "When I get back, I expect to see you and all your shit gone!"

I went to a friend of mine house and pulled out my bag that I always keep in my car. I know you got the same bag in your car too. The one with an extra pair of drause, towel, rag, soap, lotion and everything you will need when the time arises. I get all settled in for the evening and Sarge is blowing up my phone, so I turn my phone off and go to sleep. I get up the next morning and go to work as if nothing ever happened. I got to work a little later than usual but my inmates knew to sit on the bench in front of the library and wait for me until I got there. This particular morning my crew was sitting there waiting and talking with ole Sarge. I walked up, greeted my crew and unlocked the door so they could go in. Sarge and I stayed outside acting as if everything was fine, he then asks, "Where were you last night? I waited up all night for you after I called all the hospitals to see if you went there after you fell. Baby, where were you? We need to talk so we can fix this." I just nod and smile and say, "We have nothing to talk about unless we are talking about how long it's going to take to get you and your shit out my house!" He was not letting that shit go. He kept on talking and talking, so I cut him short and told him, "Look I need to get to my inmates before they be going half on a baby." I walked off and left him standing there looking stupid. I was still mad but not as mad as I was before. I was already moving on mentally and soon to be physically.

When I got in that night, he was still there as I had expected, but I didn't say anything to him. He wanted to talk and I just wasn't in the mood to talk. I had heard enough lies. He pulls out a piece of paper and shows that he has been switched from day shift to midnight shift and was trying to push the issue that we need to really work on us. You already know my mind went into overdrive. With him being on midnight that gives him the ultimate playground for cheating!! Ohhh no, we gotta end this and we gotta end this soon. I wasn't happy and not only wanted out of that relationship and that damn prison. Being that I had a one bed room I made him sleep on the couch. When I noticed my couch sinking in from the continuous use, I allowed him back in the bed but he couldn't touch me. We stopped having sex. I stopped talking to him and kept looking for another job.

One day I went into work and noticed one of my inmates wasn't there. I asked the other inmates where was she before I called her in missing to the command center. My crew stood there looking at me and then looked at each other rather oddly. One inmate said, "Ms. Betty you don't know what's going on?" I'm normally in the loop and paying full attention to everything, but apparently I missed this. I respond, "No baby, I don't know what is going on, please fill me in!" I start walking around the group of inmates standing there, waiting for them to bust out laughing because we always played jokes on one another but no one started laughing, so I say in a stern voice, "Spill it and all of it, no bullshit!" One inmate starts crying and then another one. I'm thinking these emotional heffas must be on their menstral as their bodies normally link up together and there are several bleeding coodas every freaking week. Finally one of my inmate says, "Ms. Betty, La'Qwanda found out you were having her transferred from the library because you knew about her side hustle in the here, so she had paid someone to make a shank so she could kill you. We saw her getting cuffed and packed up last night with the inmate that made the shank, we just assumed you found out about it, told the inspector what she was doing and got her busted, we thought you knew!"

I remembered an inmate sliding past me one day on her way to the inmate canteen and whispering something really quick. She was a fairly decent inmate who was always helpful and never gave me any issues. When she told me, "Watch your back someone wants you to take a nap!" I knew what she was saying, I just didn't know who at the time. I also know that inmates don't like to be labeled a snitch, so asking her who it was would have been like chasing the wind. Sarge and I were on good terms before everything went downhill with his cheating, so I went home and told him what was said, but didn't think any more of it, as all the inmates I wrote DR's on were short timers and never gave me any more problems. La'Qwanda, which was the inmate that wanted to kill me, was in for life on her first time for a botched 7-11 robbery that resulted in the murder of the clerk. She didn't commit the actual murder, but Florida has a Principal law that if anyone is murdered in the commission of a crime, whether you committed the actual murder or not, you will be charged with the murder. I didn't think any more after I told Sarge, He didn't take the threat seriously either and we both laughed it off about me being mean and not even an officer. The inmates put in to tell me how the entire compound went into recall after dinner time, which is exactly the same time I leave at 5pm. Recall is when the compound is on complete lock. No inmate movement. The water to the entire prison is shut off to ensure no contraband is flushed. The dogs are brought in and all inmates must be sitting on the side of their bunks with feet down with a continual count every 5 minutes. Once the compound is on lock, a controlled search can be conducted and whatever the officers are looking for and with whom can usually be located with ease or force it out of an another inmate as they hate recall. During regular working hours if they called recall, ohhhh my word, you would have thought I had just won the lottery. I would get to jumping, propping the door open and snatching inmates up by their drause throwing them out like yesterday's garbage. They only had a certain amount of time to make it back to their pods and on their bunk beds before the count started. The compound was on lock from 5pm that night until well after 1am. The rest of the day I'm walking around Thanking God for saving my life, yet once again and also trying to figure out how the attack was thwarted if I didn't know anything about it. I let it go after I developed a headache. It seem like that incident made me mad and meaner than ever. I started writing inmates up left and right and even rotated some of my staff out for new staff. I kept all of my ole timers and a few crack heads who use to tell some of the funniest stories, but those who seemed as if they didn't appreciate being in the library, I switched they ass out real quick for some of the inside grounds crew who was getting tired of being beat down by the horrid south Florida summers.

One of the inmates I kept had been in prison since the early 90's for murder and was due to be released in 2035. She was originally set to serve life with no release date in sight. She was one of 2 of my best law clerks out of 6, who actually had helped to reverse a few inmates sentencing, including her own. She fought her own case, went back to court and received a release date. She wasn't easy on the eye due to the freak accident that occurred to her face during the crack cocaine fueled fight that lead to her committing murder, which garnered her the nickname Pug. In her relationships Pug was considered the male or more dominate one and had a reputation for handling business if her girlfriend got out of line. The current girl she was dating was a little red head, petite white girl from central Florida that was in prison for killing her infant son. She had one child when she met and married her then husband who didn't have any children at the time. She lived the good life as a housewife, never having to work and soon became pregnant, giving birth to another son. A healthy, beautiful, bouncing, black baby boy! The husband was livid of course and started beating chunks out of her and neglecting the children. One day she goes to the mall with her children. Calls 911 and tells them a black man has just kidnapped her newborn son. A massive manhunt ensues for this black male who has just kidnapped a white woman's young infant son. After a few weeks the case starts getting cold and looking very odd to the police. The police turn their sole focus to the mom for more answers and possible clues as things are not lining up. She finally breaks and confesses to killing her son because he was bi racial and her husband neglected the child she made when she cheated on him. She felt no other recourse to try and save her marriage. She stuffed the baby in a black plastic garbage bag and let the baby suffocate in the hot garage while her and her toddler son went to the mall. The husband divorced her during her trial and she is sentenced to 35 years in prison. This is just a little background on Pug's girlfriend, whom we will see again.

Every month when it was one of the girl's birthdays, I would close the library early and let them have a birthday party filled with homemade prison desserts that were actually very tasty. Music from the radio or pull out the CD's that I had locked away for security reasons and the green colored paper cut into dollar bills so they could make it rain on who ever decided to give a lap dance. Normally it was the hot tamale young girl who had been locked up since she was 14 years old for killing her father's pregnant fiancé with her twin brother. At this time she was 23 or 24 and just as hot in the ass, yet a cool level headed and highly respectful inmate. Time had rolled by and it was now Hot Tamales birthday which is June 6, 2006. The law library was slow that day as it was her birthday. I ensured not to schedule the law clerks any appointments after lunch so the girls could enjoy Hot Tamales birthday with prison desserts, listening to their old school jam of Black Street "Don't leave me" and making it rain. Once

I get my slice of cake, I normally go back to my office, which is a circular office made of glass so I can watch everything around me. My inmate law clerk Pug came in that morning on 6/6/2006 and had a look of desertion on her face. I don't pry in anyone's business, inmate or free person. I went about giving everyone their assignment for the day and went back to my office to start going through inmate grievances so I could respond to their idiotic complaints and do my usual of job searching for anything out of this damn prison. As I was about to stand and pull the 33-8 off the shelf, Pug knocked on my door and asked, "Ms. Betty is it is ok if I come?" I wave her in and tell her, "Pull up a chair Pug, I'm just about to go through these inmate complaints and you might be able to help with the 33-8. What's going on baby?" Pug had this look on her face like she had nothing in the world to loose and that started to bother me. Not in a manner that I was scared for my life, but like she just had a death in the family and felt as though she didn't have anywhere else to turn. We made small talk for a few minutes before she said, "Ms. Betty I just want to thank you personally for coming into the devils den and actually caring about us convicts. Most people and officers don't see us as people. They see us as the scum of the earth and wish we would die for the crimes we have committed, not fully understanding there where circumstances out of our control that contributed to the crimes we committed. You came here and treated us like somebody and for that I want to tell you thank you and I love you. I never want to disappoint you, so always know I love you!" She stood up and kissed her hand and placed it on my forehead. It is forbidden for staff and an inmate to touch. If seen touching or hugging an inmate, the staff would be labeled an inmate lover and the inmate would be thrown in the hole. I didn't know what to do, but my spirit was compelled to give her hug. I grabbed her hand and pulled her close to me and gave her one of the best hugs I could. She grabbed me tight and leaned down on my 5'3 frame and cried on my shoulder. We stood there for a few minutes and I just let her cry with no regards to the rules. When she composed herself, she didn't say a word she just grabbed the cart with the books already pre stacked on it for deliveries to the infirmary, the hole and the psych ward. She turned one last time and said "Thank you." My spirit felt something but since I couldn't figure it out, I went back to what was I doing. You already serving time with 3 hots in a cot, free laundry service and no worries or concerns about bills. An hour or so had passed since I talked to Pug and it was about time to clear out the library and get my staff lined up to be escorted back to their pod for lunch, when an older inmate who worked insides grounds ran into the library crying, screaming and frantically screaming my name, "MS. BETTY MS. BETTY MS. BETTY OHHHHHH MY GOD

MS. BETTY. I look up from my desk trying to figure out what the hell is wrong with her. I don't see any blood dripping from her body or anything that looked broken, when she busts into my office and screams, "Pug just killed Bobby Anne, Ohhh my God there is blood everywhere, Pug just killed that girl under the pavilion!" I grab her while giving her my cold Pepsi to try and calm her down. All the inmates in the library rush to the south window facing the pavilion to see what is going on. All you see is inmates running away from the pavilion and screaming, officers running up to assist then running away throwing up and the medical personnel running up carrying stacks and stacks of towels. I lock the doors to contain the small amount of additional inmates I have in there and keep them calm while I ask the uncontrollably crying inmate what happened. She takes a big sip of the Pepsi, wipes her overly red face with the tail end of her shirt and says, "We was sitting under the pavilion waiting to be called for our medical appointments when we saw Pug walk by going to the hole to make her deliveries. She went in real quick, came out and pulled the cart up to the pavilion when she sat next to Bobby Anne and was holding small talk. An officer came out and asked Pug why she was blocking his sidewalk with her book cart and not at work? Pug answered quickly and got up to leave. As she was leaving she lifted Bobby Anne's head with her left hand and said I Love You and then sliced the girls neck from ear to ear with the sharpest shank I have ever seen with her right hand." As soon as she finished telling the story she broke back down into heavier tears and so did the rest of the inmates. I was the only standing there with a dry ass face. I was in shock, disbelief, hurt and waiting on those faithful words to be uttered through the intercom, RECALL! I tried to consul as many inmates as I could because all were crying. Not for Bobby Anne, but for Pug. She was truly a great person, she just got caught up in this thing called life that we all go through. Just as I was about to hold a Prayer with the inmates, those life saving words came and in a voice that let you know they meant business, "RECALL RECALL RECALL!" I didn't throw my inmates out that day as I normally would. I held the door open and told them to Pray and let them know they were loved. I had never seen the officers move inmates so quickly. It was like the inmates were on conveyor belts moving to their dorms. I stood in the South window watching everything like I was watching a movie. Bloody towel after bloody towel was being discarded as new fresh white towels was being ushered into the pavilion. Not even 2 minutes after the compound was cleared, you heard the blades of a helicopter. Broward General Hospital Trauma helicopter could not land on the compound for fear of a possible escape and safety reasons. The helicopter landed outside the compound and sent the emergency personnel in with a gurney and other lifesaving paraphernalia to get the inmate. I'm standing there with my face glued to the window. The emergency personnel rush out on the gurney with the inmate, one pressing hard as she can on the gapping, bleeding wound and the other squeezing the ventilator. The next sound you hear is the helicopter revving its motor to rise up and then I see it fly away into the horizon, never to be seen again. Back on the compound you see fellow officers helping and assisting those who have become sick and crying uncontrollably. Medical personnel cleaning up the spilled blood and placing the bloody towels in red bio hazard bags. It is then I break down from my frozen state and cry like a newborn. No one there to hold me or help me to understand what has just happened to another human being.

Some officers and medical personnel finish trying to clean the blood from under the pavilion while some other officers are carried outside the compound to regain their composure that is when the real deal investigation begins. Inspector Englund armed with his black inspector gadget bag, walked tall onto the compound right behind the SRT fully loaded with thigh holsters, face masks, riot gear and the whole nine. Once on the compound, SRT split into 2 teams. One team going to the east and the other to the west. My tears dried up like the Sahara real quick. I did not want to miss any of the action that was about to unfold. Them boys looked damn good in full riot gear moving with surgical precision throughout the compound looking and waiting for whatever was about to pop off. I see Sarge leading the charge and his ugly ass has never looked so sexy to me, but he still ain't shit, ole bastard. There were some officers combing through the grassy knoll in front of the library looking for something. One of the officers found something and called over another officer and placed the item in the bag and scurried off. SRT officers are going in and out of all the dorms coming out just as empty as they went in, when all of a sudden I see all the SRT officers run to the east side of the compound and reappear in a few short seconds later with Pug in cuffs, being led by Sarge. She was sweaty, dusty, dirty and out of breath. Sarge looked just as clean as he did when he left home the night before and still full of energy. Shortly after Pug was escorted to the admin office, another inmate was escorted out of her dorm on the west side with no incidence. She was an older inmate who had been in prison since the late 70's for shooting at a judge and her son's defense attorney. I don't remember if the judge and the attorney lived or died, I just remember she had been down for a long time and wasn't afraid of doing time whether it be in the hole or on the compound, she was a true convict to her heart. The older inmate was under arrest for making the shank made to cut Pug's girlfriend.

The compound was on lock down for 2 entire days; those were the easiest and happiest 2 days of my life. On the 2nd day I was sitting out on the bench reading a magazine while sipping an ice cold Pepsi and eating a Stouffers French bread pizza, enjoying the nice cool, crisp wind right before a good ole fashioned storm blew in, when a few officers walked up with Inspector Englund. I looked up briefly from my magazine. They had come right when the gossip was getting good. I greeted the crew, "Hey fellas, what's going on? What brings you to this side of the tracks?" Everyone had a slight chuckle then they looked at each other as if the one who drew the shortest straw was taking too long to speak up and tell me what he needed to say, so we just sat there looking at each for a few minutes before I look back down at magazine and go back to reading when Inspector Englund clears his throat and says, "Betty, we are here on official business. What we have to do its protocol and nothing personal. We need to search your entire library looking for any clues and contraband due to the assault the other day." The Inspector and I were good friends and he know how I go off like a hot pot when they come sideways about me being dirty with my job. An inmate had once accused me of bringing in cell phones and chargers, when Englund came to me with that I went off and was getting ready to walk down to the dorm where the inmate was housed and tear off into her ass like something good to eat, when Englund snatched my arm and said, "Betty, Betty, BETTY calm down, I know you ain't bringing nothing in, but when your name is mentioned in the midst of an investigation. I have to do my job and get all the facts. Trust me, I already know who is bringing all the contraband in, it's just a matter of time before they get caught!" I calmed down and let it go and it wasn't long after that an officer was caught sleep in the inmate's bed with the inmate after having sex. The inmates went and called the Major on the shift and told her what was going on. They never stopped him during the act, they let it play out and he just dozed off for some reason. They didn't wake him up either. They stood there and waited for him to wake up! When he woke up and opened the door, that's when reality hit his ass in the face like a ton of bricks. He not only got charged with sleeping with an inmate but he was also charged with bringing in the contraband. I obliged and gave them the keys to enter the library. I stayed out on the bench enjoying my free time and peace. They tore my library to shreds. Books where strolled all over the place. Desks drawers on the floor, desks turned over, cleaning linen all over the place, papers were laying on the ground as if it has snowed. It looked like a hurricane had just come through there. The officers came out about an hour or so later with their heads hung low with nothing in their hands or bags. Once they left, Englund called me so we could do our taped interview. He asked all the important questions which I had no answer for because I knew nothing of her planned attack. Once the interview was over and Englund turned off the tape recorder, he filled me in every thing that happened and why. The little prissy white girlfriend had been sleeping with a few male officers for items such as chewing gum and nail polish and the other inmates told Pug who didn't do or say anything. She just sat back and watched everything unfold. When the girl came in the dorm the other week with a hickie on her neck claiming it was a mosquito bite; that is what sent Pug over the edge to commit such a horrific crime. The item that the officers had found in the grassy knoll in front of the library was the actual shank used by Pug to cut the girls neck. I didn't see anything that happened so I was unaware it was out there, but from what Englund told me was, Pug cut the girl, ran away from the scene ditched the shank and went into hiding on the compound like she was never going to be caught. Rick James said it best, "Cocaine is a helluva drug!" We talked for a few more minutes but he could tell I was shaken up by everything, so Englund offered drinks and dinner at our favorite after work spot, TGIF which was right up the road from the prison. I agreed and we peeled out of there at 4pm.

Things between Sarge and I never got back on the right track and neither did things at the job. Sarge and I were talking and spending some time, but it never was the same especially being that he was still married to old girl. Shortly after the gruesome attack on 6/6/06 another inmate was attacked with a tube sock full of combination locks. She was one of the inmates I wished bad things happened to, so when she was in the hospital barely making it I was not the least bit sad. The inmates who had to clean up the dorm where the attack happened said it looked like someone just threw gallons and gallons of blood all over the place. The inmate who was the assailant was one of the coolest inmates who didn't bother anybody but was funny as hell with those of us she did have a connection with. When she first came on the compound, all the other inmates knew her because she had been in and out of prison for years and they called her "Lemon Head." I always thought it was because she was a cute light skinned big head girl. One day in passing I stopped her and asked, "Why do they call you Lemon Head?" She was soo cool in her response and said, "I don't want to disrespect you Ms. Betty so I'm not going to tell you now but in time I will." A few weeks rocked on and she felt more comfortable with me and came to the library one day when it was slow and no other inmates were in there except those who worked for me, she says, "Ms. Betty I know you want to know the meaning of my name. The reason they call me Lemon Head is because my head is so bitter sweet!" I fell out laughing and gave her a high 5 when one of my inmates from the back hollered out, "It damn shol is!" I was too through and after that Lemon Head and I were extra cool, so it bothered me that she had just picked up another charger to her already 10 years in prison. The compound was once again on lock for 2 days and I was not one to complain. It gave me time to search for jobs and put in applications. I was looking hard as hell to get off that compound. It had become too dangerous and I was tired of seeing Sarge at work when I'm coming on and he is leaving and when I make it home.

A couple of months had passed with no more incidents. My new crew was blending very well with my old crew and was highly appreciative to be inside the cold ac doing office work verse cutting grass in 105 degree south Florida weather. In order to see my law clerks I set up a system where you made an appointment and I would allow my clerks to determine who they saw and when. I always wanted them to be comfortable in providing the most exemplary customer service to those in need as you are dealing with someone's life. One day my oldest, sweetest law clerk came to my office right as I was getting to line them up to send them back to their dorm for lunch with a serious look of terror on her face. I ask her a few questions to make sure it wasn't a medical emergency, she says, "Noooo Ms. Betty it's not a medical emergency but I need you to walk me to my dorm." I'm looking at her like "Bitch, I can't fight all these hoes in here to keep them off you, just give up the ill nah nah!" I ask her, "Why?" Just as I'm asking her why, she places a napkin full of weed in my hand and not that bullshit weed either. It was that oooooo weeee stanky anky weed. I'm freaking out in a calm manner to not alarm the other inmates to what is going on. She describes the inmate who came in on her law library appointment and gave her the weed as payment to do extra work on her case to expedite her getting out of prison. Now you know I lose all my common sense and had the slightest idea of what to do. I keep her behind, call Inspector Englund. I walk her to the dorm as if I was making sure she had all her law papers and ran back to the library to wait for Englund. When he got his ole slick oil can ass there, the first thing he says is while laughing, "The library ain't never been this live til you got here. What you got going on today Betty?" While giving him some serious side eye with a smirk on my face. I unlock my desk drawer and pull out the weed. His eyes got big and my eyes became stuck. Englund looked at me, I looked at him and he kept looking at me and asked, "Where in the hell did this come from?" I explained the entire story to him just as my inmate did, with full detail and description of the inmate. Englund just kept looking at me shaking his head and laughing the entire time. Hell I had to laugh too because I already knew the drill, lengthy reports to write, another interrogation with the black bag, my library tore to hell and back and pop up shake downs. After lunch the compound was on RECALL again. This time they brought 4 dogs and more officers to do a thorough search which resulted in more weed, a few gold necklaces, a phone and a bunch of other contraband. The inmate who gave the weed to my law clerk had just got there and apparently was not searched properly. She claimed that not only her, but a couple of other inmates stuffed the weed in the vaginas. At this point, I was too through and ready to leave the prison and Sarge.

I Prayed for no more incidents to go down before I left and for a short while my Prayers were answered, well at least for me and my library crew. I remember I kept getting inmate requests from this one inmate who normally was in the library every day, laughing, talking and just really being pleasant. One day I stopped and paid full attention to where the inmate requests were coming from and why, she was in the hole. I didn't think anything of it, because I knew she was a little scrapper who often had to defend herself because she was so quiet and didn't bother people. When she came to the library, she said she felt at peace and ease to be herself without judgment. At the time she was in there, she couldn't have been any more than about 25 and had been in prison since she was 15 for killing her mother and her mother's boyfriend. She claimed that her mother's boyfriend was raping her repeatedly and when she went to her mother for help, her mother beat her for lying. Her and her then teenage boyfriend plotted to kill the boyfriend but when her mother got in the way and tried to stop them from killing him, she blacked out and killed her mom for not protecting her. To hear her describing how she bashed her mother's head in repeatedly and the gruesome way she tortured her was unbearable for my ears and made my stomach become nauseous. I never looked at her any different after she told me that story. I have said before and will continue to say, my best inmates were in there for murder. My heart just went out to her especially after my law clerks confirmed her story to be true. Every crime that has been committed can be located with all the evidence and circumstances in law books. One of them looked it up, confirmed the story and actually offered to help her get a new trial.

A month passes and she is finally out. Just as she is released from the hole being escorted to her new dorm, an officer sees her and drops right there on the compound with a massive heart attack. Well, see what had happened was, the male officer who she was sleeping with gave her an STD. He kept promising her that he would bring in the medication she needed, just don't tell and everything would be fine. When he didn't bring the medication and her infection was getting worse, she went to clinic to get checked and treated and told the medical personnel that she had been bumping coodas with her new girlfriend who had just come to prison. They knew she was lying and figured if they put her in the hole she would break. NOT! They couldn't keep her in the hole for over 30 days because they couldn't actually prove that she was having sex nor could they prove who she was having sex with, so they had to let her go. When he saw her on the compound, he just knew she had snitched on him and dropped with a massive heart attack. His ole nasty, dirty dick ass didn't die, but at the age of 32 he had a pacemaker put in and retired on full disability. When my staff told me this story I was in tears from laughing. The officer was a good looking, slim, caramel colored, deep wave low hair cute, real bow legged dude who had a fiancé on the outside and was sleeping with 2 other officers on 2 different shifts at the prison. Brick ho house at its finest.

It was the end September and I had already been on a few interviews. Some twice and still no word. I was growing more and more frustrated because I was now starting to feel as if I was an inmate with no options or place to go. Sarge and I had fallen back into our pattern of not talking for weeks on end and I was truly just done. Same foolishness just a different day. We was both cheating and lying. On a Thursday afternoon just as I was about to walk out of the library for lunch my office phone rings. It's a job offer! The lady said the agency and salary and I told her my start date before she could utter the words. I hung up the phone and ran through the Sally Port like a gust of wind, met up with my homegirl and made a mad dash to Red Lobster to celebrate. Normally I don't bring anything into the prison, because I'm not trying to be stopped for a search or thought to be bringing in any contraband, but on this day I brought in my food from Red Lobster because I had plans to continue eating and celebrating. My inmates return from lunch and are being silly as ever which is normal for us, but on this day I knew all hell was about to break loose. The inmates were trying to come in, I told them that we were closed for the afternoon due to inventory and I called my staff into the main library and told everyone to have a seat because we needed to talk. Everyone started looking around at each other kinda crazy because they had already finished inventory and re cleaning the library after every single search and pop up shake down that seemed to be happening every day for the past few months. I started with, "You guys know I care a great deal for you and have had some of the best, worst and scariest times of my life right here in this zoo with you, but the time has come for me to move on. I have a new job and my last day with you guys is today!" You had never seen so many tears and loud screams in your life. At first I was calm while trying to keep every single last one of them calm before the officers came running over thinking something was wrong. Each one asked if it was something that they did, because they would change. I had to laugh at that because I'm thinking, "Are we in a relationship or something and I ain't know nothing about it?" It wasn't them per se, it was more so the entire Florida department of corrections and their crooked ways of handling staff and the inmates. Then you put ole skillet breaking Sarge in the loop and it was bound to explode eventually. I explained that it wasn't them, it was me and I needed change with better opportunities. Damn, that does sound like we were all in a relationship! It wasn't that, I just treated them like they were somebody, showed them respect and I got the same in return. Just as I was about to finish my talk with them, my supervisor Asst. Warden Hall called me to confirm some things because I only gave them a few hours' notice of my resignation and really didn't give one dry fuck. If I had not told the lady I would start the next day, Friday, I would have been stuck in that hell hole for another 2 whole weeks and that was not about to happen. When I got off the phone with Asst. Warden Hall, my youngest law clerk, Hot Tamale ran into my office face red, tear soaked prison blues and grabbed me and hugged me so tight and just cried. That is when I broke down and cried too. She said, "I love you so much and I don't want you to go, nobody is going to treat us like you and protect us from the officers. Will you promise me that you will at least write and keep in touch?" I had to walk out the office on that because it was getting to be too much. When I walked back into the main library, everybody was hugging and crying like they were at a funeral. I couldn't take it, God knows I couldn't. I knew we had become close and had a great time together but I didn't know I had made such an impact on these women's lives. I was just being my usual goofy, ignant self. The time seemed to have flew by. It was now time for them to line up and be escorted to their respective dorms. I hugged each and every one of my girls. Gave them kisses on their cheeks and told them I loved them as we all cried. I hugged the young one of the crew again and she snatched away from me, cussed like a sailor in between her sobs, knocked my fucking Red Lobster on the ground and ran through the library like a fool. I froze like a statue when I see my cheddar bay biscuits hit the floor and they seemed to hit the floor in slow motion with me screaming NOOOOOOOOOOOOO. I wasn't yelling no at her ignant ass for being upset. I was screaming no because I ain't want my good food to go to waste. My tears dried up real quick when I seen my food on that damn floor. I was mad as fuck bout my cheddar bay biscuits and grilled lobster, ole bitch. The officer comes to the locked door, peers in and bangs hard to get our attention. I don't let him in. I hug the girls one last time and bid our final farewells. They walk out the library still crying and each telling me that they love me. I wave the officer off to let him know all is fine and not to say anything to anybody. I clean up the library, write out detailed instructions for whoever will be coming in to replace me, gather my belongings, return my keys to the officer in the Sally port and peacefully walk out of Broward Correctional Institution Brick Whore House, never looking back.

Its early October Friday morning and I leave my apartment in Ft. Lauderdale at 6:15am to ensure I'm at my new job with DCF in Belle Glade Florida by 8am. It's a 75 mile ride one way and I want to make sure I'm on time. With Sarge and I are still at odds and not talking, he does not know that I have resigned from BCI and taken a new job with DCF. Especially with him being on midnights, it's not like he will know or notice the difference. 2 months have passed and I'm almost finished with training when Sarge keeps blowing up my phone one day. I finally take a break and step into the hallway to take the call. At the time I had a pink flip phone, so I flip it open and in a gentle, soft voice say, "Hello, what do you want?" This nigga jump right off the bridge with, "Where the fuck are you at? I call the library to ask you out on a date and one of the classification officers answer the phone and say you don't work there anymore. What the fuck is going on? Why didn't you tell me you don't work there anymore?" He went off so quick fast and in a hurry I couldn't respond all I could do is laugh and say in a hurried fashion, "We will talk when I get in later this evening. If you're sleep, we can talk this weekend when you have some down time." I hung up the phone quickly as my special little friend was beeping in at the time and I needed to hear his voice to calm me down from the bullshit I had just heard before I went back into my training class. I get home that evening and have a long heart to heart with Sarge and break all that shit down to his ass about his habitual cheating, lying, still being married and my desire to be happy and see other people. We agreed he would move out within the week and keep it moving with no hard feelings. Sarge moved out without incident and we lost contact with one another for a couple of years.

Sarge and I reconnected about 2-3 years later by happenstance; we went out a few times while I was dating Cleophus, but nothing major. We had a few dates, hung out with his kids and just kicked it ole school style like 2 friends even though every few minutes he would let me know how much he fucked up in letting me get away and cheating on me with the zombie looking Earlene. I had my fun hanging with him from time to time but I had set my sights on something else that captured my attention, so we lost contact again for another couple of years. Don't worry; we'll see Sarge again and in full force! ~~Ain't That Bout'a Bitch~~

CHAPTER 9

HOES TO HOUSEWIVES

The latter part of 2010, I broke up with my live in boyfriend of almost 4 years Cleophus. We had lived together for 3 of the almost 4 years we were together and I had, had enough and I refused to take it anymore or I was going to end up in jail for killing his ass. Cleophus was a tall, dark, thick good looking, hardworking, fully domesticated, habitual lying, and cheating lieutenant with the Miami Dade Fire rescue. When we first got together everything was absolutely wonderful. I met Cleophus February 2007, just 2 months after breaking up with Sarge. It was a breath of fresh air to meet a man who didn't have the prison, ho hopping mind set. When we first begin dating, I use to work in Belle Glade Florida and he would come to my job all the way in Belle Glade to bring me lunch, send flowers or ask for me to hide my house key so he could come and cook for me before I got off, so that whether he was there or not, I would have a hot meal ready for me. My job finally with the Department of Children and Families finally transferred to Ft. Lauderdale, which made it a lot easier for us to see each other and spend time due to his crazy work schedule. Firemen work 24 hours and then they have 48 hours off. There were plenty of times he would pick up OT and be gone for damn near 4 days, so we would get our time in when we could. After some long and deep discussions we decide to live together 10 months into our relationship, which made sense being that he was already paying bills, cooking and cleaning at my crib.

All is great for the first year and a half as we are truly in the honeymoon phase of our relationship. We're spending quality time, traveling and I'm eating good coz he can cook his ass off just like his Georgia born and bred mother. Shortly after we have been together for the year and a half and living together, I have caught him texting with a few hoochies from his route at work. We argue, fight and work it out. It stops for a while and then it starts back up right around the time I take a promotion in 2008 as a Sr. Fraud Investigator. With my promotion, we move to Boynton Beach because trying to do field work in Boca Raton, Delray Beach and Boynton Beach and traveling back and forth between Ft Lauderdale and WPB proved to be too much. This is when all hell breaks loose with his lies, baby mommas and continued cheating. Yes, I did say baby mommas, as in 4 of the most ignantess, evil ass women you would ever want to meet and we ain't even finna get into looks and personality.

I loved being a Sr. Fraud investigator. There is so much access to any and all kinds of info and networking with others who have higher and more in depth access into the world of nosiness. As I said the cheating kicked back up and I was trying to get concrete evidence so when I busted his ass this time, I would have black and white not just some he say, she say. In talking to one of my investigative friends, I learned how to get his cell phone bill monthly, get into his email and text messages all without him finding out. OMG it was on now. Inch High Private Eye Firm was in business and ready for clients.

We had been together for almost 2.5 to 3 years when we finally started sleeping in separate rooms and spending less and less time together. We had been living separate for some time now when he comes home one day and want to have a heart to heart after I found out about him paying $150 to busted can of biscuits looking chick that he met on South Florida Back Page. This is no lie, the type of women Cleophus would cheat on me with were not attractive, educated or had anything going for going for themselves besides selling pussy. It use to bother me, but then I had to step back and realize that he has some serious self-esteem and self-love issues more than anything and this was not my fault by far.

When the Super Bowl was in Miami in 2007, it was straight pandemonium. It was such a blast with friends who packed themselves in my 2nd floor, tiny one bedroom apartment and the many new friends I met that weekend; that is all I talked about for months. That was also the same weekend I got my 1st tat of praying hands, with rosary beads on my right shoulder that weekend. When the NFL announced that they would be having the Super Bowl in Miami again in 2010, the party was already planned and in full effect before February 2010 could even get here. I requested 7 days off because I already knew it was gonna be crazy as a baby momma trying to locate her baby daddy for child support and similac, plus my birthday was right around the corner from Super Bowl and I had all intentions of partying like a rock star.

My sister Lucy and my niece Brooke decide they want to come south and do the super bowl festivities with me. They come to town late Thursday night, early Friday morning in preparation for the weekend as we plan on tearing Miami up; well at least my niece and I do because we already know my sister starts nodding off and slobbing faithfully at 6:59pm. When we get up later that Friday morning, Cleophus has cooked breakfast for us before we head to the hair salon. My stylist Nia at Dolly's New Image in Sunrise, who by the way is one of the best in Ft Lauderdale and can lay some hair down is located deep in a hood shopping center, where you will be met by the local nickel and dime dope boys on one corner, the BBQ/soul food stand with the nasty attitude and horrible customer service but the best food. On the other corner you have the projects, hourly gun fire, the local crack head who comes in and out the shop selling 600 thread count sheet sets, Oneida silverware, Patron tequila and toothbrushes (and he takes orders). All this is going on while the local Haitian Baptist church and tax services is right next door. My sister is looking at me like "Who finna get their hair done in there?", my niece is doing the bank head bounce like she know where the hell she at and I'm saying a silent Prayer that nothing goes off. One night while in the shop getting my weave sewn in and having a few drinks, bumping the ole school radio station the ambiance was disturbed by gun fire. At first we was cool, because it was just a pistol being shot BUT when we heard the semi-automatic being let off, we threw those cups up in the air and jumped on the floor like we was in basic training with Rambo and crawled on our bellies to the back of the salon behind the dryers until the gun fire stopped. Soon as the gun fire stopped, which seemed like an eternity, we quickly packed up our shit and ran out the salon and finished drinking and doing my hair at her house.

My sister, niece and I walk into the salon. I introduce everyone and let my sister get washed up1st, since my niece has already had her hair done before she left town and I need some time deciding on what color weave I want try. Never who you might run into on South Beach!! While my sister is sitting under the dryer, Benny Hill the local crack head comes in selling sheets, silverware and deodorant. My sister asks, "How much are you selling the sheets for?" Benny Hill was a true crack head to his heart. Clicking and constantly twitching with every word responds back "I will sell you all this shit right here, this shit right here for $20." Benny Hill had some name brand 600 thread count sheets and very nice silverware still in the wrapper and box. My sister was trying to pull money out her pocket so quick, she busted her head against the hair dryer and almost fell trying to get up like somebody was finna slide up to Benny Hill and yell SAFE like a damn umpire. My sister then tells Benny Hill, "If you come across some more sheets before the weekend is over, please get in contact with my sister and I will come buy what you have." Benny Hill happily agreed and clicked and twitched his crack smoking ass out the shop. A few hours have now passed, as we all know every black stylist books 6 people for the same one hour slot, everybody is chilling and getting their hair done when Benny Hills pops back up and this time with some toothbrushes, liquor and something else that was odd. My sister, who is sitting in the chair getting her wrap pressed out, says; "Hey buddy, did you get some more sheets?" Everybody is looking and listening because they want to put in their order too. Benny Hill said when he went back to the store and was digging for the high thread counted sheets, the store rep came up to him and said, "If you're looking for some more high count sheet sets, we don't have any more because you have stolen all of them." Everybody fell out laughing and some chick offered to take him to another store way across town to fulfill her order.

I finally get in the chair and get some honey blonde weave bonded into my wrap, trying to see if I want to make it a permanent change. We leave the hair salon, run around site seeing and grab some jerk pork from this awesome Jamaican restaurant and some chicken gizzards from this soul food restaurant that is so addictive, but they are in a part of town you hate to go to because you never know if you have to strap up like the crew from 300 or get a formal escort by SWAT.

It's getting late and we need to head back to my house, which is located in Boynton Beach, so we can rest up and get sharper than a mosquito's dick and hit the streets of South Beach. When we arrive Cleophus has not made it back in yet, so everybody is doing they own thing in preparation for tonight. Now remember, I told you Cleophus is highly insecure, so when he sees my hair, instead of him pulling me into the room to discuss the change, he tries to show out and get loud in front of my family, which sets off a shit storm of an argument and almost gets his ass whipped. I come from a family of nothing but women, who are known to jump a nigga or 2 if they get out of line. We don't have any brothers or uncles to call on, so we pack our pistols and hammers and get the damn job done. Once him and I argue, my sister and niece are like "Wassup, we greasing his ass or what?" I calmly reply, "Nah, we gonna let him slide for now, I got something far better for his ass." I know my sister ride with her Glock 40 at all times, my niece keep her .38 on her at all times and my pistol is always ducked off somewhere for quick reach just in case I need to correct a nigga on site without warning. We get dressed and leave the house. Leaving his period having ass laying across the bed like a pouting ho watching TV.

The traffic going into Miami was horrendous yet fun as hell, because we are seeing some of everyone and everything all the while laughing our asses off. By the time we get across the bridge onto South Beach, parking has gone up from the regular $20 to $40. We pay, park and Lawd Geesus. The streets are packed with some of the friendliest, fun going, partying people from all walks of life. We try to get a drink from Wet Willies, but the line is as long as a lie from a nigga who just got caught coming in the house at 6am with red lipstick on his boxers. The same keeps occurring at every name brand bar on the strip, except for this one lowly gay bar at the end of the Ocean Drive if you're heading north. We go in, sit right at the bar and start talking with a very friendly and social butterfly bartender who made some of the strongest and best drinks I have ever wrapped my lips around, so you know that he got a damn good tip from my alcoholic ass. After we get our drinks, we head back to where all the activity is and lose our damn mind when we walk right into that 35 degree Hawk. With the wind coming off the water, it felt more like 20 degrees. As were walking and sucking down them strong ass drinks trying to warm up and enjoying the sites of famous ball players walking up and down Ocean Drive, famous actors and actresses and all types of people from everywhere enjoying life and then of course you have the local yocals who act as if they have never been past the stop sign in their neighborhood. We walk, take pictures, keep going back and forth to the gay bar for the best drinks and clean bathrooms.

Finally one of us looks at a watch and realize it is 4 or so in the morning and we need to be heading back so we can get rested and do this all over again late Saturday evening in hopes of finding a free Super Bowl Party we can crash, eat and drink for free all night. As we creep back to the car in the parking garage, our bones are stiff as concrete from that cold weather, I meet this very handsome, good hair, dark mocha latte colored gentleman who is not only very easy on the eyes, but music to my ears with the words he is serenading me with. Jordan is a regional director for the Department of Homeland Security. He's 46, divorced, single and his only 2 children are grown and out of his home! My sister and niece ain't trying to hear none of that, they run to the car and turn the heat on full blast while waiting for me and Jordan to finish our conversation. Jordan and I stand in the freezing car garage for another 20 - 30 minutes just talking and enjoying one another's company when I hear 2 horns honking uncontrollably. My sister is laying on the car horn like it's a Sealy Posturepedic mattress and the fella Jordan was with was hitting the car horn too. We laughed, exchanged numbers and parted ways with a sincere promise to see one another again and soon. Uhmmmm, damn, if only for one night!

I finally get in the car and speed back to the house. Laughing about all the crazy stuff that has happened all night, yet still thinking about

Mr. Jordan. We get back to my house; now remember it is cold as hell in South Florida. Anything below 60 degrees is freezing to us. I turn into the complex and get ready to park, when I notice that the windows are closed. I'm thinking that Cleophus closed the windows and turned on the heater because it's freezing cold, so I shake it off. I walk up to the apartment and reach to open the storm screen door and to my dismay, it won't open! I'm, thinking maybe I'm really cold, still drunk and my hands aren't working properly due to possible frost bite. I look down at my hands and move my fingers to make sure I'm not dreaming, blow in my hands a couple times and I try it again and that's when it hits me, this raggely mutha fucker has locked me and my family out the house! My sister and niece fall out dying laughing because they think this is the funniest shit ever. I start cussing and going off because now I got to walk around the back of the house, through bushes, grass and dirt to go knock on the window and wake his ignant ass up, all the while I'm dressed in all white. I walk around the back of my house like Sophia did through the corn field in The Color Purple, use a rock to knock on the window to get his attention. I hear him rumbling around in the bedroom and I start arguing with him through the window to so he know it's me and that he understands he needs to hurry the hell up and come open this door. By the time I walk back around the building, he has finally come and unlocked the storm door, let my sister and niece in and rushed his black ass back into the bedroom because he know its bout to be on. My sister and niece are doing what they need to do in order to get ready for bed, but also standing on ready just in case I yell "REGULATORS, MOUNT UP".

Cleophus and I are arguing like 2 crack heads over who smoked the last rock and who got to ante up some ass to get some more crack, when I hear CLICK?!? Now remember, I told you it was cold as hell in South Florida. The temp that morning when we returned home was every bit of 20 degrees. My eyes have now grown to the size of semi-tractor tires when I ask this dumb mutha fucker, "What in the hell is that noise that just clicked on? I know it better be the fucking heater. Its cold as fuck in this mutha fucking house?" This bitch runs into the bathroom and starts brushing his teeth and answering me through each brush like a little child in a low voice and said, "It's the AC." I was so mad but I didn't want to raise my voice because I knew my sister and niece was on straight "Correct a Nigga Mode!" I ask him in a low, calm voice, "Why in the hell is the AC on when it's cold as Eskimo nutz outside and what possess you to lock the screen door when you know I'm out entertaining my family?" This nigga had the audacity to tell me he got hot and locked the door because he wanted to go to sleep and feel safe while sleep. Now mind you, we live in a very nice, upper middle class part of Boynton Beach, Fl and have never had any issues in that area for the entire 2 years that we lived there. I couldn't do nothing but blink my eyes fast as hell and swing my arms back and forth like a windmill slapping myself on the hips and looking crazy and I tell him, "Hurry up and get ready for work and get the fuck out of my sight before I lose it on your ass and end up in jail dancing for a honey bun and postage stamps."

For the rest of the weekend, that my family was there, Cleophus pulled OT all weekend and did not return until Tuesday morning. My niece and I went out again Saturday night and didn't return until 7:30 the next morning. My sister stayed in the house and watched movies and TV all night but then want to know what we did all night, who we met, what we saw and everything. We told that lazy, nosy ass heffa, she shoulda been there to see everything because we was too damn exhausted to fill her in on all the happenings that night. All I can say is, it was colder, more crowded, some of the ignantness ass people I have ever had the pleasure of laughing my ass off too. They left that Sunday and I went to the Hard Rock casino and watched the game with the coolest group of dudes I met from New York and had a blast. Till this day we are still in contact.

At the time that all this is going on and that disastrous weekend happened, Cleophus had been saving up money to buy a house and add all the additions he had dreamed of. Marble floors, granite counter tops, new doors, pool and all the trimmings, and at the same time he kept trying to work things out with me so that we could finally be a family and live happily ever after. Well, at least that's how he was trying to sell it to me, but unknown to him, I was still doing my monthly digging. During this last and final investigation I found 4 chicks. Chick 1, was 38 at the time. Works at Publix and never advanced pass cashier in the 14yrs she was there. 3 kids, learners permit, no car, lived in a rough housing project in Miami and very unattractive. This is the one he called and texted the most. Chick 2, was 27. Worked at Home Depot, 2 kids, live in boyfriend who had just got out of prison and a decent car. This one couldn't keep a job to Free Willy if needed; her work history had more jumps than hop scotch. This one looked like a busted can of biscuits that had been sitting in a 300 degree dumpster. He talked and text this one every once in a while but not that often as her booty bandit man had just return home from prison. Chick 3 was 21. No job, no car, no school no nothing but she was fine and lived in the Pork and Beans projects in Miami. He was always trying to get with this through text, but she was strictly about her coins and wasn't trying to hear shit else about how much he liked and wanted her, unless he was going to break the piggy bank. I totally respected her to the upmost. Now

Chick 4 was my favorite. She was in her late 40's. 1 teenage son, owned her own home, 3 cars and was a police officer for Miami for the past 20yrs. She was a very pretty lady and seemed to have a certain aura about her, that let you know not to fuck off.

I know you're probably trying to figure out how I know all this, especially how they look. Simple, after I investigate my potential fraud clients, conducted field visits and built my case against them, I investigated my fraudulent boyfriend and find out all the latest and greatest and built my own case against him. Once I ran the numbers and got names and other information, I did pop up visits to every single last one of their homes and always asked for Michelle. I was never angry or mad or wanted to fight any of these chicks. The nosey nature in me just wanted to see what they looked like. Now, trust me I did run up on some that made me sit in the car around the corner, bang my head on the steering wheel and look at him and shake my damn head and wonder how did his dick even get hard for them. We break up, he moves out and moves on with his life as I move on with mine and neither one of us could be happier.

Cleophus and chick #1, She'rilla make it official and she moved into his brand new house and they marry in 2012. I didn't dig and find this out. After 2 years, he reached out to me and apologized for all his wrong doing and was asking if there was a way for us to work things out. He was truly sorry and missed me terribly. You know that look you get when that first doo doo pain hit and its crowning right at the edge of your asshole and you're in that long line at Wal- Mart and the clerk has just called for a price check? That is exactly how my asshole felt and my face scrunched up to match it. I explained to him I was seeing someone, pregnant and expecting to get married soon because I didn't want to give birth to a bastard. Now, I was lying my ass off on part of that. I was seeing someone whom I cared a great deal for, but I was far from preggo and I was not about to stop working and sign a pre-nup just to get married as he had damn near demanded (long story for another time).

Now let's fast forward to 2013. I'm in a deep committed relationship with Linus. You will get his story in a few minutes. Cleophus started sending me text about how much he misses me and wants to talk. One day we're talking, he just busts out and said, "I think she is cheating on me! I go to work and come home and find new tooth brush wrappers in the garbage can and ain't no new toothbrush in the house between me, her and her kids. Its new sheets on the bed fresh out the pack." I stop him right there and ask, "How in the hell do you know they are new sheets fresh out the pack?" In a somber lowly voice, he says, "Because I know everything in this house and the sheets on the bed the night before I went work were freshly done laundry, she must have fucked on them, made a mess and changed the sheets plus they still have the packaged creases in them." A huge part of me wanted to scream in the phone "GOTCHA GOTCHA GOTCHA BITCH" but I didn't. I held my composure until he told me, "You know I added her to my cell bill so it would be easier and somewhat cheaper for her to pay the bill." That didn't make sense to me but I rode with it and kept listening. Then he says, "6 months into our marriage, she started cheating. That's when I started seeing her talking to the same number morning noon and night and the nights that they didn't talk all night, are the nights she must be with him somewhere!" I'm trying to keep from busting a gut from holding my laugh in, so I just tell him to call the counselor he drug my ass to weekly for 5 months and work it out. He doesn't feel that counseling will work as she is not use to anything and really don't know how to communicate with anyone. Now, this is burning me up on the inside, because I'm trying to figure out for the life of me, why in the hell would you want to be with and marry someone who does not know how to communicate. I asked him, "Cleophus, tell me something please? Why did you marry her over me, especially if she doesn't know how to communicate, no license, no ambition to advance pass cashier or anything?" He paused, took a long dramatic deep breath and replied, "Because I thought I could change and control her!" I didn't have one thing to say after that, my thoughts from earlier about his low self-esteem was right on the money. I told him "You can't change anything or anybody but your drause!" What was he thinking? He continued to vent about his frustration in her and their relationship as she doesn't like to do anything or go anywhere, when they go to the restaurants she don't pronounce the food incorrectly and how she only orders shrimp and other common food because she has never experienced anything above Chilli's or TGIF. After a while I got tired of hearing the same ole and I told him good night and I Pray all gets better for them and bid him a farewell.

A few months pass by and we haven't talked or text. One morning as I'm walking down the stairs heading to work, I get a phone call, but I can't tell who it is. I have my hands full with coffee in one hand, purse on one shoulder, laptop on the other shoulder with my lunch bag, trash bag in the other hand and my earbuds in my ears and the phone tucked in my bra so I just tap the button on the earbuds to answer the phone and I say, "Hello" in my most seductive voice. I'm not sure if it's my honey calling to check on me. The voice I get in return makes me stop in my tracks, especially with the words that were spoken, "Good morning is this Ms. Betty?" In a quick and instant defensive black woman fashion, I put that trash bag down, put my hand on my hip, rotated my neck and pressed my lips together and responded, "Yes this is and who the hell are you and what do you want?" My heart actually sank when the caller finally announced who they were, "Good morning Ms. Betty, this is Chief Walbanger with the Miami Dade Fire rescue and the reason for my call is, Lt. Cleophus failed to report for duty this morning, nor has he called out and he is not answering the one and only phone number we have for him. The purpose for this call is, he has you listed as an emergency contact and we need to know if you have been in contact with him, because we are about to send the police to his home in Weston." Ok, now remember we haven't been together in years. He is now married to poppin fresh no car, project bus catching hoochie ass heffa and I've moved on. I start to remember being the sole beneficiary of his $500,000.00 insurance policy which doubles if he is killed in the line of duty!!

My mind is moving at the speed of lightening and I instantly respond to Chief Walbanger, "Please sir, please don't send the police to his home. I was just texting with him last night and want to be the 1st one on the scene if there is something wrong. By the way, you do know he is married?" The Chief was so cool, I didn't have no choice but to respect his response and chuckle. The Chief responded, "That may be so and I'm happy for him, but we don't have that info on file therefore she can't be of any service to us if we don't know who she is!" I shook my head, laughed and simply responded "Yes sir, I understand. I will give you a call back in about 20 minutes to this number that populated on my phone and let you know what is going on."

My heart is racing like Jeff Gordon is driving around the race track and about to win the NASCAR championship. I call my supervisor to let her know what is going on and why I will be late. As I pull up to the dumpster, my heart goes back a normal rate because I start to think of all the things I can do with that $500 grand after I give his kids and mom some money. Then I start to remember some very artistic and crafty plastic surgeons in the Miami area that I could get to lift these sagging potato sack tiddays and suck some of these thighs down, the truck I have been wanting to get for some time and a nice little waterfront condo. Man, I chucked that garbage over the fence into the big dumpster without looking, ran back to my car, threw on my seat belt and channeled Jeff Gordon my damn self-trying to make it to the other side of town to see if this fool was dead.

It seemed like every blue knuckled, grey haired shuffle board player was on the road that morning. If it wasn't the old people that slowed me up, I caught every single red light even if I ducked off on side roads. On the way across town to his house, I kept thinking that She'rilla has caught him cheating and killed him and how am I going to react when I get to the house and break in and find him and his blood sprawled across the floor, his brains on the wall and the stench. How would I call his mom whom I love and respect dearly and break the news to her that her son was murdered? Then my mind somehow or another slides over to where did I place the insurance papers? Will I have to call up my family to help me fight She'rilla and her family about this insurance policy? How soon can I slide up into the plastic surgeon office? I know, Pray for me because my mind was on everything else, but not really giving 2 dry pussy fucks about his ass being dead. I finally get to his house and see both of his cars backed in the driveway. My heart really starts racing. I'm preparing myself to see the worse and notify all the necessary people. I speed into the middle of his yard and hit the brakes hard, leaving some skid marks, jump out and rang the doorbell 1st. I don't hear any movement. I'm prancing and dancing like I have to pee because I'm nervous as hell. I hit the doorbell again and do a police knock. This time I hear some slow deliberate foot dragging with mumbling, I'm prepared to see him open the door bleeding, gasping for air with his hands stretched high to the heavens begging me for help.

When the door finally opens, it's a tall, slender, very musky odor smelling teenage boy who answers the door and says, "Yeah, can I help you?" This is the 1st time I have ever seen one of She'rilla's kids and I was kind of taken aback, so I said, "Good morning sweetie, is Cleophus home?" He looked at me crazy, which I would have done the same thing if another woman came to my momma husband house asking for him. I'm in fight mode and a fight stance just in case she come running her ass out the door with some stupid shit. Again, I hear some slow deliberate walking so I think it's his stanking ass again but I'm ready for whoever come out this door. The knob turns and the door swings out fast and I got my shit ready when Cleophus half dead ass comes out and looks at me crazy. Before he could speak, I through my hand up as to say HUSH, in a low calm voice I tell him, "You know I wouldn't dare come to your house if this was not an emergency. Your battalion Chief Walbanger called me because you did not show up to work, nor have you been answering the phone when they call. Plus you still have me listed as your emergency contact, so they were about to send the police over here to do a wellness check and I told him I would do it and call him back. Are you ok?"

I have been on this front porch for about 5 minutes or so and she has not darkened that damn door step nor did any window blind in the living room or front bed room move. It would have taken Jesus and all his 15 disciples and his momma Mary to keep me from going out the damn door and finding out what the hell was going on. He reaches to hug me when I throw my forearm up and back away giving him that ole mean momma look. He thanks me and explains that he had one too many drinks, over slept and forgot he had to work. I can totally relate to that. I said to him, "Ok, well I'm going to call Chief Walbanger and I'll talk to you later, take care of yourself." As I'm walking off calling Chief Walbangerback, something tells me to turn around and Cleophus is standing on the front porch looking a little lost kid being dropped off to kindergarten on the 1st day.

He calls me later that night after he made it work and thanked me profusely for coming to his rescue. I had two burning questions to ask him and you know I asked him. I said, "Cleophus why do you still have me listed as your emergency contact since you're now married?" This fool had the nerves to say, "I never thought of changing it and you're still the beneficiary of the insurance policy too, I hope you know that. I know I fucked up in letting you leave me, especially with all the wrong I did but I know you will make sure my kids and mom are taken care of if something did happen to me." He is absolutely correct. Even though I don't have respect for any of the mothers due to how they use the kids as pawns, I would most definitely make sure they are set as well as his mother. I love that spunky, out spoken old woman. My last question was burning a hole in my tongue; I couldn't get it out quick enough. I asked, "Cleophus, what did She'rilla say when you went back inside the house?" He claims she didn't say or ask him anything. If you let him tell it, all was cool and calm and she waited until he went to work and then she texted him asking who was I and why was I at the house. Cleophus claims he told her everything I just told you and she was like, Ok! I think he was telling me the truth, because he would have been venting about what all she don't do and she ain't got no right blah blah blah. I give Cleophus one last piece of advice and we bid our farewells.

Now we fast forward to Sunday 3-9-2014 night when he calls me again after not speaking for a few months, because I told him he needs to take his vows serious and do what a man is suppose to do, especially with this being his 3rd marriage as the 3rd time is the charmer. ROFLMAO . . .

I wake up Sunday morning, all refreshed and ready to go to church when I check my phone for texts, missed phone calls and other alerts because I turn my ringer off at night so I'm not disturbed. I go through my texts when I realize I have one from Cleophus from earlier in the damn morning about 7am. The text reads, "She didn't stay here last night, there was no condensation on the car when I got home this morning, every car in the neighborhood had it except hers, I really need to get that GPS ASAP!!" I'm laughing and damn near in tears as Mrs. Cleophus, the one he couldn't live without when we was together, the one he stayed on the phone with night and damn day talking and texting when we was together, is running nothing but raw dick up his ass with no Vaseline for all the shit he took me through. After I take a long, relaxing shower feeling completely free and open to speak open and bluntly to him, I send him a reply text while sitting on the side of the bed and ask, "Tell me this, you already know she is cheating why are you going through all of this verse letting her go and moving on with your life? She got a man or men running all up and through your house, she don't cook or clean soooooooooo what's the point of being married and unhappy? Don't get mad at me boo, I'm just asking?"

I went on to church and have an awesome time as I do every Sunday from the teachings of Dr. Clover. I came home, chilled and did as I normally do on the weekends. Its late night and my phone rings, as I reach for my phone to ignore the call because my favorite show is on, re runs of Martin. I see it's Cleophus and I think really hard if I should answer or if I should just roll over and keep watching Martin. Like a fool, I answer and he tells me, "You know I haven't been able to sleep because I know she has been at another man's house fucking and sucking all night." I say a quick and "Uhmmm mm well only you know the situation and what you really want to do in order to be happy." Cleophus gets very angry with me and says in an aggressive tone, "I fell as though you don't care what's going on with me and I really need you. I'm going through something." Now you know me and my mouth so I quip back," I don't give the slightest fuck about you or ya fucking mammy especially when you was cheating on with me with this no nothing ass bitch." Something tells me to switch gears and just shut up, so I say, "Cleophus, my bad its late honey what's wrong?"

Now I'm hoping you are sitting down with a strong drink in your hand when I say these next words. Remember I'm lying in bed chilling on a Sunday night when this Georgia inbred bitch say to me, "I need you to help me buy a state of the art GPS for the Honda because I want and need to know where she is going when I'm at work especially since it's my car she is using to go see another man!" My face has gotten tight, twisted and cocked like a stroke victim with severe paralysis. I am totally quiet when this bastard said this. I can hear him breathing hard in desperation. Here go my ignant ass, "What the fuck you expect me to do, I ain't fucking you or your ugly hoe ass wife. WTF I look like buying you a got damn GPS for a bitch you cheated on me with and married the hoe??" I'm hot now and sitting up in my bed ready to fight this lame ass sucka duck ass nigga. He doesn't say anything for a few minutes, I guess he is trying to gather his thoughts so he says, "When I came home the last Monday morning, I took my shower and was sitting on the side of the bed rubbing Vicks vapor rub on my feet before I went to sleep, you know it actually helps my athletes feet. I'm done with the left foot and I'm getting ready to rub my right foot down when I see something sticking out from underneath the bed. I get off the bed and look under the bed and it's a shop rag." I'm like whoopty doo, you left your shop rag in the room. He goes on to say, "Betty I don't have any shop rags. I haven't used those in years and on top of that it was hard and stuck together with like a cum stuck!" I'm crying laughing but at the same time I'm trying to be supportive and said, "Well sweetie, maybe she brought it in from work and it fell out of her work uniform." He took a deep breath and said, "Betty she works in the fucking bakery, what do she need a fucking shop rag for? Huh, they using shop rags to make the fucking doughnuts? To decorate cakes? It had cum on it Betty, give me a break!"

I kindly tell Cleophus I'm not about to buy him no got damn GPS, but I'm be more than happy to help him research a good one and take him to pick up his Honda because once he pull off, I plan on sitting there to video everything that happen from the time she walk out the door and see the car gone til the time he pull back up in the Honda. He got mad at me when I told him this, "Cleophus, I ain't even mad at She'rilla, because the bitch got mad skills and is playing the game very well. You thought you had the game down and a dumb bitch on your team, but she has played the game like a true master and if I ever formally meet her, I'll introduce myself to her and take the bitch out on a date."

I know you are trying to figure out how a Lt with the fire department who makes close to $100k a year, doesn't have enough money to buy his own GPS? Well it breaks down like this and I'm going to look stupid as hell in this too. Cleophus has 6 kids and 4 baby mommas. By the time I found out about all the kids and baby mommas, I was already vested in and said what the hell. I'm good, because all was fine and dandy in my house and I wasn't lacking anything. WELLL until the child support kicked in. Cleophus roughly grosses about $6000.00 every 2 weeks, but he pays $383.59 bi weekly in arrearages for his 2 oldest sons from his 1st ex-wife. Then he has a teenage son with some white girl who can't collect child support because she stay in and out of jail, but he does send the boy whatever he asks for within reason, so that's about $200 or so bi weekly. Then you have his only daughter from his 2nd ex-wife, who get $446.65 bi weekly. Last but not least, he has 2 little boys from Biggie Smalls little sister, that he made while he was married to the 2nd ex-wife and those two little boys get just about $371.32 bi weekly. When you add all that up it comes to a whoopin $2,803.00 a month or $1401.56 every 2 weeks. In the state of Florida if you work for the state, city or county you have to pay an additional 3% into your retirement, so that is a nice little chunk of change coming out of his check every 2 weeks as well. For years they could never find him to make him the arrearages for his 2 oldest sons, as soon as we get together and start hitting the rocky patch in our relationship the arrearages hit. I'm like, cool we can manage and still be cool. Almost a year to the day that the arrearages start, the 4th baby momma with his 2 little boys come for child support. I guess she had been in the system it just took them some time to find him. Not even 6 months later, here come the 2nd ex-wife with her child support claim. The amounts he is currently paying for child support is not the court ordered amount, as the state of Florida cannot take more than 50% of your gross pay. Meaning that arrearages are currently building for his last 3 children, which are all under the age of 10! Now I'm pretty sure you have already added that up. Now take out his taxes and remember he can't claim any of his kids as dependents, so Uncle Sam is chewing on his ass like a tender T-bone steak. Cleophus still has a mortgage payment over $1,100. A truck note, insurance on both of his cars and other miscellaneous bills, and there you have why a Lt. with the Miami Dade Fire department cannot afford a $150 GPS tracking system for his cheating wife.

Being the good supportive girlfriend, I hung in there as best as I could. I knew he wanted a house and was picking up as much OT as possible and saving all the money he could for a down payment at the same time doing whatever I asked for and still buying pussy online. That was the only reason I stayed, because I felt as if I kicked him out when he was on the brink of his breakthrough, my blessings would have been blocked. He bought his house and I had my priceless peace of mind back.

Cleophus called me on day and told me he had found a GPS on Ebay for $40 and asked would I be willing to help him out this one time. He was getting ready to go to Georgia for a week to see his family for Memorial Day but She'rilla wasn't going because she couldn't get that much time off from Publix. I told him to let me think about it and I would get back with him. I thought about it for a few days and hit text him back that I would, send me the item info so I could easily locate it on Ebay and get this ball to rolling. Don't look at me like that. You know damn well you want to know just as well as my nosey ass do who this girl is sleeping with when Cleophus is at work. I do wonder if it's someone from her past. What he looks like? Will Cleophus and the dude fight? Will She'rilla jump in the fight and help her side piece beat the shit out of Cleophus? OMG so many questions and not enough answers. I order the GPS one Saturday morning and texted him that it was ordered, when he texts me back and says, "You know she came home with a hickie on her neck and she wasn't even trying to hide it!" I was walking down the hall to the living room when I read that and fell all over the arm of the couch and bust out laughing. My retarded ass text back, "Maybe she allergic to something or a mosquito bit her."

Cleophus overlooked my comment and went on to say how she how wasn't even trying to hide the hickie, she came in the house and just chilled like she was daring him to say something. Since he is being so honest I figure why not ask a serious question. I ask, "Cleophus are y'all still having sex and if so, are you using protection?" This fool said, "She always brush me off when I ask for sex and say she ain't in the mood. We haven't had sex in almost 2 months and hell no I don't use protection with her, that's my wife!" All I could do is say, "OK" and make a quick excuse to get off the phone. I can honestly say I love She'rilla, she is my new hero.

I check my Ebay daily for shipment and arrival of this GPS because now it's getting to good and I'm ready to sit outside ole boy house and record the goings on of what happens? Cleophus is steadily texting me every day asking about the whereabouts of this damn GPS and it's starting to get on my nerves because this ain't my fault that you going through this. Cleophus texted me on Thursday asking about this damn GPS and I lost it. I quickly texted back, "WTF you mean what is wrong with me? You got urself in this mess with this ho, now the whole world has to stop bcoz YOU are going thru something . . . GTFOH dude seriously . . . aren't you at work. DID I not say WHEN I GET IT AND IF NEED BE I'LL BRING IT TO UR JOB????????? Damn man, I didn't even go pick it up bcoz you said you were with ur daughter." He so busy trying to get the GPS because he was about to go out of town for a week for Memorial Day holiday and wanted to know her whereabouts. After I went off he called me with major attitude and said, "Why you acting so stuck up and mean, all I was doing was asking if you had it on you coz I was going to come by your job and pick it up but fuck it, I don't need you or anybody and you can best believe you want ever hear from me again. FUCK YOU!" and hung up the phone. I cried laughing because how you actually have the unmitigated gall to sit on this phone and say you don't need anybody? You don't have any friends, hence why you call me, your ex from years ago and confide in me about your marital problems with the chick you was cheating on me with. Hilarious if you ask me. Unscrew your face, you already know I sent that damn GPS went right back to the company and I got a full refund with no worries. There is far more to ole Mr. Cleophus than this story.

As of this writing, I have not heard from Cleophus anymore and to be honest I'm not upset at all. Even though I do wonder whatever happened with him and my new hero She'rilla? I also wonder if he ever changed the insurance policy and emergency contact information? Hmmm ~~Ain't That Bout'a Bitch~~

CHAPTER 10

TUCK DUCK AND ROLL

After breaking up with Cleophus December 2010, I started back celebrating my birthdays with big parties with all my friends and family. When we were together, it was mainly dinner and gifts. My birthday is February 12th which is 2 days before Valentine's Day and our anniversary was February 21st so it was always something intimate, never ever a full blown out birthday party. Shortly after Cleophus and I broke up, Leroy a very good friend of mine wanted to throw a birthday party for me in Gainesville at Club Envy, a new snazzy club that had just opened up. Since I'm known all over social media to be the University of Florida Gators biggest hater, he figured this would be a good way to get the UF/FSU crew together and have an awesome time celebrating Ms. Betty's birthday. FSU had beaten the snot out of the Gators. Trash talking was at an ultimate high. The venue was set. Fliers made up and spread across every social media outlet and windshield in Gainesville. Dress paid for. Hair appointment on deck! Money right! Turn pike bound February 10th.

I make a pit stop in Coleman, Florida at the Coleman USP Federal Penitentiary to see Sincere for a surprise visit. It had been years since I had last seen him. I don't do well with prison visits. Especially seeing someone you love caged like an animal when you know they aren't an animal. I get cleared, escorted down a long side walk in the freezing wind to the visitors pod. I sit. Wait. Wait some more. I go to the guards desk and ask is there an issue. The guard had forgot to summon for him. Something tells me she has a thing for Sincere. She smirks her lips and rolls her eyes like a common ho. He is known to charm the ladies, which is the main reason we aren't together. Well that and his lengthy prison sentence. When he finally comes through the door, I turn from my seat so he can see me. We lock eyes. Fast pace walk run to one another and embrace until the officer commands we break it up. He is excited to see me. I'm overjoyed to see him. All those lost, dead and buried emotions come flooding back in such a whirlwind, I start crying. We sneak a quick passionate tongue kiss and quickly sit down. When he dropped his head to fix his clothes, I quickly wipe my mouth and have a Cheshire grin on my face when he looks back up. Y'all know I worked in a prison!

Now to be completely honest, I don't see Sincere as being a catcher. I see him more so as a pitcher. Just in case you're confusing the terms pitcher and catcher with baseball, you're already lost. In prison terms, if you're a catcher that means you are the woman and take the dick If you're a pitcher that means you are the man and give the dick. Sincere is a fighter. He comes from a long family of fighters. I know deep in my heart, he could only beat his dick for so long. Sincere had 15 years in the federal penitentiary and there was only so much dick beating you can do. We talked. We laugh. We reminisce. I tell him all about my big birthday party and explain that is part of the reason why I'm there seeing him. He gives me the usual prison lesson. If a dude has cuts in or arched eye brows, that means he is a "catcher". What this is or who did what to get in prison and what he does now while in prison. It had been years since I had seen him and I forgot, that it's not safe to make sudden hand movements, because they could be misinterpreted for gang signs. If someone in the visiting room saw me making sudden hand movements, which I do naturally, when he went back to his housing unit, it could cause tension, when all I was doing was being me. Sincere says, "Baby! You know you can't make hand movements like that. They will think I'm in a gang. They also have hired a dude from Miami who can read lips and tell if what we are talking about!" My nerves have just shriveled like bacon that's ready to be taken out the hot frying pan. This is why I stop working at the prison, far too risky over dumb shit. We go outside and walk around the make shift park for visitors, when Sincere decides to break the news to me. Since he has been locked up, he was served with paternity test papers and 2 more kids have been linked to his happy, go lucky dick. Now he has a total of 5 kids that were made while we were together. What can I say? What am I supposed to do? Nothing but I gave him a hug, got a quick feel on each other and kept that shit moving. As much as I miss and still love Sincere, I can't take the visit anymore. I hate seeing him locked up like this. For all the wrong he did to me and the other women, he never deserved to be in a place such as prison. I explain to Sincere it is time for me to leave. I still have a ways to make it to Gainesville and I still have a few things I need to do before the big hoorah! Tears well up in our eyes. We hug and take our last picture together, snuggled up in front of a honeymoon backdrop and say our farewells, never to see one another again. A few weeks later I receive a letter from Sincere with the picture we took. He was being shipped to another prison in Missouri. He had been in a fight and hurt the dude pretty bad. To this day, Sincere still holds a major part of my heart, but we could never be together.

I arrive in Gainesville early evening. The temp is decent for early February. I make a post on Facebook. Make a few phone calls. Send multiple texts. Start my quick visits to a few friends I haven't seen in years and get them pumped for tonight. I do some last minute errand running. Make the call and head to Leroy house that is throwing the party for me. I have been living in South Florida now for over 8 years. Anything below 60 is freezing to me. The temp has now dropped to 40 and steady dropping. I call Leroy as I turn into the apartment complex to make sure the heat is on and to tell him to have the door open. I park quickly. Grab my shit and Carl Lewis run in his house. To my surprise, there is a huge birthday sheet cake on the table for me. It is the prettiest, sweetest cake ever. The music is pumping. We are sipping drinks. Showering and getting dressed. Everybody is dressed, smelling and looking good. Unfortunately we have to take separate cars. I have my niece Brooke and homegirl Stoney to pick up. Leroy has to be to the club early to make sure the DJ gets in and does sound check and get my cake there in one piece. Phone calls are coming in left and right, checking to see if I'm really in town and to let me know they are on their way to the club. I left Gainesville in 2002 after the Feds picked up Sincere, so I don't come to Gainesville often. I scoop the girls. Crank the music up. We sip on our drinks and head down University Avenue to Club Envy. I have on a fitted red dress. Black heels with the matching black clutch. Hair freshly dyed and hanging on my shoulders. We park and quickly run across the street to the club as that Hawk is head busting that night. When we walk in and the ambiance is electric. The club is semi packed. The music is bumping, with a strong bass beat stomping through the speakers. Everyone seems to be enjoying themselves and appear even happier when I walk through the door.

There are a few people on the dance floor getting down. I haven't had enough drinks in me to take my heels off and put on my Dr. Scholl's so I could join them. The drinks start coming from all my friends and more and more people are coming into Club Envy. I'm opening gifts and steady throwing back shots and drinks. That liquor is starting to talk to me and tell me that my toes ain't crunched up in my high heel shoes like 300 Mexicans on an old school bus trying to cross the border. I get out on that dance floor and baby, momma is tearing it up. I dance to about 3 or 4 songs back to back before I beg for my niece to get my Dr. Scholl's out my clutch. I slide them puppies on and hot damn, I'm on! The night goes on with more drinking. More friends and strangers showing up to the club. One of those strangers was this fine, thickly built, brown skin Adonis. He is in the back of the club holding up the wall, wearing me down with his eyes. That liquor tells me to go over there strike up conversation and it goes from there. We start to dance and really get into the groove with one another's body when I start seeing paper falling all around me and I hear my niece Brooke screaming "BACK UP BACK UP BACK UP". It startles me, so I push old boy to get him away from me so I can see what is going on with my niece. Brooke is bent over on the dance floor picking up the paper and stuffs it into my bra and tells me to go back to dancing. I know I'm still trying to figure out what is going on when the sexy Adonis grabs my hand and asks for a slow dance. We dance and in the blink of an eye, he is gone! The music is still pumping. The club owner sends over a magnum bottle of Moet with the sparkler on it. I'm so drunk and into the mood that Leroy has to run up on stage to grab the bottle. I'm lifting it up to take a picture but I'm about to set off the automatic sprinkler system. Hell, they should know not to give a drunk some fireworks around open sprinklers. I open the big bottle of Moet and share with all those in close proximity to me. Now it's time to cut the cake. I hear singing of Happy Birthday and my eyes well up with tears. I'm so overfilled with love and of course, liquor. We cut the cake, open gifts and get back to the party.

The clubs close in Gainesville at 2am, so by 1:30 they are calling for last call of alcohol and trying to usher people out the door like cattle by 1:45. I vaguely remember people trying to get me and my stuff together to leave the club but the music was still pumping, somehow or another the liquor was still flowing in my cup and that liquor told me it was not time to leave MY birthday party. I'm still jamming with my Dr. Scholl's flats and drinking. The next thing I remember is picking my shit up off the sidewalk. It isn't until the following week that Brooke and Stoney tell me the entire story and I just die from embarrassment. Security picked me up under my arms, turned around, had someone open the door while he carried me and my shit out the club, put me on the sidewalk and slammed the door behind me. How the hell I get put out my own party? At least he didn't throw me down on the sidewalk. Ole too tall, hungry hippo nose, thumb built bastard. Remember the paper that was falling and Brooke stuffed it in my bra? Somebody was behind me making it rain and Brooke made sure no one picked up my money. When I finally got up the next day and remember that she stuffed something in my bra, I started digging and pulled out a total of $280! ~~Ain't That Bout'a Bitch~~

Birthday 2012 rolls around and I want to do it bigger and better than last year when I was personally picked up by security and placed out on the freezing sidewalk with all my shit. Gainesville was very cold February night. FSU has once again annihilated the Gators. Obama is still president. Gas is still high as giraffe pussy. A dozen eggs and a loaf of bread cost you an arm, leg and 2 pinky toes, but I'm still going to have one helluva birthday blowout regardless of a recession. It's me, my niece Brooke and my homegirl Renee drinking, laughing and getting ready to have the best night of our life or so I thought. The night starts off with some strongest shots you have ever wrapped your lips around. The liquor is strong; it fights off the cold Hawk that is beating down the front door of Brooke's apartment trying to gain entry. The laughing, joke telling and gossip continues as Brooke, Renee are almost ready for the VIP birthday party at Club Vault.

Upon arrival at Club Vault, we are escorted upstairs to VIP where there is a table full of top shelf liquor, ice and a vast array of chasers to our liking. We instantly start pouring drinks and flicking it up. The night goes on and on with awesome music being spun by the Dj. People from all over the club coming to the VIP section and showing love to the ladies, especially me, the birthday girl. This is where everything starts taking a turn for the worse. You see, Brooke punk ass is suppose to be the designated driver for me because it's my birthday, but Brooke gets straight twisted and curls up on the couch in VIP and starts snoring louder than the music. Renee is raping all the men that come by and daring they ass to say something like she is the prison bully on Oz and my poor little ignant ass is drunk as hell, still flicking it up not thinking the worse is yet to happen. I can deal with a sleeping drunk and a heffa trying to give away a little drunk cooda. Seems like a normal night, right?

It's now about 1:45 and club security does a walk around telling everyone it is now time to go; "You ain't gotta go home, BBUUTT you gotta GET THE FUCK OUTTA HERE". As those words are being spoken, I'm shaking Brooke like she is a Yoohoo. She is in a deep comatose sleep on the couch and I can't get her to wake up for shit. Renee has a cool homeboy of mine hemmed up in the corner trying to give him some drunk pussy. All I can hear is my homeboy screaming, "Yooooo B! Come get cha girl!" in his thick New York accent and his hands in the air. I throw my hand up at him like I'm swatting flies and I continue begging for help to get the drunkards down stairs. How I make it to the car and able to drive it to the back door of the club, only God knows. As I'm driving up, security is carrying Brooke, my niece old drunk ass downstairs and somebody is escorting Renee drunk fighting ass to the car. Brooke is placed in the front seat and continues her slobbing and snoring expedition while Renee is fighting everybody like an Alley cat and throwing up at the same time. Finally the fighting and throwing up stops, but the snoring has increased from Brooke.

I pull out from the club and join the growing traffic on University Ave as all the clubs are letting out at the same time. I'm pumped and ready to continue celebrating my birthday but how so when I have Mike Tyson in the back seat ready to fight, continuing to throw up and my snoring drunk ass designated driver niece. All I keep thinking is "Go as fast as you can to get them home, and then hit the streets DOLO". Renee decides that traffic isn't moving fast enough for her, so she decides to open the door of the stopped car and fall out right in the middle of University Ave by Gator Beverage. I start screaming and asking for help to get her back in the car. I'm drunk as hell and don't want to draw any unnecessary attention to myself from the infamous Gainesville police department. Two sweet men assist me in placing Renee back in the car and all is fine for a few minutes. I pull up to the red light at the very busy intersection of University Ave and 13th Street. I'm the first car at the red light. Once the light turns green for me to pull off, I punch it to 25mph. Renee decides she wants to open the door again to feel the fresh air directly and falls out face first and tumbles down University Ave like a stunt double for Starsky and Hutch.

I'm so damn drunk and don't realize what has happened until I hear tire screeching and loud screams. When I hear the screams and tire screeching, I realize the dome light is on in the car. Even though I don't know Brooke's car that well, I know the dome light shouldn't be on. All occupants are in the car and the doors are locked and shut. I stop looking up at the dome light that is on and focus my attention on the open back door and wonder why its open when all I of a sudden I see the seat is empty that should be holding Renee. The tire screeching and screams make sense now as I pull over and run back to help Renee drunk ass out the middle of University Ave and 13th Street. In my drunk thinking, I figure I can run back 15 – 20 feet, pick up Renee, put her back in the car and speed her home as if nothing has happened. By the time I run this play through my head and actually make it in front of Renee, it's about 1000 GPD officers already on the scene. Being the true, drunk driving friend I am and not wanting to get hit with a DUI on my birthday. I pick Renee up under her arms. She is heavy as shit but I walk her ass like a refrigerator over to the corner and politely prop her up against the pole. Some big fat white, Buick body built ass heffa had the nerves to say to the police, "I think someone pushed her from a moving car!" What the fuck? Heffa don't say that shit, that somebody pushed her from a moving car. She was about to get a straight Rodney King beat down, but the Po Po was standing there. Renee is swollen, bloody and banged up pretty good looking like she just went 5 rounds with Mike Tyson and Thomas "Hit Man" Hearns and lost. All she can say as she is looking up to me is, "I'm sorry for running your birthday Betty. Betty please forgive me because I'm really sorry Betty!" I clinch my teeth so hard they are about to break and I scream whisper to her, "Shut the fuck up and stop saying my damn name!" Once I make sure she is ok and being tendered too by the police and EMT's on the scene, I hear her telling the police she is ok, she just wants to go home. A GPD officer out the blue asks me, "Is that your car parked in the middle of the road?" I gently answer, "Yes sir." I slowly walk away trying not to be detected as a potential DUI offender. I get into the car and easy as Sunday morning, blend in with the traffic and bend the corner by the church on University Ave across from the University of Florida. Just as I bend the corner, and see a set of frantically flashing lights behind me. I start to freak out. The cops have caught me and I'm going to jail. I pull over. Get out the car and have my head hung low when I hear a familiar voice say, "Betty, get that liquor out of your car!" I'm already in panic mode and say, "Where the fuck DID THAT LIQUOR COME FROM?" We put the liquor, well actually, Kong put the liquor in his car and we split up like Vivica Fox and Jada Pinkett did in Set It Off because the police are now circling the block real slow like they are looking for me.

I'm ready to shit a golden brick. Instead I find some bushes and trees and duck off in the dark of the night with the drunk ass Brooke still snoring, slobbing and farting in the passenger seat. Brooke only woke up once during this whole ordeal to say "Calm down Betty, everything will be ok" and then drifted back into a deep drunk sleep. I so desperately wanted to 1-800-CHOKE DAT HO but I didn't. How I found these bushes is still beyond me. I found some bushes and trees that were directly in front of some duplexes in the student ghetto. I was able to slide the Nissan Altima right into a tight spot right in the front door of someone's apartment and hide from the police. I'm hiding in the bushes with the heat blowing and jacket covering the dash board in hopes of not give away our location just in case the PoPo was riding and looking for me. I called one true homeboy who I love to death and will give that nigga whatever he want for saving my life that night. Trick Daddy Dollars got out of his bed at 3:30am in 20 degree weather, found me ducked off in the bushes like a slave chasing freedom and followed me to Brooke house so I can drop her drunk ass off, hop in my own shit and find something to eat. Now the entire time I'm on the way to Brooke house, I'm on the phone with Brooke's baby daddy, Alejandro Mexican ass. I'm crying and telling him what has happened and that I need him to meet me down stairs and help get drunky poo up the stairs. For some reason I can't find my shoes or purse and I'm hysterical.

I'm crying and losing my damn mind. Something keeps telling me I hear an echo and snickering on the phone the entire time I'm on the phone with Alejandro but I don't pay it any attention. I'm just trying to get from the East side of town to the west side without seeing any GPD officers. I make it to the house. Get this drunken sleeping heffa up the stairs. I see the smirk and damn near uncontrollable laughter that is trying to escape from Alejandro but I don't pay his inner tube floating ass to America no attention. I hop in my car and hit the Sports bar, but it's kinda dead or maybe my nerves were too bad to fully enjoy the atmosphere. I run over to Ihop have breakfast then head back to the house.

I'm pretty sure you can only imagine the true hysteria going on that night, with all the crying, screaming, ducking and hiding in the bushes hiding from the police. The next morning, Brooke and I check the booking blotter to see if Renee has been arrested and call the area hospitals trying to locate her, being that I did leave her ass on the curb with da PoPo. While Brooke and I are trying to locate Renee, Alejandro is trying to be funny and has the TV turned to the show Jail and the volume turned to the max. I almost called INS on his ass since he wanted to be a comedian. I get scared all over again and decide to leave town for a few hours. I head south to St. Pete to see my dad and hide out just in case they call out the SWAT looking for me and I have to shoot it out like the OK corral.

A few hours later Rene calls and states she is fine. She is still highly apologetic, hurting like a mutha fucker and don't know what made her open the door and decide to tuck, duck and roll out of a moving car like an unpaid stunt double. She is looking for her jacket, purse, phone and the Mack truck that ran over her ass. I explain to Renee that I'm not in town and I can have Brooke meet her somewhere to drop off her personal belongings, you know to keep the police from knowing where I'm staying for the weekend and to keep my niece out of any trouble or possibility of having to snitch on me. While we are talking, I'm sitting in my dad's ice cold house dropping sweat the size of a newborn baby trying to figure out if Renee is trying to set me and my family up or is she genuinely just trying to retrieve her belongings. I tell her to sit tight and I will have Brooke call her and set everything up. I spend some more time with my dad and step mom telling them what happened. In between laughs, they tried to show some concern, but I saw right through that shit and knew them Negros was dying laughing at me. I get on the road back to Gainesville about 8. Brooke and I have plans to hit the streets again but without Renee and go to Ocala. I call Brooke and give her all the details of the call and she assures me not to worry. She will handle it.

I make it back to town and just as I'm sliding into town a friend of mine calls and wants to meet so he can give me my birthday present. We meet at Dunkin Donuts on Archer Rd. He gives me an awesome gift and we grab a cup of Joe as I put in to tell him about the night before. As I'm telling him the story from the night before, my phone rings and it's Brooke. I panic. I start sweating profusely again and my heart races. I answer the phone and all I hear is the background conversation of her and Renee. I sit quiet for a few minutes listening to the conversation. When there is a pause I say, "Brooke is that Renee? Is the police with her?" Brooke apparently has her ear piece in and responds real quickly, "Yes and No!" I take in a deep breath and exhale with goose bumps all over my body. I'm still listening to them talk, but Renee sounds muffled or if there is something wrong with the ear piece. I ask Brooke, "How does Renee look?" Before I can get the last word out good, Brooke responds with a, "DDDAAAAMMMMMMMMMNNN!!!" I fall out laughing hysterically. I can only imagine what the hell this heffa look like 24 hours later. I feel better about everything now and tell Brooke I'm on my way to her house so we can get ready to go out. Brooke responds, "10-40 Shawty" and hangs up.

I'm so relieved the police ain't looking for me. I make it to the house and ask Brooke to tell me how Renee looked. I was crying, laughing, farting and gasping for air. Brooke say Renee look like she got in a serious fight with the concrete and the concrete went MMA on that ass with no mercy. Renee mouth was swollen to the size of a cantaloupe and she was trying to conceal it with a rag. Her head had multiple lumps like she was a male deer trying to sprout antlers. When she said that, I was too done and had to go lay down and try to get my energy back so we could go out that night. When Brooke and I went out that night in Ocala, we didn't have any problems or accidents. Everything was going to smooth for me, so I asked that we go get something to eat and go home. It had been a long birthday weekend and I just wanted to make it back to Ft. Lauderdale safe and sound without a felony!

Renee understands why I had to leave her on the curb that night and beat it like Michael Jackson. With my job as an assistant supervisor for the Department of Children and Families, I couldn't and still can't afford an arrest or blemish on my record. When she held her own against the police who kept badgering her to tell her what happened, who was driving and she didn't budge, she earned a place in my heart forever and can get a kidney if needed! Till this day we are all still very close friends and we talk all the time and hangout when I come to Gainesville, but Renee can only ride with us if she is in a booster seat, seat beat and the child safety locks are on the door with the windows rolled up and locked. Ain't nobody got time to be fucking around with her wanna be stunt double ass or the police.

When I have to travel down NW 13th Street and University Ave I cringe and then I bust out in a thunderous laughter and thank God for his favor.

Brooke is still with the ole wanna be Mexican. Remember I told you I heard an echo on the phone when I was talking to him. Well it turns out Alejandro was recording our conversation on his Iphone and played it back for us that Sunday when we were looking for Renee in the local hospitals and jail. While Alejandro monkey ass is playing Dj with the recorded conversation, Brooke is all over the floor laughing uncontrollably while I'm trying to laugh in between a river of tears. Have you ever seen someone crying with the dry heaves and trying to laugh at the same time? If you have, that was me that morning. If I could have and not got cut in the process, I would have jumped on the little illegal alien for playing so damn much and having that incriminating evidence. As much as I love my niece and still kick it with her when I come to town, she can't ever be my designated driver to a damn place, ole drunk ass heffa ~~Ain't That Bout'a Bitch~~

Chapter 11

CRYSTAL BALLS ON THE WALL

It's early spring 2012. I had been single for some time and everybody was trying their hardest to hook me up with friends, cousins, uncles, brothers or even the local dude on the corner who looked like he didn't have shit else to do at the time. I wasn't dating anybody seriously but that didn't mean I wasn't getting some special attention every now and again.

I have always had 2 stylists. It depends on what type of look I'm going for. Every day wear or if I had a special black tie affair to attend as to which stylist I would go to. When I want my nice classic, clean cut wash, hot oil deep condition, wrap, up do or roller set; I would always hit up my good and faithful stylist Nia at Dolly's New Image in Ft Lauderdale. We would have a drink; catch up on the gossip all while getting my wig split and just enjoying sisterly love. Now, when I want the braids, buns or the latest hood style, but in a classy way; I hit up my girls Ashley Sweets or Crystal at 5 Star Spa and Salon in Delray Beach, Fl. Ashley Sweets is fire on a sista head with braids, sew-ins or anything you can think of. Just show her a picture of what you want and she got you. Now her momma Crystal, is the female Edward ScissorHands with some hair shears. You want a tight, slick, sleek cut, see Crystal and I promise you won't be disappointed!

One day I went in for some goddess braids and got to telling the girls about my latest man drought and how I had went bowling with some busta who was so cheap he felt that since had paid the little $7 for us to bowl, I should buy all the alcoholic drinks and food for the evening. Now I'm nice, don't get me wrong, but got damn mutha fucker, you only paid $7 for bowling which included shoe rental and now you can't spring for a few drinks and something to chew on while I bust your ass in bowling!

156

Needless to say, we never ever went out again and hell nah I ain't buy his ass one damn drank!!

In the process of telling my story, I see Crystal face change instantly from laughing with tears, to her face scrunching up like backed up traffic on 95 South at 5pm on a payday Friday afternoon. Ashley is putting that fire to my head putting in my goddess braids, so I'm sitting there trying to be cool and not show that I'm about to cry when Crystal says to me, "I have the perfect guy for you. He is tall, likes to work out, owns his own home, has 2 cars and works at the cement company so you know he making that money." He is sounding good as hell on paper. I ask all the important questions such as is he married, dating, girlfriend, crazy baby momma, any kids, how many kids, has he been to prison and is he gay or bi and does she have any pics of him for me to see. Crystal come back with a smirk on her face, I should have known then something wasn't right with the way she came smirking and telling me about this perfect man. Crystal responds, "No he isn't married he just went through a very messy divorce but he ain't bitter. He has kids and they are older so he ain't paying child support and no crazy baby momma drama. Trust me boo he is really good people and the only pics I have of him are on his Facebook page that he don't post on that much." I jump up out the chair and ask her to pull up his page so I can see what I'm working with. He is nice looking, tall, a lot slimmer than what I prefer, but something about the pic of him in that tux and the pressure from them goddess braids Ashley is putting on my head that makes me have a temporary moment of insanity and say, "Send him a pic of me, see what he say and lets go from there!"

I send Crystal a few recent pics from my phone to hers so she can send them to him. I sit in the shop having a few drinks and talking while we wait on him to text back. Time rocks on and I have stuff to do, so I tell Crystal to hit me up if he hits her back.

I get a phone call from Crystal about an hour or so later and she is screaming in the phone, "Girl, Ariel just came up here in the cement truck asking if you were still here because he wanted to meet you in person. He say he was in Broward making a drop when we texted him earlier and couldn't get to the phone quick because they aren't allowed to use the phone while driving. He asked me to ask you, if it was ok for me to give him your phone number?" Well now I'm flattered and amped up to meet him. I tell Crystal to give him my number and let's see what is really going on.

That particular night, I had a date and wasn't readily available when Ariel called, but the voice mail he left was very nice and intriguing. I couldn't wait to call him the first chance I had. Before I could get up the next morning, my texts alerts start going off like crazy. I turned the ringer off and went back to sleep. My ass was dragging. Not dragging in a good way, but because I had to get drunk in order to deal with my online date from the night before. I had been cat-fished in a major way and had to get drunk in order to show my face in one of my favorite restaurants. You already know I was not about to leave without getting my belly full and my drink on. His online profile made him seem like an Adonis, especially with the pictures he posted of a tall, thick, fine, pissy red ass man with his shit together. The phone conversations and texts were always on point. He really knew how to make a sista feel damn good. As bad as I don't want kids. I thought about it with him. He was saying, looking and doing all the things needed, or so I thought. I get to the restaurant a few minutes early to survey the scene. To see and be seen before my actual dates get there. You never know what other potential mates may be lurking. Once I survey, get my eye full and fill up plenty of eyes, I venture back outside, post up in my curve hugging, deep v cut, brown and white striped, sleeveless dress with coordinating brown platform stilettos and clutch. I have these curves shining in the moonlight, so when he walks up all he can do is drool. I see this man pull up in an old Buick with dents, faded paint with smoke coming out the back. He pulls up to valet to have them park this shit. I laugh and say to myself, "Go head playa, I ain't mad at cha." I don't pay him any attention. My date drives a Jaguar. I turn my head back to the beautiful scenery not thinking about the Buick or the man who just got out of it, when I hear someone say my name. I know that I have surveyed the scene inside the restaurant and no other car has pulled up. In dramatic white woman movie form, I dramatically turn my head to have my hair flow and blow in the wind and have that dramatic flair.

When I finally finished with my Gone with the Wind head turn, I damn near broke my neck and ankles trying to get a better look at this short, stumpy, gimp wanna be cool pimp daddy walking monstrosity. Girl, he was short, round, with a George Jefferson hair doo. His slacks were 2 sizes too big and wrinkled, his shirt didn't match and was made of ribbed stretched material had the beaded knots on it from washing the cheap material too often and was 3 sizes too small and had the nerve to tucked into his pants with a belt on that was cracking and old as hell.

Now this is a pivotal point, where some serious decisions need to be made. Do I stay eat, drink everything on the menu for wasting my time and energy to get here and getting Ms. Sunshine all ready for a possible long night of ecstasy only to be let down by Yoda who apparently thought he was going to get lucky that night by the Grinch smile he had on his face. Little did he know that if ever did dare to touch me, I would stick his little stank ass itchy dick in the nearest electric socket while he stands in a bucket of water. He grabs my arm and slides his hand down to try and hold my hand. I close my hand to make a fist. I'm about to hit this fool with a serious right upper cut and then a quick gut check. I'm steaming. I just want this part of my night to be over, when I say fuck it, let me make Yoda look good and at least get something out of this besides being hotter than a volcano.

The hostess remembers me from earlier, smirks with her eyes rapidly moving back and forth like the ball in a pin ball machine and asks us where we would like to be seated. Remember I had already surveyed the scene earlier when I got to the restaurant and noticed that the outside by the water was pretty empty. I spoke up and suggested we sit out back by the water so we could have more privacy to become better acquainted. Low and behold, the patio area has become quit crowded. The hostess slowly walks us through the entire restaurant. By the bathroom, through the kitchen, the bar and then seats us dead smack in the middle of everyone who seem to have stopped eating, chewing and breathing as they see this monstrosity of a date walk behind me. I was so embarrassed. Our waiter came very quickly and before he could offer a formal greeting and tell us his name, I blurted out, "Hi love, may I have a double shot of chilled Patron, salt and lime and a double of Titos vodka with 3 ice cubes and a splash of pineapple juice. By the time you come back, we will be ready to order!" This bastard actually had the nerve to say, "I love a woman who knows what she wants and isn't afraid to go after it." What kind of trouble do you think we can get into after dinner?"

You know my jaws got tight and hard like I had a mouth full of rocks because I was just about to cuss his natural born ugly black ass out when the waiter walks back up with my drinks and asks if I was ready to order. I ordered the Osso Buco, rice pilaf and seasonal veggies. He ordered fish. Conversation was very nil during dinner until I just couldn't take it anymore. I had to know why he posted pictures of someone else online, got me all gassed up and thinking I had found someone I could actually chill with and see what develops. This fool said, "Most the time the women that I do meet, look just as fucked up as I do, so we end up dating and kicking it a little while, I get some. Then after awhile we get tired of one another and break up, then I'm back on line. When I met you, I thought and figured it would be different, like I had met a real woman, guess it's over now huhh?" He was trying to look and sound pathetic, that shit didn't work. I summoned the waiter over to bag my dinner and bring the check. I waited until that check was paid for and said, "Nigga you have literally snatched the drause off Geesus if you think I'm about to date your lying, ugly ass. It's not that you're ugly. You're a big ass liar and I don't have, space, time or energy for that shit." I had to ask him one more question before I left, "Who was the person I was talking to on the phone, because your voice sounds different?" He said it was him and that he works very hard every day looking in the mirror talking to himself getting a certain talk and sound down. I had heard enough, I got my semi drunk ass up, sashayed through the restaurant to valet. I didn't even let the baby go get my car. I saw it, asked for my keys, tipped him and did the 100 yard dash to my shit. I was so fucking mad at him, I could have been out somewhere else doing something else. My biggest pet peeve is wasting my damn time. Time is the only thing in this world that is priceless and that we can't ever get back once wasted.

When I finally get up a few hours later and turn my ringer back on, I notice I have a few missed calls and waiting texts from Ariel. I hit him back and tell him that once I'm out the shower and have eaten I will call him. When I do call Ariel, he has this sexy baritone voice that most definitely matches his pictures. We talk for almost 2 hours and I'm enjoying his conversation. He is telling me all about himself and what he likes to do and just the normal stuff you talk about when you first meet someone so it was cool. With him living in Delray and me in Lauderdale, it's only about a 20 minute ride, but for some reason it wasn't always easy to coordinate time to hangout due to my work schedule, workout routine and him always having something to do with the fellas or going out of town with a homie or anything that prevented him from seeing me in person. Even with me going to church in Delray proved to be taxing to see him. We keep talking and a few weeks have rolled by and we are in contact, just yet to meet. One night during conversation the subject of sex comes up. I figure we are grown and can talk about anything so I tell him what I like and that I love head. This bastard makes a vomit sound. Twice. I get concerned and yell in the phone, "Ariel ARIEL are you ok? What's wrong sweetie? Are you ok?" He clears his throat and said, "Just at the mention of eating pussy I get sick. I have thrown up on a girl when I tried to eat her." My whole world just got flipped upside down, but hold on, it gets worse. I'm stunned and not really knowing what to say. He starts the conversation back up and asks me, "Betty do you like anal?" Now I'm putting 2 and 2 together and I ask him the million dollar question before I answer him, "Have you ever been to prison?" Like it wasn't nothing Ariel says, "Yeah, I been home almost 2 years after serving 13 years in the feds and I had also been to the state for 5 almost 6 years."

Now it make sense as to why he never has any time and is always hanging with the fellas verse trying to make time with me, why he vomits at the mere mention of eating pussy and why he likes anal this bastard is gay as hell. I just say, "Ohh ok, well lemme hit you back in a few minutes I need to take care of something before I go to bed." When I hung up the phone, you know he went on block instantly. I texted Crystal, "The very next time I see you Missy Poo, oohhhhh Imma put a whole bucket of perm on your eyelashes!" She replies, "ROFLMAO what did I do?" I didn't even respond. I just showed up there that Saturday and told her and everybody in the salon the story. There wasn't a dry eye in there, including mine. We was laughing soo hard, we were crying because they all knew him. We had a blast as usual in the salon, but today was different. I gave Crystal a hug and told her, "If you ever try to hook me up with anybody else, I promise to hang you upside down to the wall by your balls! Keep on."

After telling the girls what happened with Ariel, my baby Ashley Sweets tried her hand at hooking me up and that shit went downhill just as quick as it went up. I was in the shop getting a sew-in, when this very handsome, 5'10, semi bow legged red bone walked in with his young son and daughter. He and the son got a haircut while Crystal styled the little girls hair. We keep making eye contact but never really saying anything to one another, just the shy smile and head nod. I whisper and ask Ashley, "Is he single? What's the deal with him?" She says, he owns his own HVAC Company and she thinks he is single. Since she is almost finished with my hair, I asked to find out his credentials when I leave, see if he interested and text me when she finished. I hadn't even made it to 95 when Ashley texted, "I didn't even have to ask him anything. Soon as you walked out he started asking about you. He is single, just those 2 kids and I already gave him your#." I was like BET. Let's see what this do.

Later that night he calls me and become better acquainted. His name is Teddy. He's 38, sold his HVAC Company, currently in school for nursing. Sounds pretty good so far right? Hold on it gets better. He only has the 2 kids I saw for right now. I stopped him right there and asked for better clarification and here comes the good stuff. He is currently in an on and off again 9 year relationship the mother of his 7 year old son and in a cool decent relationship with the mother of his 4 year old daughter who is currently 5 months pregnant with his child now. Not only is she preggo. She is relocating from South Carolina to be closer to him and is cool as hell with his current on/off again 1st baby momma. This fool say, they hangout and kick it like best friends. I couldn't even hide it. I was straight up and said, "I'm really happy for you and your family but I don't have time for this. Thank you for your time and I wish you the best of luck." I couldn't press the end button quick enough to get his silly cock slanging ass off that phone. I knew right then and there, homie had a dick that was out of my league. Let me stay in my lane in the pee wee league. Fucking with him and that major league dick would have me pregnant, hop scotching backwards down 95 in rush hour traffic, butt bookey ass naked, baying at the sun, looking for him with a flood lamp in the day time. Ohhh No ma'am Pam that just ain't gonna work for me.

I went back to the shop again, this time to threaten Ashley, that if she ever listened to me again about hooking me up with anybody, I would put perm on her eyelashes and hang her and her momma to the wall by their balls if they ever tried to hook me up again. When I told them the twisted fantasy ole boy was living, nobody wanted any parts of that dick either. ~~Ain't That Bout'a Bitch~~

CHAPTER 12

IT'S ELECTRIC

Since moving to South Florida, I searched endlessly for the right church home. I went to church after church, never ever really feeling like that is where God and my spirit joined as one. One day at work I was talking with a coworker and she started to tell me about the sermon from the previous day. We both laughed about the humor the pastor chose to use to bring the message home and agreed that we all need more love in our life with understanding. She then proceeded to invite me to her church, "I would love for you to come visit my church one Sunday. The name is Church of Christ in Delray. Here is the address and my cell number if you get loss!" My eyes beamed with delight. I was having a terrible time finding a Church of Christ home. The 1st time I went there, I sat on the 2nd pew with my coworker and the rest of the older ladies and I have been there ever since and that has been since 2008. The tutelage I have received from Dr. Clover has truly been instrumental in the development of my growth and well-being as a Christian and all around better person. All Glory to God for choosing this man to deliver his word. The bible states, "Many are called, few are chosen!"

At Church, I sit directly up front on the 2nd pew with all the sweet, classy and well refined older ladies. You can best believe that they give me a good laugh every Sunday. One Sunday, one of the ladies of the church stood at the front of the church and gave out handmade felt crosses and little bows that you could pin on yourself. She gave me her humble gifts. I gave her a hug and quickly went to my seat as church was getting ready to start. On the seat with me, Mr. Kenny sits on the end, Mrs. Dolly sits on his left and I sit next to her. On the pew behind us sits Ms. Berta Mae and Ms. Mae Belle. I call them Thelma and Louise because they are very outspoken, funny and keep the song leader and preacher in line. Mrs. Dolly and her hilarious husband Mr. Kenny, both who are up in age about late 60's early 70's. They are one of the sweetest couples I have ever met and the epitome of marrying your best friend. I can only hope and Pray to one day have a marriage like them. Now Mrs. Dolly is the truly a southern Church going woman, with the big, oversized hats, 20lb brightly colored Church suits, her matching bag and shoes. You can best believe don't nothing be out of place with her or her outfit and please don't think for one minute that Mr. Kenny don't be clean as the white walls on a 57' Chevy.

Service is almost over and I'm fumbling with my felt cross that the lady gave to me earlier in the morning before service started, when Mrs. Dolly leans over to Mr. Kenny and asks, "Kenny, where is your cross? Without missing a beat Mr. Kenny pats his crouch and says, "It's right here baby and whenever you want to pray, it'll be right there!" Before I knew it, I had laughed so loud and had to duck my head in embarrassment. Mrs. Dolly laughed and hit Mr. Kenny in his arm and told him, "Tighten up Kenny!" It was too late; Mr. Kenny had already spoke his peace and meant every word of it.

Its mid-2010. Close to the time Cleophus is about to move out. Cleophus and I had been living in separate rooms for some time now and I was well on my way into moving on with my life and had already started dating. I met a few people online as usual and others at various places that I would go. I'm pretty sociable and rarely ever meet a stranger. I'm very fun and open person. One day after church, one of the older single men in the church approaches me and ask for a few minutes of my time to talk. I oblige him. I had seen around the church on the usher board and a few other ministries, not to mention he was a fairly decent looking older man. You can tell that he was truly the business back in his day. He was about 6'2, dark skinned, slim build with some of the prettiest salt and pepper hair you had ever seen and in his mid to late 60's. He seemed like a man's man. I never really saw him caught up in Church foolishness and gossip, so that made him even more attractive and appealing. He asked if we could exchange numbers and maybe do lunch one day. Now you already know once he mentioned free food, I was all ears. We exchange numbers and talk later that evening and became somewhat better acquainted. He was originally from South Carolina. Older children, paid off home and 2 cars. Our initial conversation went so well, we decided to meet for lunch at Olive Garden the following Tuesday. In preparation of this date, you know I hit the mall and got this hot all white Capri jacket suit set. I paired it with a silk ruffle red shirt, matching shoes and coordinating clutch. I'm thinking a man after God's own heart, older, ready to settle down and just live the good life, let me get my shit together and make it happen.

During the day he can't text or talk because he drives a cement truck and I totally understand and respect that. The day we decide to meet for lunch he is off, so we are texting back and forth getting ready for our 1pm date. 1pm arrives and I'm almost to the restaurant. I can never leave on time. My job as Sr. Fraud Investigator kept me busy and running and not always on my time. I only had so many days to start, build and close a case. I get to Olive Garden and he is there waiting for me looking rather dapper and better outside of church. We hug briefly before the hostess takes us to our table. We sit down; talk a little more when all of a sudden I'm hearing a real thick deep south Cackalacky accent. Those from the north and south Carolinas speak Gullah or as we like to call it, Geechee. Don't get me wrong, there isn't anything wrong with it. I just didn't hear it in our original conversation and it's now starting to throw me off. The waitress comes back and takes our order. I start with Kendall Jackson Chardonnay, the soup and a nice veal parmesan. He orders the soup as well and a chicken dish.

We are still talking, but I'm starting to get aggravated. His accent is coming out really thick and it's hard to understand him. I play it cool and squint my eyes real tight like that's going to make it easier for me to understand what he is saying, but that didn't work. I take the last sip of my wine just as the waitress comes by to check on us and I request another glass. The waitress and I turn to Mr. Carolina just as he is turning up the soup bowl to his lips and sucking out the rest of the soup. I damn neared cried a river so I could swim right up outta there. I was so embarrassed I didn't know what to do or say. The waitress turns to me and is looking at me like, "Where the fuck you got this nigga from?" Instead of him handing the freshly sucked clean bowl to the waitress, he plops it back down on the table and of course, just because this is the way my luck is set up, a nice size amount of soup jumps out and on the sleeve of my all white jacket.

I'm done. I'm not sure if he was nervous or if that was just him, but I'm totally turned off and ready to go back to work and listen to more lies from clients who are trying not to see me in court! The meal comes and I just nibble on it a little bit, to try and get this date over. His meal has pasta which I didn't know until the server brings it. When I see pasta, I instantly get scared and with reason. This fool removed the spoon that goes with the pasta to help you wind them up on your fork. Girl listen, when I saw him toss the spoon to the side and ask, "Why would they bring you a spoon with some noodles? I don't need no spoon with my noodles!" This Negro slurped and sucked that pasta as if it was the last and best piece of cooda he has ever had. It wasn't a normal little slurp and sucking, it was the loud sucking slurping sounds you make when you are home by yourself or amongst friends who just overlook yo ignant ass. I ate a few more bites, waved for the waitress to come and asked for a to go box and the check. She nods like, "I got you sis, it's been time to take Koonta home and put him back in the field!" She brings back the to go containers and before she can hand him the check, he is already standing up ready to walk to the front. The waitress and I are looking at each other the "WTF" look on our face when I ask him, "Uhmmm baby, what are you doing? Where are you going?" This fool opened his mouth and said with the most sincere voice, "I'm going up front where we came in at to pay for our meal!" Did this fool just say pay for our meal like we are at Morrison's cafeteria? I just close my eyes, bow my head and say in the calmest voice I can muster up, "You place your form of payment in the bill holder. Give it to the waitress and she handles everything from there." He obliged. I picked up my stained jacket, clutch and Olive Garden bag. Walk out the front door and wait for him on the bench. He comes out shortly and said this was the best date of his life. I don't say one word. I give him a hug and tell him I will call or text him later. I speed walk to my truck. I don't remember cranking her up but somehow or another I jumped the curb backing up and hit another 2 curbs driving out the parking lot. I texted him later that night after I got my thoughts together and replayed everything making sure I wasn't over reacting. I told him I really thought he was a very special guy and he deserved better than I could offer and I hope that we could remain friends. He never responded nor said anything to me in church. Shortly after our little date, he relocated to Miami and then back to the Carolinas. I vowed then to never date another man from the church I attend ever again, I was too embarrassed.

Welp that was short lived. You already know I don't think there is anything wrong with a swagged out jitta bug, who knows how to dress, act in public and talk with proper pronunciation; but there is nothing like his smooth, clean cut, spottie ottie, suave daddy, uncle or granddaddy. To me, older men have gotten a lot of that bullshit out of their system. Have righted their wrongs, learned what it takes to actually please a woman and keep her happy and not just sexually. A lot of the younger guys say they know and understand what it entails, but I don't think they really have the slightest idea what it takes to maintain a real woman and how to keep her attention and focus at home. I may be wrong; I just ain't the one to find out, unless he has a strong back that knows how to curve it like a snake at the right time with a deep thrust to make me want to switch religions and buy his ass the latest Play Station with all the latest games.

I had been going to Church of Christ in Delray Florida for about 5 years and I loved it. I don't know what I would do without my Pastor and Church family. I have grown so much from my Pastor's tutelage and teachings. Since I was a small child going to Church with my grandmother, she would always say, "You go to Church to get God's word, bless the Lord and receive your blessings, so you go in the front door and right out the back door when service is over because some of the biggest lies are told on Church grounds." To this day I live by those same exact words. I walk in the front door of the Church, give my hugs, love and kisses, take my seat and Speedy Gonzalez my fat, black ass right out the back door with no hesitation. When I hear about the gossip or the happenings of the Church, it's during Prayer request and I get the entire scoop from the older ladies I sit up front with.

There is this older more mature, yet very handsome man who attends my Church and fits the bill to a T. He drives a newer model Cadillac. Always dressed sharp, with just the right amount of jewelry on his short, pissy red bow legged ass. During praise and worship he is always full of the spirit, singing and in full brigade for the Lord and not caring who sees him dancing or singing off key. That is a major turn on for me, along with his demeanor and style.

I noticed the spottie ottie always looking at me, smiling and nodding like them ole school players do, but never really paid him any real attention as I didn't want to date that close again, just in case we break up I don't want to look at his ass every damn Sunday and wish you would just stop breathing voluntarily. One day in the spring of 2011 after a great sermon, I'm running out the back door when he runs up behind me, grabs my arm and says, "Sista (with that ole man moan), I have been watching you for over a year now and I love everything I see about you and would love the opportunity to get to know you better." He extended his hand to shake and said, "Hi, my name is Sylvester and you are?" I'm looking around like I'm about to make a drug deal checking to see who is around. I don't like people, especially Church folk in my business unless I put you in it. I extend my hand and say, "Nice to meet you Sylvester, my name is Betty. Thank you for the compliments, hopefully I will see you again next Sunday." He smiled at me all the while still holding my hand, but when I see his teeth I jumped slightly and played it off like something was biting me, so I could free my hand from his grasp because his teeth look like piranha teeth. I guess I never noticed it before, because of how he would always smile just enough to show that he had teeth but not show how he could possibly pull your uterus out giving you a full hysterectomy with one swift bite.

Upon letting my hand go, he stated, "I was hoping I could take you out sometime and talk over a nice dinner and drinks." You already know free drinks and dinner is right up my alley, so I played coy and was like, "Sure sweetie, give me your number and I'll call you soon and set something up." Lil buddy was already set and ready to go, he handed me a business card from the Cadillac dealership where he is a manager and said, "I look forward to hearing from you soon and spending some quality time together getting closer." Being that you know my history with dudes and their teeth, I was not really feeling this but I was like, what the hell. I'm fresh out of a 4yr relationship. Dating but nothing serious, I was tired of seeing chicks who look like a busted can of runny biscuits out with their man and I'm over here with Jethro and his Soul Glow dripping all over my nice clothes and name brand handbags, so what the hell. Let's see what he is talking about since he is a manager at the Cadillac dealership. He looks and dress nice and is on fire for the Lord.

We talk on the phone a lot and text getting better acquainted and as it turns out, he isn't a bad dude. He is pretty cultural and highly intelligent. He is originally from Baltimore and lived a pretty rough life, which lead to becoming one of Baltimore's biggest drug dealers, getting high on his own supply and eventually in prison for a lengthy amount of time. Normally I get the twisted face when a man says he has been in prison. We all have seen Oz! But he states upon his release many years ago, he relocated down to Florida; got his self-cleaned up, finished his education and became a productive citizen. We talk a little more and finally decide to meet up for dinner and drinks at one of the local restaurants in Delray by the beach. He gets there before me and grabs us a table and a simple appetizer. The conversation is going very well between us, just as long as he didn't smile too much, but aside from all that all is fine. Sylvester then expresses his desire to see me again and possibly make me a home cooked soul food meal. I agree and say we will talk later in the week to set up a date.

The following week was particularly grueling for me. I couldn't catch a break for nothing. If it wasn't real deep fraud being committed, it was deadlines to be met for cases being prosecuted and needed all my unwavering attention to ensure the state gets their money back one way or another. Sylvester and I had been texting but had yet to get together for our 2nd date. Finally, I catch a break and hit him up. We agree to Friday night at 8, which gives me plenty of time to get home, relax and get all dolled up. I get to his house and you can smell the groceries out the door and what a wonderful smell it was. He greets me at the door looking very distinguished and it was such a turn on. I walk in and see a house decorated with the most eclectic art work, well-coordinated furniture with the proper accent pillows and decorations. I was highly impressed and turned on at the same time. I didn't want him to know I was turned on, so I grabbed his hand and said, "My love, you have such a wonderful, warm and inviting home. I love it!" He smiled and I winced at the sight of his piranha teeth but tried my hardest not to show my disgust. He gives me a tour of his home and each room is just as incredible as the last. We walk back into the living room where he has the quiet storm playing on the radio. I take a seat on the couch and he asks, "What would you like to drink? I don't have any alcoholic beverages. I'm a recovering addict." On the inside I'm cussing like a sailor. For one, you ain't but a buck twenty with boots on. You was in prison, so I know that didn't work out to well for you. Secondly, you're a recovering addict, which means my alcoholic ass can't get have a taste or two for fearing of your little ass falling off the wagon. His stock has already plummeted and the more I thought about it, it wasn't looking good for pops. I gracefully nod my head and ask for ice tea. He returns and places the glass on the coffee table and we have decent conversation while we wait on dinner to finish.

We are enjoying one another's company, when Sylvester grabs my right hand. Looks me dead square in my eyes and says, "There is something I really need to talk to you about and I'm not sure where to start but I don't want to scare or run you off." You already know I'm thinking the worse but my thoughts stop mid-stream. I feel something in my hand that feels familiar, yet very strange. I don't remember seeing anything wrong with his hand. I try to pull my hand away from him, but he grips my hand while still looking very intensely in my eyes. I try to remove my hand again, this time Sylvester finally speaks up and says, "I have been watching you for some time now and I'm really digging your style. I know I'm older and maybe out of your league but I'm willing to do what needs to be done to get and keep you!" He is still holding my hand when I try once again to remove my hand from his and see what this is in my hand. He finally lets my hand go and says, "Please don't open your hand until I tell you what I have to tell you. I'm in my late 60's. You already know I have been to prison and I'm a recovering heroin addict but there is something I really need to tell you, so you will know what your man is bringing to the table. My dick don't work and I have to use a penis pump whenever I get ready to have sex and I also have to wear a pamper for various health reasons. Go ahead and look in your hand now." I move one finger at a time, with my eyes solely focused on him because I don't know what to expect after all that. I open my hand and there is a fresh, crisp one hundred dollar bill in my hand! I'm confused as to why he put a $100 bill in my hand when I'm only here for dinner and he just told me about his medical conditions. I know I have my blonde moments from time to time, but I'm having a severe blonde moment for real, so I ask him, "Sylvester why are you giving me money?"

Girl, when this fool said these next few words, I felt like running out his house like Penelope Pussycat in the Pepe LePew cartoons. Sylvester cleared his throat and said, "I want to make love to you so bad and taste you but I know I would need to sweeten the deal and make it worth your while. While you sit here and think this over, let me go check on these pots." He walks into the kitchen and I hear him in there banging those pots around a little. The entire time I'm trying to think of an exit strategy that won't have me looking for another church home.

I text 4 people and told them to call me ASAP and act as if something is bleeding and hanging off and they need me to come and run them to the hospital. None of them raggedy bastards called me. I'm still looking for them till this day. So that strategy didn't work. I thought about falling off the couch and pretending I needed immediate medical care, but I'm a punk and too damn scary to hurt myself, so that was out. During all this thinking and plotting, I hear a noise that sounds like a washing machine in his bed room. I don't remember him telling me he was on a breathing machine, iron lung or any other apparatus. I get up look in the kitchen and notice he isn't in the kitchen anymore. I slowly creep down the hall towards the noise to get a better listen and possibly see what is making this noise. The closer I get down the hall, the louder it sounds and baby when I tell you, whatever it is, it's really working and putting in some serious work. It had the sound of a washing machine hooked up to a 405 big block engine in a 57' Chevy. I tip down the hall slow but fast and as quiet as I can. Baby, I bend the corner and see him sitting on the side of the bed butt bookey ass naked working the hell out of that damn penis pump. I'm thinking to myself, it's gotta be electric because ain't no way in hell he is making that much noise with a hand pump, cause he was going to got damn town with that thang. He has a big, pretty piece of red meat, long as it was in the clear sleeve with the suction making it hard. Just as soon as he thought it was hard enough to raise hell, he would pull off the plastic sleeve and that thang would fall over like a newborn baby. He went back and forth with this about 3 or 4 times and he was truly going hard in the paint with sweat on his brow and all. When it appeared that he was about to try it for the 5th time, I slid my fat ass back down that hall to the living room, stared real hard and intense at that $100 bill trying to make a real pimp decision. If he did get hard, it ain't like it would be the worst I've ever had? Maybe he could just eat it?!?!

I placed that $100 bill on the coffee table under one of his very pretty table decorations. I thought about his teeth on my sweet innocent Precious and threw up in my mouth. I unlocked the door as quiet as I could, not that he could hear me over that 405 big block engine in a 57' Chevy penis pump he had roaring in his bedroom. I locked the door and slid right up outta there with ease. I was expecting him to call or text that same night, but he didn't. I went to church extra sanctified that Sunday. When I walked in, I saw him deeply engaged in conversation with one of the brothers of the church. I roller bladed to my seat real smooth, yet quickly. I sat down and tried to appear extra busy filling out my tithes and offering slip before service started. He came over and tapped me on my right shoulder, as I had turned my body with my back towards the congregation. He asks, "What happened and was everything ok?" I looked up at him like I was looking over the rim of some glasses, looked around real quick to see who was looking and sized him up real quick as to say, "If you don't get yo Its Electric, extra small Huggie pamper wearing ass the hell from in front of me before I cut up in the sanctuary, I know something". He never called or texted me again and we have remained silently cordial with one another.

Till this day, we still attend the same church. We don't speak and rarely make eye contact; if we do it's a simple old school head nod and nothing more. Don't get me wrong, there isn't anything wrong with wearing an adult diaper or needing to use a penis pump, just don't bust out the adult pamper, desitin and electric penis pump on me all at once. Shit, work everything in one at a time playa, one at a time or offer more than a measly $100 dollars. Had he offered $1000 that might have made me think a little harder and reconsider some stuff! When I do see him, the thought that runs through my mind is, if we would have hooked up, would I have him stand in front of me to put on the desitin and pamper or place him on a changing table? Was that pump hooked up to an electrical socket or big block engine? Did he know how to work that real pretty piece of meat he has if it ever did get hard? Damn. ~~Ain't That Bout'a Bitch~~

CHAPTER 13

DREAMED DEFERRED

I want to say it was the end of February early part of March 2012, because I remember still being in fear of my life after the whole tuck, duck and roll incident. For some reason I really felt as though the police was coming to my house or job and drag me to jail like Renee had drug herself down University Avenue that night. A week or so passed and I was kind of tired meeting the same ole same running the same ole same game, so I signed up for one of those dating websites whose commercials kept coming on what seemed like every 30 seconds to remind me of how pathetic my dating life was and they could guarantee me a rescue from the walking dead. I answered all the questions, placed some bio information and posted some of my more professional and sexy pictures to elicit some classy and more elite suitors. Once my profile was approved in a matter of minutes, I started receiving flirts, winks and emails. One of the suitors was this good looking, well versed and on paper, highly accomplished man in his late 40's, no kids and all of his teeth. I email him a thought provoking response and it takes off from there. We exchange numbers. Finally hear each other's voices, converse a little more in depth and I'm really digging his convo and what he is representing at this moment.

After talking on the phone, he tells me he is a Colonel in the Air Force Reserves and currently an airline pilot (starting to look damn good to me). He owns a house on the beach, several cars, loves to travel the world and is really ready to settle down and have a child before he turns 50 (SCCRREEEECCCCHHHHH) I almost ran on that comment because you already know I don't want no damn kids, but I'm looking at this from the white woman stand point. Get married, spit out a baby or 2 and become a housewife and live out my days drinking Mojitos by the pool. Anywhooo, we decide to meet for dinner once he flies back in from California. He gets there before I do and is sitting in a black newer model BMW midnight black SUV. He gets out. I get out. We walk across the parking lot and instantly embrace as if we have known one another for years and missed each other tremendously.

The dinner date was filled with great conversation, laughs and speaking of the possibility of a future together; but there was some body language that stood out and didn't really sit too well with me and his odd attraction to a woman having a hairy ass, but I rode out with it until he left the door open and said, "I'm really enjoying your company Betty and I want you to feel free to ask me anything you would like to know since we are finally face to face!" I put the cutest smile on my face, lean in to make him feel more comfortable and ask, "Are you gay, bi or curious?" This mutha fucker got the biggest smile on his face, clutched his chest like he had a triple strand pearl necklace around his neck and said, "OMG! I use to be when I was a young boy and experimented in college. At first it was just touching and feeling, then it got into sucking each other off and penetration!" I'm about to jump out the window of the restaurant and run like a runaway slave with massa and da dawgs on my ass. I don't know what to say or do. I'm sitting there with a half-smile, half gas face looking at this man, who just moments earlier told me how beautiful he thinks I am and how he could see us getting married by the end of the year and having a kid!! He then leans in and states, "The best orgasms I have ever had, have been with men. You know men are either a top or a bottom and I prefer to be a bottom. The pressure you feel when he is in you. The milking of the prostate makes for one helluva orgasm!!" All the while he is telling me this, his eyes have lit up, and his smile is wide and bright as 10 million Christmas lights. I summoned the waiter over to the table and asked for a double shot of chilled Patron, salt, lime and a double shot of Tito's vodka. My stomach is jumping and twirling like Gabby Douglas is in there practicing for the next Olympics. I want him to tell me more because never in all my life have I had a man, who is trying to date me, tell me he likes to suck a dick from time to time.

I get my drinks, finish off my dinner, because you already know I ain't bout pass up no free liquor and dinner. He then asks me if I have ever been with a woman or wanted to be with a woman and I answered "No, I have the same thing they do and don't want those kinds of headaches!" He chuckles and had the nerve to ask me, "Have you ever used a strap on?" When he is asking me this, I'm actually taking a big sip of my vodka and damn near choke trying to take in what he just asked me and drink at the same time. I cough and pound my chest like a gorilla. Tears well up in my eyes, because all I can think is, "WTF did he just ask me? Does he know that all I date is black men who would gladly take a murder charge for beating my ass like a Piñata on Cinco De Mayo?" My passage clears and I'm now imagining myself butt ass naked, walking into the bedroom with a big black strap on, all greased up and asking my man is he ready? After I visualize my funeral, I quickly abandoned that thought.

He states, "I haven't been with a man in years, I mean years but there is this HAWT GUY who is friends with a mutual friend of mine and I swear if he gives me any inclination that he is down, OMG I don't know what I will do!" I'm confused as hell, because not too long ago you were talking marriage and kids, now you're all ready to bust out some new Sears Craftsman knee pads and suck the skin off this man's dick. I ask him, just being the ass that I am, "If we were together and in a serious relationship, would you cheat on me with a man?" He responds, "No, I would never ever cheat on you with anyone, but this one man makes me so hot and weak in the knees. I would just have to come home and ask you if is ok if I go suck his dick and invite you to come along as well." Baby, I swear at this time I'm waiting on Ashton Kutcher, Jaime Kennedy or any damn body to come from any damn where and scream YOU'VE BEEN PUNKED and give me $10k for being a good damn sport. I didn't know what to say or what to do. I'm completely stuck with a stupid ridiculous ass grin on my face trying to think of something to say or do, but nothing happens. I have truly heard all I need and want to hear. I promise, I ain't never ever heard anything like this in my life. I end the conversation with how nice it was to finally meet him, how I have thoroughly enjoyed the evening but I must be leaving now as it's late and I have small drive ahead of me. My drive was less than 20 minutes. We had dinner in Boca Raton and I live in Pompano Beach, Florida. I was just ready to get the hell away from dancehall twerking queen.

He walks me out the restaurant reiterating how he is so into me and he would love for us to go out again and see about a possible marriage and kids. All the while we are walking out the door he is holding my hand and being a complete gentleman. While we are standing outside, we see a few unsavory guys approaching us and he takes a defensive stance like he is gonna hold it down. All I can do is reach for my hammer in my purse just in case I have to fight for the virginity off my asshole and save him as well. He then tells me he wants to teach me how to fight and whenever I'm out at night I need to call him and talk to him until I get in my car and have made it home safely. If you could have seen my face as he is telling me this foolishness. Why in the hell does he feel the need to teach me how to fight? Who the hell am I protecting, my anus or his? I turn and look to him and say, "You really seem like a nice guy, and you if you were to treat me . . ." before I can finish my sentence, dudes voice went all deep high pitch and he shouts in a very serious manner, with his eyes wide, grinning from asshole to appetite and blurts out "I can go suck a dick?" All I could do at this time is lower my head, shaking it in disbelief. I give him a hug, kiss on the cheek, not that it matters if I kiss him on the lips, because we both suck dick. I thank him again for a lovely evening and drive down 95 South in total amazement of how in the hell I meet the one and only gay, white dude on a straight black dating website . . .

He texts me later that night to ensure I have made it home safely and once again to let me know how serious he is about us dating and having a family. Once again, the "Dream Life" flashes through my mind before I go to sleep and I say what the hell, "Let's go out again!" . . . WTF was I thinking?

A couple of months pass before we are able to go out on our next date. He has been traveling all over the US and even down to South America for various job requirements with the reserves and his regular pilot job. Finally he makes it back to South Florida. We chit chat and set up our next date. I go and get a fresh perm. My hair is fried, died and laid to the side to go along with my new outfit. I had on a low cut, curve hugging, long red, spaghetti strap maxi dress with some really cute well-coordinated wedges and small clutch. I figure I might as well look cute with the night I'm expecting to have. We have dinner at this really cute, cozy authentic Mexican restaurant in Boca Raton, right off of South Dixie highway. The setup is in an old house, sitting close to some rail road tracks that has been converted into a restaurant with all old country Mexican artifacts. Everything is going well with us. The conversation is fun filled, pleasant and full of "I've missed you" and other nice pleasantries. The owner of the restaurant is the one who seats us, took our drink order and told us our waiter would be with us shortly. Everything is going wonderful. We are talking about continuing to get to know one another, meeting each other's family and what religion the child(ren) would be raised up in. I'm Church of Christ and would most definitely need my child(ren) raised knowing about Jesus. With that part of the conversation set up perfectly. Now is the time I ask him the million dollar question, "Honey, how we would conceive our children? Naturally or via invitro?" I had taken the biggest swig of my margarita in preparation for his response. At the time he was about to answer my question our waiter had walked up.

Our waiter was a very handsome model type. About 6'3, very nice muscular build, dirty blonde hair that was cut in a very cute Tom Cruise style. Electric blue eyes. 100 million megawatt smile, who was a thorn in my black ass. As soon as their eyes met, my date, future husband, baby daddy, dream life come true; forgot who I was and that I was even there. They are doing the flirty eye thing and talking, all while my date is clutching his got damn chest like a cheap ho trying to get a happy meal. I'm sitting there with my head going back and forth from my date to the waiter like I'm at the got damn US Open and I'm watching Serena tear the competition to pieces. I tell you no lie, 3.5 minutes have passed when they finally realize I'm sitting at the table and decide to include me in the conversation and ask what I would like to start with for an appetizer. I go along as if nothing has happened, smile, nod and order an appetizer and a double shot of Patron. I can already tell this is going to be a very interesting night. As our waiter is closing out his description of the night's specials and turns to walk away, he does a Kenya Moore "Gone with the wind" fabulous twirl; my date is following his very toned muscular ass every move. I start a conversation just to see if he is paying me any attention and all he does is nod his head in agreement. All I said was, "I miss the ole Looney tune cartoons."

Our conversation picks up again, as the main attraction has left to go fill our appetizer order and my drink request. Since it has been a couple of months since we last saw one another and spent some time, or talked that much due to his hectic traveling schedule, I wanted to know how things had been. So I asked, "How has your dating life been?" He had the most serious look on his face and became almost manly in his actions as he was about to respond to me, but what came out his mouth, I would have never ever expected to hear in my entire life. In his most serious Colonel voice he says, "My dating life has been shitty. You would think it would be easy to find a man and explain to him that you just want to hook up a few times a week with no strings attached. I give you some head and my hole and everybody goes their separate ways!" Baaaaaaaaaaaby, just as the last words fell off his lips, the waiter returned with my drink and appetizer. I immediately requested he bring me another double shot of Patron and this time also bring a double of Tito's or Ciroc, 3 ice cubes and a splash of pineapple juice. They get back to making googly eyes and flirting. I clear my throat and tell him, "Uhmmmm excuse me! I need my drink right now and I'm also ready to order my entrée if you have a few minutes for me!" He notices my displeasure and takes my order and returns quickly with my drinks. My date is now looking at me like he sees a ghost. I have to know and I ask him, "If that is what you're looking for and desire from a man, what would be the point for me being in your life?" This bastard had the nerve to say in the most serious manner, "I need a good woman in my life who would be able to give me stability, a family and bring some form of normalcy into my world!" With a slight chuckle, I ask, "How would I be able to do that when you're still very much attracted to men and want to have sex with them several times a week with no strings attached?" Girlllllll, I promise God has a serious sense of humor when it comes to me, because this date went from bad to horrible with his next sentence. His response was classic, "I know my lifestyle is not one you may be use to or even thought of actually being in, but you seem like a really good, strong woman who I would love to share those experiences with. I don't mean join in or anything, but I would love for you to come along, watch and see what my life is all about. Grab a snack or something and just enjoy the show." What is a girl to say after her dream life has just crashed and burned like Chernobyl.

I so badly wanted the answer to my question earlier, regarding how the child or children would be conceived, so after several long eternal minutes of silence, I brought the question back up and I promised myself, that after he answered this question, I would not ask any more due to the fact my face muscles couldn't take any more abuse that evening. Here comes my cute, I can't wait to make babies with you face and I sincerely ask him, "Baby, how would we conceive kids with you having a strong desire to make love to men?" Without skipping a beat, nor missing a bite of his food, this fool said, "Invitro of course. I don't think I'm able to perform adequately with a woman!" I'm about 3 sheets in the wind. When I hear him say that I'm ready to do a hearty belly roll laugh and say "Thank you GEESUS". The waiter comes back and offers us dessert and checks to see if we will need any to go trays. My date and I both agree to no dessert, but say that we need to go trays. When the waiter returns, he immediately starts to wrap up my dates food with such an electric smile, so me being me, I sit there so cavalier and await him to do the same thing for me. Well to my surprise, I have to bag up my own damn food and my date does not part his perfectly lightly tinted glossed lips to correct our waiter's actions or lack thereof. I continue to hold pleasant conversation while packing up my own damn food, slide out the booth and tell my date I will wait for him outside. I figured, I would be respectful and allow them to have a private moment and exchange numbers.

He comes out to the parking lot 10 minutes later. We hug and he moves in to kiss me on my lips. I do an exorcist move and turn my head quickly so that he kisses me on my cheek. He walks me to my car. Tells me how gorgeous, sweet and kind he thinks I am and how he would really love to see me again and really work on this even though we have two totally different backgrounds, beliefs and "orientations." I lean my head slightly to the left, fling my hair back and say as polite as I possibly can, "I like you. I like you a lot and I really think you're an amazing guy who deserves the world, it's just that I can't give you what you want, need and desire. I need my man to be a man. I don't want to be giving you head and you stop me and say "Betty you're doing it all wrong, let me show you how it's done properly!" He laughed so hard, tears actually ran down his face and he coughed several times. At first I thought I had offended him, until he put his hand on my shoulder and said, "You are so fucking funny, because I have stopped a woman from sucking my dick before because she was not doing it right. I thank you for your honesty and I would really love to remain friends, if you're totally cool with that?" We hugged, shook hands, spoke our last pleasantries, got into our respective vehicles and rode off into the still dark summer night like the wind.

Till this day, we are cool. We text/talk from time to time. He is still single wishing that we had worked out. How the hell are we gonna work? What the hell we gonna do? Have dick sucking and bootay twerking contests and shit???Damn, my moving on up to the eastside on the beach, world travel, housewife has become a dream deferred ~~Ain't That Bout'a Bitch~~

Chapter 14

LOVE OR LOVE OF CONVENIENCE

Before I got into my relationship with Linus in October 2012, I went on two dates that just made me look up to the sky and tell God, "I know you doing this on purpose, just so you can have something to laugh at. Enough is enough. I give up, you win!" As you can tell, I have had some of the most interesting experiences in this thing called dating. Some good, some bad and some that made we want to look for their parents and slap they ass dead square in the face with a hot shovel for not finding something else to do besides make this man. Couldn't they have found anything better to do than to come together and spawn a seed that would grow up, come into my life and act a complete fool?

I had met this pretty cool guy online. Yes, my retarded ass went back online. I haven't the slightest idea what made me do that silly shit again. From our initial email exchanges, he seemed alright and that led to our trading of numbers. He wasn't exactly what I'm attracted to. He had a nice personality. He was gainfully employed as a high school honors teacher. It made up for the fact that he had a pug puppy face and was shorter than me! At one time I was asking myself, "Is this Kevin Hart after a few iron skillet shots to the face?" After two dates, he invites me over to his house for a home cooked meal. I go and had a really nice time and complimented him on his culinary skills. So he says, "One day whenever you're ready, I will come to your house, bring everything and cook. We can even cook together". Me being me, not knowing how to cook and never ever turning down a free meal agreed and set the date for a week or 2 later. He comes to the house with all this food, wine and cheesecake from this really nice boutique bakery. He cooks and I mean he threw down. While watching TV, his stomach starts to rumble. It was loud to make me look out the window to see what car needed a new muffler. He asks if he could use my bathroom. With a mean mug on my face I ask, "For what? Do you need to boo boo? He responded "Yes", with a life or death desperation look on his face that was truly priceless. In the nicest way possible, I then asked, "Can you please go home and take care of your personal needs because I'm not comfortable in letting you take a shit in my house?" Dude looked at me like a little lost puppy and asked "Are you serious right now?" I try to remain as pleasant as possible. I give him a firm, serious, "Hell yeah I'm dead ass serious. Don't nobody take a shit in here but me! You may want to leave now since you have such a long drive ahead of you!" He picked up his keys and left. As he was speed walking the down the stairs to his car, I told yelled out to him, "Call me later and let me know how you're doing." Now granted, he left all the food, a half of bottle of wine and an entire cheesecake, was I wrong for not letting him boo boo in my house? Hell nah, coz don't nobody drop a stinky load in my house but me! I didn't even know or like him like that any damn way, Ole stanky booty lil boy. ~~Ain't That Bout'a Bitch~~

A few months had passed since I out on the date with doo doo boy. Hell it had been months since I had went on a date with anyone. I closed out my online account and just went into chill mode. It's normal to talk to my dad once a week and not really miss a beat. One night my dad calls and tells me that one of my cousins in South Dade had passed and that he and my step mom were coming down that weekend to stay with me so we can all go to the funeral. I'm like this with all of my family and friends, whenever you are in town you don't ever have to get a hotel room, you just let me know ahead of time and you are more than welcome to stay with me. I'll give you the guest key and you come and go as you please! All I ask in return is that you burn a few pots while you are here and leave plenty of leftovers.

My parents get in early Friday afternoon and here comes that infamous 60 gallon marine cooler filled with all kinds of good southern, home cooked goodness that I have truly missed. I don't cook like my parents. I'm always on some form of a diet, so you never ever see that type of food in my house unless my parents have shown up. We get everything upstairs and once all settled in. My step mom gets the stove and oven going and the house quickly fills with the scent of some collard greens, seasoned with some pig tails. Hog maws in another pot. Is that my Auntee Jerry famous sweet potato pie I smell in the oven? Auntee Jerry is my step mom's baby sister who can cook any dessert from scratch with her eyes closed and hands tied behind her back. We eat and head down to 67th street off of 27th Ave in Miami to my aunt's house who has just lost her 3rd child in 2 years. On the way down, my step mom makes me promise to take her to Calder Casino, The Hard Rock and the Isle casino by my house before he head in for the night. I agree and we ride out, speeding down 95 listening to some blues. By the time we got to Miami, the fish grease was already hot and popping. The music was blasting. The liquor was flowing. Greens, rice, chicken, salad, rice and peas, jerk pork/chicken, BBQ and any kind of food you could think of was in the backyard and there was never any worry of running out. We stayed a couple of hours, mingled with family and had a great time reminiscing about times of old and planning future family outings besides always hate getting together for funerals.

We get up early and get ready for the funeral. We have a 45 min ride down to Miami so we can let the family know we are there, but we head to the church and get a seat before the rest of the family arrives with the procession. The service was a lovely home going service. The pastor preached a life sermon which moved everyone to joy and laughter verse tears. I needed that. I'm a big water bag anyway and don't deal very well with death. It was an open casket ceremony, but we didn't get up to walk by and pay our last respects as the church was filled to capacity in the 2 story church. My cousin who died, only son got up, walked up to the casket kissed his mother and pulled the blanket up over her and closed the casket. I lost it. They had to carry me out the church and damn near call 911. He was her only child. To have to kiss and tuck your mother for the last time was just too much for me. I needed a break and an entire bottle of any bottle of liquor to calm my nerves. We skipped the gravesite and rode down to south beach and just had a mommy, daughter, father moment before we headed back to the house for the repast. We get to the house about an hour or so after everyone has returned from the gravesite. We grab a few chairs, some food and chill out. I feel a pair of eyes on me that are wearing me out from top to bottom. I ask my mom if she knew who he was and she said no. He kept looking and smiling. Not bad looking with an electric smile. I grab one of my cousins and ask her if she know who he is. She puts in to tell me he isn't any kin to us. He is the brother to my cousin's ex-wife. BINGO! No relation. It just so happened that I parked the car not too far from his car. When I see him walk over to his car I get up and slowly walk pass him on purpose going to my dad's car for absolutely nothing. I'm just trying to catch his attention in hopes he will speak first. BOOM! Not only does he speak, he offers to walk with me over to my father's car and assist me with placing my phone on the charger. I have full charge and don't need to do a damn thing, I just needed to catch his attention to spark up conversation. The things we as women do to catch the attention of a man.

We walk back to his car and he asks, "You look pretty stressed out, would you like to have a drink with me? I agree and we stand over by his car swatting bugs, drinking, talking and becoming better acquainted. Eventually he tells me that he works for the garbage truck company for 19-20 years, drives a 2010 BMW, older kids, divorced, owns a home in South Carolina and has a pretty cool personality. We are having drinks and have a great time at the repast, of all places. He asks me out for a date and of course I agree. We spend the 1st week just talking and texting as our schedules are completely different. We finally coordinate our schedules and have an awesome 1st date that was really nice. We had drinks, great food and I agree to see him again. Baby, ohhhhh baby that 2nd date, not so well. When he comes to pick me up, he has been drinking and says I need to drive the Beamer. So I gladly hop in and flush it to CheeseCake Factory at the Sawgrass Mills Mall with no conversation as I'm highly pissed that you came to pick me up drunk and not to mention late. I park the car. I pull down the visor and open the mirror to fix my hair and make-up as the wind was whipping since I had all the windows down and the sunroof open. As I'm doing what I need to do to ensure my face and hair are on point before I walk into the Sawgrass Mall, he asks me to give him a napkin from the back of his seat in the pouch. I reach back there and hand him a few napkins, not really paying him any attention, I reapply my powder and as just as I'm about to apply another coat of lip gloss to make sure these lips are popping, I hear "Pffffffftttttt." I look over to see why he just made that noise and to my amazement this nigga just spit his dentures into the napkin and started rubbing them off. My jaw drops and my eyes have grown to the size of semi tires. At this point I'm so out done and don't know what to do. I want to reapply my lip gloss, but I'm afraid I will look like a Parkinson patient just applied it because I'm in straight shock mode. This nigga with his lips balled in around his gums asks me, "Baby, hand me that black bag in the back please?" Without looking or taking my eyes off of him, I reach in the back, grab the bag and hand it to him with disgust.

I don't care that he has false teeth, but please use decency and order when dealing with personal hygiene as such and handle that shit before you go out in public. I'm still sitting there looking at him like "WOW did he really just do this in front of me?" Just as I'm about to turn my head and attempt to finish putting me together, this fool as the nerve to say, "Girl just wait til I get you home, pull these teeth out and eat dat pussy! Imma give you the best head you eva had!" He said all this while putting a fresh set of poli grip on his dentures and a serious look on his face. I respond real quickly while beating this face to sleep, which is what I'm wishing I was doing, "UhmmmmNahhhhh I'm cool."

I get out the car, run into CheeseCake Factory, order a double shot of chilled Patron with salt and lime, followed up with a glass of Kendall Jackson Chardonnay and that's what I drank all night with dinner. Just when I thought the night couldn't get any worse, this fool after studying the menu like it was a study guide to a final exam asked the waiter, "Do y'all have Colt 45?" I swear I wanted to shrivel up and blow away like a grain of sand. The waiter looked at me with a "WTF" and I looked back at him with a "Don't ask me" and dropped my head. After I got drunk, belly full, ghost rode the Beamer one last time. I made him drive his drunk ass home and never called him again or answered any of his texts or calls. Is he on block too? Hell yeah and with ease! After this date, I vowed never ever to date again. I was too through and just knew God was punishing me for something I did a long time ago. ~~Ain't That Bout'a Bitch~~

After those last two dates, I told myself that I was giving dating a huge break and let the dating pool get a thorough draining, cleaning and new filtration system. After my dates with Mr. Shitty Drause and Snaggle Puss, I couldn't take anymore disappointments or severely embarrassing moments. My plan was to fall back into chill mode and just enjoy single life. If you are friends with me on Facebook, then you already know I'm a severe goof ball and stay on Facebook posting jokes and true life events. When I make my daily posts, it is just a way to give a smile to a friend who may be going through something and on the verge of jap slapping the hell out of someone. I can relate to that feeling, because I'm normally on that verge daily and keep my Ike Turner pimp hand ready to issue one on demand, so I make myself and others laugh as a way to deal with life. This last relationship started on Facebook and most definitely ended my social media/online dating.

One night I was in Wal-Mart in the check-out line when I see a midget check out and start walking out the door, when this little boy in front of me with his uncle asked the question, "Unk, where do midgets come from?" His uncle without missing a beat in answering the question and placing his items on the conveyor belt answered all in one breath, "Midgets come from shawt dicks!" The look on his face was serious and priceless when he answered the baby. I tried my hardest to contain my laughter and keep from hollering. All that went out the window. I laughed so hard and damn near uncontrollably as I kept thinking there should be a world filled with midgets because I know plenty of shawt dick men! I put my previous night experience on Facebook and my friends and I had a time laughing and throwing out various versions for midgets, when he comments on my post and asks me a direct question, "Now, what's the rationale for women midgets? IJS?" Now, don't get me wrong Linus has commented on plenty of my other posts, but this particular day I finally see his post in time and respond timely. Me being me, I respond in typical Ball Bustin Betty fashion, "Well, being that I have AWESOME pussy (THANKS MOM) and working plumbing that could very well produce the next Nobel Prize winner, and which have resulted in stalkers, kidnappers, wanna be domestic violence situations, hundreds of marriage proposals and other crazy out of this world shit, the only thing I could come up with is, MEN WITH SHORT DICKS are the result of midget women as well. That's just my synopsis!"

From there the in boxing started that Friday with Linus stating, "And the audience gives a standing ovation!!" By the time I notice I have an inbox message and from him, I'm busy as a one legged man in an ass kicking contest on a wet oil slick. It takes me a minute to respond and it's something small and simple just to show that I'm paying attention and not trying to be rude, so I say, "LMAO, you have me rolling in here right now. Thank goodness my co-workers know I'm slightly off and don't pay me any attention." I don't think much more of it. Everybody on Facebook is use to me and know I crack jokes all day, but he sends another message "You're good, I recently transitioned to south Florida from Gainesville, so I'm sure our paths will cross one day. I won't stalk, attempt to kidnap, or request any babies from you!" I'm laughing as he has actually paid attention to my post and let me know I'm safe from danger. I respond, "I did not know you moved down here. We will most definitely have to meet up one day and hang out. Please call me when you get a chance and let's talk. 987-654-3210." I go back to playing assistant supervisor and trying my hardest to not slap fire out of my staff, as its Friday and for some reason they all have amnesia on how to complete their assigned work. He sends me another inbox with his number stating we will most definitely get together soon.

The Friday I started talking Linus was the same night I went out with the BMW driving, several property owning, free will money spending teeth spitting garbage man who wanted to eat my cooda with his teeth sitting on my dresser. Just saying that to you has made me weak in the knees. All I can see is his teeth in a glass on my dresser talking to him saying, "Eat it dawg, make us proud, woof woof woof!"

Saturday is normally my college football day from August to December. I hate to be disturbed, but the garbage man is steady calling and texting. I refuse to answer my phone nor do I respond to his texts or call. I can just imagine are his gums being attached to my sweet little innocent cooda because he has an excessive amount of Poligrip on his gums. Right before I get ready turn to my phone off. I get a Facebook alert letting me know I had just received an inbox. Lo and behold, it's Linus. He states, "I know you're in Facebook football mode right now, but I just wanted to give you a quick shout and say Hi!" That simple message brought a smile to my face in a time of frustration. The Gators were up in the 2nd qtr. I sent a quick response to show my interest, but let him know not to respond back. Keep watching Facebook. That is where he can keep up with me. I Swype back real quick, "Yes baby I am. I'm getting ready to jump off in their ass real good. Thank you for understanding LOL . . . Maybe we can catch a game at a sports bar or something." I'm pissed as hell. The Gators have just scored another touchdown when he sends his last message stating, "Sounds like a plan, can't wait to make it happen."

Sunday afternoon, I'm home after church, trying to nurse Saturday's hangover of food, FSU and drinking! Linus calls asking how I was doing and just generally holding small talk. I'm so damn sleepy and tired that I'm not even holding the phone with my hand. I'm lying on my right side with the phone resting on my face saying the occasional "Uhmm mm", "What", "For real", "I know what you mean". I tell him I'm going to get up, do laundry and that I will call him in a little while once I'm finished. Linus asks real quickly, "What are you doing later once you finish your laundry?" I'm saying to myself, *Sleep nigga, I gotta get this hangover off my ass, shit!"* I quickly respond, "Nothing but rest. I have missed 2 days at the gym, but we can meet up if you like and watch the game?" He agrees and we decide to meet up at TGIF at 8. As usual, my ass is late but hell, I'm trying to stop my head from spinning and gather up some energy. I never asked what type of car he was driving or what he would be wearing. I get to TGIF get out the car walking up to the restaurant and ohhh my word, here he comes out of nowhere. This mass of tall, thick, sexual chocolate thunder in some nicely creased cargo shorts, crisp white Ralph Lauren Polo shirt and Jordan's. I stop dead slap in my tracks. My head stops spinning and I start grinning from ear to damn ear. We walk towards each other and hug. I held onto Linus so tight and he held on to me just as tight and for a long time, planting one of the most sensual kisses on my forehead. Not only was Linus a very handsome, good looking man but he smelled so good wearing that throw back cologne, Curve. We finally let each go of each other, step back and marvel at one another. I had my hair pulled up in goddess braids, a long beautiful multi colored strapless sundress and coordinated sandals truly looking the south Florida part. Linus grabs my hand and says, "Wow! I finally get to meet the infamous Ms. Betty and what a pleasure it is." I laugh it off and start walking towards the restaurant and holding small talk with Linus just trying to get a better feel for one another. We are vibing as if we have been friends forever. We are seated and start talking about everything from Facebook, sports, our college education and past jobs that we have held at similar places in Gainesville, such as Meridian and a few other places. He then tells me that he has just taken an Assistant Head Coach at a college down here, which is what prompted his relocation to South Florida.

The fun filled night continues with more energetic conversation and some serious mutual physical attraction between the both of us. I break the tension by focusing my attention on the game and trying to motivate the NY Giants to stop that slave ass whooping they were getting that Sunday night. The staff came in and alerted all the customers that people were breaking into cars and that we needed to check on our cars to ensure they were safe. Once we checked on our cars, we went back in and grabbed a booth to finish watching the game or should I say massacre of the Giants. I turn to Linus to talk to him about the game when he grabs my hand and holds it gently, yet firm enough to let me know that he is really into whatever it is I want to talk about. I grip his soft, masculine hand back and continue my conversation as we are massaging each other's hand. When I get too turned on and my hand starts to sweat from excitement, I pull my hand back, regain my composure and get back to talking about the game which is almost over. He has paid the tab. We walk to the door, holding hands. When we make it outside I'm sweating like a taco stealing gator running from the police down University Avenue with the K-9 on my heels. We are still holding hands when I look up at his tall, dark chocolate sexy ass and say, "Thank you sweetie for inviting me out for such a lovely time. I had a so much fun and I'm really looking forward to hanging out with you." I was expecting Linus to say the same but he didn't, he just leaned his 6'3 chocolate thunder ass down and gave me the most passionate kiss. We both stood there enjoying the moment of each other's soft lips and tender embrace. You know it had been about 6-8 months since I last had sex and a good couple of years since I had some real intimacy with some monkey, wall climbing, ceiling hanging love making, so I can't even sit up here and lie, I was too gone. Not only from his kiss and the passionate way he knew to hold me in the small of my back and pull me close to him but just how genuinely he was into me, Betty!

I pull away quickly to avoid any more tension because I was about to tackle his ass like a quarter back sneak. My spirit wouldn't let me, even though my flesh wanted to eat his ass up like a fresh out the grease pork chop sandwich on 2 of the softest pieces of white bread and mayo. Linus is married with 2 older daughters who are in college. I established from the beginning that we would just be friends who hangout from time to time watching the games, throwing back a few drinks having a smoke and just enjoying the camaraderie of two friends as I don't date married men. He agreed and we never had that discussion again. We part ways and I speed home to clean up the massive flood in my panties caused by hurricane Linus, when I get a text. I check my phone and it's Linus! When we left TGIF it was already 11:00pm, when we finished texting it was 1:15 Monday morning. We talked about everything that night like 2 giddy teenagers deep lust. I had all intentions of keeping my daily appointment with the gym at 5am til 6:30 especially being that I had not been there in 2 days. We eventually stop texting and I went into deep sleep thinking about Mr. Linus.

I'm awakened early Monday morning by phone alarm at 4:30am. Well as an early morning motivational text from Linus at 4:45am. His text gave me the energy I needed to get up; hit the gym do cardio, strength training and cool down with another round of cardio. We talked all day and saw each other later that evening once I returned from my 2nd round at the gym. We met up had some wings and Monday night football. More talking and feeling at complete ease with one another and even some tension building touching! We finish eating wings and watching the game. Linus walks me to my car and here his ole sexy good smelling ass come with another hug and kiss. This time the kiss we shared was deeper, more tantalizing and intense. He asks, "Would you like for me to come over and chill with you?" If I was to let my raging hormones take over, there wouldn't be anything chill in my house. Everything would be hot as fire. The thoughts I had running through my mind was nowhere near chill. I decline his offer and tell him that my house is a mess with my wet, sweaty funky gym clothes hanging all over the place to dry. He understands and we part ways only to be on the phone til the wee hours of the morning again.

Wednesday is my one workout weekday at 5am and then let my body rest. I go to the gym twice daily 5am and 7pm Monday, Tuesday, Thursday and Friday. Linus and I are hot on each other's trail. Wednesday were texting all day, when he asks if he can come over and chill. Aww what the hell. I give in and give him directions to my apartment and the code he needs to use for me to buzz him in at the gate. We agree to 8pm so I can work my OT and have my apartment ready for company. It is storming badly that night. I mean cats, dogs, elephants and a giraffes are falling from the sky. I park in a guest spot so upon his arrival we can switch parking spots. But when Linus gets to the house, it's raining too hard to switch parking spots. I'm like bump it park in my spot and run upstairs. The brown Lexus, with rims slow rolls into the parking lot. I direct Linus to my parking spot from inside my cold, dry apartment. He gets out the car and runs upstairs with the quickness. I'm standing in the door waiting for him with a warm dry towel. Got dammit man! Linus looks good as hell in his camouflage cargo shorts, red shirt and white Nikes. Ohhh Lawd, peace be still. I was looking at him so hard, I forgot he was standing in my breezeway. He walks in, I give him the towel to dry off and warm up as I like to keep my apartment cold as hell. We hug and ohhhh Lawd do we hug and kiss. I break away and offer him something to drink and eat, Linus declines. I sit in my big oversized chair in the corner to finish watching the game that had started and let my pressure calm down while Linus makes himself at home on the two seater. We are having so much fun talking, watching the game and really continuing to grow on one another like we have been down with one another for years.

I'm getting nervous because the rain has stopped, there is only a few minutes left in the game and Linus hasn't said anything about getting ready to leave and call it a night. I really want to tear his head off and fuck him to death and back to life, but I'm trying to play it cool. I keep waiting on him to say he is leaving. Those words never leave his lips. I get up to get something out of the kitchen when Linus gets up and walks right in front of me, palms my ass and kisses my neck with fire and desire in his soul. That was it. Fuck it. I'm all in! I grab ahold of his ass and walk backwards slowly towards my room. We are at the foot of the bed, we never stopped kissing or holding one another. I take his shirt off and my word, there stands before me a mountain of well-built chocolate. I kiss his chest and suck on one of his nipples while rubbing his throbbing growing dick. Linus pulls my dress up over my head, throws it with great force onto the floor, picks me up and lays me down in the middle of the bed and begins to kiss, caress and massage my entire body with his very soft masculine hands. Even though my AC is on 75 and the fan is on high, I'm sweating like 30 Mexicans in an 84' Hyundai trying to cross the border. This man gives me fire with the way he pays very close attention to my body while he snaps my bra off and starts sucking on my titties and massaging my clit through my panties. He sucks each tittie with the same attention and passion he has been giving my entire body. Linus reached for my panties which are barely there. Precious overly aggressive ass had already started chewing through them. He pulls my panties off and buries his face so deep into Precious. I'm trying to scoot away because the hurricane tongue he has is driving me crazy. I keep scooting and scooting until Linus got tired of my running. He hooks his arms around my hips and puts me in my place and damn near ate me into a coma! When he finally comes up, I'm the one out of breath with the dry mouth. Linus is looking like a fresh out the oven glazed doughnut. I'm ready to go to sleep after that intense cardio workout, but not before I put the hurricane tongue back on his ass. I had to teach Mr. Man about messing with grown people. I started sucking his dick slowly. Licking the shaft and getting it sloppy wet and going to work on that dick while massaging his balls. Once I get his dick hard as cement and wet as a water park, I slide down and start gently sucking on his left ball. I glide over to his right ball and suck on it gently while jacking his throbbing dick with my right hand. All ten of Linus toes popped like a case of firecrackers while moaning and groaning and gyrating his hips letting me know he is enjoying this. I place both of his balls in my mouth and suck gently, hum and slide back up to his dick to suck it real good while roller coasting my tongue on the head of his dick then deep throating it before going back to his balls one last time. Linus couldn't take it anymore. He grabbed me under my arms, threw me on the bed and beat this pussy like she owed him back taxes. Linus and I was on every inch of my bed acting like wild savage animals in the jungle. We dare not get on that floor. Wood floors don't give a damn about how much passion we have.

Once Linus and I had finished, cooled off and caught our breath Linus gets up. I'm thinking he is going to the bathroom but he stands in front of the bed to the side. He calls my name so I can look at him and gives me a round of applause with a standing ovation and says, "Betty, I have never been made love to like that, I must admit! You are awesome." I think he is playing. I start laughing and he just stands there for a few minutes and said, "Betty, I'm not joking." I'm blushing. I roll up out the bed, grab him and pull him back to bed. We lay there in complete silence just holding one another and drift off into a deep, somber peaceful sleep. We awake the next morning at 6am to get ready for work, we go over our schedules as Linus plans on coming back before he leaves on Friday going to Tallahassee scouting JUCCO players. We hug, kiss and both exclaim how we thoroughly each other the night before. Linus goes down stairs. I start my shower when I hear a loud pounding knock on my door. I look through the peephole and its Linus. I guess he forgot something. Actually, we forgot to move his car once it stopped raining the night before and his car was towed. I felt horrible because they hadn't been towing cars for several months and the one night I decide to break the rules, they want to tow. To get his car back was $160. Once he paid and got his car back I gave him a hug and told him I will give him $80 towards to the towing because I genuinely felt bad. He gave me a hug, kissed me on my forehead, patted my ass and said, "Have a good day at work baby. I'll call you in a lil while." I get two texts from Linus all day; I just knew it was over before it started due to his car being towed.

Being that I didn't go to the gym that morning, I got off early so I could hit burn off some anxiety. Just as I'm walking out the gym my phone rings and its Linus. He asks, "Hey baby. How was your day? Are you at the gym or home?" I quickly say, "I'm just leaving the gym headed home about to shower and crash. Why, what's up." In the cutest voice Linus says, "I was coming over to spend time with you, you know I'm leaving town tomorrow for my business trip for the weekend." The biggest smile came over me as my heart started racing, I told Linus to come on over and meet me at the house so we could chill. Linus beat me there, found a guest parking spot and greeted me at my car when I parked. I didn't want to hug him. I had just finished an entire hour of fast paced cardio, but Linus wasn't hearing that. We hugged and kissed right there in the parking lot with my sweaty, musky ass grinding all over him. I turn the TV on for Linus while I take a shower and get comfortable. It's late and I know he needs his rest and should be leaving soon. One thing I love about Linus, we could always talk about every and anything and be able to have an open, healthy dialogue regardless of opinion. It's almost midnight when I say, "Babe it's getting late and I know you have a long trip ahead of you tomorrow, so I'm not going to hold you any longer." Linus looked at me strange. Took his shoes off and said, "I was wondering when you were going to get ready for bed." He got up, turned the light on in the bedroom, came back into the living room and turned that light off. I'm in my big easy chair watching him do all of this like WTF? Linus grabs my hand and walks me into the bedroom. DING DING round 2!

When Linus left the next morning, he went to Gainesville to see his wife and kids on his way to Tallahassee. I wasn't upset or concerned. Hell what we had going was most definitely not planned it just happened spur of the moment, so there was no reason for me to get upset but my curiosity was getting the best of me. See, Linus was living with his wife's sister in Ft. Lauderdale, so for those two consecutive nights that he was not at his sister in laws house, what was he telling his wife? We talked on the phone for a long time before his youngest daughter and wife came home. My mind still spinning but like I said, that ain't none of my business. Once he reaches Tallahassee and throughout the weekend, there was more of the same. The conversations were always fun, full of life and entertaining. I worked OT that Saturday and of course my FSU football mixed with hanging out. I'm beat when Sunday comes. I just want to go to church, rest and recoup so I can get my gym time in and get ready for work. Sunday night about 9pm I'm lying in the bed sipping wine flipping channels when my phone rings. It's the front gate! Linus is back in South Florida and right back to my house. I didn't know he was coming over, so I didn't get a guest parking spot. Linus rode around the complex for 15 minutes until he found one. He came through the door with his bag, took a shower and snuggled right up next to me and said, "Ohh how I've missed you baby!" DING DING round 3! This goes on for two weeks straight with no break before Linus says to me one night, "I think I need to show my face a little more around my sister in laws house. Amethyst is asking in a roundabout way where I've been." I hadn't thought about a sister in law, his wife Amethyst or nobody for that matter. It felt so damn good to come home to a man whose company you enjoyed and looked forward to being with and just finally being able to exhale and be happy. What can I say? Nothing. I'm lying on Linus chest when he tells me this. I rub his stomach and chest and say, "You do what you have to and need to do, no worries from me." It wasn't even two days and he was back!

We are having the time of our lives. We are going out to dinner, movies and even going to the gym together. Sometimes he would go with me at 5am or he would wake me up at 4:30am so I could go and roll his black ass back over and go to sleep. Football season is now in full swing and his season has yet to start. We would lay in the bed Saturday watch the games holding hands and drift off to sleep. Wake up holding one another's hand ask did you see that hit, take a sip of our drink and drift right back to sleep holding one another's hands. We were very happy and at peace. Linus is buying groceries, cooking and cleaning and I'm beaming brighter than the sun. Even though this relationship is wrong as hell, I'm just so happy to be off that damn dating merry go round. It's now the end of November. Linus texts me saying that we needed to talk when we get off that night, I'm like cool. He gets in after me and has this horrible look on his face like someone has just died. I give him space and time to feel comfortable. I sit in my big easy. Take a sip of my wine, watching the game and wait. Finally, he parts his lips and says, "I know we had plans this weekend but Amethyst is coming to town for her birthday and to celebrate our anniversary." I'm thinking he was going to tell me his sister or one of his kids was hurt. What was I supposed to do or say, tell him that he can't go or that she can't come down here? Hell she needed to come check on her husband and help give my sweet little Ms. Precious a break, shit I'm tired. I'm so into the game because Clowney has hit a boy so hard, not only did the boy helmet fly into the parking lot, I know I saw a bolt of lightning when Clowney hit his ass. I simply say without taking my eyes off the TV, "Ohh that's cool babe. I'm working OT and the fellas are going to tail gate the Miami game, so go do your thing and have fun." He appeared to have relaxed after I said that. But I noticed that anything having to deal with her, it was going to be hell to get him to tell me for fear of what he thought would be a problem or a bad reaction from me. I would never react in a bad way or cut up, unless he starts lying then we have a serious issue on our hands.

The weekend is here. Amethyst came to town that Friday evening. Linus and I didn't text again until the next day before one of his basketballs games. We were just having general conversation and joking as usual, when he says, "It's almost game time baby. I'm going to head down to the gym and I'll try to hit you later. I miss you. Hugs, kisses and that other thing." I'm confused because I don't know what the other thing is, so I ask him "What is the other thing" it was the cutest thing ever, Linus says, "What are those 3 special magical words you always tell me when I'm having a real deep, special, intimate conversation with Ms. Precious?" He was trying to tell me he loved me without saying the words. Get the teary eyed look off your face. Why in the hell tell me that when your wife is in town. You could have told me that another damn time when it would really mean something, not because you're feeling guilty. Amethyst leaves Monday and guess who is back home Monday night? What was I going to say? Not a damn thing but, "Hiiiii baby, I missed you so much. Glad you're home!"

Christmas break is vastly approaching for all the schools especially college meaning all the kids will be returning home for the holidays, when Linus texts me saying we need to talk, again! I'm ready for this one. I don't know what it is but I'm ready. He gets in that night about 9. I'm home from the gym chilling trying to rub a cramp out. He sits on the bed trying to assist but it seem like he made it worse or I'm just a big ass baby. Linus says, "You know school is about to let out for Christmas and my sister in laws son will be coming home for the break, is it ok if I stay with you during that time?" The cramp mysteriously disappears instantly because I want to kick him in the side of his got damn throat for asking me that dumb shit. You already live here. Buying groceries, cooking, cleaning and washing yo ass here, so what did he just ask me? I don't say one thing because I still want to kick his ass in the head for asking me that. I let a few minutes pass then ask, "What day do you want to move in?" He said the weekend of the December 14th. Which happens to be the weekend I will be out of town with my family. Every year, the weekend before Christmas my mom, sister, niece, nephew and I get together at a designated family members home and celebrate Christmas together since we are all spread out over the state. Whoever is hosting that year, we go to their home for the entire weekend. Friday night is just regular gathering and eating and cutting up with food and chilling. Saturday is the big dinner with gift exchange and Sunday is the day reserved for whatever else we want to do together before we all depart. I explain that to him and that I will be out of town, but I will get a copy of the key and a gate card so he can come and go with ease while I'm gone because I may not be by my phone to buzz him in. I made room for his clothes in the dresser and closet, so when he comes with all his clothes they would not be lying around my house all over the place. The weekend with my family goes off perfect as usual. I head home on that Sunday the to spend some much needed quiet QT with my baby before he heads to Gainesville for the 2 week holiday break.

Linus leaves December 20th heading to Gainesville for the holidays. We talk every single day that he is gone, even on Christmas. I normally turn my ringer off at night so I'm not disturbed in my sleep with alerts from Facebook and late night texts, but something told me not to on Christmas Eve and I'm glad I didn't because he called me first thing that morning and said, "Merry Christmas baby. I miss you so much and I love you!" I melted instantly when he said that. As he was going around town visiting family and just enjoying himself he was constantly in contact with me, we didn't miss a beat on Christmas. I noticed the day after Christmas he was extra chatty but I didn't pay it any attention because I was back to work and damn near bout to snatch a panda patch out of one of my staff's ass. I get tired of going back and forth in email with this one heffa and start to write her up but my mind is not flowing because I'm so got damn mad I can't even see straight. Linus calls and I tell him what is going on and he helps me write her up so pretty. That write up sent a 22 year veteran back to program office for additional training and assistance in properly running her cases, I bet she won't question me "why" ever again. Due to the days hang ups, I don't get off until 7. I go get a lip and chin wax and head home, the whole time talking to Linus and he is steady asking me where I am. Since he doesn't know the streets of Ft. Lauderdale that well, I tell him a familiar place that we have either been to or rode pass so he will know. I finally pull into my parking spot when Linus abruptly says he has to go and he will hit me later. I think nothing of it because I just want a drink of wine and my bed. I'm walking up to my apartment and notice that my blinds are closed which alerts me that somebody has been in my house, because I don't close my blinds. I have my keys in my left hand. I reach into my purse and pull out my hammer and mace. Once I unlock my door, I swing it open with force and stand back with the mace in one hand and my hammer in the other, when the light clicks on. It's Linus! He is in my kitchen cooking a half a bushel of crabs! I stand in the door for a few minutes looking at everything in excitement but trying to calm down from fight mode because I was ready to bust a head open and give somebody a nice dirt nap. He came home a week early to surprise me, spend the rest of the holidays with me and exchange gifts. With him leaving his wife and kids the day after Christmas just to come back and be with me after only being gone for one week, something doesn't seem right. I don't say one word. I just keep listening and watching because something just ain't adding up.

Linus and I bring in the New Year at the movies and a passionate kiss in the middle of the road on our way home as the clock struck midnight, 2013. Our year starts wonderful and continues on with Linus staying at my house 5 days a week and 2 at his sister in law house. The 2 days that he is not with me, you can best believe we are either on the phone talking or texting until it's time to go to bed, not once did he let doubt or fear about infidelity enter our relationship, well at least not early on. Not once has his wife come down, popped up or call late at night since she was there in November, so I ask him one day out the blue, "Do you and your wife have an open relationship" he responds "No." That doesn't satisfy me so I ask, "Are things happy and all well between the two of you?" he responds "Yes, we are normal and have our ups and downs, but for the most part we are ok" I ask one last question, "Do you think she is seeing someone else?" He shrugs and hesitantly says, "Nah it ain't in her." I don't ask any more questions and leave it alone, because Linus cooks, cleans, brings groceries, helps pay bills at my house and fixes things too, so who am I to question why about anything? As I can also see he don't know women either.

His basketball season is over but the season is just now starting to heat up for his oldest daughter who goes to school out of state. With her season picking up and her team going into playoffs and finals, his travels to Gainesville increase so him and Amethyst can travel and watch their daughter play which is only right. The oldest daughter has a phenomenal season and wins big and everything returns to normal. It's now March and we have now been together for 5 months, with no arguments, no disagreements, spending plenty of fun and energetic time together and having the best sex damn near daily but my spirit is in complete turmoil. I know the relationship I'm in with Linus is not one I should be in. Every week I'm breaking up with Linus and with every breakup here he comes with why we shouldn't break up. How much we love one another and I have no worries about anything with us. I think back to that dating merry go round that I just got off and I shake the thought of breaking up, yet my spirit is killing me. My drinking increases from 1 or 2 drinks a day to drinking over half a fifth of vodka in a day. My cigar smoking increases from once every few weeks or once a month to almost every day to calm my mind, nerves and get the guilty thoughts out of my mind. Long as I had a silencer for my spirit and thoughts I could handle this and keep it moving. I'm off the merry go round of dating right?

Linus is in Gainesville once a month every month since April, for no more than a week due to his basketball season being over and there was no way he could possibly justify his presence in South Florida since recruiting wouldn't start until July with him and his head coach traveling all over the United States watching countless recruits in various tournament games. Granted there was work to be done in the office, but not a lot of work for a D2 school. July comes and he is in Gainesville to see his family and to participate in a family reunion on his father's side before he heads out for the entire month of July to recruit. We spend the entire week and weekend before the 4th of July together with no break because he will be gone all of July traveling and recruiting and he wanted to ensure I knew how much I was loved and would be missed.

We are talking and texting every day. If I didn't awake to a beautiful text, one was sure to follow shortly after I got to work to let me know how much he loved and missed me and to let me know how the recruiting process was going. At times he would send me snippets of the game he was watching of a particular recruit so I could weigh in and help him in his recruiting process. Much like what he would do when I was having a tough time making an administrative decision at work. His time away was not easy for either one of us. My soul and spirit was at total ease and peace. Even though I was missing him and our daily physical interactions my soul, my spirit were in a great place. My drinking and smoking even decreased because I was at peace. I was in such a great place I decide to try my hand at dating again. I knew it was only a matter of time before I had to get out of this relationship. I couldn't continue to live like this. Happy but not at peace.

I met a few cool people while out and about. The first guy I met, was about 5'8, slim, clean cut, no kids and funny as hell. I liked him because he kept me laughing and seemed like really cool people. We go out a few times and have a blast. One day he invites me over to his apartment. What the hell, I ain't doing nothing else. I go and we have a good time until he tries to make a move and get some! He moved in closer to me on the couch. Started rubbing on my thigh and tried to move in for a kiss. I backed up looked at him crazy and asked, "What the fuck are you doing dude?" He had a burning fire in his eyes when he slides closer to me and says, "I have wanted you since the first time I laid eyes on you. I just want to eat you and eat you some more then make love to you!" Apparently he didn't think this all the way through. If he had he would know that you clean the damn apartment first. Have some smoother more original lines and have an actual bed! How the hell you plan on eating and beating me on a got damn air mattress when you drive a brand new fully loaded 2014 Dodge Challenger? If he didn't go sit his crazy ass down somewhere and learn life, I know something. Needless to say, we never saw each other again. My purpose for dating while Linus was gone, was not to have sex with other people, but to see what was out there and to weigh my options, if I should sit and wait on him as he had asked me time and time again or move on.

The next fella I met was very suave and handsome. He was about 6'6. 250lbs, light brown, bald head and a decent build with a British accent. He had a nice job selling high end cars in Miami or at least that's what his business card said. We talked and texted for a while due to our busy schedules, but I was really trying to rush this date because I only had 10 days before Linus was due back home. We finally decide to meet up for dinner one Sunday evening, his original choice was to go to one of my favorite restaurants, JB's on the water but I wasn't in the mood to dress up and drive that far plus my spirit was sitting right about something. Even though I'm not a big fan of Applebee's, I suggested we go there especially since its right around the corner from my apartment. Linus had been texting and calling me all day for some reason, I didn't pay it any attention as this is what we do when he is in the airport. I try to keep him company the best way I can and we keep each other abreast of what is going on. I know he was heading to Washington for another recruiting tournament and was tired of the road already. So we keep texting and talking when I tell Linus to hang tight I need to season my salmon and asparagus, which is really what I had all intentions to do until I remember I had a date. I put the food in the fridge and make a bee line to Applebee's texting Linus the entire time. For the first time ever, I actually get to a date early, so I knew something was bound to happen. Linus is steadily texting me and calls just as my date walks in, I let the phone ring and go to voicemail when he calls right back and I do the same. This time Linus texts and asks me, "Can you do me a favor and look out the window and tell me what type of BWM it is our neighbor drives?" I replied a 528i, I knew what it was because it was the same BMW that the denture spitting garbage truck man drove. This calling and texting and date goes on for 2 hours! The guy and I had a great time talking, laughing and getting to know one another better when I say, "It's getting late love, I need to get going." He agrees and asks for the check. We continue talking when the waiter comes back and says, "Sorry sir your card has been declined!" I grab my shit and scoot to the end of the booth. He tells the waiter to run it again. This time the manager returns with the excessively smoking declined card and says, "Sir we have ran your card 3 times and each time it is declined. Do you have another form of payment?" This raggedy bastard pulls out his wallet and it is completely empty! There is no money, no other credit card, nothing. He turns to me and asks in an even thicker British accent, "Would you happen to have your card or any money on you? The bill is only $67!" Without missing one beat I say, "Hell nah, I don't pay for dates. Thank you gentlemen. Have a lovely evening!" I grabbed my phone, purse and leftovers and casually sauntered to my car. I was so pissed! How do you supposedly sell high end cars in Miami on Brickell Ave, wear three piece suits, smell like an expensive cologne store but can't afford a $67 meal from Applebee's? Get the fuck outta here with that!

I rush home to get a drink so I can calm my damn nerves, cook my salmon and asparagus so I can have my lunch for the week when I walk into my dark apartment and see Linus sitting at my desk with his feet propped up on the couch! The lump in my throat was the size of an elephant and was just as hard to get down. I stand there for a few seconds in total shock. I'm trying to figure out what the fuck is he doing here. He is supposed to be in the air somewhere on his way to Washington D.C. What am I going to say about this Applebee's bag in my hand and no salmon being cooked? I throw everything down and run to him and give him a big hug and try to kiss him when he backs up from me and says, "Damn you smell like a brewery! What were you doing?" Whewww saved by the liquor. Linus and I had talked some months back about why my drinking had increased, which was due to the stress of this relationship. There was no stress from him, just the stress of being in an inappropriate relationship and happily living with a married man. I had agreed that I would slow down then stop drinking, but that didn't exactly happen. I explained to him how a few friends had called and wanted to go out and since he was supposed to be out of town on business I figured what the hell let me go kick it with the fellas. He was hot, you could see it all in his body language. I was trying to play it cool even though ole Mr. Smoking Declined Card was blowing my phone up. I ask Linus, "Baby what are you doing home? Aren't you supposed to be in D.C?" Without moving from his spot or moving his lips Linus says, "Yes, I am supposed to be in DC but since the tournament starts later due to unforeseen circumstances I came home to surprise you and spend some time with you before I fly out tomorrow but I see I'm the one who got the surprise huh!" I apologized profusely as I pan seared my last piece of salmon and pulled the asparagus from the oven. I walked over to Linus, grabbed his hand to pull him up out the chair and gave him another hug as I slow walked him into the room. We stood there forever just holding one another and me telling him I love him and I'm sorry I didn't tell him the truth about going out for drinks and dinner with the fellas. I pushed him down on the bed, climbed on top of him and had the best non fighting make up sex ever. Linus left the next morning at 4am to catch is 7am flight out of West Palm Beach but not before another round of he still wanna act like I'm mad at you sex. He leaves and soon returns by the end of the week to stay for good. It seemed like after that one little episode, Linus started to change and not for the better either.

Linus holds basketball practice at 3pm and is normally over by 5pm. Of course there is paperwork, phone calls and emails to be returned which puts Linus in the house no later than 7 - 7:30pm, most definitely no later than 8:30pm. There were plenty of times he would beat me home, but as of late Linus is coming in a tad bit later about 9 or so and steady texting. I let this go on for a week or so to make sure I'm not imagining anything. One night I'm sitting in the bed next to him working as we always did. He is texting and giggling his ass off when I say as peacefully and calmly as possible, "I don't know who Missy Poo is but you and her are going to respect my house. All y'all texting and talking stops when you darken that door step. When you take yo ass to Gainesville I don't fuck with you because I never know if and when Amethyst is with you and don't even try to sit up here and say that your texting with Amethyst either. If that was the case she would have been had her black ass down here to see about you and you damn shol can't say it's your players. They are young and trying to give away more head, booty and cock than a little bit, so whoever the fuck Missy is, get that shit together and get it together now! If you don't remember nothing else, remember this, I ain't new to this I'm true to this!!" He put that phone down so got damn quick and started talking about everything under the sun, never ever once denying or admitting anything. So this is how we gonna do it huh? I put my work aside for a few minutes and sit Indian style in front of Linus and say, "Baby listen, I know how it is to want to be on your own and not live with anyone even someone you love. We don't have to be together. You can see who you want and do whatever in the hell you want to do and we can still grill and chill out watching the games with no sex, no strings, no worries or pressure! Just call me ahead of time before you want to come over to ensure I don't have any company" Linus went off quick fast and in a hurry, but that wasn't nothing but a poor smoke screen he put up to try and deflect what he was already doing.

Things get back to normal for about two weeks and then he starts coming in my house around 10 – 10:30pm. I light into his ass again and tell him it is over. He thinks I'm joking because I use to break up with Linus almost every week but we never ever broke up, that was just my way of trying to get that guilt off my ass, but this time the break up was for real and I meant it. Whoever Missy Poo is or was that you just had to be with, by all means go there. This was the longest break up we ever had of two days and it was only because he went to Gainesville to a funeral of a friend of his who had hung himself. Linus called me Sunday afternoon after he figured I was out of church and talked to me all the way from Gainesville to Lauderdale about our relationship and what he wanted us to do and continue to be with one another. That Sunday in mid to late August when Linus came back from Gainesville, he never left my side again and things were back to how they use to be in the beginning, or so I thought.

Remember, Amethyst the wife, does not come down to Ft. Lauderdale. If there is a late night call he may answer or he may not and if he do the conversation is over just as quickly as it started. Which got me to thinking, if Linus was my husband and he was supposed to be staying with my sister but he ain't never ever there, I would have popped up to that nigga job with a fold away chair and cooler. Propped up outside on the passenger side so he couldn't see me when he came out. Soon as he hit the alarm on the car, I'd ease my ass up like a jack in the box with a big kool aide smile on my face and tell that nigga, "Where ever YOU go to lay your head down is where US is going to lay our head down and you bet not touch that phone while we riding to US sleeping place." Ain't no way in hell I would have let my good looking husband run loose in the new common day Sodom and Gomorrah of South Florida and I not come down and see about him. I asked him once again why she doesn't come down here. Once again claimed he didn't know. Fellas when a woman asks you a question, you can best believe she already knows the answer, we are just waiting on you to tell the truth and shed a little more light on the situation. I had already been reading his text messages for some time and could feel the cold shoulder she had been giving him. One weekend she went on some trip with her sister to Savannah, not to south Florida but to Savannah Georgia. He would send sweet loving texts to her and Amethyst reply would simply be "Awwww" or "Oh Ok" nothing more. I didn't say one word, I let him keep up his shenanigans. One night he ran into the house looking crazy and said, "Shit, she will be here tomorrow!" Not knowing or understanding what the hell he was talking about asked, "Who is she and why is she coming here?" She was Amethyst and her sister was having an emergency surgery so she was coming down here for the weekend. Once again, what can I say? I just sat back and asked myself, "Betty are you in this because of love or love of convenience?"

Our 1 year anniversary weekend is here 10/12/13. We have finally made it to a year and what a year it had been. We talked about the things we had discussed all year and where our progression was as far as with being together and moving forward with one another. One of the promises made by Linus was, once he went D1, no matter where he went I would follow and not work. He was going to put me back through school for my Nursing Degree. We had agreed on marriage and most definitely no more kids. He already has 4 and you already know I ain't spitting out nann! Yeah, I know you're trying to figure out where that 4 comes from. Linus has 2 girls from his wife. She already had one daughter from a previous relationship, so that's three right? Well two years into Linus's marriage, he had a son by a white co-worker! Linus never told me about the son. I found out about him by accident a month or so after we met. I was investigating someone else and stumbled upon this kid. One thing about me, Betty love the kids. I may not have wanted to give birth but I do love kids. I'm Auntee Betty to a host of kids and love them to pieces. I'm the aunt that will let you cuss, have a sip or two of my drink and have the real deal conversation with them about life and whatever else they want to talk about. I'll babysit from birth til two years old. After that don't bring they ass to my house until they have a job so they can let me hold a little something something and car so they can drive my ass around. Ok back to Linus. No matter if the girl got pregnant on purpose or kept the baby on purpose that's still your kid which you don't deny regardless of whoever. The entire time Linus and I are together I know about the little boy. I would just say crazy shit like, "Linus with your athleticism, smarts and my good looks let's make a little boy so he can take care of his momma in my old age playing basketball." Linus would do a quick "Ha" and change the subject just as quick as I started it. Even though Linus and I had talked about marriage, not having kids, relocating with him and living out the rest of our lives together, something wasn't right.

We had an awesome anniversary weekend. We went to see Rickey Smiley in West Palm Beach. Exchanged some nice gifts, once again was back to how we once use to be. We laughed til we cried about the things I use to do to Linus in the beginning of our relationship. The 1st time Linus and I made love. We cuddled until we both fell into a coma but I broke loose and threw my right leg over his body and went on a farting spree. He took every green fog producing fart for that first week we were together, the following week he woke me up out of a sound sleep and said, "Baby, baby BETTY are you ok? What did you eat because you are over here killing me?" We also cracked up about the first time I tinkled on him. Yes I got drunk and peed in the bed but I didn't have him doing the back stroke like the other little buddy in the previous story. Stop laughing, it was a small little tinkle that never ever touched him and he wouldn't have known about it had he got his ass up and went to work early like he was supposed to. One night we were watching his daughter play basketball when they did a special segment on her coach who once swam for the Olympic swim team and won. My retarded drunk ass went to sleep and dreamed that I was an Olympic swimmer in the race of my life. I was on the platform in position. I heard the starter gun go off. SPLASH! I was in the water, swimming like a fish. For some reason I was swimming very slow and what I felt holding me back from swimming as fast as I knew I could was the gas that was forming in my stomach. While swimming I figure if I fart really quick and kick at the same time so the judges and camera won't see the bubbles I'll be ok. I swim, kick, swim harder and kick harder and fart. Well a fart ain't the only thing that came out, it was pee. Just as soon as I fart in real life I pee at the same time all while kicking. I feel the wet spot, jump up without alerting Linus and put a towel down. I was too out done and laid there without cuddling with his snoring ass for about an hour or so thinking that he will get up before me and go to work. SYKE! This was his late day. When he stays in bed late watching the news and chilling until later in the afternoon. When I finally realize he ain't going to work, I damn near lose my mind. I get up. I slide out the bed like a slinky, throw the covers over the towel, take a deep breath and say, "Linus, don't make up the bed please." He looked at me a kinda funny because he always made the bed when he left after me. I took in a deep breath. Dropped my head and told him about my dream and what happened. I almost hit his ass in the head with a brick because he was laughing just too damn hard for me. I had a feeling he was going to leave me then for sure. To my surprise when I came home on lunch to take care of everything, Linus had already taken care of the bed, laundry and everything for me. We laughed a good while about that even though at the time it wasn't funny at all. He was good to me like that in many more ways than one!

A week or so after our anniversary I get a phone call from a very close friend of mine. He used to be my biggest and best frenemy during college football season. He is a Gator lover and I'm a Mighty Sexy Seminole Squaw. Now, he is my evangelical friend who is always there even when I don't call him. God will place me on his mind and the words he speaks to me can only come from God. On the day he called when I was busy in and out of meetings. Our entire admin was getting ready for a state audit. I answered real quick and told him I will call him back shortly as I was getting ready to go into a meeting. Hours went by and I never did call him back, so he sent me a text that read, "God told me to tell you He hears you but He will not bless or heal you until you honor the promise you made to Him years ago!" I stopped dead in my tracks with tears running down my face and Goosebumps raised all over my body. People were asking me what was wrong but I couldn't speak. I ran to my office closed the blinds. Put a do not disturb sign on my door, shut and locked my door and called Evangelist Kerry back. We sat on the phone for almost 2 hours of him telling me every single thing I have prayed to God for. No one knew of these Prayers especially not Kerry, but when he got to the promise I made God years ago, I broke down and told him everything. As we were talking, God was steady talking to him and easing my soul and spirit as God is the only one who knew my heart's desire and Prayers. The promise I made years ago to God was if he was to get me through and out of my relationship with Cleophus, I would never in my life date another married man. Cleophus was married when we got together. When we started living together 10 months into our relationship Cleophus had already filed for divorce. The relationship grew horrible with all of his cheating, my cheating which he never caught me doing, the child support and all the baby mommas. I wanted out of that shit with the quickness, but God didn't let me out until I learned my lesson.

I was married man free for two years and proud until Linus chocolate thunder ass came along!

Linus had developed a very bad habit of not wanting to tell me when he was going to Gainesville. The rule in our house was I needed to know as soon he knew he had to go to Gainesville, no matter what the reason so I could be mentally prepared, well as make arrangements to do other shit besides sitting in the house. At first that rule worked fine until one weekend I picked him from the airport fully dressed, face beat to the gawds and a doggy bag from one of my favorite restaurants that him and I had never been too. After that Linus would tell me 1-2 days before he was supposed to leave and that would start shit in our household when we normally didn't have that type of energy in our house. It's now November, just about a month after our 1 year anniversary and I'm at work on a Monday afternoon and had just finish dealing with a telecommuter staff who does not like to follow policy when Linus texts me and says, "You know we have that week long tournament in Orlando this week and after we finish I'm going to drive up to Gainesville for a surprise visit for my step mom that all my siblings have put together." When I read that shit I got hot as hell and wanted to call him and go off but he knew he was safe. I'm not one to show out in public and especially not at my place of business. Instead I sent him a hot ass text going slap the hell off but also explaining to him that I need to show him old texts in my ole phone where the entire family was just with her July of this year for the family reunion and that if he is going to Gainesville for his anniversary with Amethyst he just needs to man up. Not only did he not call back, he didn't come home that night! Being that my job is flexible I worked from home that Tuesday because I had a feeling he was going to try and pull a junkie stunt and show up when he thought I was at work. He didn't show Tuesday nor did he stay there Tuesday night, so I worked from home again on Wednesday and parked my car in the back of the complex again. Just as I was about to get up and make me another cup of tea and watch a little TV, the brown Lexus with rims comes slow rolling in and parks in his parking spot. I back away from the window where my desk was situated. I jump in my big comfy chair in the corner and wait for him to open the door. When Linus opened that door he stopped. Gasped for air and asked, "What are you doing here?" I snapped, "Bitch, I live here, what the hell you doing coming here when you think I'm at work? Where have you been for the past two day's coz all your shit is here?" Before he could even speak, my stomach sank to the pits of my bowels because I knew he was lying when he said, "I been at my sister in laws house!" How in the hell was he expecting me to believe that bull shit when you haven't stayed over her house since we met and all your shit is in my house. When you leave town, you leave from here when you come back into town you come here, so how in the hell you been gone from her house all this time and then you can just pop back up over there easy like Sunday morning. I went off about telling me last minute about the trip to Gainesville and grabbed my old cell phone which I had been charging since Monday to show him a previous text about being with his step mother, he didn't want to see it so he walked off. He tries to spend a lot of time with his step mom since his father died and ensure she is ok and to let her know she is still loved.

We went round and round over him telling me at the last minute about his trips, being honest about what is really going on. I can't really tell him that I know what is going on because I have been all through this texts and voice mail! The argument gets so intense and heated that I finally break down and tell him about my spirit being in turmoil, the conversation with Evangelist Kelly and this relationship has really been about convenience for me. He shuts up. Stops and looks at me like I just gave him a gut punch to rival that of Mike Tyson. We sat there in silence for a few minutes when he asks, "If this relationship was only of convenience to you, why did you stay with me for this entire year? Did you love me like you said you did, what the?" I could have slapped his ass because this relationship was convenient for him too, he just didn't want to admit it. I respond, "Linus I do love you as a matter of fact I love more than I ever thought I could. When we first started I was in a very vulnerable place and you fitted everything I look for, love and desire in a man it's just that for the past year I haven't met a man who was able to do what you did and do. It seems as late with all the changes going on between us and I have talked to you on many occasions about how things have changed and not for the better, things will get better between us for a minute but then it goes right back to the bull which I refuse to put up with especially in this type of relationship. Can I have anyone I want? Hell yeah, I can have any man I want but for the past year I have wanted you but things keep changing and not for the better. I have offered you the opportunity to just be friends with no strings and no benefits and still allow you to come over and chill. You didn't want that. I offered an open relationship, you didn't want that so that leaves nothing else for us to do, I'm tired of this bull. You claim you're going to see your step mom when we both know that's a lie. Its Amethyst birthday and your anniversary, just tell the truth." He didn't say anything, he just packed up some clothes for the week long tournament and some hangout clothes for when he went to Gainesville. He never said another word the whole time he was packing up some clothes. When he got ready to leave he stopped at my desk pulled me up from my chair gave me hug and said, "I love you Betty and I never wanted anybody else or any of those other scenarios in our relationship because you are who I love, want and desire to be with. Not to mention more than a handful to deal with. We will talk more about this when I get back because we have a lot to deal with, and FYI this relationship was not convenient for me. I really do love you." I didn't say another word. He walked out the door and I finished working. That was Wednesday early afternoon when he left for Orlando with his team. I didn't hear from Linus until the following Tuesday. No phone call. No text the entire time he is gone. I see Linus don't think fat meat is greasy.

Linus and I talk Tuesday night to check in and let me know he had just got back that and that things have become highly complicated between him and Amethyst and we need to talk. I'm so sick and tired of talking but I ask him when and he says sometime this week as they are preparing to play against a pretty tough opponent from Puerto Rico so he was going to be in the office late tonight. How are you in the office late for a team that was 4-13? Ok, Imma play the part. We talk during the week and decide we will break up but he still wants to talk. That was cool but I needed him to come and get all his stuff out my house since we are going to break up. I'm knocked out when Linus comes through my door at 12:15am Thursday night, drops his dirty clothes in the hamper like all is fine and gets in bed giving me some of the best make up, I miss you sex. When he left the next morning, he didn't take any clothes with him. He did his usual routine of standing on my side of the bed until I get up so we can hug, kiss and say our daily morning "I love you!" Before Linus leaves he tells me one more time he loves me and we will talk tonight because this isn't over. We talk Friday morning but Linus is a no show with no call or text that evening. Here go that lying bullshit again. He had a game Saturday against Puerto Rico and normally I would have attended but after last year season I stopped going. Them heffas wasn't winning enough games for me to be driving from Ft. Lauderdale to downtown Palm Beach with gas still high ass giraffe pussy. We talked before the game and I texted my weekly spirit fingers in hopes that would help. They lost. Linus was texting just a tad too much that night yet he wasn't really saying anything worth texting about. We talked about how FSU had whopped another team and little non-essential stuff. I received my last text from him about 7:45pm. By 9pm Linus is not at my house to talk or collect his belongings. I call him at 9pm. No answer, no return phone call or text. This goes on until 11pm with no answer, no return phone call or text. You already know I'm hotter than the blue flame of a fire. I walk through my apartment for a few minutes. I'm burning the hell up with anger that I had not experienced since my days with Sincere, so you know I'm ready to fight!

The phone rings three times when a voice answers rather hastily, "Hello?" I take in a deep breath and say, "Hi sweetie. Is this Amethyst?" She responds in a very nasty attitude, "Don't call me sweetie!" I wasn't in the mood for that type of attitude, so I quip back, "You may want to kill the attitude sweetie, my name is Betty and I'm your husband's live in girlfriend! Have you talked to Linus today?" She got quiet. A minute or so passed and she responded in a calmer nicer tone, "Yea, I talked to him once, earlier today." I asked, "Have you talked to your sister?" Amethyst replied, "Yes about 30 minutes or so ago?" She is quiet and I'm trying to pace the questions as to not lose her in any of this. I then ask, "When you talked to your sister was Linus there?" She was slow in her response, "Actually no, he wasn't. Why?" I said real quick, "Because he isn't he here and I was just wondering if he was at your sister's house." Amethyst and I said at the same time, "It must be someone else!" Amethyst and I stayed on the phone and talked for about 30 - 45 minutes. 10 minutes into our conversation my phone beeps. Low and behold it's Mr. Linus. I interrupt Amethyst and tell her that it's Linus calling me and she said, "I know because I just texted him and told him I was on the phone with his live in girlfriend!" I laughed, never clicked over and got back to talking to her. Our entire conversation was me asking her all the questions I had asked him the entire year we were together. The answers she gave me, made me feel so bad for Linus. You could tell this was a woman who was tired, fed up and meant every word she said to me.

The main question that was burning me up and I had to know and asked was, "Amethyst, why haven't you come down here more to check on Linus?" There was no hesitation when she responded, "Because I refuse to put any wear and tear on my car. Waste my money or time coming down there!" Pineapples, PINEAPPLES! I was nowhere near ready for that answer, but I kept right on asking questions. I asked what if he went D1, she flat out said she was not going anywhere he goes. She is happy and fine right there where she is. I had to ask about the outside son I asked, "I don't mean to be funny but why doesn't Linus talk about or recognize his son? Is it because you don't accept him?" She was so cool and almost sounded heart broken when she answered, "No, I accept his son and have said he can come around. It's Linus who acts as if he don't want him around." Since I had her on the phone with so many burning questions I kept asking and she was pleasant in her response. I asked, "If Linus was supposed to be living with your sister and he hasn't been there in months, that didn't bother you or make you want to come down here on a surprise visit and find out what was going on?" I had to laugh to myself and respect her answer when she said, "No not really because my sister was only letting him stay there as a favor to me. When he left she was happy because she wanted her space back. I always told Linus that I'm a God fearing Praying woman and whatever he was doing would soon be revealed to me plus our marriage has pretty much been over way before he left here in August, so I guess you can say I was living free and enjoying my life. That's why I'm not moving down there, that's why I'm not relocating with him if he ever does go D1 or anything else. I make enough for me and my girls. He don't pay any bills here and his name isn't on my house so I'm good! You have actually been a blessing to me tonight and I appreciate you calling, and no, I'm not seeing anyone."

That last statement caught me off guard. I never asked her if she was seeing anyone. It wasn't my business and I really didn't care. Untwist your face, because mine was most definitely twisted when she said that. If I am doing dirt the last thing I want to do is add anymore sunlight to an already beaming situation. With her not coming down here, calling or doing pop ups that was evident enough for me, but none of my business. We talk a few more minutes before she asks me to call her tomorrow so we can finish talking because she has to get to work tomorrow and those 12 hours ain't no joke. When we get off the phone, I sit there thinking real deep and hard about what this woman and I just shared with one another and I asked myself again, "Betty are you in this because of love or love of convenience?" I was still asking myself that same question an hour and a half into packing all of Linus shit up and placing it in the living room. I was tired. My little buzz from my liquor was gone. I was sweating like a slave but in a good place mentally. I wasn't mad nor angry I was actually at peace, finally!

That Sunday I was home working OT, which is rare for me because I never like to miss Church for anything. I had moved my car to the neighboring complex the night before in preparation for Mr. Junky Stunt pulling Linus. I got up at 6:15 am made me hot pot of water for my tea and promptly started work at 6:30am. I was in a calm, peaceful mode all morning. Linus knows I go to Church every Sunday and leave my house no later than 9:30am to make it to Delray Beach on time for Church. His retarded ass sends me a text at exactly 9:45am stating, "Good morning. Not sure if you are home or not but I'm on my way to the house and will leave the key if you're not there." I don't respond because I don't have time, the brown Lexus with rims is slow rolling through the complex. I slide back from my desk that sat directly in front of my living room windows as he pulls directly in the handicap parking spot. He sits there for a few minutes and looks up to see if he can see anything. He gets out the car with his duffle bag and proceeds upstairs and opens the door to see me. He turns white and doesn't say one word as he sees all his shit in the living room taking up major space. I immediately light into his ass and start going off. He never says one word. I ask, "So since you are all of a sudden a mute, can you unmute and tell me why you lied this entire time?" He doesn't say one word. I ask, "Where were you last night?" This nigga had the nerve to say, "I was at my sister in law house chilling watching the highlights from all of the games." I lose it, get up from my desk and stand directly in front of him and scream at him, "You lying mutha fucker do you not remember I was on the phone with Amethyst last night, huh? You don't remember that huh? She had just hung up with her sister who said yo black ass was not there and we already know you wasn't at the head coach house because his wife is pregnant again and your frat brothers all got they own shit going on, so where the fuck were you?" He stops gathering his already packed shit, looked at me and said with the straightest face ever, "I was at my sister in law house!" He was not going to budge off that lie, instead of answering any of my questions or finally coming clean since the entire truth was already out there, this negro started humming church hymns. When he did that I just laughed. It took him 7 trips to get all of his belongings out of my house and an additional 2 trips to get my key, gate card and parking decal out of his car.

When Linus left that morning we were both burning with a heated anger that would not be quelled for some time. I was supposed to call Amethyst later that Sunday but I didn't. I had already found out what I needed. I found out why she wasn't coming down here to check on him and that he had not been to his sister in laws house those 3 nights he claimed he was there, so there was no other reason to call her. I know you're sitting there scratching your head trying to figure out why I called her in the first place. My intentions of calling her had nothing to do with ever breaking them up. If she stayed after he had a son with a white girl two years into their marriage, what was our 1 year of being in a relationship and living together supposed to do? Not a damn thing. When he got too comfortable with our situation and felt like he could play me like he play Amethyst, I had to correct his thinking and let him know I ain't new to this but true to this! Plus I had far too many questions and no answers. He was not cooperating like he should have especially when I'm giving you plenty of options with no problems. Had Linus been straight up with me as I was with him, I would have covered for him to the grave but like most men, they get far too comfortable and think they got all the sense in the world when in actuality they ain't doing a damn thing but spinning their wheels in the mud!

That Sunday afternoon after I simmered down a tad, I started scrolling through my phone trying to find someone who could come and change my locks because I was getting ready to go out of town that Wednesday for Thanksgiving then head up to Gainesville Friday for my annual FSU/UF rivalry party and wanted to make sure I didn't return to a surprise. I scrolled through my phone 3 or 4 times before my finger stopped on a name. The name of a person I had not spoken to in years. Instead of calling, I decided I would text just in case the number changed or someone else owned this number. The text read, "Hi Sarge! How are you? I hope all is well." Not even a minute later I get a reply, "Hi baby. I'm good how are you? Where are you?" I text back and forth with Sarge before asking him if he knew how to change door locks. He was too excited to come and change the locks, so I told him to let me go get what I needed and I'll meet him at a gas station and have him follow me home. When we get to my apartment and Sarge gets out the car, he has a walking cast on his left foot. I ask Sarge, "What happened to you?" He had just had surgery on his foot to repair a tendon he tore years ago, it had become too painful to walk or do anything but he came to my house and changed that lock with no problem. Sarge and I started hanging out daily and just catching up on everything and enjoying one another's company. One night while Sarge and I are hanging out having a drink my mind wonders back to the prison and I get a little teary eyed. Sarge asks while rubbing my arm, "Betty, baby what's wrong?" The tears don't fall but my nose got stuffy and I sounded funny when I responded to Sarge and said, "I just want to thank you for saving my life when La'Quanda the inmate had plotted to kill me!" I'm over here in a tender moment reflecting on life when this black bastard had the nerve to say, "Awww I wasn't going to let her kill you when I wanted to kill you my damn self. Hell, she couldn't have all the fun! All the shit you took me through, ohh you know I couldn't let anybody lay a finger on you if I haven't." He always did know how to ruin a wet dream.

Sarge and I continue to hangout for some time never ever once being intimate. For one he has a girlfriend of 5 years and secondly I never double back and sleep with an ex. You are most definitely an ex for a reason. One day Sarge calls and tells me we need to talk and to meet him for dinner. I select one of my favorite steak houses, J Alexander and tell him to meet me at 8pm. I actually get there on time and see Sarge there already with this look on his face like someone has died. I know his brother is a crack head but they don't die they just multiply, so it ain't him. I know his mother is older and had taken ill sometime back but he would have called me ASAP if something had happened to her. We finally get seated, hold very small talk which is most definitely not Sarge, so I ask him in a very concerned manner, "Sarge, what is wrong? What is going on? Are you ok?" Sarge looks up from the table looks me right in my face, grabs my right hand and says, "I never ever want to hurt you again. How we broke up all those years ago still haunts me because I lied to you and I felt your hurt that night we had the fight and all these years later, so I want to come clean to you now. When everything first jumped off all I could do was see your face and think about you" I'm getting frustrated as hell, I squeeze his hand and forcefully say, "SPILL THE FUCKING BEANS MAN!" Sarge looking sick as hell in the face finally continues, "You know me and old girl have been together for 5 years and for the entire time I have always been able to shake her grip when she talks about marriage. Now that she is older, all her friends are married and keep asking her when we are we getting married she put the pressure on me. I swear Betty I didn't propose to her because I never saw myself getting married again. She hit me with the ultimatum and I told her to handle all the details. She got the rings, the clothes, honeymoon planned out and paid for everything. All I had to do was fill out the marriage certificate. We are getting married 2 weeks from today, Friday July 25. I'm sorry!"

I can't front and lie, my feelings were hurt. Not because my ex, Sarge is getting married but because I ain't getting married. I can't be that bad of person that a good man doesn't want to marry me. My standards aren't that high that a man can't jump up and grab the bar and pull himself over to meet my few little measly standards. I drop a tear as those thoughts roll through my mind. This retard has the nerve to say, "Baby if you had waited on me, you and I would be getting married, not me and her. I never stopped loving you and I will always love you!" Did this mutha fucker just say, "Had I waited on him we'd be getting married?" Girl fix your wig. I had to pat and scratch my weave when this Negro said that shit. I took in a deep breath and went off on his ass reminding him why the fuck we broke up in the first place, "Bitch wasn't you married and didn't tell me? Had me all up in that woman face looking like a damn fool and then you cheated on me the crypt keeper from Tales from the crypt and Lord only knows what else you did to me that I don't know about, so wait on you for what?" He didn't part his lips, he just ordered another double shot of Tito's vodka for me and sat there quietly until I decided it was safe for conversation to begin again. Did this bastard just say, I should have waited for him? Where is my skillet when I really need one?

Sarge and old girl get married as planned. Sarge and I hung out one last time at a fight party the weekend before his nuptials. We have not seen nor spoken with one another since that weekend.

Linus and I have not spoken to one another nor seen each other since that Sunday morning. I spoke with a mutual friend of ours a few months ago who died laughing when I told him the real and complete story about everything. When he finally stopped laughing he said, "You know Linus didn't tell me all of this. He left a lot of this shit out but I knew you would tell the whole story." I had to chuckle at that my damn self and said, "I'm pretty sure he hates me and wish I was dead but oh well!" This was the only time our mutual friend was serious and said, "Betty to be honest. He doesn't hate you. He ain't even mad. He said he got caught at his own game and misses you tremendously!" When our mutual friend used that big word, I knew that came from Linus and no one else. That Negro always likes to sound highly educated like he has all the sense in the world.

Till this very day I still think of Linus and wonder if he is ok and how is he doing. There are times I especially miss him like during football and basketball season when he would help me to come up with quick quips to all the Gator and Heat fans. Grilling our favorite foods before the games and just being with him in general. With me getting back into this incest infested dating pool, I most definitely think of him. Normally I tell guys that they were a complete waste of time, but in my time with Linus even though he was married it wasn't a total waste of time. It was another great learning and growing experience that allowed me to re-experience what I had been missing for so long. A man that knew how to create a stable, safe and secure environment for me to be me, grow and change on my own without him trying to change me as so many other men have tried to do. Linus always took care of me and that's just one of the many reasons our break up affected me as it has. Our good times greatly outweighed our bad times, because we didn't have any bad times until the end when he tried to be slicker than a wet oil slick and that just wasn't about to work with a woman like me. "Betty was you in this for love or love of convenience?"

Remember Charles the love and lust of my life from chapter 3? He is back in the states and currently coaches college basketball. A couple of months after Linus and I broke up, Charles came to Ft. Lauderdale on business. We made plans to see one another the entire week and weekend that he was here. As I was taking my shower getting ready to go see him, my heart broke and I cried like a baby. I didn't leave my house. The Holy Spirit said not too.

Charles is now married with children and there was no way I could promise God or myself that nothing would happen, especially with the emotions that were instantly were stirred up upon hearing his voice. All the memories started flooding back into my mind and the fresh break up from Linus didn't make it any better. When we spoke the next day, Charles understood exactly where I was coming from because he felt the same thing and was unsure if he could remain committed to his marriage vows had I come to his hotel. I want my own husband. I had to be obedient and repent for the thought of even wanting to go over there, especially with what I had just went through with Linus and the horrible way we broke up. ~~Ain't That Bout'a Bitch~~

CHAPTER 15

BACK TO THE BASICS

After Linus and I had our 1st, only and final major argument; I swore off online and social media dating and said let me get back to the basics. The basics of getting to know myself all over again, knowing what I want, don't want and desire in my life. And even though I was going to Church and paying my tithes faithfully, I also needed to get back to the basics of my relationship with God.

When Linus and I broke up in late November, it was close to my annual FSU/UF rivalry party that I throw every single year in Gainesville Florida so I wasn't sweating the break up. I was gearing up for my event. As usual, my party went off like a BANG and we had an awesome time. FSU beat the snot out the Gators. That year I had people fly in from California, Georgia and from all over Florida. We have a blast and shut the city down. Even though I was in Gainesville and its Thanksgiving weekend and I know Linus was there, he never once crossed my mind.

I make it back to Ft. Lauderdale early December; and get a phone call from Jordan. You remember Jordan right? The handsome mocha latte, good haired, divorcee who I met during Super Bowl 2010 when Cleophus just so happen to lock me and my family out the door in the freezing cold. Well we remained in contact this entire time but it was always hard to coordinate our schedules due to his grueling work and travel schedule. When we did manage to spend time, he always made sure it was romantic, fun filled and all about Betty. Damn, if only for one night! Jordan calls to ask me over to watch the FSU ACC Championship game with him and just kick it. Jordan is a huge FSU fan like me which of course you know I love. Not only is Jordan a huge fan of FSU, he also graduated from FSU and pledge Omega Psi Phi. You know I happily accepted his invitation and sped my ass down to Homestead and had a great time smoking my favorite cigar that he keeps stocked in his humidor just for me, drinking wine and watching FSU pluck the feathers out of Auburns War Eagle. Becoming the 2013 National Champions! When Jordan and I are together we always have this electric chemistry between us that makes the time we spend so much fun and mind blowing! If often makes me wonder, what if?

I text my hair stylist Nia in Ft. Lauderdale and ask her to set my appointment for the 2nd Friday in January. When she calls me and tells me some very devastating news about her mom. Ms. Dorothea. her mom had been in a devastating car accident and passed away. Ms. Dorothea was the type of woman who never ever met a stranger. She would feed you, give you somewhere to sleep and just an all-around good, God fearing and God loving woman. If you were ever able to be blessed to have her wash your hair in the salon, ohh my word, you ain't never had a feeling like that. I remember one day going in there for a regular wash and set but my head was hurting so bad, that I looked Chinese because my eyes were half closed. Ms. Dorothea always talked loud but with the most electric and contagious smile and said, "Baby come on in here and let me see what momma can do for ya." When I got up from that shampoo bowl my eyes were open. My body felt calm and relaxed and my head ain't never felt better. I use to love to walk into the salon and see Ms. Dorothea; I would speak to her first and get the biggest hug from her. Going to the salon on Friday nights just aren't the same with her not being there, she is truly missed. Nia calls telling me when the wake and funeral services are, I tell her I'm here for her in whatever way she needs me. I saw her mother as my mother too.

I get off Friday night about 7pm. Still dressed in slacks and a Polo pullover shirt and flip flops. I had been in my loafers all day and needed to let them dawgs breathe. I park in another business parking lot, 4 lots over. As I'm walking up I'm seeing people from all walks of life standing outside. Some older and dressed more respectfully. Then there was the crew who looked like they had an AK or SR on them and will use it with no hesitation. I clutched my purse a little tighter under my right arm and walked a little faster like I was in a speed race. As I'm walking up to the funeral parlor, I see a big, tall, dark chunky dude with a mouth full of gold wearing me out with his eyes. I'm scared as hell. The way he is looking at me is like he is about to jack me right at the front door of the wake. I clutch my purse even tighter and walk like my feet are on fire and a puddle of water is just a few feet ahead of me. He starts to walk towards me. I make a mad dash to the right into the parking lot over a yellow parking bumper. There are people standing on the sidewalk talking and I think I have shook him, when he appears directly in front of me in the parking lot. I freeze as if he has pulled a gun on me. He comes close and wraps his right arm around me and says, "It's been a long time since I last seen't you. How you been?" I quickly respond while pulling away from his ferocious grip and say, "No sweetie, we don't know one another. I'm not from here." I start walking towards the funeral home to make my quick entrance and exit just as quickly as I entered. I don't deal very well with death and I turn into a water bag very quickly. Just before I reach the door, here comes the Michelin man ass talking about, "Yo, I taught you were a chick I went to sc'ool wit and all I was doing was try'na speaking. I won'ta know mo bout ya if ya don't mind lil momma? Oh yeah my name is'a Dunna Man, wut cho name iz?" Yeah, you just read that slang and broken English exactly how it was spoken to me. So don't be looking at me all crazy like I don't know how to spell. The way you looking right now is the same exact way I was looking when he was talking to me. I never made any facial expression to let him know that I was lost as hell. To get out this situation with him, I say, "Hi, nice to meet you love. My name is Betty. That's cool sweetie, we can talk soon as I leave the wake, I just want to see Nia and let her know I'm here for her and the kids."

I finally get away from him and draw some strength to actually be brave enough to walk into the sanctuary and give Ms. Dorothea the proper respect she deserved. She was truly good to us all. I see Nia and the girls and they are doing fine, actually they are doing better than I expected, so I grab Nia and pull her to the side and ask, "Do you know a dude name Dunna Man?" Her eyes got big, she gave me a big ole smile and said, "Girl yes I know Dunna Man, he use to run with my husband back in the day before he got locked up!" I know Nia through her husband and Sincere who use to run dope from back in the day. When she said the Dunna Man use to run with her husband, I was extra done. I hung out a little while longer to lend my support to Nia and her family and to shake the Dunna Man who was running straight Top Flight Security on the front door of the funeral parlor. I looked for a back door exit. It was hooked to an alarm so that killed that idea of going out the back for an easy unnoticed escape. It was getting late, my stomach was starting to chew on my left pinky toe. I hadn't eaten since earlier in the day and I wanted to ensure that I didn't get sick while at the wake and lose my food. I give my love, hugs and kisses to Nia and the girls and get a running jump start out the door, when the Dunna man catches up with me and walks me to my car talking the whole time. I don't respond or say a word. I can only catch on to a few words that he says, so I just nod and say "uhh hhh." We finally make it to my car and I'm looking around constantly. My head is on a swivel. I don't know if this is a jack move or not and I always keep something on me just in case. We are talking and he is just talking me to death telling me, "I ain'gunna lie, I use to be all up in dese screets makun mad money and living all big Willie style but once a nucca seen all my boys fall'wen off with mad long crazy time I knews I had to make a change or sumthing cuz even tho I was in dem screets and was ready for wut'eva, I won'st tryin to be off in no damn prizzun, feel me?" Of course you know I agreed with everything he said. He went on to tell me he has 3 kids all girls. He owns a store that sells hair and hair care products, a mobile and stationary mobile detail business and something else that I didn't understand nor did I ask for details. He went on to tell me that he has 5 cars, lives on his own in a condo and he is completely legit just looking for that rock so he can get married and settle down and then he says, "You know by next year, I won'na hav'a mor'garage, stop paying rent and just live big!" I can't fault him for that, hell all of us are out here looking for love, marriage and a house with a double garage. He asks me about myself and I try my hardest to dumb it down as much as possible. Not trying to make it seem as if I'm from the streets or uneducated, but just by not using big words. I have already detected him and the proper use of English diction are not on the best of terms right now. I explain to him that I'm an Assistant Supervisor with Department of Children and Families and have held various professional positions in my 37 years. No criminal history with a strong desire to go back to school for another degree, this time in nursing.

Dunna Man had the biggest smile on his face and grabbed me and gave me the tightest bear hug I have ever been in, in my life and said, "I won'na help you get dat da'cree so den you can take care of me!" I didn't say anything. I wiggled out of his arms and looked down at my phone to check the time. Dunna Man, then says, "Have you eaten? Lets go grab some food. Where you won'ta go get some food from?" I promise you it was taking every fiber in my body to keep me from beating him in the head with a dictionary and praying that the words just leapt into his brain. I kindly declined and started digging in my purse for my keys, when he said, "I aint tak'on no for no answer. Where wuld you like to go?" I am hungry as an Ethiopian hostage and it ain't like I got shit else to do. I agree to go have dinner with him and I tell him to meet me at TGIF over on West Broward Blvd in about 30 -45 min. I always said one day I was going to learn my lesson about always going out with someone trying to get my grub and drink on and boy did I learn this night.

You know I can't get no damn where on time. I showed up about 15 – 20 minutes late. I took a shower and changed into some jeans and cute little sweater with my same ole work flip flops. I pull into the parking and see the prettiest copper brown dunk with the nose raised up and the ass dropped low just bamming out. I'm so busy looking at the car and trying to park that I didn't even notice it was the Dunna man. I get out and start to walk over, he hits the gas to let me know how that big block engine sounds and ohhhh did she sound good as hell with the pipes, music and all. Dunna cleaned up pretty nice and was smelling pretty good too. I'm thinking maybe I was a little quick on the draw to try and dismiss him, let's give him another chance and see what happens. We walk into TGIF holding small and simple conversation. I don't want either one of us to get lost on each other's words. We are seated at the bar because I wanted to watch the basketball game. I start out with my usual drink of patron shot and Tito's vodka. We are having a decent time and I'm actually starting to enjoy myself, mostly due to the liquor. The waiter returns to take our order and he starts with me asking, "What will you be having this evening ma'am?" Still looking down at the menu I look and respond, "I will have the Grilled Salmon with Langostino Lobster seasonal veggies and rice pilaf. Thank you." The waiter repeats my order back to me. We agree that the order is correct, he then turns his attention the Dunna man. I turn my attention to the basketball game. It's now getting intense. Chris Paul has just broken 2 sets of ankles and makes the 3 off the dribble, SWOOSH!! When I hear the waiter gently cough and say, "Uhmm excuse me, can you repeat that please?" I take another sip of my vodka and turn my head towards the Dunna man who says, "Yea, I want da Sa'mon but I don't want no los'ta, just the Sa'mon." Just as I'm about to slide down my chair and out the back door like a slinky the waiter turns his head to me and we get into the biggest argument with our eyes. This fool has the nerves to look at me and raise his eyebrows saying, "This yo mutha fucking man, what in the hell is he saying?" I raise my back with a smirk on my lips saying, "This is ain't my fucking man, I just met him but ain't you the professional? Don't you know how to read between the lines and take peoples orders? Imma do this one time and one time only, you bet not ask me for shit else." The waiter rolled his eyes at me. I rolled my eyes back at him to let him know I will be meeting him in the parking lot when he got off, with a real nasty dirty south Florida ass beating. I take the rest of the vodka to the head because I'm going to need it. I take in a deep breath. Look over at Dunna Man and gently rub his right thigh with my left hand and say, "Baby, just point to what you want to eat." This fool points to what I had just ordered but was adamant about not having the los'ta on it because he is allergic to shellfish.

Come on now, straighten your head up and unscrew your face one more time. I know, I know it's hard to understand. What he was trying to order was the salmon without the lobster. If you could have seen the waiters face when he tried to place his order, the waiters face was priceless. There wasn't enough money in the world to ever recreate that look. The food some came, our conversation was small and pretty much on the basketball game and other little small stuff, so we could both be on the same page with one another A commercial came on regarding buying homes, when the Dunna Man turns to me and says, "I can't wait til I get my mor'garage, that's when I knows I dun did tha thang then." Going off of what he has just said to me I ask, "Once you get more garage space, how many cars do you plan on placing in there? I know the vert is going in there for sure." He looked at me crazy and rubbed his chin like he was disgusted with me and said, "I'm not get mo car space. I'm finna stop paying rent and get a mor'garage and own sum shit shawty!" I didn't know what to say or even how to play this one off. I sat there quiet for what seemed like an eternity trying to come up with a smooth mellow way get out of this. Nothing! I flagged the waiter down and asked for a to-go box, smiled at the Dunna Man with childlike innocence and finally said, "Honey I hope you find the house of your dreams and live like a King for the rest of your days." He smiled grabbed my hand and said, "Thank you, hope'ully you will be der too living like da Queen you is!" It finally dawns on me, mor'gararge is actually mortgage. Uhmmm

I wasn't trying to be funny or mean towards the Dunna Man, but with the way my luck runs I could see the 1st time we had sex I would get pregnant with triplets and they all slide right up out my little cooda with a mouth full of gold, speaking broken English and asking, "Yooooooo ma, y'all get dat mor'garage set up?" Nah, I'll pass and just keep my little cooda to myself and keep it moving. The waiter finally came back and politely bagged up my food, Dunna man paid for the food. He actually tipped the waiter very well, when he wasn't looking I slipped in an additional $5 because of what he had to endure. Dunna walked me to my car and asked when would he see me again because he was really feeling me. I didn't have it in me to tell him this was our first and last time ever ever ever doing a got damn thing together. I told him let me check my schedule as I work a lot of OT and I'll get back to him quickly. I got in my car, listened to the pipes of the vert one last time and put his ass on straight block. For almost a month I didn't go get my hair done by Nia for fear I would run into him and have to explain why I put him on block. I do wonder how he is doing from time to time and if he ever got that mor'garage, then again no I don't. Back to the basics 1, Betty 0. ~~Ain't That Bout'a Bitch~~

A few weeks, almost a month have passed since I have last seen or heard from Mr. Mor'garage and I for one was not upset or concerned.

I will admit, Linus had scrolled through my mind a few times. I get off one Saturday evening from working OT and have a strong taste for some chicken gizzards. I slow roll over to the hood and pick up my order and just roll through Sistrunk Ave taking in the sights of my people hanging out and enjoying their life to the fullest with a game of spades, checkers and dancing under the tree at the park, when I see something so fine and dressed sharp. As I slowly pass by him standing in front of a Tahoe, I mouth "DAMN!" He yells "Turn around cutie." You already know my hot ass bent that corner so quick, crept back up to him and hopped out the Suzuki like I was the jump out boys from SWAT. He walks up to me, wears me out with his eyes, shakes my hand with a firm grip and says, "Hello beautiful, my name is DeMario. What is your name?" He has 4 golds on the bottom of his mouth, yet speaks perfectly good English. I respond, "Hello DeMario, what a pleasure it is to meet you. My name is Betty." We have great conversation for about 20 minutes building a comfort zone and feeling one another out. I have to admit, I was feeling his little chocolate drop ass. DeMario was about an inch or 2 taller than me, dark chocolate, some very pretty well manicured low cut waves that were freshly lined up. He had an electric smile even with the 4 golds at the bottom of his mouth and a very taunt, well defined body either from work or the gym. Either way, his little black ass was sexy. DeMario is a supervisor the city of Ft Lauderdale and has been there for 15 years. He has 3 kids all whom he claims to have an active role in their lives even though he also claims to not have any sexual or physical contact with their mothers. When asked about a girlfriend, he stutters and stammers around then eventually states he is single but lives in the house him and an ex bought together, but she don't live there. Uhmmm mm ok! We find out that our birthdays are just one day and one year apart, with me being the oldest. His is February 11th and mine is the 12th. I make the suggestion, "Since you are the young gun, you should take the ole lady out for her birthday." We both laugh and he says, "As soon as I get back from cruise, we can do whatever you want to do, all on the young gun since that's the name you have for me." We share a few more laughs before my stomach rudely starts joining in on the conversation. We exchange numbers and plan on becoming more acquainted.

We talk and text all that week. Our schedules are completely different. He gets up at 4am gets off at 3 or 4pm and is in bed early due to his schedule. I'm knocked out until 7am knowing good and got damn well I need to be to work 8am but I don't get off until 8pm. I'm always working OT, so for the moment all we can do is text and talk on the phone. The 2014 Super Bowl was vastly approaching and I didn't want to watch it at a sports bar or home alone. The year before Linus was home with me watching the game, chilling having a great time eating fresh grilled burgers and wondering who in the hell came up with those whack ass commercials. A few of my friends was doing something but I didn't want to go there either. DeMario called me and told me him and his crew was about to do it big and asked me to come through and watch the game with him. I'm ready. I got my hair done that Saturday, toes done, eyebrows arched and a fresh new cute little strapless dress. Remember I live in Ft. Lauderdale, our winter is only 4 days long and that is broken up over the months. It was a beautiful weekend to go cute and strapless. I get the directions to the party and ironically it's the same park I met him at. I circle the block twice because I see a small TV, some tower house speakers and a bunch of people. If you're not from Ft. Lauderdale, you won't understand why this was a problem for me. I'm not stuck up or snobby in any form of the word BUT there are certain places in ever bodies town that you don't go in after a certain time and Lincoln Park on Sistrunk Ave is one of those areas. I bury my purse in the Suzuki. Put my hammer in my tiddays. Make sure my hair and make-up is on point before I walk thru the dirt and grass to the party. There is a tent set up with chairs underneath which happen to be filled with his friends and a few homeless people from the neighborhood, multiple orange extension cords running from the TV, the turn tables, the tower speakers to the concrete light poles stealing the city's electricity. The 32inch TV somebody has brought from their living room has the volume turned down, while the music of Uncle Al, Uncle Luke and other south Florida artist blare through the speakers. DeMario greets me as I walk up with a hug and a kiss. He introduces me to all of his friends and finds me a seat under the tent as it was starting to drizzle. Once I take my seat DeMario asks, "Baby are you hungry? I got a bunch of chicken from Churches and I got your drink in my cooler in my truck." I ain't got nothing against Churches chicken but can anybody tell me when a chicken wing has started getting big as car doors or when a chicken breast is actually a size 42DDD and in dire need of an underwire bra from Lane Bryant? Not to seem too prissy, I ask for a wing but I need my drink first so I can become a little friendlier. There are more homeless people coming up with milk crates, sitting walkers, fluffed up newspaper placing it on the wet ground for cushion and protection from the hard ground. Demario was very sweet and dutiful to my needs well as making sure the party didn't stop. Dj Frog was on the ones and twos making the crowd hype. The liquor made me loosen up just a tad but not too lose that I noticed the homeless people was all over the chicken like flies. My appetite went right out the window. We talked, dance, had drinks and really was enjoying one another and his friends until Denver loss. DAMN! The party had thinned out except for a few people who have moved in closer to watch the 32inch living room TV. A few times during the night I notice Demario either get in his truck and talk on the phone or walk a great distance off from everyone and talk on the phone, each time was some long conversations. I don't think much of it until he is trying to rush me from up the spot, saying it's late and he know I have to get up early. Wait a minute bastard you wake up at 4am. I'm just rolling over good and farting at that time of morning so what the hell are you talking about. I don't fight it. We hug give each other a quick kiss and I leave.

We chit chat and text sparsely during the week with no question and answer session about him requesting I leave the park quickly. I set my weekly Friday wash and set with hot oil treatment with Nia. I get to the shop and Nia has a very pretty yet very pregnant lady in the chair. I greet everyone with pleasantries. I head to the back of the shop to the fridge, grab some ice, make my usual drink and sit down and listen to the girl talking while she sits in Nia chair. I almost dropped my cup of good liquor when she said, "I know Demario fucking round on me and when I catch his ass and her, Imma beat both they ass!" I take a big ass gulp of my drink and say, "I don't mean to get in your business baby, but don't get mad at the chick. She may not have known anything about you or him being in a relationship with a new baby on the way. Charge her ass full tax if she disrespect you or attempt to fight you. 9 times out of 10 she don't know anything about you." Ole girl think about it for few minutes and say, "You are absolutely correct, because the last chick I found out about, he told her we only bought a house together and that it wasn't nothing. Imma see what is really going on because we just got engaged and supposed to be going on a cruise next week for his birthday." I'm sitting there boiling but trying to make sure she don't know a got damn thing about me. She keeps talking as Nia is flat ironing her very long, thick and pretty hair. During her conversation with Nia, she mentioned the super bowl party that he kept telling her not to come to because it was too live and he didn't want his seed in the park and on and on. All I can do is take the rest of my drink to the head, take a deep breath and put another win in the column for back to the basics.

When the lady left, I wished her well with the wedding and birth of the baby. All which was supposed to happen soon. The baby was due the end of April and they were due to get married in March. When the hair salon cleared out, I filled Nia in on everything and she burst out laughing saying, "You one cold bold bitch. How you talking to the girl giving her advice and shit?" Nah, I ain't cold or bold, I'm just real. How in the hell was I supposed to tell this girl her man ain't shit when she is already knocked up, tied up in a mortgage and money spent on a wedding? I wanted to bust

Demario in the face with a hot shit brick and make him eat it. He put me in harm's way with angry disgruntled pregnant woman and lord only knows who else. I stopped texting, calling Demario and instantly put his black ass on block. I recently rode by the park where I met him at and noticed he wasn't there. Guess the baby came and the wedding was off the chain. Back to the basics 2, Betty 0. ~~Ain't That Bout'a Bitch~~

With my birthday coming up within the next week, I wanted to do something, but was afraid to go out because you know I like to drink and with that DUI scare last year on my birthday I was kind of leery. I said what the hell and set myself a 3 drink limit. I went to Wal Mart earlier in the week and bought all of hygiene items and noticed that Caress had a new body wash and it smelled great. I figure what the hell. I buy it and keep it moving. I can only use Caress due to my very very sensitive skin and body Ph. Hell to be honest, I can only use a certain laundry detergent, lotion, deodorant, dish detergent and all. I love perfume and Victoria Secrets body sprays but they can't go on my skin. It has to be sprayed directly on my clothes or you will see me scrubbing my ass on some hot concrete to get any kind of relief. My birthday weekend comes. I get off early head home and start getting ready to club hop, drink, meet new people and party like its 1999. I went out and had a blast all weekend long now it's back to the daily grind at the zoo. I'm sitting at my desk minding my own damn business when Ms. Precious decides she wants to start a forest fire and ring the alarm! I go use the rest room and do a quick little cold water wash off until we can get home and fully check the situation out. That worked and she piped down for a little while. Girl by the time I had gotten off at 5pm I had a full 5 alarm situation going on in my drause. Smoke, fire and the fire department was all in my drause trying to contain this situation. Just because I had a fire in my drause every light and bad driving ass bastard was on the road and of course in front of me. All I'm trying to do is get to Wal-Mart so I can buy some cream and burn the rest of the Caress body wash they had on the shelves. I finally make it to Wal-Mart 35 minutes later when the drive there from work is 15 minutes, slide into the first parking spot I see and hell no, I didn't park Suzy Suzuki correctly. Fuck her, if I hadn't gotten out of her quick enough we all would have blown the fuck up.

I want to speed walk and do the crossed leg hunch move as I Carl Lewis run my ass into Wal-Mart, but I don't. I play it cool and walk good enough where I can squeeze my muscles to take care of the itch until I can make it to the cream isle and Lord why is it's bunch on non-English speaking Haitians blocking the entrance and exit doors. Under normal circumstances I'm more polite and nice, not today. I pushed through they ass. Didn't say excuse me or sorry and I was waiting on one of them to say something, I would have shot a cannon ball from Ms. Precious on they ass and ruined everybody day. I make it to the cream isle. I grab 2 boxes, panty liners, my regular Caress body wash and knock that other bullshit on the floor and walk off. Since I'm in Wal-Mart I figure let me go and get a few other items I need because I don't plan on coming back anytime soon. I make it to home wares, push my buggy out the way and stand back looking for a particular jars to put some stuff in, when this very handsome white guy approaches with his buggy and says, "Excuse me" me being me, I move my buggy over just a little more, not that it could move anymore and say, "I'm sorry sweetie, I didn't mean to block your way." I get back to searching for my jars and squeezing my muscles when I notice that he does not move, he is still standing there and says, "I noticed you when you came in and I really think you are so beautiful. Would you like to go out for coffee some time?" I'm flattered and on fire at the same time. I play it coy and clutch my chest and say, "Awww thank you sweetie. My name is Betty and you are?" He tells me his name is Eric and that he is here from New York to take care of his father because his mother just recently had surgery. I empathize, nod my head and squeeze some more. I agree to go to coffee and we exchange numbers and just as I'm about to bid him a pleasant good bye, he starts a whole new got damn conversation. I swear we stood there for what seemed like an eternity but it had to be about 10 – 15 minutes. His conversation was so long, I was about to throw my left leg behind my head and play a strong cord of Hambone Hambone on my little charred cooda OMG. I finally get him to stop talking and promise to talk to him tomorrow so we can set up our date. I don't even remember if I paid for my shit or not, but I do know I flew home and doctored on my little cooda, have a bottle of wine and rested my nerves. When I got up the next morning to get ready for work, the first thing in the garbage was that half full bottle of Caress body wash. I don't buy their new fragrances for fear of dying the next time.

Eric calls me early morning the next day and we talk for a little longer today, because my fire was put out. He tells me he is 50, divorced, and owns a construction company in New York, 5 kids which are all grown except for his daughter who is 15. He felt as though his ex-wife got pregnant with her as a last ditch effort to not have to work for as long as possible. He was not sure how long he was going to be down here in Ft. Lauderdale because he needed to really get back and check on his business to make sure everything is running smooth as possible. I tell him about myself and we are actually hitting it off. You already know I had to ask him about his sexuality. Since the last white guy I talked to wanted to suck a dick and give up his hole from time to time. When I asked him that question he just laughed and said no but my youngest son is and I support him to the fullest! My hat went off to him for fully supporting his gay son. He made a joke and said, "I'm not that good of a dresser, so I will go to him and ask for fashion advice and he always makes me look super!" We agree to meet later in the week for dinner at Bone Fish Grill. I only set the date for later in the week because I didn't want to be out somewhere and set off the smoke alarm from Ms. Precious, so I had to make sure she had fully recovered. We meet and actually have a wonderful time at dinner. He was very charismatic, humorous, and highly intelligent and someone I could see getting to know a lot better and seeing where things could go, even with the distance.

He showed me pictures of his business and how he was one of many construction companies at ground zero. As he was describing his experience there in great deal, of seeing bodies, the smell and how the horrible unnecessary terroristic event devastated him right then and there. I had to change the conversation because I'm such a water bag and didn't want to mess up my makeup, so I ask the million dollar question, "Being that you're divorced, are you seeing anyone?" I took a bite of my salmon and had a sip of my wine awaiting his response as he fumbled with his napkin. He finally responds and says, "I am seeing a very nice lady. She's a few years younger than me. She is Vietnamese and we live together but that doesn't stop the fact that I find you to be so beautiful and I'm really attracted to you and would love to spend more time with you." I don't say one word. I keep eating, ordered another wine and just sat there for the longest thinking and wondering "What in the holy heck can be so wrong or disturbing about me that I can't find a single, straight man to save my life." He reaches across the table, grabs my hand and asks, "What's wrong? Have I offended you? If so, that was not my intentions I just wanted to be completely honest with you and hopefully not lose your friendship." The best response I can come up with is, "It's not you love, it's me. I have thoroughly enjoyed getting to know you and I wish you and your family well in all you do." We finished up dinner with small talk, a few chuckles and another round of drinks. It was a pleasant end to an uneventful evening. When we left the restaurant that night that was the last time I ever saw Eric. We did talk daily while he was still down in Ft. Lauderdale taking care of his parents. Once Eric went back to NYC a month later that ended the calls, text and friendship. Back to the basics 3, Betty 0. ~~Ain't That Bout'a Bitch~~

My birthday has passed and was ok, nothing to really brag about. My little Ms. Precious cooda is finally out of the ICU burn unit and has made a full recovery and I'm once again working OT like crazy and maintaining. A few months have passed when a friend of mine in Gainesville invited me to her all white birthday party that was set to go down in April. I agree to come up and kick it Bruce Lee style, but as I'm looking for what I want to wear to her party I can't find a suitable all white outfit, so I call up my seamstress, whose name is Betty as well and the owner/operator of Dovely Designs. I tell her my idea and she was right on! We made an appointment for me to come through for measurements and to check off on the awesome sketch that she texted me. I slide up over to Bettys house one evening about 8 when I get off and park behind a really nice, newer looking black BMW. I get out and make a mad dash to the door to get out the rain, when I hear a very deep, masculine voice call out from behind me and say, "Hey Ms. Lady how you doing?" You already know I stopped once I made it onto the porch out of the rain, did a cute little head spin to make my hair flip in the wind and coyly respond, "Hi sweetie, how are you?" When I stopped being all dramatic there stands my weakness. 6'2 about 185lbs of pure light bright, damn near white sexiness. I didn't want to make it appear as if I was staring so I ducked off in the house real quick, gave Betty and her family a hug and went straight into interrogation mode about the white chocolate knight outside. Betty ain't no damn good, she gets to laughing a little too hard for me and says, "Who that lil young ass white boy out the door? Betty you too much damn woman for him, do you know he is 23!" I flopped down on her couch and said Ain't that bout'a bitch! I forget about little the cute tender roni out the door and get down to business with Betty because I need this outfit in a week. We make some minor tweaks to the sketches, take my measurements when one of her grandkids walk into her studio and say, "Excuse me ma'am, Carlos told me to give you his number and tell you to call him." I don't know no damn Carlos, so I take the number and thank the baby for bringing me the message. I instantly look at Betty who is sweating like she in the cotton fields and laughing a hard as hell. I ask Betty, "Who the hell is Carlos?" Betty finally musters up enough strength to say, "That lil white boy you was asking about earlier. One of the kids must have said something to him and he felt like he could talk to you. Betty don't put that cougar pussy on him, he is only 23!" I brush Betty off and get back to my outfit, after I cuff his number into my bra.

We finish up and as I'm walking out Betty house I say my good nights to everyone and start walking to my car when I hear that sexy voice again and then his megawatt bright ass pops up from behind a car. He asks, "Did Man Man give you my number?" I felt like I was back in elementary school at Stephen Foster when he asked me that, all I could do is smile and very nicely respond, "Yes I did sweetie and I will be in contact shortly!" I get in Suzy Suzuki and peeled out. I get home, take a shower, get something to eat, fix me a drink and get in the middle of my bed flipping channels when

I decide to give the Thunder Cat a text. Before I could put the phone down, he text right back. We hold simple convo for a few minutes as my old ass need some sleep so I tell him I will hit him tomorrow and hopefully we can plan to do something this weekend. Linus is running through my mind like a got damn marathon, I take sip and that running immediately stops.

I awake the next morning to a sweet text from Carlos that reads, "Already at work thinking of you. Hope you have a great day Betty!" Awww how sweet, yet in my mind I keep thinking of him as my nephew. My sister Lucy and I are 13 years apart with her being the oldest. My sister has my niece Brooke who is 29 and my nephew Morgan who is 21, so that would put Carlos right behind my club hopping, non-designated driving niece Brooke. Uhmmmm mm not a good look or feel. A couple weeks pass before we can actually see one another and then I head up to Gainesville for the party, which I missed but I still had a blast in Gainesville seeing friends and clowning them bum ass Gator fans. I make it back to town and we finally make plans for a date on a Friday night. By the time Friday comes I'm so got damn tired from working all the OT, traveling and partying. For the life of me, I can't come with any damn where to go and eat even though my stomach as eaten all my organs and started chewing on my clothes. Carlos finally says, "Meet me at Ihop on Broward Blvd and 441 and we'll go from there. Meet me there in 20 mins lil momma." I kinda like that. He has the take charge attitude and didn't back down when I spoke up. I'm glad I had already taken a shower when I got home earlier, all I had to do was throw on some clothes and ride out. There was no make-up that night. Truth be told it was about to be a glasses, house dress and hair scarf night on his ass, but I didn't do the baby like that. I put on a an all-black maxi skirt, black tank top and my famous don't give a hot got damn flip flops. But in my defense they did match my outfit because they were zebra colored.

I pull into the parking lot of Ihop and there he sits, in his freshly washed BMW waiting for my late as usual ass. I pull up next to him and we both roll down our windows and smile like crazy, he says, "Baby you look like tired. Get in the car with me and I'll drive and make sure you are well taken care of." Ohhh shit, little tender just don't know what he working with. I hadn't had sex in a minute and just the mere sight of him was not making this easy especially when he stepping up like a man. I roll up my window, reach in the back for my purse and as I turn around my car door opens. Its Carlos opening my car door to escort me out, he then locks my doors and shuts it behind me. We stand there and hug for the longest, damn not only did he look good but he smelled like an Adonis and felt like one. He escorts me to the passenger side of the car opens my door, puts me in the car and ensures I put on my seat belt before he shuts the door. He gets in and takes off like a bat out of hell. I can't even lie, I was sitting in that passenger seat pressing an imaginary brake pedal, the whole time Praying we didn't crash. He wants to hold conversation while I sitting over there grabbing on the handle over the door. He finding this shit funny while I'm bout to pass out. We finally put up to this BBQ joint named Father and Son on Sunrise Blvd. He gets out, comes around to my side and does the gentleman thing, when all I want to do is roll out the car and kiss the ground for making it there safely. I get out and as we are walking up to the restaurant, there are some old heads sitting out on the porch area of the restaurant playing dominoes. Carlos is walking in front of me just by a few feet, when all of the old heads respectfully great us, but I can feel those eyes wearing me out. We go in, place our order to go and sit at the hi- boy chairs to catch some of the game as we wait for our food. The food is ready, Carlos goes to the counter to pick it up and I exit the restaurant thinking he is right behind me because he had already paid for the food. I get outside and pass the old heads who bid me a good night. But one of the old heads stands up and says, "Baby if you don't tell, I damn shol won't tell and I got long bread!" You already know me, I coyly laughed it off and replied, "Thank you sweetie, but I'm good. I'm seeing someone." He was persistent as hell with his old drunk ass. He pulled out his old man knot and said, "I love a woman shaped like you with that cute babydoll face, I can really take care of you!" I'm about to sneak my number to the old head when I hear, "Pops, she good! I got all she need and then some. Y'all gentleman have a wonderful night and take care!" Baby when I tell you the rest of the old heads clowned ole buddy and said, "Young blood handle ya business."

Ohhhhhh shit girl, I wiggled these hips a little harder to that BMW passenger door. Gave him a succulent tongue kiss and waited on him to put the food bags down and open my door. Once in, I grabbed the bags placed them on the floor between my legs, leaned over and opened his door for him. Once again his ass peeled out the parking lot but not before he rolled down all the windows and kissed me on my cheek in front of all the old heads! I can have a conversation with him now because I'm not seeing him a child anymore. We ride out to Ft. Lauderdale beach. Park and he pulls out a nice beach ensemble. Towel, cooler, chairs, food and me. It don't get any better than that. I had the absolute best time with him sitting on the sands of the beach, having a night picnic and having some interesting conversation. He tells me he works at Goya and is currently in school for business. He told me about his past scrape with the law for a burglary he claims he didn't have any part in, which he also says was his one and only time. Side eye to that for sure!

The night continues on with more talking and laughing when a drunk crew of white people walk by on the sidewalk and are talking very loud about finding somewhere to get a quick fuck. I squeeze Ms. Precious tight because I been thinking about throwing his ass on that oversized beach towel and fucking him to sleep several times that night. We laugh it off and he suggest we get out of those foldable chairs and get more comfortable and stretch out on the beach towel. Girl the ocean ain't have shit on me with the wetness at that moment. I get up and he folds the chairs down and helps me down on the towel. I cuddle up right next to him and place my right hand on his left thigh, while he places his left arm around my waist. Just from conversation I'm really enjoying him and his future ambitions, when I ask him about any desires to have kids. I knew the answer to that but I had to ask. He wants 2 kids, a girl and a boy. I explain not only am I older, pushing 40 but I have never ever had a desire to have kids. When I was 15 I asked for a hysterectomy and was dead ass serious. At 16 when they discovered I had gallstones, which hurt like a mutha. The nurse who was rolling me into surgery said, "Baby, the pain you're feeling from the passing of these gallstones is equivalent to childbirth." At the time she was telling me that, a stone was passing. Soon as it passed, I was in the operating room, I grabbed her hand and my doctor hand and said, "Since the passing of a gallstone is the equivalent of childbirth, you can snatch all my reproductive organs out." I wasn't even bullshitting, I was dead ass serious and as you can see they left me with all my working plumbing, ole bastards. That conversation puts us on the subject of sex. I'm ready and prepared to tear his head off with pleasure! I was telling Carlos how I love head, head and more head, foreplay, different places, positions, in the car, the pool among other places. He agreed and stated very somberly, "I love the feeling of my skin on my lady skin, sweating and just being with one another in our own world making passionate love." I think nothing more into what he has just said because the wind coming in off the water was so nice and relaxing and really had me feeling some type of way, especially with what I had just told him, I turned my own ass on. Just as I was about to lean in closer, rub on other body parts and give him a very passionate kiss Carlos says, "Betty I'm really attracted to you and I want nothing more than to make mad passionate love to you, but I have only had sex and ate pussy twice in my life." I stop dead on a dime. I don't look at him and say, "Its ok sweetie, you still have your whole entire life ahead of you to experience more love making." At the same time I'm saying this to him,

I'm thinking to myself, "Training Day was a fucking movie, not what the fuck I'm supposed to be doing with you!" My nick name should be Steve Irwin with the way I hunt head. Shit that's an automatic prerequisite. I was too pissed, mainly with myself because I had forgotten that he was 23 and had the possibility of being my middle nephew. I let out a huge sigh and said, "Honey I have had such a wonderful night with you and I hate to end it, but you know I have to work tomorrow and I don't want to mess up my OT." He looked at his watch and said, "OMG my bad I lost track of time because I was lost in you." Little Negro please, you ain't got lost yet. Had I put this grey haired cougar pussy on yo ass, you would have been lost for real then.

We pack up all the stuff. Throw away the trash and walk back to the car hand in hand never ever saying another word. He is still the consummate gentleman opening the door and making sure I put on my seatbelt. We cruise down the beach taking in the sights and people watching before we head back into the city. Remember earlier when he was driving out to the beach I was pressing the imaginary brake pedal? This time I was laying down on the gas pedal trying to get back to my car ASAP before Chris Hanson jump his ass up out the trunk. We pull back up to Ihop and sit in the car for a few minutes just stating how we really enjoyed one another and how he hopes to see me again. You know my famous line, "Let me see how my work schedule is looking and we will work something out." I never had any intentions of seeing that little sexy, make me weak in the knees baby ever again. He gets out, opens my door again helps me out and then opens the driver door to my car and gives me a good night kiss. We text and talked back and forth for a month or so until he got tired of me coming up with excuses as to why I didn't have time. I didn't want to be the one who turned him against women, because I could see me cheating on him and not being happy. For one, I wasn't comfortable with his age and then the lack of sexual experience was the nail in the coffin. Back to the basics 4, Betty 0. ~~Ain't That Bout'a Bitch~~

CHAPTER 16

OLE FAITHFUL

After all the bull was said and done and said again with going back to the basics of dating which kicked my ass up and down the road, I fell back on a guy who I had been seeing for about 7 – 8 years. I can't call him a boyfriend because I never saw him like that, but I could always call him when things were not going the way that I wanted or needed them to be. Kane was a pretty decent dude. He had transferred his job with the USPS as a sorter supervisor to Ft. Lauderdale from Chicago. We had arrived in South Florida about the same time, but didn't meet until years later.

One day in 2006 while in my least favorite place to be, Wal-Mart. If it's not enough checkout lanes open your bound to get in a traffic jam down one of the isles and experience some form of road rage. Just as I'm about to karate chop this ole lady in the motorized scooter for throwing gang signs at me as she almost ran over my feet, he walks up behind me and says, "Excuse me ma'am but I couldn't help but notice how beautiful you are. My name is Kane and you are?" He wasn't the ugliest dude I have ever seen but he would do until someone else came along to fill the spot. I shoot grandma a quick unit to let her know I will see her in the parking lot. I turn my full attention to Kane and say, "Hi love, my name is Betty. Nice to meet you." We strike up small yet pleasant talk while standing in the middle of the isle before eventually exchanging numbers. When Kane and I met, I was dating Sarge and told him that from the gate. He said he was cool with it, he just wanted to get to know me better. BET! Kane is about 5'10, 300lbs, caramel complexion, low haircut, walks a little humped over but I think it's just the way he walks and he has a very pretty smile. He wasn't much to write home about but he was nice, ohhh and the deal breaker is, he was Muslim. I believe we can all co-exist with respect for one another's spiritual path, but I'm Christian and didn't go along with a lot of his 5% practices. None the less I did appreciate him not giving up eating pussy.

Remember when I busted Sarge in the head with the frying pan for cheating on me and still being married and for having me all up in the woman face? Remember I went and stayed at my friend house? Kane was that friend who I stayed with and who greeted me with open arms and a warm inviting safe environment and some of the best head in my life. He didn't even want to have sex. He just wanted to please me and make sure I was ok. When I cut the phone off that night at Kane house, I let myself fall off a cliff deep into ecstasy. After Kane ate me for what seemed like an hour, he gave me a few minutes to get myself together before he pulled me on his chest, held me tight and rocked me to sleep. That is how I was able to go back to that hell hole of a prison, face Sarge and be walking on cloud nine. Kane was always there for me during any and all my men situations, never ever putting any real expectations or demands on me, my time or commitment to him.

Kane was with me through Sarge, Cleophus and all my meaningless dates but the only one I didn't run to Kane about was Linus. We would text and chit chat from time to time but I never had any reason to run to his arms when I was with Linus. Shortly after everything went down with my last four dates, I fell right back into ole faithful arms. I called him up and told him I needed a small get away to get my mind off of some stuff. Out of concern he asked, "Betty what's wrong? What do you need and what do you want me to do?" I don't even why he asked such a silly ass question when he already knew exactly what I was about to say, "I want you to kiss it and make it all better daddy! Ohh and a home cooked meal with some ice cold vodka fresh out the freezer please." Kane just laughs and tells me that I'm crazy and to swing by the house as soon as I get off. I get off of my usual time of 8pm because you know I be trying to kill all the OT I can get. I get to Kane house about 9. Soon as I walk in I'm taken aback by the entire romantic set up. Kane has some very nice slow music playing in the background at a low level. Candles lit all over the living room and bedroom. Dinner smelled like Wolf Gang Puck had come and personally cooked for me. The table was set and looking like something out of a magazine. Kane grabs me and gives me the sweetest hug and kiss before he leads me to my seat at the table. He goes into the kitchen with my plate and comes back with baked chicken, asparagus and sliced baked sweet potatoes. My drink was right behind the plate because it was truly needed. We had great conversation that night. We didn't talk about work, family or anything negative. We didn't even talk about the reason why I was over there, hell to be honest I forgot all about it once I walked through the door. Dinner was over, Kane cleaned off the table and started to clean the kitchen. I walked into the kitchen and offered to assist and he told me no, so I sat at the bar and kept talking to him as the conversation was actually going good.

When Kane finishes cleaning the kitchen, I'm still sitting at the bar in the kitchen, he comes and tops off my drink, asks if I need anything else when I say no, he goes into the room for a few minutes. Kane returns to the living with a weird look of confusion and certainty on his face. Kane drops to one knee, pulls a box out of his right pocket, opens it all while looking me in my eyes smiling hard as hell as if he is being electrocuted. The ring is a beautiful 2 carat princess cut with 2 rows of baguettes on each side. I'm just sitting there with a deer stuck in headlights look on my face, wondering if this is really happening. I've been proposed to plenty of times before and you remember I was engaged to Sincere and I always said the next time I get engaged it would truly be right and with someone I know I can't live without on good or bad days. The oncoming headlights of that semi finally pass and I can think clearly. I grab Kane by his hands, pull him up to me, give a great big tight hug, kiss him on his forehead, grab my purse and walk right out his front door never to look back.

Untwist your face, take a sip of your drink and understand where I'm coming from. I never loved or even saw Kane like that. He is a sweet guy who was always there for me when I wanted and needed him to be there, nothing more nothing less. You know how it is when you have a drought season or you're not getting the head and dick you like or need in order to get that nut off your chest and you call that one who can always provide that home run and make you feel as though you have just ran a marathon when he is finished with you? That's all Kane was to me. He was just always my ole faithful! I know I could never be happy with Kane. He is Muslim and would kill my mood very quickly when he would make statements like, "The white man is the problem in America. We as a people will never be able to prosper as long as the white man has his foot on the black man neck, raping our black women and killing our black babies." Who the hell want to live with that every day? Proverbs 17:1 says, "Better a dry crust eaten in peace than a house filled with feasting and conflict" With that being said it ain't a damn thing wrong with my fried bologna sammich at my house which is always filled with peace! Kane lives up to his name with his racial and political views. When I'm with him, he would chill on them a little bit but that's get old with me. I have my own views of the world but I don't try to impart them on anyone for any reason. Kane came running out the door asking what was wrong, all I could do was tell him, "Kane it ain't you, it's me. I'll call you a little while and we will talk about it." I never called or texted him again and yes, he is on block! ~~Ain't That Bout'a Bitch~~

I went home that night more confused than before, because it just seems like love is not in my favor at all. I fixed me a night cap. Got in the middle of the bed, flipped channels and soon went to sleep. The next morning I arose feeling like the world was on my side and was looking forward to going to work. I get there, my staff is actually pleasant and all smiles. I make me a fresh tea pot of hot water for my daily black tea. Soon as I sit down and take my 1st sip, he peacefully gallops through my mind as usual. I pick up the phone, press his speed dial number and on the 2nd ring he picks up and says, "Good morning my heartbeat. I miss you!" I melted like butter in a hot skillet on Sunday morning. With all my 30 teeth showing, I respond, "I miss you soooo much Jordan. I can't wait to see you baby." We run over our schedules, actually we go over his schedule when I say, "I don't like what you're telling me. I don't want to wait that long I need to see you now." I almost pulled out my umbrella and walked over all the cubicles in my building singing when Jordan replied, "Baby I tell you what, why don't you come home tonight and I promise to have a surprise for you." We coordinate the time we are getting off, my drive time from Lauderdale to Homestead and how much time he will have in between to coordinate whatever it is he is working on for that evening. I didn't work OT that night. I really needed to see Jordan. Something deep inside me was speaking but I couldn't quite understand it. I go home, shower, get dressed, throw my black bag together and hit the turnpike heading south with the wind in my hair and the oldie but goodie station which happens to be playing one of my favorite Luther song, "If only for one night."

I call Jordan just as I get off the exit to let him know I'm almost home. You can hear the excitement in his voice. It takes me forever to get through the got damn gate almost causing me to just run through it and deal with the repercussions later. I turn into the driveway and the front door opens slowly and there stands my sexy, handsome, mocha latte baby. He greets me at the car with a huge hug, kiss and smile. Jordan grabs my bag from the backseat and we walk in the house together to some slow music, low lighting and Chinese takeout. I wasn't mad at all, I just wanted to be with him. Something about being with Jordan always makes me feel fully complimented and covered. It's just his hectic work and travel schedule that will keep him gone anywhere from 2 weeks to a month and has always made me wonder and question if there is a 2nd family some damn where that I may need to knock off CIA covert style. Not only his job, Jordan is part of a band and plays the guitar so there are times when he is home and has to go do a gig when all I want to do is snuggle and cuddle in front of the big screen in the den and watch action movies or sports. We are catching each other up on all the latest, constantly hugging and kissing just thoroughly enjoying each other.

It's getting late and we both have to rise early the next morning for work, when Jordan starts shutting down everything and takes me by hand and leads me upstairs to the bedroom, pulls out the guitar and serenades me with all the oldie songs he knows I love. That's another thing that makes me love him so much. The simplicity of all the things he does to show how much he cares. I'm lying in the bed making dreamy eyes telling him to come to bed, I'm ready. He strikes the chord of a very familiar tune. I sit up, squeeze my eyes real close to catch it but he is mixing the chords so well and fluently that I don't catch the song until he sings it to me and you already know I melted like a snowball in hell. My baby was sanging Lootha, "If only for one night."

That night Jordan and I made love for the very first time the entire 4 years we had been together. Jordan took his sweet time and kissed every stretch mark, licked every jelly roll, sucked every toe, rubbed my hairy ass, caressed me like I was new born baby and made love to me with his mind first by engaging me in conversation as to not get lost in the act of making love but the art of making love. It was as if he was learning my body and how it responds to him and the things he does to me. Sucking each of my fingers while rubbing his body against mine, with our underwear on so Ms. Precious wouldn't jump up and attack his ass, because she is aggressive as hell. He gave me a full body massage, still talking to me and revving up my heart rate with each touch, kiss, lick and dick thrust with our drause on. Jordan pulls my panties off with his teeth and gave me the best wall climbing head ever. It was one of those that I never stop cumming, my legs were shaking uncontrollably and my mouth was dry as the Sahara from all the deep heavy breathing. I'm begging and crying pushing Jordan's head away trying to make him stop. It seemed like the more I pushed him away, the more and more he ate my pussy. I couldn't take it anymore. I scooted and scooted until I fell off the bed. I was ok, I didn't break a hip, leg or anything. Just as I was about to get up, dust my ass off Jordan fell his crazy ass right on top of me and put the whammy down. My word, that man flipped, fingered and fucked me every which way but loose. I knew I was flexible but Jordan had my body so loose and limber from the ever stimulating foreplay and head that I felt I could have been a performer in the Cirque du Soleil. He had my legs pulled, twisted, crossed and pushed every whicha way with ease as he beat this pussy for the old and new.

Jordan's dick is the perfect length and width to my pussy. It slides in like a hand to glove. We started out on the floor on the right side of the bed by the chaise lounge with him on top going to work like a damn jack hammer; we end up on the back of the chaise lounge with the fiercest doggy style. How my leg was able to get up on the back of that chaise I'll never know and I don't want to know. Before we get to the dresser, I tell him to stop so I can suck his dick. Jordan picked me up put me on the dresser and went to work. Loose change, watches, car keys, DVD's and anything on the dresser was now on the floor. Just when I think I can't take anymore, Jordan gets his stroke right. He is breathing hard, stroking me hard, breathing harder and stroking me even harder when he grabs me around my throat and gently yet kind of strongly chokes me. I think Jordan was letting his inner porn star out by looking in the mirror at my body and his body intertwined and the choking just brought it on home. How did he know I love to be choked when I cum? I don't know but he choked me and we both bust nuts so hard and together that the dresser was full of our cum with some dripping down the ledge. With his hand still around my neck and his dick still inside of my pussy, Jordan kissed me like it's his last as I milked that dick by squeezing my muscles and kissing him just as passionately.

My legs are wobbly like a newborn fawn when Jordan helps me down off the dresser. I slide my fat old ass over the edge of the bed to try and catch my breath and bearings. Jordan comes with a warm rag, lays me down and washed my entire ass. I was too tired to tell him No! I just laid there, held my legs up as if he was changing my pamper and thoroughly enjoyed him cleaning Ms. Precious up. I don't look for my drause. I just roll over to climb in the bed under the covers when Jordan comes around to my side of the bed and sits on the chaise lounge with the guitar again. I get up out of my comfortable position in the bed and sit on the edge of the bed with baited breath waiting for Jordan to say or do something. Jordan starts to sing the lyrics from another one of my favorite artist, *"I ain't like most men, I ain't like the others you have dealt with you in your past. Just have some faith, that's all I ask, believe in me."* Jordan puts the guitar down, grabs my hands and comes sit right next to me on the bed still looking me directly in the eyes and says, "Betty, baby we have been going back and forth for the past 4 years or so and I'm tired of the back and forth. I'm ready to settle down. I'll be 50 soon and you getting up in age as well. I've been crazy about you ever since I met you on South Beach in the parking garage when you had on all that white. I'm ready for it to be you and I. I also want to have one more child. Wait wait wait, I know how adamant you feel about not having children, but I want to have my final child and I want it to be with you. Do you want me how I want you?" I have tears running down my face like a river. I suck the snot back in nose, wipe my tears and kiss Jordan ever so passionately while telling him, "Yes, yes baby I do want you just as much as you want me!" How did he know I love Rahiem DeVaughn and his song "Believe" was another one of my all-time favorites?

We got settled into bed, I whispered, "You know we gotta talk about this baby thing seriously, because I already know it will be a girl, shaped my like me with your hair and skin color. Soon as she pop out the cooda, Imma put her ass in a head lock and let her know that her momma been there done that so don't try me lil girl". He laughed at me and called me crazy as usual. I snuggled right up to Jordan's right side, I throw my right leg over his body. Dug my head deep in his chest holding him just as tight as he holding me. Jordan gave me a good night kiss on my forehead and said, "I'm looking forward to forever with you. Good night, my heartbeat!"

I didn't fall sleep right away. My mind was racing and steadily trying to wrap itself around having a baby when I quickly dispose of that idea like I'm throwing out the trash. My mind then wonders, was love in my face all along or not? ~~Ain't That Bout'a Bitch~~